FEB – 4 2010

ST. H

MW00679684

DISCARD

ST. HELENA PUBLIC LIBRARY
1492 LIBRARY LANE
SAINT HELENA, CA 94574-1143
(707)963-5244

Books by Robert Lynn Asprin

Non-Series Novels
The Cold Cash War
Cold Cash Warrior (with Bill Fawcett)
The Bug Wars
Mirror Friend, Mirror Foe (with George Takei)
Tambu
For King and Country (with Linda Evans)
License Invoked (with Jody Lynn Nye)
E.Godz (with Esther Friesner)

Phule's Company Series
Phule's Company
Phule's Paradise
A Phule and His Money (with Peter J. Heck)
Phule Me Twice (with Peter J. Heck)
No Phule Like an Old Phule (with Peter J. Heck)
Phule's Errand (with Peter J. Heck)

Thieves' World Anthologies
Thieves' World
Tales from the Vulgar Unicorn
Shadows of Sanctuary
Storm Season
The Face of Chaos (with Lynn Abbey)
Wings of Omen (with Lynn Abbey)
The Dead of Winter (with Lynn Abbey)
Soul of the City (with Lynn Abbey)
Blood Ties (with Lynn Abbey)
Aftermath (with Lynn Abbey)
Uneasy Alliances (with Lynn Abbey)
Stealer's Sky (with Lynn Abbey)

Griffen McCandles Series
Dragons Wild
Dragons Luck

Duncan and Mallory Series (with Mel White)
Duncan and Mallory
The Bar None Ranch
The Raiders

Myth, Inc. Series
Another Fine Myth
Myth Conceptions
Myth Directions
Hit or Myth
Myth-ing Persons
Little Myth Marker
M.Y.T.H. Inc. Link
Myth-Nomers and Im-Pervections
M.Y.T.H. Inc. in Action
Sweet Myth-tery of Life
Myth-Ion Improbable
Something M.Y.T.H. Inc.

Myth Adventures Series (with Jody Lynn Nye)
Myth-Told Tales
Myth-Alliances
Myth-Taken Identity
Class Dis-Mythed
Myth-Gotten Gains
Myth-Chief
Myth-Fortunes

Time Scout Series (with Linda Evans)
Time Scout
Wagers of Sin
Ripping Time
The House that Jack Built

Wartorn Series (with Eric Del Carlo)
Wartorn: Resurrection
Wartorn: Obliteration

ElfQuest Series
The Blood of Ten Chiefs (with Richard Pini)
Wolfsong (with Lynn Abbey & Richard Pini)

Catwoman Series (with Lynn Abbey)
Catwoman
Tiger Hunt

Books by Eric Del Carlo

Wartorn Series (with Robert Asprin)
Wartorn: Resurrection
Wartorn: Obliteration

Books by Teresa Patterson

The World of Robert Jordan's Wheel of Time (with Robert Jordan)
The World of Shannara (with Terry Brooks, illustrated by David Cherry)

NO Quarter

by

Robert Asprin
Eric Del Carlo
Teresa Patterson

DarkStar Books
Bryan-College Station, Texas

NO Quarter © 2009 by Bill Fawcett & Associates,
Eric Del Carlo, & Teresa Patterson
All rights reserved.

Cover painting and interior illustrations by Nathan Smith
Cover design by Jason Carranza
Book design by Tom Knowles
Set in Adobe Garamond Pro

This book is printed on acid-free archival paper.

No parts of this book may be reproduced in any form or by any means, including photocopying and electronic reproduction, without written permission from the publisher.

This book is a work of fiction. Names, characters, and places are the product of the author's imagination and any resemblance to actual persons, living or dead, business establishments, events, or locales is entirely coincidental.

ISBN: 978-0-9819866-0-9

Library of Congress Control Number: 2009927674

Published by DarkStar Books
P.O. Box DS
College Station, Texas 77845
www.darkstarbooks.net

Produced and printed in the United States of America
by Tops Printing, Inc.
www.topsprinting.com

Dedication

Here's a toast to the memory of Robert Lynn Asprin. To those of us who knew him, Bob *was* the Maestro. He created much of what is best within this book. His spirit lives on in its pages and in the hearts of his many fans and friends.

Special thanks go to Fahy's, The Fatted Calf/Yo Mamas, Marie Laveau's House of Voodoo, and all of the people of the French Quarter who inspired the characters within this story. Without them, there would be no story to tell.

And to Tom and Bill, thanks for believing in this book enough to give it new life.

Once Upon A Time, Before Katrina ...

After you've lived in the French Quarter for a while, you develop the cynical belief that you've seen it all ... that nothing can get to you anymore. You and your bar acquaintances tell yourselves and each other that you've gotten so used to the drunken tourist idiocy and random acts of violence ... that it doesn't bother you.

That's bullshit.

Sunshine

Unsteady on her sandaled feet, Sunshine climbed the stairs leading up from the French Quarter levee to the Moonwalk. A bit high and more than a little distracted, she tripped and almost fell. She hesitated on the walkway, looked out across the Mississippi at the riverboat *Natchez*, a glittering beacon of lights sparkling against the dark water. Live jazz music drifted across the distance in cheerful waves. *The Big Easy* was a city that never slept, not even on Sunday night. That positive energy was one of the things she loved about New Orleans. The southern nights could be as warm and seductive as a lover.

She'd discovered that those southern nights, and the Big Easy itself, could also be as dark and as cold as the Mississippi depths. Sunshine was her real name—her middle name, anyway. She liked it better than the first name her mother had inflicted upon her. She'd left that behind, along with her old life, even before she'd chased her elusive dreams to San Francisco. She hadn't found her pot of gold at the end of that particular rainbow, either, so she'd left California behind, had come to New Orleans to build a new life in the bohemian atmosphere of the French Quarter. Unfortunately, that smaller, simpler dream had been more difficult to find, to hold on to, than she'd expected. Her hopes, her plans, her dreams had shattered in the atmosphere of plentiful booze, all-night parties, and easy drugs that permeated the Quarter. Trapped amid the "easy" of it, she had sunken into a cycle of despair and anger. She'd lost everything that she'd brought with her—love, friendship, and finally, hope. She'd lost her way.

She would change all that tonight. She had a new dream, and she would make this one work.

Shoving her shoulder-length, bleached-blonde hair out of her face, she looked to the right, toward the bright glowing lights of the Aquarium of the Americas and the Riverwalk shopping mall where the Moonwalk began. Like the riverboat, it cast an almost magical glow, just out of reach—just like the life she wanted so badly.

But she finally had a chance to put it all back on track. Sunshine squared her shoulders, wiped her sweaty palms on her jeans, and took a deep breath. At last she had a real shot at happiness—if she could just get through this night, this one last task. She turned to the left and looked down the path to where the concrete ribbon of the Moonwalk disappeared into the shadowed darkness behind the Jax Brewery. Only gutter bums and the occasional street musician hung out beyond the lights. Most who knew the Quarter avoided the dark end of the Moonwalk at night, especially if they were alone. Sunshine told herself she wouldn't be here either, if she thought she had a choice.

Something on the ground caught her attention. She moved closer. Someone—probably a tourist—had left one of those fake voodoo dolls lying on the walkway. She walked over to it and poked it with her toe, trying to ignore the feeling of dread that crawled up her back. It was just a toy, nothing more. Drawing in another deep breath, praying she wasn't making a huge mistake, Sunshine walked into the shadows.

* * *

Mouse just wanted a place to sleep where no one would hassle him. With a bottle of his favorite juice to keep him company, he headed for a secluded spot down by the river, a safe place hidden deep in shadow. But when he pulled the hedges aside he found someone was already there, sleeping in his spot.

His first reaction was indignant anger. It was still early by Quarter standards. No one should be crashing in his spot. He pulled out his little flashlight and flicked it on, meaning to wake the bitch up and make her move on. But then, when he saw the blood that stained her face and soaked her t-shirt, he realized that the blonde girl wasn't just sleeping. It took a few seconds more for his fogged brain to notice the fluffy bits of red-streaked white that lay scattered around the girl's thin body. In morbid fascination he picked up one of the pieces. The bloody head of a decapitated chicken stared back at him. Mouse jerked back, throwing the gory thing down. Scrambling up the bank toward the light, he left a trail of scarlet footprints as he ran. His prized bottle, forgotten, stood amidst the destruction like an offering left on a desecrated altar.

For the first time in his life, Mouse actually wanted to find a cop.

Chapter 1

Maestro

Before I came to live in the French Quarter, I believed that the number one recreational activity in the Quarter was drinking—usually heavily—often followed closely by losing the ability to walk upright or talk. For many, the next step involved becoming closely acquainted in a personal manner with gutters and pavement. Among the tourist crowd, that proved mostly true. But among the people who live and work within the Quarter—those known as "Quarterites"—the most popular recreational pastime (that you can do in public, anyway) is shooting pool. I can't think of many other athletic competitions where you can smoke and drink heavily and still be a champion. We have pool-playing leagues here—one for eight ball, one for nine—and our teams shoot out of the participating Quarter bars. It's more social than competitive. At least it's supposed to be. I had been playing for several years, had proved myself a "fair stick" (as good pool players are called) to the point where I was co-captaining a team. It had proven to be a great way to meet people and to blend myself into the local scene.

Of course, while some people use pool league as an excuse to get together and drink, some of us actually like to win. Winning requires practice. This particular Sunday we had a late practice scheduled at Fahey's bar. I wanted to stop off on the way to show Padre one of my custom cues. Unlike my usual cue stick, which broke down into several small sections, this one had been carved from one solid piece of mahogany and inlaid with Mother-of-Pearl. Despite the fact that it was a sweet shooter, I didn't use it often because I don't like carrying a full-sized pool cue around the Quarter. Even in its case, something that long draws too much attention. But I had promised to show it to Padre and let him try it out.

I left my place around 11 p.m., carrying my cue stick packed lovingly in its own soft-sided cue-case, and headed down the sidewalk towards Fahey's. Within the Quarter, the "sole express"— foot power—is the preferred manner of transport, followed closely by bicycles. The narrow one-way streets and scarcity of parking make automobile travel largely impractical. So, like most Quarterites, I walk everywhere. I no longer even own a car, using a taxi or a streetcar on the rare occasions when I have business outside the Quarter itself. After all, walking is not only great for keeping fit, it allows me to keep close tabs on the "feel" of the neighborhood.

2   Asprin-Del Carlo-Patterson

There was no moon. Deep shadows lurked in the doorways and recesses along the street. But the streetlights still provided plenty of illumination to spot trouble, for someone who knew where to look.

"Did you think you could do me like that and not pay?" The voice, originating from a deeply shadowed alcove just ahead, sounded loud, angry, and male.

A second angry, male voice joined in. "You're gonna pay tonight!"

A third voice replied, "I didn't mean anything! Come on, take it easy!" That voice was female, very frightened, and quite familiar to me—Ruby Rose, one of the Tarot Readers who worked the Square.

Without altering my pace or manner I quickly checked to be certain my knives were within easy reach (I rarely leave home without at least two or three concealed blades), shifted my cue case to a more comfortable position, and chose a path that would take me right by the alcove. I knew from the voices that there were at least two guys, but there could be more. As I reached the alcove I turned into it, as if on purpose, then feigned casual surprise to find it occupied.

"Oh, I'm sorry. Didn't know somebody was here." There were only two of them. Late twenties or so. One was tall, dark haired, and very angular, and he had Rose pinned against the wall with a long, wooden walking stick. The other—a short, very stout guy—looked like he could have been a college linebacker if only he'd laid off the burgers and fries. He leaned in close to Rose, trying to loom ominously over her. Rose had at least two inches on him, which ruined the whole threatening henchman effect and left Burger-boy looking a little ridiculous.

Ridiculous or not, I could see that Rose's fear of him was very real.

"Maestro!" She seemed relieved to see me.

"Hey, Rose, I've been looking for you." I improvised madly, determined to keep this from escalating into something nasty, but I was equally determined to get Rose out of there. "Didn't we have an appointment for a card reading?"

"Yes, we did!" Rose was quick to see where I was going. "I ..."

The stout one said, "The bitch ain't goin' anywhere till we're done, old man."

The tall fellow stared at me. "Maestro? Are you the one who ran the sword club? That Maestro?"

Nicknames are a way of life in the Quarter. At first you're surprised at how few people you know by their real names, but after a while you get used to it. There's Bicycle Rob and Jersey Rob, Puerto Rican Rita, Aardvark, Confucius, Little Jim, etc., etc. It's almost like hanging with my old Outfit.

Here in the Quarter I'm known as Maestro. It comes from when I started an informal sword club, which I ran for a while, teaching both traditional fencing with foil, saber, and epee, and the more flamboyant forms with rapier and dagger. My students took to calling me Maestro, even though I tried to deflect it.

"Maestro" is a particular title one has to earn as a sword instructor, one that involves passing tests for certification. I'd never done any such thing, and I winced when people assigned me the unearned rank. I tried to discourage it, but I gave up when it got to the point where even the Quarterites who had never been in one of my classes started using it.

Honor is well and good, but sometimes you have to yield to reality. If they were going to call me Maestro, that was the way it was whether I deserved it or not. Nicknames are usually self-chosen down here, but not always. Just ask Snuggles. *He* didn't pick that name.

The guy in the alcove knew my nickname, so I decided to make it work for me. "Yeah," I said. "I used to run a fencing club." I wasn't sure where this was leading.

"Great!" He lowered his cane from Rose's chest. "Then we can duel for the lady! That will be almost as much fun as cutting her up!"

He pulled his cane apart to reveal the long, nasty blade hidden inside. I immediately recognized it as one of the more flamboyant—though impractical—sword canes they sell at the weapons gallery on Royal. Usually only tourists or collectors buy sword canes ... them, and the idiots who seem to think they can channel Errol Flynn.

He brandished his blade a few times, proving to me he knew very little about fencing. That actually made him more dangerous because he obviously had no control over the three feet of edged steel he was slinging about. He dropped into an exaggerated enguarde position and waited expectantly. *What the heck?* I started to tell him I didn't have a sword, then I saw him looking at my cased cue. I realized he had mistaken it for a sword.

"Fine," I said, "but I don't duel just anyone. You have to prove you're worthy. Let her go first, then I'll be happy to fight you."

He looked doubtful.

It was critical that I get Rose out of there. She was within easy range of that blade. The weapon had a wicked edge, which wouldn't require a lot of expertise on the part of its owner to be lethal. "Look," I said, "if you win, you will have bested me, and you will have a reputation. You won't need her." *And when I win you'll wish you had never bothered her,* I added silently to myself.

After another moment of deliberation, he signaled to Burger-boy, who backed away to let Rose get past him to the street. She hesitated and gave me a questioning look. I grinned at her—the grin that shows all my teeth and isn't at all friendly—letting her know I had it under control. She nodded and disappeared down the street.

"Give me a minute to get my weapon out." I backed out into the light, turned partly away from the wannabe Errol, and made a show of kneeling and fussing with my cue case. "You're really gonna love this baby. She's a beautiful piece." I bubbled with enthusiasm, and as I hoped, both Errol and Burger-boy stepped forward. One step, then another, I slowly unzipped the bag as they came closer. Errol bent over for a closer look—just as I stood up and snapped my elbow back, slamming the butt of my cue into the bridge of his nose. He went down onto his knees, shrieking, dropped the sword cane, and grabbed his nose with both hands.

"Oops. I'm sorry. It slipped."

Burger Boy, perhaps smarter than he looked, moved fairly fast. He grabbed me, pinning my arms in an attempt to keep me from using the cue on him the way I had his friend. He had quite a bit of weight and muscle on me. I went very still.

"I'd let go if I were you," I said.

"What makes you think I'd let you go now, old man?" He tightened his grip, no doubt meaning to crush the breath out of me.

"Look down," I said.

He did, and his eyes got big as he saw the knife I held in my left hand, blade back, positioned only a hair's width from his gut.

"Why don't you two just walk away?" I said in my most reasonable tone. "We'll call this an accident. Errol there tripped and fell. I won't tell anyone, and neither will you."

Burger-boy nodded, carefully released me, and stepped quickly back out of range of my knife. He didn't realize he was still in range of the pool cue.

"And you both promise to leave the young lady alone," I said. "If not, you get to find out what I'm like when *I'm* the one picking the fight." I grinned dangerously. "Oh, by the way," I said as I picked up the sword cane, "I'll be keeping this. Don't buy another one unless you plan to keep it at home. Otherwise, you might get to find out how it would feel jammed up your ass."

I sheathed the blade and watched as Burger-boy obediently gathered up his wounded friend and made a quick exit. I watched for a moment to be certain they were headed away from the Square, then I slid both the sword cane and the cue stick inside my case. I would now have to backtrack to my apartment to get rid of the sword. No reason to court trouble by taking an illegal weapon into a bar. Padre would just have to wait to see the cue another time.

So much for getting out early.

Chapter 2

Bone

Cop-car lights, red and blue—they were something for the eye to follow. They sped fast along Decatur, silent but for the gunning motors. I didn't see the first, just glimpsed the second squad car. Red and blue lights splashed the building fronts and colored the windows of parked cars, and were gone.

I had three plates stacked up my left arm, from hand to elbow ... a balanced load, if you know how to do it, but the dishes made three hot spots that would start burning if I left them there. In my right hand I carried a fourth, and I had a fifth plate on my right arm.

I dealt them off onto the table clockwise, making certain each diner got his or her proper plate without me needing to double back. I had taken the orders for the table, complete with multiple substitutions, without writing anything down. I can remember almost anything I hear or see—if I want to. It is my one special skill, often good for tips. But for this group, it was a wasted effect. All four of my feeders were craned about, looking past the restaurant's front windows after the police lights.

"See?"

"*Two* of 'em, even."

"Wonder what they're after ..."

"Aww, I don't believe any of it."

"See?" Again, said like a point was being made.

I *had* nearly burned myself, but my face stayed neutral. Never flinch. Somebody brands the back of your thigh with a careless cigarette or coffee pot, don't cringe, don't respond. Nobody likes to hear about a waiter's problems. Certainly not your customers, who want a dining experience where they and they alone matter in the universe.

"You live 'round here?" I was being addressed by the *See?*ing one. Addressed flat and direct, the way lords of the manor talk to servants in period-costume dramas. A demanding voice.

"I do," I said.

"Here'n the French Qwardah?"

"Here in the Quarter." I waited by the table. I had two other parties—two-tops, locals I knew. I'd already brought out their plates. They were eating, happy. They would tip decently.

My foursome here were out-of-towners, but Southerners. I can't distinguish the subtleties of cracker accents, so I couldn't say from where. Two couples, middle-aged, dressed for the heat. The women were heavy, the men heavier. Drunk, the gals would make public nuisances of themselves, and the guys would become belligerent. I could extrapolate their behavior at a glance. Luckily they weren't drunk—not yet, anyway. This late-night supper would fortify them all the way back to Bourbon Street. They were off the normal tourist beat here at this far end of Decatur Street, near Esplanade, here at this restaurant that's mostly a locals' hangout.

"Tell me sump'in'." He leaned toward where I was standing. Latent aggressive air. "What's it like? Inna Qwardah, livin'—acsh'ly *livin'* here. What's it like?"

I don't know what tourists see when they come here. When Sunshine and I arrived two years ago, we got busy scrambling for jobs, hunting up an apartment—not much sightseeing time. The Quarter very quickly became, simply, our neighborhood. It was real. It was where we lived. There are a good many residents here, more than you'd guess, residents to whom Bourbon Street is just a *street*. The endless stream of tourists—and regardless of the season, they never really stop coming—have different expectations.

I offered my table a smile that didn't involve my eyes. "The party never stops in the French Quarter," I said with a leer in my voice.

What they wanted to hear. They grinned, cackled. People in their forties, aroused by the decadence we sell by the glass here. There are strip joints, adult novelty shops, and bars, bars, bars. It was giddy culture shock for these four, reminding them of younger days—the males: tireless stud-machines; the females: slim and beautiful, with their pick of dates. At least, that's how they would remember it. They were cutting loose.

"Y'er skinny," the woman with the other man said it at me the way you'd point and comment, "That dog has a fluffy tail."

I slid my eyes toward her, held there briefly, while she laughed at her own wit. I thought of telling her I had cancer. But you're working for tips—their tips—the money they'll leave you for good service, but more for letting them enjoy themselves however they want to.

"But those po-leese, they jus' went by—what's going on, who're they after?" It was the man again. He had a thick, graying mustache that looked like it grew right up into his flared nostrils. They all had their individual physical characteristics. My mind recorded just enough while they were here and would attempt to erase them when they left. Of course, they would always be there, somewhere in my head, locked in with all the other things I could not completely erase.

8   Asprin-Del Carlo-Patterson

The two squad cars had been heading down Decatur—toward the Square, toward Canal. No sirens, just lights. Whatever it was had already happened. I shrugged, "Parties get rowdy sometimes."

More cackles at that. Give them what they want. Right, right, it's Mardi Gras every day of the year. Go buy yourselves some beads, join the fun.

"Y'er *real* skinny." She found it funnier this time, laughed longer.

I *am* thin. Gaunt, if you must. Not due to dieting, not to exercise. I've got a junkie's body, but I never have used junk and never will use it. What I do have is a persistent lack of appetite. I don't normally get hungry, or I'm not aware of getting hungry, so I miss meals. I'm not anorexic and wouldn't expect any sympathy if I was. I simply don't *understand* food, why people make such a big deal out of it.

Which makes being a waiter an odd job choice, I suppose. I'm good at it, though, as much as I well and truly loathe it. I stopped by the kitchen and rattled off the dessert orders for my last group, aware of the grumbles from the cooks.

"Why can't yuh just write it down like everybody else?" Joe moaned. A common complaint from him, but I didn't take it seriously for a four-top. If I have a group of six or more, I usually speak nice and slow to give the kitchen time to make a list. I never write anything down unless the cook needs crib notes. My memory for detail makes me especially good during slam times. Unfortunately, numbers are not my thing. If I had any skill with math I could maybe count cards in the casinos instead of waiting tables.

I kept my eye on my other two tables, aware of the other waiters and their tables. I heard the hurly-burly of the eight-top, a party of eight college-age yahoos that Nicki had got stuck with. Nicki was young, cute, sweet—too sweet, too nice—and judging by the hoots and grunts coming from her big table, the yahoos were hassling her. I was aware of football jerseys, meaty faces, pitchers of beer on the table—loudmouths, MTV-bred, hormonally overwrought. They were of a type. When they find out they can't get laid, they start a fight.

But it wasn't my table. I had my own customers and my own hustles to work. My four tourists finally settled into eating, the two guys arguing. "It's alla put-on, Harry, like Disneyland," and, "Naw, the pahwty never stops, you *heard* 'im."

I made my rounds. Cleared plates, poured coffee. I chatted with my two-tops, more sincerely than with my tourist feeders. I knew these folks, from the restaurant, from around the Quarter. We could talk about common things.

I was getting twitchy for a smoke.

Midnight had come and gone. I knew that much, as I slipped past the waiters' station of cutlery, coffee pots, and menus, but was surprised, turning the corner and lighting a cigarette, to see the clock reading past one-thirty. It was Sunday, technically Monday, but it's not the next day until you've been to sleep.

A radio played from the kitchens, loud, drowning some of the chaos—steam and clatter and greasy smoke. Even when it runs smoothly, our restaurant—like any restaurant—is chaotic. There's a kind of bored frenzy to it.

I puffed fast and deep, knowing cigarette breaks never last. I felt the sweat sticking my black T-shirt to my back, despite the air-conditioning; felt my aching calves and sore lower back. I felt—probably more than anything—that sickly sense of indignity. I was at the end of my night, worn-out. Easy to feel lousy about spending these past hours of my life toadying and scraping and degrading myself, kowtowing like a goddamned manservant! *Did I do good, boss, suh I live only to please, yessuh.*

Christ, Bone. Lighten up. You're just a waiter.

I sucked smoke into my lungs. I patted my apron pocket, feeling the bills there. My tips. All for the money, that's why we humble ourselves. I wasn't taking new tables. I was done for tonight, would finish up the ones I had, total my checks, cash out. Leave Nicki and the other kid, Otis, to handle the graveyard. Employees come and go: waiters, cooks, dishwashers. The flake factor is high for jobs in the Quarter, astronomically high in its restaurants. I expect to see several new faces every week, and expect they'll be replaced before I get to know them.

The party never stops.

I pitched my smoke, relishing that lightheaded rush you get when you haven't had one in hours, and started back toward the floor. Ours is a good restaurant—less pricey than a lot of Quarter joints, sizable portions and, like I said, a locals' haunt. *Real* people come here, people who read Tarot cards in the Square and work at the gift and T-shirt shops and tend bar and sell Lucky Dogs from vending carts on the street corners and eke out livings like people do everywhere. Locals, keeping the French Quarter functioning for your amusement.

I felt a snit coming on. Familiar pointless anger tingled my raw nerves. But there was nothing to do with it. Nowhere to aim it.

Now that I'd had my smoke, I wanted a drink. Before I could reach the dining room floor to get to my tables, deliver checks, get my customers and myself out of here, this week's bicycle-delivery kid came toward me. Our eatery is open twenty-four hours and we deliver free in the Quarter. What more could you ask for?

"Hey, Bone!" A kid, yes, but sometime during the last few years "kids" had somehow become twenty-five-year-olds, which this one was. His head was shaved, the lack of hair compensated for by the junkyard's worth of ear piercings and the compulsory goatee. What was his name ... ? I accessed that memory file.

I retrieved the name. "Hey, Spit." No lie, it was his handle. People get called what they want here.

"Somethin's goin' on down by the river. 'Round the Moonwalk. Cops. Lotsa cops."

I shrugged and went past, and he went to the pickup window. If you've got a bike, the stamina, and a willingness to carry a wad of cash through the streets at night, you can make very respectable money doing deliveries. A percentage of Quarter-dwellers become shut-ins on their days off. They order their cigarettes and beer from the corner grocery, they have their meals delivered at night from the restaurants and delis. Quarterites usually know how to tip good. Hell, half of us are waiters and bartenders ourselves.

By now I needed to get back onto the floor. My tourist four-top was nearly done feeding. My other two tables looked ready for their checks. But Nicki came rushing off the floor past me, a petite hand over her mouth, tears in her eyes. I saw her college-boy eight-top getting up, shuffling out, still hooting and hollering and blustering. *Neanderthals.*

Customers come first, yes, but Nicki had worked here awhile. I actually knew her. I turned, followed a few steps, and gently touched her elbow.

She spun, hand moving from her mouth to cover her eyes. Her other hand was a fist she knocked against the wall by the coffee pots.

"I'm not crying 'cause I'm hurt, I'm crying 'cause I'm *mad.*" Which apparently made her madder. She thumped her fist harder. "Fuckin' ... fuckin' ... *creeps.*"

I squeezed her elbow and backed off. She didn't want to be watched, and I understood. I went out to my tables. It didn't matter really what the yahoos had said. What mattered was that they *could* say it ... or thought they could. Thought they had the right. *Hey, fuckit dude—she's just a waitress, ain't nothin'.*

You're working for tips, their tips, you just take it. Take it.

I wanted that drink more now. Wanted to do other things as I tracked the eight Neanderthals past the windows, out of sight along Decatur. But what was there to do? Take it. Nicki, me ... all of us who do this shit for a living.

The yokel with the mustache wanted me to recommend a place for him and his plump friends to go drinking. *An authentic New Orleans waterin' hole.* I thought of several places I might send them ... thought wickedly, hidden under my servile face. Thought of all the authentic New Orleans experiences they might find ... *interesting.*

"So skinny," the woman said, with feeling, just in case I'd missed it.

I recommended a nice, safe tourist club, collected my tips, checked on Nicki before I clocked out and left. She looked through me with cold, bitter, red-rimmed eyes. I lit a smoke and walked out into the hot summer night. It was almost two.

I thought briefly of Sunshine. If we were still together, I'd be going home to her. I immediately wiped it from my mind—it had been a messy breakup, and our last meeting had been even worse. Instead I would collect Alex, who would be getting off from her own job about now. We would probably go hang with the regulars at the Calf in an attempt to erase the day.

The party never stops.

* * *

Excerpt from Bone's Movie Diary:

> *Remains of the Day*—Anthony Hopkins' finest screen performance. Far superior to *Silence/Lambs* & his campy Oscar-winning Hannibal Lecter. *Remains'* Hopkins is an ice-stiff English butler who gives his soul to serving, sacrificing every human privilege, including the possibility of a wife, & never blinks. Yet we can see his feelings, deep, painful. He knows what he lacks, but he's too dedicated to change. It's fabulously bittersweet, not schmaltzy. Appraisals: *Remains* * * * ½; Hopkins * * * *

Chapter 3

Maestro

I dumped the entire case, newly-acquired sword cane and all, back at my apartment rather than take the time to repack it. Normally I would be worried that word of my altercation might get out and ruin my deliberately low profile, but I knew that Rose hadn't actually seen anything. The two fools were unlikely to brag about a fight they'd lost—especially to an "old man."

That still rankled. I may have a little silver in my hair, but I really don't think of myself as old—just more experienced. And in the Quarter, experience counts.

The brief practice went well, even though I arrived later than planned. Afterwards I relocated to the Calf, along with my pool team co-captain, Padre, who tended bar there. A month ago the owners had changed the name of the bar to "Yo' Momma's," but the regulars, in true Quarter fashion, hadn't accepted the change. I was no different. In my head it was still the Calf—same bar, same bartender, same regulars, so why call it something else?

By around two-ish in the morning, early by Quarter standards, I had settled in at the bar to wait until the lingering tourist crowd thinned enough so I could talk pool-team strategies with Padre. Besides being a great co-captain, he was also my oldest friend in New Orleans. While stalling, I joined a group of regulars indulging in one of my favorite pastimes, talking old movies. I had gotten to know a number of them because most of them lived and worked in the Quarter and tended to frequent the same bars I did—probably for the same reasons. The Quarter doesn't lack for watering holes, but I tend toward the quieter places. Since dance and jazz clubs and bars that cater specifically to the tourist trade are usually loud, I go where the locals more or less "own" the place.

We were in the middle of casting a fictitious remake of *Gone With the Wind*. Tom Cruise and Mel Gibson had both been proposed for Rhett, though there was a faction pushing for Harrison Ford. Gwyneth Paltrow was penciled in as Scarlett, with Oprah as Mammy. No one could decide on Ashley.

"Hey, where's Bone?" T.J. remarked. "He's the Master of Moviedom. He should be in on this!"

I agreed. Where was Bone? He would have plugged right into the current debate. Bone was never so opinionated as when he talked movies. He usually showed around this time of night to collect his friend, Alex, who worked the gift shop at Pat O.'s, a tourist hot spot across the street. Most nights they met up here after work, hung around for a while to decompress, then walked home together since they both had apartments in the same building.

Bone was a relatively new acquaintance, but we'd hit it off quite well, despite our age difference. I don't know where he got the name, unless it was because he was thin as a ... well, I'd never asked.

The first time I saw him I mistook him for a low-level pool hustler. He was shooting late night racks for a dollar. I watched him take four games in a row, only to find that no one in that bar wanted to shoot against him for higher stakes. I eased over.

Like anywhere, people here are usually friendly if you're friendly to them first, even after midnight in a bar. We were both warmly cocktailed, and he wasn't at all hostile when I offered pointers. I didn't lecture on technique. He had a fair arm, even if he didn't know where to point his elbow. What I passed along was a little sage advice about pool hustling—advice that with my old crowd up North would have been *da-da-goo-goo* baby talk.

"You're showing too much too soon, and too cheap." Meaning he had a decent game, but shouldn't flaunt it right away, certainly shouldn't give it away for a dollar.

He stared back at me for a few seconds. "Should I know what the hell you're talking about?"

Turned out he was a waiter and shot games more for fun than cash. "Not that I couldn't use the money," he said, but he knew he wasn't anywhere near as good as some of the hot sticks in the Quarter. We had a laugh, and I bought a round for the misunderstanding.

Pool may be the basic sport of the French Quarter, but for me it was mostly just something to do. Just like coming out to the Calf to talk tactics with Padre and have an Irish whiskey or two and maybe bump into Bone were things to do. I was dug in, in the Quarter. I liked it here.

I ordered another Irish, still waiting for Padre to get some clear time so we could talk. The regulars moved on to another of our favorite movie-related bar games. It's gotten to be fairly popular, as any number can play regardless of qualifications, and it never really ends. Simply put, one reflects back on the old film greats, then tries to identify who has emerged from the new crop of talents to take each individual's place. Case in point: Who would you say is the new Jimmy Stewart? Our answer: Tom Hanks. The new John Wayne? Try Arnold Schwarzenegger. Actors are fairly easy. Actresses can drive you nuts. This can and does go on for hours, as everyone has his own opinion and there are no clear-cut right or wrong answers. The bartenders love it because it keeps people hanging around and drinking, which boosts their rings on slow nights.

We all had our reasons for drinking. Some were social, some not. This was one of those nights when we were all feeling our drinks, but more on the euphoric than depressant side. That is, it didn't actually improve our humor, but we appreciated each other's jokes a bit more than usual. Bad humor is the standard language of Quarter bars. If you aren't witty, you ought to at least be quick with your comebacks. Some nights the puns and crude double-entendres fly so fast it can make your head swim.

Somebody slotted quarters into the bar-top video-trivia game, and the gang went over to kibitz. I already knew Bone had all five high scores in the movie category. Any two players working together were lucky to make a third of his recorded low score. I'm a movie buff myself, but Bone was more like a fanatic.

It was well past two by now. Where was he?

At that moment a young man came through the door and beckoned Padre over. I recognized him as one of the waiters from Poppy's, the diner a few doors up St. Peter.

Like every other local, I maintained a casual scan on everyone entering the bar, and while the waiter was a known quantity, something about his manner caught my eye.

How does a Quarterite know when there's trouble brewing? Hey, how does a bug know when it's going to rain?

After talking intently for about thirty seconds, the waiter headed back out. Padre remained where he was, leaning on his side of the bar, his head bowed slightly.

I hadn't joined the others at the trivia machine. "Bad news, Padre?" I slid down the bar to him.

He looked at me a moment without speaking.

"You know Sunshine?" he said finally. "The little waitress from Big Daddy's?"

There was pun potential there. Protocol called for a wise-ass answer. His vibe didn't.

"Yeah. I know her." A local, Sunshine was a cute little bundle of irrepressible energy. Big Daddy's was a strip club, but she worked as a waitress, not a dancer. A casual bar buddy, she had actually called me very late the night before and left a message on my answering machine—something about wanting to talk to me at noon the next day. Of course, I didn't get the message until I dragged

my night-owl self out of bed at three o'clock that afternoon, well after the re-
quested time, so I didn't ring her back. Figured that by that time she had either
handled whatever it was herself, or had found someone else to hold her hand.
Otherwise, she would have called me back. I wondered if this had something to
do with that call.

"What's up?"

Padre's eyes were grave. "She's dead. They just found her up on the
Moonwalk. Somebody stabbed her. Rumor is it may have been some kind of
voodoo thing."

Suddenly, the rest of the bar receded a million miles away as a collage of
film clips played in my head. *Sunshine, flipping back her impossibly blonde hair,
laughing at one of my notoriously bad puns.* Or hunched over the drink of the hour
with red-rimmed eyes as she shared the latest train wreck in her life. I'd sat and
listened to her emote about whatever guy she had just broken up with at least a
dozen times. She had notoriously bad taste in men. Once upon a time, I'd made
my own interest known to her. She had looked shocked, then she'd gently but
firmly rebuffed my advance.

I wasn't put out. At my age, hurt feelings, particularly over a female's
friendly brush-off, are rare. Since then we'd drifted into being casual bar buddies. Along with a couple of other Quarterites, I took turns watching over her
when she was too drunk to repel the random guys that endlessly hit on her. We
often poured her into a cab to get her home, even if we had to spring for the fare
ourselves. Locals tend to watch out for each other, especially for those who don't
always handle their drinks well.

Now she was dead. Nothing could change that. No sense second-guessing
myself. Right. *Of course.* She'd called me late on Friday night, and I wasn't there
to answer. Now, it was late on Sunday, and she was gone.

Too late. Let it go. *Sure.*

As the bar swam back into focus, I saw the news traveling. Padre poured
drinks, the regulars all raised glasses to Sunshine. The night's earlier euphoria
began its slide into maudlin morbidity. It was going to get ugly.

I wasn't eager to join what was going to quickly become a grief-fest. Part
of me still felt the shock. But I also mentally noted that murders in the Quarter
were rare—very rare, compared to the homicide statistics for the rest of the city.
The French Quarter is a vast source of revenue for New Orleans, so City Hall
takes a pointed interest in keeping it safe.

I also noted that Bone knew Sunshine—knew her well, if I recalled correct-
ly from previous conversations. I had the vague sense that they'd been a couple

once, but that was long over before I really got to know either of them. Bone was from the West Coast and had known Sunshine out there. This would probably hit him deeper than those acquainted with her only casually from the bars.

Right then he stepped through the door, his face grim, and made a beeline for the bar. He didn't look like he'd heard, more like he'd had a bad night at work. Before Padre could work his way back down to this end, I edged over.

Earlier I had been looking forward to seeing him. Now, given the sad occasion, I figured he might as well hear the news from me.

"Maestro," he said curtly as he lit a cigarette. "Jesus, what a night," he grumbled.

"Bone," I said, nodding a greeting. Then, with no easy way to say it, I simply told him. "Sunshine's dead. Murdered." What else can you do in such a situation? The bereaved either handles it or he doesn't.

Bone didn't exactly handle it. His eyes went wide and still, and his cigarette dropped from the corner of his mouth onto the bar top. I put it in an ashtray.

"You're sure?" He spoke in a strained whisper, like he couldn't find the strength for anything else.

"That's the word. You can call it scuttlebutt if you want. But I doubt seriously anybody would make up a story like this." I didn't say anything about voodoo. It was probably just wild talk and rumor, nothing Bone needed to hear from me.

He stepped back suddenly from the bar. "Then I'm finding out for sure." He stalked toward the door.

I moved fast. No time to think it out or even examine closely why I was doing it. I caught Bone by the upper arm as he stepped out onto the sidewalk. He was headed toward the river.

I don't lay hands on people without cause. Anyone who does that around here quickly unlearns the habit or gets himself painfully rehabilitated. But I had figured out where Bone was going and didn't think it was a good idea. I applied just enough pressure to stop him briefly, which he did, rounding on me with a snarl.

There were several ways I could manage him if he got violent. His balance was off, stance bad. You learn a lot from fencing.

"Look," I said in a calm, reasonable voice, "you don't want to go to the crime scene." I let go of his arm.

He stayed put for the moment, though I could practically see the fight-or-flight adrenaline pumping through him. It was hot out here on the street, especially after the Calf's air-conditioning. The humidity was high, even this late at night. That's how summers are in New Orleans.

"I've got to find out!" he snapped. "I'm not going to sit around wondering if her getting *killed* is just a rumor!"

"I know she's your friend ..."

He rounded on me. "She was my *wife!*"

"*What?*" I couldn't hide my surprise.

"We got divorced after we moved here. She didn't want anyone to know." He looked away. "The Quarter life changed her. Took her away from me. I couldn't make it work for her. I'm not proud of that." He looked up, met my eyes. "That's why I have to see for myself."

Things fell into place. The occasions when Bone had been the one insisting Sunshine be poured into a cab when she'd had one too many. That strange way he looked at her the few times they were both in the same bar—and the way she pretended not to notice him, pulling away from him—just a little—if he got too near.

"And that's all the more reason to stay away from the crime scene."

"Why?"

"Most folks around here may not know you two were married, but the cops will damn sure find that out. They'll also be keeping track of anyone who shows their face down there. You think it won't send off alarm bells if the ex visits the crime scene? Do you really want to become the prime suspect? You're already likely to get questioned once they discover your relationship."

"So? *I* didn't kill her." But he didn't seem to like the notion.

For me, avoiding the police is a matter of course—and good sense. I put a hand on his shoulder, this time to show support. "Look, Bone. Go back in, sit down. Get a drink. I'll go find out what's happened. But I'd advise you to start getting used to the idea of Sunshine ... being dead."

He was thinking it over, looking like he really needed that drink, when a cheerful voice hailed us. "Hey, you two!"

It was Bone's friend, Alex, coming across the street from Pat O.'s, still in her work uniform. She obviously hadn't heard. I used the distraction to do a fade, throwing her a quick wave. Bone could pass the word on to her. I set out toward the river.

* * *

I'd left my drink on the bar top and the heat was terrible, but good deeds are their own punishment.

The Moonwalk runs along the Mississippi River for about three quarters of a mile from midway through the Quarter to the Aquarium of the Americas and

Riverwalk shopping mall. It sits on the edge of the river, just beyond the levee wall built to protect the Quarter from floodwaters. Among New Orleans' quirks is that the city is several inches *below* sea level. The Moonwalk's west end, by the paddlewheel riverboats and the Aquarium, is well-lit and patrolled by bored security men on electric carts. It's popular with lovers and people looking for a pleasant stroll toward Canal Street. In the summer, the breeze off the river makes it about the coolest place to be found in the Quarter, if you don't count the air-conditioned bars.

Though pleasant by day, the other end is poorly lit at night and tends to attract only those who don't want to be seen. Wiser heads tend to avoid that area after the sun goes down.

I was curious to find out exactly where it was on the Moonwalk that Sunshine had met her untimely end. She knew the "safe zones" as well as any other Quarterite.

Unlike Bone, I didn't doubt the rumor. Grown men will gossip like hens about who's sleeping with who, who made a drunken ass out of himself and so on, but news like this wouldn't travel unsubstantiated. *Somebody* had actually seen Sunshine's body, probably after the police arrived, before they covered her up and hauled her away.

If she was still lying down there by the river, though, Bone didn't need to see it. He was wound up, ready to do something stupid, and stupid could take a lot of unproductive forms. I didn't want him getting in trouble. My protective instinct had kicked in surprisingly strong, and I still wasn't sure why.

The nearest point of the Moonwalk was only about three or four blocks away from the Calf, if you count Jackson Square as a block. I wasn't about to go to the river myself. I'd just as soon have the cops notice *my* face as little as possible. Starting across the Square I could see the cluster of blue-and-whites gathered across Decatur, next to the Jax Brewery. That was down near the Moonwalk's east end.

I turned to wander casually across the Square and spotted a familiar face. Despite the hour, Rose was still manning her table, along with a few other psychics and artists. Anyone who thinks that street entertainers don't work should come down to the Quarter and note how many of the artists, mimes, and tarot readers are still at it in the wee hours of the morning, long after everyone except the graveyard-shift bartenders have called it quits.

"Hey, Rose."

"Maestro!" She scooted around her table and greeted me with a warm hug. I allowed myself to enjoy the moment. I normally don't like being touched, but I make an exception for hugs from the fairer sex. "You're okay? Those guys ..."

"Realized they made a mistake."

She stepped back and gave me a measured look. "You didn't fight some crazy sword duel, did you?"

"Would've been kind of difficult with a pool cue. We had a nice chat, shook hands, and went our separate ways."

She seemed a little disappointed. "Still, it was kinda nice to have somebody come to my rescue. It's more than that poor girl got." She gestured across the street toward the Brewery and the gathering of police vehicles. "Murdered. They say some voodoo cult may have done her. Stabbed her and then held some kind of ritual with voodoo dolls and liquor and a couple of dead chickens. 'Course, it's just another crime stat for the Chamber of Commerce to play down."

"Any word on who?"

"Word is it's Sunshine. You know, the little blonde waitress from Big Daddy's?"

It's an exaggeration that everyone in the Quarter knows each other, but not much of an exaggeration. No six degrees of separation here. More like a degree and a half.

"Yeah. I know her ... knew her. Damn. She was a nice kid."

"Well, *nice* don't cut it for armor around here."

"Nothing much does except for maybe eyes in the back of your head. Did you see her before it happened?"

"Not that I know. I had a couple of readings so I wasn't watching real close, but I don't think she came by here."

"Too bad. Well, I just wanted to check up on you. Watch yourself, okay?" I started to leave.

"Hey! I owe you. How about a quickie reading?" She stepped back around her table and reached for her cards. "On the house. Payback—for saving a foolish damsel in distress."

I hesitated for a few beats. Normally, I avoid the cards. If anything, these days I believe in them too much, and sometimes getting a warning in advance only makes you so wary and nervous that you end up precipitating the very thing you're trying to steer around. Still, turning down a free anything from someone you know in the Quarter is a sure way to ruffle feathers, and if she felt it would balance the scales, I owed her the chance.

"Sure. Why not?" I slid into the customer's chair, trying to appear casual. "So what was that guy mad at you for, anyway? Did you get his reading wrong or something?"

"No." She started shuffling the deck. "Problem was I got it *right*. Cards told me his girl was steppin' out on him. I told him. He insisted I was full of shit—refused to pay. I let it go. Then, when he found out it was true, he came after me. Said I put some kind of mojo on her to make it happen." She snorted. "And some people think denial is a river in Egypt!" She set the deck in front of me.

I did two fast cuts and set it back on the table. Like I say, I believe in the cards. Shuffling doesn't really do much. If they have something to tell you, they'll rearrange themselves to deliver the message no matter what you do to the deck physically.

Rose peeled off the top three cards one at a time. It's an old quickie reading she's done for me before, considerably faster than the complicated spreads she does for the tourists.

"The Moon," she said as she glanced at the first card. She knows I can read the cards myself, but is in the habit of doing her readings out loud. "A dangerous undertaking."

I silently absorbed that.

The Two of Cups was next.

"Lovers or partners," she pronounced, "someone new in your life, or an old friend at a new level of awareness. Looks like it will work out pretty well."

I nodded.

When she turned the third card, we both stared in silence for a moment.

The Nine of Swords.

People who don't know the cards are always afraid of the Death Card. They shouldn't be. All it means is the end of one cycle and the beginning of a new one. The Nine of Swords, however, is the one I always dread. I stared at the card, a very distressed man in bed with nine swords around him—the Lord of Despair and Cruelty. Also known as the martyr's card, it can mean many things, both internal and external, almost always bringing changes borne out of conflict and suffering. All swords indicate some level of change, but the nine of swords usually involves a *lot* of change. I have reasons for wanting things unchanged, and I've never been a big fan of suffering.

"Well ... it could mean worry or anxiety," Rose suggested, then glanced up guiltily. Never kid a kidder. We both knew it could also mean downfall, death, or imprisonment.

"Yeah. Well, thanks, Rose. I've got to get going."

I stood up and put a fiver on the table. Even if the service is free, it's always good to tip well. Besides, the reading had been interesting. I wandered on and hung a right onto Decatur Street as if that had been my destination all along.

I considered the area where the police lights gathered. That was important. I knew where Sunshine worked and vaguely where she lived. The end of the

Moonwalk nearer to the French Market was not along any remotely logical route from her work to her home. Whatever happened, it probably wasn't random violence, like running into a mugger. It looked like a deliberate act aimed at her. What's more, odds were she knew whoever had killed her. Why else would she travel so far off her normal beat? But the whole voodoo thing didn't make sense. So far as I knew, Sunshine had never been involved with any of the religions in the Quarter. She certainly never mentioned any interest in *Voudon*. Had she gotten mixed up with some kind of cult? Was this whole thing some ritual gone wrong? If so, the Moonwalk seemed a particularly poor location for it. And from what little I knew of the tradition, stabbing was not normally a part of any of its standard practices—but then, neither was murder.

When I got back to the Calf after making a long circle, Padre was waiting for me with a slip of paper. He didn't look happy.

"Found this after you left."

He handed me a folded piece of paper with *Maestro* scrawled gracefully across the outside.

"I let the new kid, Hound, watch the bar for me for a few while I grabbed some stock from the back. Says some girl came by around eleven looking for you. She left this, said she had to go. The kid forgot about it until I found it under the edge of the register."

I unfolded the white paper and read the brief note scrawled inside:

Maestro, we need to talk.
It's important. Please call me.

Sunshine

I stared at the signature. For a moment, I couldn't breathe. My fingers felt like they'd frozen to the paper.

Chapter 4

Bone

Tripwire ...

I ordered two rummincokes from Padre, made sure Alex got hers to her lips. Her small fingers wound tightly into mine as we sat on our stools. Her eyes were wet, and I kept thinking irrelevantly, inappropriately, about Nicki back at the restaurant, pissed off and crying. Impotent anger. Maybe a special kind of anger only a waitress or waiter knows.

I wasn't crying. I didn't know if I would later on or not.

I had stammered out the news to Alex—babbling but hitting the high points. *Sunshine* and *dead* and *stabbed*. And as I did, I realized it was true, all true. Maestro was right, and this wasn't a rumor.

Sunshine had been murdered.

Or, less passively: Someone murdered Sunshine.

"It's ... awful," Alex choked out the words.

"Yes. It is."

I had known Alex since before Sunshine and I were married, back in San Francisco. Alex was a transplant herself, from the Southwest, the desert. She'd come alone to California, fleeing the smoldering rubble of a divorce.

She had become Sunshine's best friend. She was the only one who'd stayed in touch after we'd cleared out of San Francisco. We had provided a safe landing for her when it was her turn to do the same. She'd crashed on our couch, and then she'd moved into the same Burgundy Street apartment building where I still lived—where Sunshine and I had lived together. Sunshine had suggested that she rent the empty apartment in our building.

No, she didn't *suggest* it. She'd insisted on it.

We three had been such good friends—but what kind of a friend had I been to Sunshine? What kind of husband?

The regulars at the Calf were all talking about Sunshine, naturally. Trading stories, reminiscing, but, really, trying to keep the dead alive a little while longer. That's another thing you do at times like these. Of course to them, she was just a friend from the Quarter. They had no idea what she had been to Alex—or to me. Some of the others might have known her, but we *really* knew her. It wasn't cheap sentiment we felt. It was genuine loss. At that moment I needed Alex and she needed me in a way that was deeper and a little different from what we had known before. Death, when it hits near enough, upsets all arrangements. You reevaluate, scared and desperate, and everything around you suddenly seems doubtful. Tenuous. The relationships you have suddenly take on an increased intensity.

Alex felt it. So did I.

I was in my mid-twenties when I met Sunshine. We were both working at a hipper-than-thou dance club in San Francisco's South of Market district. I was bar-backing; she was a cocktail waitress. I was probably the only straight male there that didn't hit on her mercilessly, which was probably why she turned to me for friendship. I'd be there while she waxed delirious about the latest love of her life, the one who was going to make the difference, the guy who was going to seriously straighten her shit out. I'd still be there two weeks later, a sympathetic ear, when the romance went completely to hell.

For her part, she kept me company when I wanted to go catch a movie or shoot pool or abuse my liver. At first, we didn't date. I didn't want to be dating. I've never had a flair for it, for the formal courtship rituals. My first marriage had ended not too long before that in a finale that combined the apocalyptic elements of *Play Misty for Me*, *End of Days*, and the bloodbath at the end of Peckinpah's *The Wild Bunch*. Sunshine had demonstrated to me, without having to try, that all women weren't emotionally manipulative furies. So, Sunshine and I nursed each other. She was witty, compassionate, alluring, energetic, and intelligent, though definitely lacking in romantic judgment. We became friends, the long-time kind, the ones who've hurt together—the kind of friendship in which lasting bonds are made.

I sympathized with Sunshine. For her incompetent upbringing by hippie parents—"Sunshine" was her real middle name, but her first name was even worse—and for her unbroken run of bad luck with guys, but more because she was a decent person. *Decent.* One not so self-involved that no one else's pain mattered. One who wasn't overly sullen or apathetic or surly or stupid or any of the other traits that our generation and the one that followed were said to possess. She was certainly more generally compassionate than I've ever imagined myself to be. We didn't fall in love, exactly, but it seemed that all our other relationships were such disasters that we were better together than apart. We understood each other.

So we got married. Not out of passion, but because our relationship worked. I wanted a permanent ally, someone I could huddle with while the rain was falling. She was that person. I was absolutely sure of it.

Then, somewhere along the way, my empathy with Sunshine had slipped over a barely definable line. I fell in love with her, and suddenly, our comfortable relationship didn't work anymore. It had been based on friendship and respect, but not passion.

I'd changed. She hadn't.

Even so, we might have made it work if not for San Francisco. That city is even less sympathetic to young newlyweds than to singles. No love lost there. Being native to the city meant nothing, not if you were trying to find a decent apartment without a six-figure income. Just a place to *live*, basic shelter, with running water and electric lights and a mailbox. Nothing extraordinary, understand, nothing unreasonable. But insatiable landlordish greed made for insanely high rents, which much richer people were willing to pay, and the whole sick, sadistic game just wore us out. So we left, disgusted. San Francisco rejected us like a pair of bad kidneys. We'd decided to try to make a go of it in New Orleans.

The best revenge is living well. We rented a spacious apartment here in the Quarter, with a monthly rent that couldn't buy you squatting rights on somebody's back *porch* in San Francisco! Last laughs sound something like this: *hahahahahaheeheehahaha* ...

The best revenge ... revenge ... *tripwire* ...

Sunshine had picked out the apartment. We were set. Life was good.

Ha! The wheels were already coming off the bus before we hit New Orleans, long before Alex left San Francisco to join us in the French Quarter.

Alex wiped her eyes with a small square cocktail napkin and numbly picked a cigarette from the pack she'd laid on the bar top. I lit it for her, lit one of my own. Alex is a head shorter than me and, if anything, scrawnier. Sunshine used to joke that Alex and I looked like matching scarecrows.

"She was my 'little sister.'" Alex's voice had a ragged edge to it. "If not for Sunshine—and you—I'd still be stuck in San Francisco. Probably homeless by now."

I squeezed her hand. When Alex had called us from San Francisco, I'd picked up the phone. I'd immediately recognized the taut, raw-nerved desperation in her voice even before she told me she needed help. She was twisting at the end of her rope, mentally and financially. She was going broke paying $1150 a month for a crummy studio apartment. A *studio*! That's a goddamned broom closet with a bedpan in San Francisco and doesn't come furnished. And she wanted *out*.

Sunshine had insisted that Alex join us in New Orleans. She'd had a blast showing Alex around the Quarter and teaching her the ropes. We had only been living in town for a few months, but Sunshine acted like a native.

I was so proud of how quickly Sunshine adapted to New Orleans, to the French Quarter in particular. It was harder for me. She seemed to fit right in.

It was probably—no, most certainly—too good a fit.

They call New Orleans the Big Easy, and it is that. Jobs and relatively cheap apartments are easy to find, even in the Quarter. The pace is Southernly slow, and there's the general sense that no one expects much of you. It makes for a kind of slacker's paradise. Sunshine landed a gig waiting tables on St. Louis Street, and I snagged one for myself just off Bourbon. Fine? Dandy? Not entirely. As we settled into the rhythm of the Quarter, Sunshine began to change.

She was better off here, I knew, than in San Francisco. Without the pressure of worrying about simple survival, I could see her relaxing, the knots untying. And it was nice, very nice having her in my life. We had a chance to actually *be* a couple. She seemed to be happy ... but we really hadn't left our problems behind us.

Patterns repeat, of course, and Sunshine had always been drawn to men—especially the bad ones. And the Quarter is full of temptation for those who look for it. I knew her eyes were wandering, like a kid's in a candy store. As our lifestyle adjusted to the nocturnal schedule required by our jobs, she began to stay out later and later, often coming home after sunrise. She stopped watching movies with me, and she slept most of the time she was home. Bit by bit she pulled away into the night, until, not long after Alex had settled into her own place, Sunshine asked me for a divorce.

"It's not about you, Bone," she'd insisted. "I just need my own space. I need to find myself, find my passion. I feel like I'm tied down. We'll still be friends."

Those dreadful words. The masquerade ended. The lights came up; the masks were set aside.

I told her that I loved her. She told me that she knew it, then she smiled, kissed me on the cheek, and walked away.

So we divorced, almost as quietly as we had married. We both agreed to keep tight and maintain our friendship. For a while, it worked.

Our marriage had not cured Sunshine's addiction to men, so I wasn't really surprised when after a month or so she found the same sort of relationship troubles here that had plagued her back in 'Frisco. Bad boyfriends were her habit. It was another of her habits, though, that started causing me to worry.

I knew that Sunshine had been a drug user of the recreational sort. Pot, painkillers, nothing stronger I knew of—nothing that showed on the surface, anyway. But if she used while we were married, she kept it quiet. She never brought any dope into our apartment. Her life had never derailed because of it, no more than alcohol has destroyed my life. Yes, I drink. No, alcohol doesn't take the higher moral ground over narcotics. Yes, a lot of the Quarter's social scene revolves around the bars, and the Quarter is where I live. Why do you ask?

After we split, I started hearing through the rumor mill that she was getting a bit heavier into the drug scene. I didn't like that—didn't like that I was *hearing* it, that is. I try to avoid bar gossip, but it's frankly impossible. Drama is a way of life for some Quarterites, usually those with the least going on in their lives. If they can't find that drama or melodrama, they invent it, and they'll do every damned thing in their power to make you a part of it. Or at least to listen to them and take their side.

This time they were talking about her, Sunshine, which was disturbing, but it was also, incidentally, a sure sign she'd been absorbed into Quarter society. She left the St. Louis Street restaurant for Big Daddy's. Again, I wasn't surprised. People bounce around in the business. No big deal.

I wasn't seeing so much of her. It was a slow change, slow enough that I didn't realize it right away. Maybe I didn't want to think she was ducking me ... actually, that's bullshit. I didn't want to think *I* was doing the ducking—which might well have been the case.

When I did see her, she was ... off. The rumormongers had it that she'd become a full-blown druggie. I made an effort not to be influenced by that. It was tough. She wasn't looking right. Behavior, familiar mannerisms, everything about her skewed just so ... out of adjustment. I tried to get her to open up. I did the good friend shtick. But she laughed it off, changed the subject. Something wrong with the laugh, too—brittle, off-key. I persisted and got told, bluntly, to give it a rest. That I had lost the right, with the divorce. That stung, especially since our parting hadn't been my idea.

Her behavior continued to deteriorate, though I couldn't have said just how, exactly, she was different. Even those changes I could see weren't extraordinary, weren't really cause for alarm. But she felt wrong to me. I saw her less and less.

I'd known her almost six years, was married to her for one. I was thirty-one. Friends had come and gone, and I was used to that, could accept the fact like a grownup. But Sunshine had been more than that to me. I didn't want to lose her ... but I sensed she was going, her life heading toward self-destructive territory well beyond her normal range—sensed, second-guessed, but didn't *know*. And I didn't have the stamina, the *cojones* to stick with it, to get her to talk and tell me what was happening to her, to offer her a hand and make goddamned sure she knew that I was still—*always would be*—there for her.

I realized in mid-sip of my rummincoke what my last memory of Sunshine was going to be, what I'd got myself stuck with, and drank off the rest of my drink in a gulp. When Padre came by to repair my glass, eyes small and distant behind his spectacles, he asked, "You taking it all right, Bone?" Padre was in his forties, fit, even-tempered, long hair pulled back into the same ponytail I wore during the summer swelter. He was a first-rate bartender, able to handle capacity tourist crowds here at the Calf without breaking a detectable sweat.

"I'm taking it," I answered. We were brothers-in-arms, service industry cousins. Sunshine, too, had been a waitress. You could say we'd lost one of our own and wouldn't be significantly over-dramatizing it. Padre poured Alex another drink as well. Of course, he didn't know what I had lost.

That last memory of Sunshine, the last time I'd actually seen her ... it wasn't pleasant. That pissed me off, and once more tonight there was nowhere to put the anger.

I counted back, fingers tapping the sweating side of my rock glass. Eight ... no, nine days ago. It had happened at Molly's, the one on Toulouse, not Decatur. Happened. The Incident. *Shit!*

I was off work a little early, just after midnight, had stopped in at Molly's to shoot some solitary practice pool, where I roll three balls at a time randomly onto the table and take them down in the best order. It gets one thinking strategically, and that's good, since I don't always leave myself a decent next shot when I'm playing.

Sunshine came in—no, came *rolling* in with that pitching stagger of someone who is too drunk to be out in public any longer but is being borne along by reflexes and remembered motor skills. You see this particular form of locomotion pretty regularly in the Quarter. It's funny—sometimes—if it's a stranger, especially a tourist, since it's like watching a child who's snuck half a beer at a Christmas party weaving and wobbling around.

Seeing Sunshine in that state made me wince. Normally she was a very capable drinker. Fact is, most of us Quarterites are. We drink—oh, yes, we do—but getting sloppy or hostile or weepy is looked down upon, and your friends will step in if you start making a habit of it, partly to spare you the embarrassment, partly to keep you from getting into *real* trouble.

There is no last call for alcohol in New Orleans, no 2 a.m. cutoff, no laws even preventing you from walking around with an open container. In short, nothing to stop you from pulling a Nicholas Cage à la *Leaving Las Vegas*—that is, drinking yourself to death. Nothing except those people that might give a damn about you.

Sunshine looked wrecked. I stared at her a few seconds from the far side of the pool table ... and God help me, my first and surest thoughts were for slipping out the bar's other door before she spotted me.

She didn't just look drunk. She was wound up, in a fumy, heaving fury, eyes spinning in opposite directions, like she was going to come apart, right *apart* and right there, in an explosion sure to take out the entire room. I had seen her angry; I had seen her distraught and hysterical. Her emotions could rev high, into the red. But this was new to me.

I quietly laid down the bar cue I was using and—yes, cowardly, totally cowardly—I edged for the door.

Molly's wasn't crowded, but when Sunshine saw me, she *shrieked*, and all conversation stopped. The juke wasn't playing, and there was only ambient street noise from outside. Inside, that sudden instant of silence reverberated.

Being a Quarterite, I've dealt with drunks. Being a waiter in the French Quarter, I've dealt with them professionally—that is, I've calmed them down with overwhelming reason, which is better, though less satisfying, than resorting to physical persuasion. Sunshine, wheeling on me with berserk eyes I didn't recognize in a face I'd known for six years, was more than drunk. There was an added tweakiness, a terrible elastic intensity to her manner—a craziness booze can't easily deliver.

Sunshine's shriek hadn't had any words in it. It was just primal sound meant to freeze me in my tracks, which it did. Long enough for her to pounce on me.

The bartender, a gal I'd tipped well for the one cocktail I'd bought since arriving, was moving to intervene, but it was a long way around the bar.

This twitched-out, hag-like, violent-ward-nutcase version of the woman who was once my wife and best friend meanwhile proceeded to lay into me. She went for my guiltiest exposed nerve—where had I been, why was I avoiding her? Who the hell did I think I was? It was a tirade, and barely coherent. She raved, her arms whipping wildly. All heads were turned in the bar, watching, and I was embarrassed to be a part of the spectacle. It was a short hop, though, from embarrassment to resentment.

My shift that night at the restaurant had been typically unpleasant. I'd wanted nothing more than a little quiet time to decompress, which I'd been managing to do before this happened. It was a nasty shock seeing Sunshine like this, and worse, much worse, that she was pulling this psychodrama on me, in public. Maybe I deserved some of what she was saying. That got me angrier, but I couldn't just stand there and put up with this shit.

So I gave back what I was getting.

"Yeah, I've been dodging you! Take a *look* at yourself, for Chrissake! *Listen* to yourself! You've become a doped-out freak lunatic I'd cross the street to avoid! You think you can talk like this to me? Me—*me?*" Or words to that effect. I was suddenly seeing red.

Tripwire ...

The bartender broke it up, and I left, and I didn't see Sunshine again. And now that was it. That was the end of all our time together, and there wasn't going to be any more.

My second rummincoke was gone, and I couldn't remember tasting it. I was reaching for another cigarette. This is what we would do tonight, I realized, Alex and me and the regulars who knew Sunshine. We'd sit in here and drink somberly, and probably more than one of us would get drunk, and there would be more tears and maybe some anger. Sunshine would remain dead, and nothing whatsoever that we did would mean anything.

"Bone ... ?"

Alex was looking at me. I had stood from my stool.

"I'm going to find out if anybody knows anything more." I heard my words like someone else was saying them. "Want to wait for me?"

"I'll wait." She looked at me, in a way that said more than her words, "Be ... careful." She squeezed my hand, before letting go.

I looked at her again, and I realized how lucky I was to have a friend like her. She'd been there for me after Sunshine had left me. She was here for me now that ...

I couldn't think it. I couldn't think of anything else. I left the bar.

* * *

Excerpt from Bone's Movie Diary:

> I wept when George C. Scott died. Brilliant of course in *Patton*, but also not to be forgotten are his performances in *Anatomy of a Murder*, *The New Centurions*, *The Hustler*, Paddy Chayefsky's *The Hospital*. For that matter he was terrific in *The Changeling* & even *Firestarter*—say what you will. I wept actual tears. I had seen him in movies since I was a kid. Maybe that familiarity, maybe having him suddenly gone from my

landscape, whatever, it saddened me. I felt it personally. I also think it points up a fundamental flaw in me: I prefer movies to people. I don't say this to sound cool; I'm not particularly proud of this trait. I know, in my head, that the real world deserves more attention than films. Movies are make-believe. Life is supposed to be experienced firsthand. Blah blah blah. Know what? I don't want to live my every moment to its fullest. I want, sometimes—and probably more often than most people—to watch others living, watch their dramas and interactions, their pratfalls and unlikely coincidences, their terrors, hopes, joys. When a film convincingly conveys these other lives to me, I'm enthralled. I'm entertained. I can feel for these pretend people, I can appreciate the craft of the performers, the talents of the cinematographer and director. I can feel emotions I might not, frankly, ever experience in my life—not with such depth or clarity, anyway. So, it's a failing on my part. I cried for George C. Scott, not because a flesh & blood person had passed from this world, not because I personally knew him. But because he had been so many different & wonderful people to me. Same when Vincent Price died. And Steve McQueen. John Candy (& if you can't enjoy him in *Splash*, laughter is a stranger to you), Rod Steiger, Audrey Hepburn, River Phoenix, Bette Davis ... my friends, how I miss you all.

Chapter 5

Maestro

I carefully folded the note and put it in my pocket, trying not to think about the fact that Sunshine had come looking for me in the last hours of her life—and I had been out dealing with the Flynn wannabe and his fat henchman. A phone call and a note, and I'd missed both. Were they related to her murder? A cry for help? If so, why me and not Bone? Especially since they had a history.

Bone was gone. Looking around the Calf I spotted Alex, sitting at the bar. A tiny thing, mostly angular bones and big eyes, Alex wore her dark hair cropped so close she almost looked like a young boy sometimes. She was one of those devouring readers that could knock out a book in a sitting—lots of science fiction and fantasy. She also enjoyed counted cross-stitch as a hobby. A knapsack full of yarn sat at her feet, her cross-stitch busywork for lulls at her job at Pat O'Brians gift shop. She looked up at my approach and gave me a wan smile.

In an odd flip-flop, I'd actually met her before I'd met Bone, and was subsequently surprised when we all crossed paths at the Calf one night. No real reason for my surprise, though. Quarterites' lives are practically braided together, whether we like it or not. That two people I'd met independently happened to be friends from the same town was nothing extraordinary. I would chat with Alex when our paths crossed, mostly the play flirting that passes for conversation here. It didn't take me long to realize that she had no real interest in me, but was totally devoted to Bone, though he seemed not to realize that. We still flirted, but nothing serious. It was just a fun way to kill some time without really showing each other any important cards.

"Where's Bone?"

Her voice was a little unsteady. "He left. Said he'd be back."

I felt a pang of unease. I had wanted him to stay put. "Did he say where he was going, exactly?" I asked, more directly than I wanted to. Caginess is second nature to me. But, then again, Alex was a good egg, and I only had Bone's welfare in mind.

"No, Maestro." Her eyes were a bit red. "He just said something about finding out what people know about Sunshine. Why don't you sit down, wait for him to get back?" She gestured toward the adjacent stool.

Padre eyed me from down the bar, to see if I wanted a drink. I did, but ...

"Thanks, darling, but no. This has been a rough night. I think I'll head home."

Alex gave me a kind of numb little farewell hug. I nodded a goodbye to Padre, leaving him to tend to the crowd of grieving locals that was bigger now than when I'd ducked out earlier. Padre and I wouldn't be talking pool-team strategies tonight.

I lit a cigarette as I stepped again into the humid outdoors. Another glass of Irish would have been very welcome, but Bone was out here somewhere. I wanted to keep him from doing anything rash or stupid, if I could ... even though I still wasn't sure where this protective impulse was coming from.

I started down St. Peter, toward Bourbon. Maybe I was doing something stupid myself.

The Quarter hasn't changed much since September 11th. That's not a sad commentary on our backwardness or tradition of isolationism. Locals themselves will tell you that New Orleans lags behind the rest of the nation by decades. Our schools and civic services are supposed to be sub-par, of Third World quality. I don't know how true any of that is. But here it's easy sometimes to forget about other places. The Quarter is its own world. In some ways it feels like the 1800s have never lost their hold on the area.

It was certainly a drastic change for me when I came down from Detroit ten years ago.

Ten years ... sometimes that seems like a lot more time than it's been. Other times, not nearly enough. I mentally snickered at myself. Apparently I'd been living on "Quarter time" too long. I couldn't calibrate myself with the outside world's calendar anymore.

Bourbon Street was winding down, though it usually doesn't completely die until sunrise. The street was littered with plastic drink cups, spilled booze, and assorted bits of trash, and reeked of stale beer—just what you'd expect in the aftermath of any good frat party. Taxis scurried up the cross streets, gathering up partied-out tourists to take them back to their hotels. Two cops rode by on horseback. To the tourists, they were undoubtedly a colorful, quaint sight, but they were out here working. The horses gave them the height to see over crowds and the maneuverability to navigate narrow alleyways. And even the largest, most belligerent drunk would have a hard time pushing around fifteen hundred pounds of horse. I slowed a bit, idly watching as a couple stumbled by across the street—a coed wearing a green boa and one spike-heeled shoe, borne along by a guy who looked embarrassed enough to be her boyfriend.

There is a strong police presence in the French Quarter, but in order for it to be as safe as the theme park most visitors seem to think it is, cops would have to be camped on every corner. On certain occasions that is nearly true. Our city hosted a Super Bowl following September 11th. And of course, every year there's Mardi Gras. Both events sprouted police *everywhere*, not to mention the Feds and the Guard. At such times I tend to lay *very* low.

But this was just a normal, lackluster summer night, with no conventions in town and nothing remarkable happening. Nothing except a murder by the river. Rose was probably right. The incident would likely get played down by those City agencies interested in maintaining a good image for the Quarter.

What else had she been right about? The Moon, the Two of Cups, the Nine of Swords: a dangerous undertaking, the appearance of a lover/partner, and the Lord of Despair. *Swell*, I thought, then pushed it out of my head. Like I said, the cards can get you second-guessing yourself into as much trouble as they can help you avoid.

I had covered two blocks of Bourbon, heading in the direction of the Marigny, taking a casual look into every place I passed. Alex had said Bone had gone out to ask around about Sunshine. I figured that would take him where the most people were. Hopefully he hadn't actually gone to the river after all.

I found myself in front of Marie Laveau's House of Voodoo, an older one-story shop on the corner of St. Ann Street. I thought again about the rumors of a voodoo involvement in the murder. Would Bone have come here? The shop was closed down tight for the night. If there were any answers in there, they would have to wait.

I looked down Bourbon at clusters of wilted balloons, remnants of some earlier celebration, that hung from the balconies. Music and laughter spilled out of the bars across the street, both still jumping despite the late hour. St. Ann Street supposedly splits the straight and gay halves of the Quarter. From what I've witnessed, though, those aren't distinct realms. I suppose I know a lot more gays here than I knew up North, and in the Quarter they don't segregate themselves. Neither do most locals give a rat's ass about anyone else's sexual orientation. So we get male bartenders with boyfriends working in "straight" bars, and heterosexual couples going into the two mostly gay dance clubs in front of me.

I didn't figure that Bone would have gone trolling for information in either club, though. I turned around to follow Bourbon in the other direction, toward the CBD—the Central Business District.

"Hey, Maestro!"

I was used to being hailed on the street, but right now I didn't have time for neighborly chitchat. I did a fast scan and saw someone coming toward me. I recognized the walk before the name came to me. Fencing had taught me to study an individual's gait and body language.

Jet had been a decent stick when he shot for several league sessions a few years ago. He'd also been a notorious bad sport who contested every close-call shot and made a general pest of himself during the pool games.

"In a hurry, Jet. Can't talk." He had asked for a spot on my team roster before, which wasn't going to happen.

I could smell the alcohol in his sweat as he stepped up, silvered hair sticking up in an unruly wad from his balding head. Jet was my age and drank about twice as much as someone of our years should. "Maestro, ya hurd?"

I guessed he'd heard about Sunshine. "Like I said, Jet, I'm in a ..."

"Somebody's lookin' for yuh."

I was turning away. I stopped. I measured him with my eyes. Jet was loaded, but not exceedingly drunk. I took a few steps away from the corner, and he followed, to a quieter patch of sidewalk.

"Want to tell me about that?" I kept my voice low and level.

He licked his lips. "Guy goin' 'round. He's askin' for yuh. By name."

That meant "Maestro," since nobody but my landlord and Padre knew the name that appears on my bogus state ID—which, of course, isn't the name I was born with.

"Did you see this ... guy?"

"Naw. I was up to the Abbey earlier, heard 'bout somebody, a guy, nobody knew 'im, and he's askin' 'Where's Maestro, any y'all seen Maestro,' like that. O'course nobody tells 'im shit, y'know. I heard he was goin' along Decatur doin' the same thing."

"This was when?"

Jet's bloodshot eyes narrowed as he thought. "Half hour. Forty-five. Not too long."

That was roughly the time that word about Sunshine had reached the Calf. Was that significant? I didn't know.

"Well, thanks for the heads-up," I said sincerely.

"Sure. Hey, I ..." I could see him getting ready to ask again about getting on the team. Then he shrugged and said, "Sure," and slipped off up St. Ann.

Jet wasn't a friend, but it wasn't shocking that he was giving me this warning. There are things that put Quarterites on automatic alert. One of them is strangers making inquiries. Some, but not a lot, of locals are ducking warrants and parole officers. Some are paranoid about the IRS showing up unannounced on their doorsteps. Whatever, xenophobia is the Quarter's most common disease—though some would argue for alcoholism. Asking questions about a local quickly causes the wagons to circle. Suddenly, nobody knows *nothing*. Doesn't really matter if you like the person or not. It's almost jailhouse code.

I certainly didn't like the idea of someone looking for me. It could, of course, be a simple misunderstanding. I counted off the bars along Decatur, thought of the bartenders I knew, and who was on what shift. I wanted more information than Jet had provided.

I was still standing there a few steps back from the corner. My eyes were darting around, scanning the people milling around the clubs' entrances, the occupants of passing cars. My normal healthy state of cautious awareness was turned up several notches, so that the sweat on the back of my neck wasn't entirely due to the heat anymore.

There were extreme possibilities here, very extreme. I forced myself not to mentally follow them to their conclusions. I'd been in danger much more tangible than this, and at just over half a century old, I was still walking and breathing.

I reversed course back down Bourbon, taking only a few steps before it hit me out of the blue where Bone might be. For a few seconds I'd actually forgotten him, which was why my subconscious had probably furnished the answer. I moved on at a faster pace, hoping I wasn't right about his whereabouts.

Chapter 6

Bone

For the record, I've got nothing against naked women, but even if I had never been married, I still wouldn't make a habit of visiting strip clubs. It's not prudishness on my part, not lingering Catholic school behavioral inhibitions. Neither do I go out of my way to object to the objectifying of women. One doesn't need to shimmy naked and publicly to feel cheap and exploited and a whore for tips. Ask any waiter.

As gentleman's clubs go, Big Daddy's wasn't at all seedy. New Orleans' romantically sleazy Storyville past is just that—*past*. Advertised as Bourbon Street's only "topless, bottomless club," Big D's was more like Disneyland—for adults. A pair of high-heeled mechanical legs, complete with stockings, swung back and forth out the front window, drawing the attention of Bourbon Street crowds, much like balloons might draw a child's attention at the fair. Inside, all was virtually antiseptic. Crisp lighting, air-conditioning cold enough to nearly freeze my summer-sweaty T-shirt to me, a bouncer's alert/disinterested eyes robotically watching, all combined to make the climate feel—what? Fake? Contrived? You mean those beautiful buxom babes aren't dancing up there strictly for my enjoyment? They ... they just *work* here? You mean this isn't real?

Pornography is as pornography does.

The patrons crowded the seats nearest the one occupied stage—frat-boy cretins that could be the same ones who'd hassled Nicki at the restaurant earlier, and maybe were, along with middle-aged and much, much older men. Their voices slavered and cheered above the soulless, bass-heavy music pounding the air. I didn't know the girl twirling around the pole on the stage, and didn't study her long enough to figure out if her bare, gravity-defying breasts were real.

Hardly a turn-on. I didn't join in the ogling, didn't want to be mistaken for one of the simps down front. Stayed instead back by the bar, ordered a shockingly expensive rummincoke from the tall female bartender, and tipped good anyway. That's ingrained. I've had quite a few years now in this industry, having no other marketable talents, and very quickly tipping becomes sacred. (If you've got no education and no prospects, go wait tables.) It works both ways, as do most things in the Quarter. When I wait on bartenders and fellow wait-folk at the restaurant, I can expect generous gratuities.

I watched the spike-haired waitress work the customers by the stage, noting and recognizing her naturally sensual movements. She came up beside me to set her tray on the bar top and place her order with the bartender.

"Bone," she acknowledged me. I saw raw eyes in her heavily made-up face.

"Chanel." I'd served her at the restaurant often enough that we knew each other's names.

"If you're looking for a job, we don't hire male dancers."

It was standard smartass banter. But her voice sounded scraped and quivery. She was just barely holding herself together; so was I. And we both were wearing our tough fronts.

I wasn't about to make it a contest. "I came to ask about Sunshine."

I said it quietly, under the music, so the bartender didn't hear as she set glasses and beers onto Chanel's tray. Chanel heard, and her painted features went still.

Finally she said, "What ... do you want to know, Bone? We only heard a little while ago. I only know she's dead. *Stabbed.*" A shrill note of anger, one I recognized, punctuated her last word. Her bare eyes drilled me.

"That's all I know too. Chanel ... *please.* Sunshine was ... she was special to me. We go back. I just want to know ..." And here my breath was suddenly gone. I locked gazes with her; and perhaps there was something to be read in my eyes.

"Who did it," she finished for me.

"Yeah, who did it." My lungs restarted. My heart beat slow and hard.

"I don't know that." Chanel took up her tray.

I nodded. "But I want to find out. I want to know who killed Sunshine." I realized the club's management might be watching, and I didn't want Chanel getting any flak for loitering to talk to me.

She stood there a moment. "Look, I'm out of here in fifteen. Okay?" And without waiting for me to say anything, headed back toward the stage where the grandly-endowed girl was mock-humping the face of a man who looked old enough to have stormed the beaches at Normandy.

I drank off my drink, too fast, feeling it in the bones around my eyes. I hadn't eaten dinner tonight—didn't like eating on-shift—and tried to remember a meal before that. Nothing came.

The dancer finished her set, and a new one appeared on the second stage, causing the college kids and old men to migrate over. While I don't knock the stripping profession, per se, I don't know if it attracts self-damaging individuals or creates them. I've known two dancers in my life who have overdosed, and one who is serving a ten-year manslaughter stretch for putting a 9-millimeter to her sleeping boyfriend's forehead and pulling the trigger. That the boyfriend used to pound her like a gong hadn't seemed to impress the cops much, but the jury took it carefully into account.

When I stepped outside, the steamy air was almost welcome after the club's deep freeze. I picked a patch of wall, leaned, and waited. Sunshine had been waiting tables at Big Daddy's, not peeling, I reminded myself needlessly. But ... hadn't she already been on a self-destructive trajectory? And, if I was going to be brutally honest, she had been since we'd moved here. For that matter, even before we got together. Bad relationship choices—so bad and so consistent, in fact, they had to be deliberate on some level. Her high-strung personality had been volatile, but not panicky. Actually she was a good one to have around in a crisis. Still, she had that penchant for strong emotions, and her flirtation with drugs had been more serious than I'd let myself think. And what of our relationship? Was I the only decent man she'd ever been with, or was I just fooling myself? That scene at Molly's between us, when she'd showed up wrecked and we'd ended up screaming at each other ... *Christ*. It still made me wince.

I want to know who killed Sunshine.

It had startled me when I caught myself saying that. It was suggestive, telling. I hadn't yet stopped to think about what I was doing—stepping out of the Calf, coming here to Sunshine's old workplace to make inquiries, to find out. She'd been killed. Stabbed. Possibly as part of some sick, twisted ritual thing. I would handle the grief of that on my own. But I needed my question answered. Who did it?

Why, though, did I want to know? It seemed if I was asking, then I meant to do something about it. Was that what was happening? I didn't know.

Was I thinking of revenge?

I absentmindedly lit up a smoke, and immediately a rancid gutter punk sprang up out of the dark and grime, looking to mooch. Beer-stained T-shirt, facial blemishes, gross ingratiating grin. It was tough to give a shit, and I didn't try, waving him off.

Bourbon, which closes nightly to auto traffic, was supporting just a few handfuls of revelers, those walking around with "specialty" drinks (puked up, they make distinctively colored puddles on the sidewalks) and oversized beers in plastic go-cups. Somebody shouted out, *"Newwwor-LEEENZ!"* at football rally volume, just in case anybody sleeping in a one block radius had forgotten where they were, and mispronounced our city's name to boot.

I love the Quarter. I truly do. But it can be a test.

When Chanel came down the front steps, I'd been waiting more like twenty minutes. The tight outfit had been replaced by dowdy civilian clothes, her spiked bottle-red hair hidden under a cap. Frankly, I thought she looked prettier this way, less mannequin-like. She fished a pack of cigarettes out of her shapeless, baggy jeans, and I lit her smoke for her.

"Okay, Bone." Her makeup too was gone. She looked tired. "Ask me."

"You want to go someplace?"

"No. I don't. I want to go home. Ask me here."

It felt, oddly, for that second there like I was at some line of demarcation, that to cross it I need only ask my first question about Sunshine—that I was at the start of something I could stop now, simply by not going forward.

I stepped off into the void. "Do you know if Sunshine was dating anybody lately?"

"Dating?" Chanel blew smoke through grimly smirking lips. "What, like going to the malt shop, wearing some guy's school pin?"

I wasn't doing banter tonight. "Like seeing somebody steady."

"Couldn't say. I had the feeling she was screwing someone on a regular basis, but who ..." She shrugged. "We weren't tight, y'know, her and me. Girls go through here, and it's usually a while 'fore I get to know ..." She didn't need to add that now it was too late to make friends with Sunshine.

"How about customers?" I asked. "Anybody showing up to see her?"

"Sure. But that goes for everybody. Not just the dancers. I get guys asking for me all the time." She said this with some professional pride.

I was hoping for something easy, I realized—one of Sunshine's standard disastrous boyfriends, maybe a customer at the club stalking her. Something—some*one*—obvious.

Chanel was already looking impatient. Who could blame her? A dead co-worker, and now my questions. Better ask while the asking was good.

"Was Sunshine showing up for her shifts on time?"

She shrugged, a bit petulantly this time. "I guess. Most of the time. She wasn't, like, a total flake."

"How about money? Was she short on cash lately?"

"I didn't make a habit of going through her purse."

I grimaced. "Right. But was she strapped, did she borrow from you, from the other girls? Did she gripe about money a lot?"

"Not to me. Borrowing? I never heard of her doing it. Look, Bone ..."

"I know." I took a last puff off my cigarette and ground it out under my heel. I did have something I had to ask, had teased around it with my last few questions. It was delicate, and I was using up the last of Chanel's good will. I didn't want to, but—I had to ask.

I drew a breath.

"Chanel, was Sunshine turning tricks?"

Those raw, tired eyes lit with a spark. She stiffened. If this was a hard-boiled gumshoe movie, I would be able to divine her body language instantly. Fact was, I didn't know if I'd bumped against the truth or just provided a point of focus for her free-floating anger over Sunshine's murder.

With studied icy dignity she pulled herself tall. "You ought to speak a little better of the dead, Bone." With a sharp flick she shot her cigarette butt inches past my left ear, and that was it. She turned and strode off, down Bourbon toward Canal, a straight crisp line.

Leaving me staring after her, alone on the sidewalk with the street's fumes and very little accomplished. Alone ... until I realized someone was standing behind me, very near.

* * *

Excerpt from Bone's Movie Diary:

A good way for an actor to grab the Oscar is of course to play a character with an affliction. Dustin Hoffman's 2nd Oscar for *Rain Man* (autistic); Daniel Day-Lewis for *My Left Foot* (cerebral palsy); Tom Hanks' double whammy of *Philadelphia* (AIDS sufferer) & *Forrest Gump* (mentally challenged); Pacino's *Scent of a Woman* (blind); etc. Not always the actor's best work, is it? Actresses fare well for awards & nods playing prostitutes & women of questionable morals. Elisabeth Shue got a nomination for *Leaving Las Vegas,* as did Annette Bening for *The Grifters,* Jodie Foster for *Taxi Driver,* & the Oscar went home with Jane Fonda for *Klute,* Mira Sorvino for *Mighty Aphrodite,* Kim Basinger for *L.A. Confidential,* Anne Baxter for 1946's *The Razor's Edge,* Liz Taylor for *Butterfield 8,* & so forth. There are good performances among those, with some glaring exceptions. Yet even the cautionary tales, the gritty & seamy ones ... they seem to subversively & perversely glamorize the lifestyle. We can safely observe and tsk-tsk the proceedings & most of these films encourage us—overtly or otherwise—to do so, but secretly we're titillated by these "fallen women." We are meant to thrill as they plunge headlong toward annihilation.

Chapter 7

Maestro

Bone turned around suddenly, but I'd glided up behind him, past whatever radar he had. He was startled and his stance was wobbly again.

"Maestro—"

"I thought you said you were going to stay at the Calf."

He recovered himself, shaking his head. "I didn't say that. *You* said you were stepping out to ask about Sunshine. Well, I did the same thing."

I glanced past him, to the entrance to Big Daddy's. "You went asking in there?" My tone was clipped.

"Right. I know one of waitresses from around. Chanel. I was just talking to—"

I'd seen him talking to the redhead. "Look, Bone, I want to talk to you about this. But let's get off the street. We'll go to Fahey's. Come on, I'll buy a round."

He looked at me funny. "Talk? Maestro, I ought to be getting back to the Calf. I left Alex sitting there. Talk about what? Did you find out something about Sunshine?" He asked it eagerly.

"Who killed her? No." No one was within earshot, but I still wanted off the street.

"Talk to me on the way back to the Calf, then. I don't want another drink. I'm going to meet Alex and go home."

For the third time tonight I put a hand on him, on his shoulder this time. "Bone, we need to talk. Seriously."

I guess I said it convincingly. After a few seconds he nodded. Tufts of his dark hair were sticking out from his ponytail, and his already thin face looked even more drawn. We hiked down to Fahey's, which is just two blocks off Bourbon, on Burgundy and Toulouse. On the way, I thought about what I wanted to say.

We stepped into the air-conditioning. Milo was bartending. I took Bone at his word and just ordered him a soda, but by now I definitely wanted another cocktail. It was quiet in the bar but I led Bone back toward one of the high tables by the poker machines anyway. We were isolated. Even both pool tables were unoccupied, which was rare. Fahey's is a little local Irish pub that never plays

Irish music, but is home base for several pool league teams and has a bank of cue lockers. There's little or no "trash talking," no big money games, but on any given night you can normally find half a dozen to a dozen solid shooters sorting out the pecking order over drinks.

"Okay," Bone said, leaving the soda untouched and lighting a cigarette. "What?"

He wanted to be direct? Fine. Now was the time for it.

"What the hell are you trying to do?"

He had the perplexed look again. "How's that?"

"Earlier you were ready to go charging off to the crime scene. Why?"

"To find out what happened to Sunshine—if it was true, and what exactly it was that happened."

"And then you went over to Sunshine's work place, asking questions."

"Right."

"Why?"

He was starting to look pissed off. "Like I said—to find out."

I took a pull on my drink. "But why?"

Now he *was* getting angry. "What the hell you think?"

"Doesn't matter what I think," I said steadily. "Just answer, Bone. Why are you asking around about Sunshine's murder?"

"So I can find out who's the motherfucker who did it!"

I saw Milo glance our way, but the bar's few other patrons didn't pay us any attention. It was mostly service industry people, familiar faces.

I leaned forward on my stool and pinned him with my eyes. "And what do you plan on doing with that knowledge, if you get it?"

He bit back on an immediate retort. I watched him think it through. He puffed hard on his cigarette.

Finally, he said, "It depends."

"On what?"

"On whether the cops know who did it, and whether they catch him."

I had him thinking in an orderly fashion now. That was good. Before, he'd been reacting strictly from the gut. Still, I had a good idea where this was going, and that *wasn't* good.

"What if the police don't have any suspects, don't pick anyone up?"

"Then *I'll* find out who killed her." His voice was a level growl. "And I'll set things right."

"Revenge?" I asked, almost softly.

"Justice ... no, you're right, *revenge*. The eye for an eye kind."

I let out a long sigh. "Don't personalize it,"

"What do you mean?" Anger flashed back into his eyes.

"Most of the murders the police get are what they call 'smoking guns,' where they know almost immediately who the perpetrator is." I spoke slowly and quietly, trying to wind him back down. Sometimes boring lectures work. "You're most likely to get killed by a family member or a close friend in the heat of an argument ... especially during the hot, humid summer months, like now. It's the cases that aren't obvious, the 'whodunits' that usually go unsolved. If they don't come up with an answer in the first forty-eight hours, they usually quit. It's not like TV or the detective novels. They're overloaded with cases and simply don't have any more time to put into any single case."

"You said not to *personalize* it." He obviously didn't like the sound of that.

"You're not giving the police the time to do their job. Realize what they're up against in every 'whodunit.' Give them the chance to check things out their way. Maybe they'll get lucky. You're already running around trying to start your own investigation. You're going to call attention to yourself, maybe end up distracting the cops. I would recommend you chill out, at least enough to think clearly. It's always better to fight cold than hot."

He ground his cigarette into the table's black plastic ashtray. It wasn't earth-shaking advice I was giving him, but hopefully I'd cooled him down sufficiently.

He looked at me, intent but not hostile now. "You didn't just happen to bump into me up there on Bourbon, did you, Maestro? You came out looking for me. Didn't you?"

"Yes," I said simply.

"Why?" He gave me a wry little smile, appearing to enjoy giving me back my own earlier question.

I'd been thinking it over, though, trying to deduce why I felt such a strong protective instinct toward this kid who was, after all, a new acquaintance and not somebody I should be too invested in.

"I'm just looking out for you, Bone."

"Why?" he asked again, enjoying it even more.

I took another healthy swallow of Irish. "Because you remind me of some-one ... someone I don't want to see doing anything unnecessarily dangerous." *Or stupid*, I added silently.

The smirk left his face. "So what do you want from me, Maestro?"

"To lay off this thing for forty-eight hours. See what the police can do."

He nodded once. "And if they don't come up with anything?"

"Then *you'll* want to do something. Presuming you're serious?"

"Very serious."

I finished off my drink. "In that case, you could probably use some help."

We stared at each other a moment across the tabletop. I thought of Rose turning over the Two of Cups.

"Forty-eight hours," Bone finally said. "Okay. Clock's ticking. Meanwhile ..." We climbed off our stools. He had Alex waiting to be escorted home.

I didn't have anyone waiting for me, but the Quarter, in its entirety, was my home, and ... well, I didn't take kindly to the murder of one of my household.

* * *

I still had Jet's news to worry about, of course. That I'd put it on hold while hunting down Bone showed how serious I was about trying to safeguard the kid. Now, however, it was time to look into it.

My apartment is maybe a little too close to the action on Bourbon, so on busy weekends, and certainly during Carnival, I get a lot of crowd noises. I don't particularly mind, though. My place is a "slave quarters" apartment, a local term I found a bit shocking when I first moved down here. It refers to a detached unit at the rear of a larger building. Mine abuts a flagstone patio planted with jasmine, where there's enough space for me to swing a fencing foil or a *baston eskrima* around when the urge takes me. The plants and vines on the perimeter also block the view from the street and the main house, which makes it a good place to practice with live blades.

Jet had mentioned Decatur Street. If somebody was going along that street tonight looking and asking for me by name, that somebody didn't know my movements. Decatur's bars are more for the younger set, though there was one bartender I knew well.

I flipped through the phone directory, dialed the number. When the Bear answered I identified myself.

"Maestro!" the Bear's gruff voice boomed through my earpiece. "How's it goin', Bro? I take it you got my message."

I glanced at the answering machine next to the phone. I hadn't checked it. "Actually, no. Somebody slipped me word on the street, something about ... inquiries being made."

"Right. An' I know how you like your privacy."

The Bear had the physical presence to match his basso-profundo voice. He was ... well, a bear of a man, except that real bears don't have shoulder-length hair and tattoos. He'd also been in my sword club when it was active and was one of a handful of people who had my unlisted phone number. The bar where he currently worked was at Decatur's far end.

"So, who is this guy?" I flexed my free hand.

"He came through here 'bout, oh, hour an' a half ago. Asked for you by name."

"Asked who?"

"Me. I didn't know him, so he got my best blank stare. He tried askin' a few of my customers, but I told him he had to buy a drink or get out. He went."

"He give you any trouble about that?" I asked.

"Naw. Actually he was well-mannered. Wasn't drunk. Was wearin' square clothes. Cheap, y'know, but neat—collared shirt, slacks."

I absorbed that. "Okay. Tell me what he looked like, please."

I could hear the bar's raunchy jukebox in the background, ice cubes rattling. The Bear was making drinks while he talked.

"White, early thirties. Light brown hair. Recent haircut—a short, cheap cut but, again, neat. Blue eyes, soft-lookin'. Narrow jaw. Wore a silver crucifix on a chain around his neck. No rings in the ears, but both lobes had multiple piercings. No tats on the hands or neck. Five foot nine. One forty—one forty-five. Not muscular. No watch on his wrist, no cell phone clipped to his belt."

It was the sort of thoroughness one could expect from the Bear. He was in his forties, easygoing enough, but he'd spent his youth in the military. Special Forces—that much he'd said, and I never asked further. I figured he had been in on some serious shit, but his past was as off-limits as mine.

I ran his description through my head and nothing clicked.

"Is this trouble for you, Maestro?" he asked after a few seconds.

"Honestly, I don't know. I appreciate your concern, though. And the info."

"It's all good. Hey, you heard 'bout the girl gettin' iced at the river?"

"Yes."

"Bummer, eh?"

Then he asked about the pool team in way of polite chitchat, and I gave him the quick low-down. He was himself a fine stick, but he'd quit playing in the league several sessions back when his chronic back trouble acted up.

Finally he rang off.

I emptied my pockets, kicked off my shoes and stepped into sandals. It had been a long night, and a sad and disturbing one. I lit a stick of incense on the small altar in the closet off my front room, sat cross-legged on the floor in front of it, and began the *Shanmatha* contemplation to clear my mind. It couldn't hurt to say a prayer for Sunshine's soul tonight.

Chapter 8

Bone

I escorted Alex back as far as my apartment. Her unit was just above mine. Once there, we discovered neither one of us wanted to be alone. Sunshine had died alone, and that thought haunted us. We spent the night on my couch, just holding each other—nothing more, just warm companionship against the dark.

I woke alone and badly, absurdly late, deep into the afternoon. I hadn't dreamt specifically of Sunshine, but I'd been trapped in seemingly endless running-in-glue type nightmares, which left me feeling limp and lousy. It was so late Alex had already gone to work. I realized I should have gotten up with her. Should have seen if she was okay. We were both grieving through the aftermath of a friend's death. Alex might have wanted some comforting before going off to the gift shop.

Nodding over my first cup of coffee, I tried to come to grips with the truth. Sunshine was gone. My head told me I should be reacting. But I felt nothing ... emotionally flat-lined. Oh, the grief was there, and the anger, but it was all limbo-like. Stalled, like a storm front. I was waiting. I had promised Maestro. Forty-eight hours, during which time New Orleans' finest might solve the case, nab Sunshine's killer and set the wheels of justice cleanly into motion.

They might ...

I've no gripes with the NOPD. I like safe streets to walk, and the thicker the police presence, the better. The Quarter's police district is the Eighth, and I've poured coffee for and chatted with a fair number of its officers who stop through late nights at my restaurant. Always civil, decent tippers to boot, they certainly appeared competent.

But they were *people*. I knew what Maestro said was true, that the police were overworked, had only so much time and manpower to devote to any single case.

I went looking for my smokes. My apartment is a comfortable place, and part of comfortable is that I don't expect to be visited by the Royal Family without adequate notice. Which is to say if a hurricane hit the place, it wouldn't make all that much difference.

I picked my way into the bedroom, found my smokes, crumpled and tossed the empty pack with a grunt. Booboo, my cat, leapt at it, bounding from whichever of her hiding spots she was favoring today, went skittering across an unexpected clear patch of floor, and crashed into a stack of videotapes.

Booboo was a native Quarterite. She'd adopted me shortly after Sunshine had moved out.

Sunshine ...

I stared a slow blinking moment at the bed, which was banked with blankets and assorted debris. The bed Sunshine had picked out for us. The same bed Sunshine had slept on with me when we were married. We'd brought it with us from San Francisco. I've never had a driver's license, so I navigated while Sunshine drove the moving van all the way. Was it too late for us to make it work between us, even then, even before we got to the Quarter?

My fists clenched unconsciously until I felt my nails dig into my hands.

Forty-eight hours ... well, minus about twelve of them now. I had agreed to do nothing, take no action. *Revenge*—so I'd said to Maestro last night, at Fahey's, and I'd meant it. Goddamned right I did. Once those forty-eight hours were completely expired and the police had nothing ... what, exactly, did I intend to do?

I drained my coffee and started finding clothes. What I intended right now was, of course, to get myself a fresh pack of smokes.

Booboo fixed me with accusatory green eyes. I checked her food and water bowls—both full. "I'm just going to the store," I told her. "I'll be right back." She swished her black tail and did not blink.

It was crawfish-boil hot as I climbed downstairs and stepped out onto Burgundy Street. The daylight shrank my pupils behind my sunglasses as I hiked up toward the corner mart. Like a whole lot of Quarterites I know, I am not naturally attuned to the daytime.

I wanted to know who had killed Sunshine so that if the cops didn't get him, I would. I'd said as much to Maestro. *Revenge*, of the Biblical eye-for-an-eye variety. Which meant, of course, that I intended to *kill* Sunshine's murderer.

This time the thought didn't startle or dismay me. I had done the math, thought it through, even as Maestro had tried to talk slow, deliberate reason at me. I knew what I meant. Knew what revenge was. I had decided without needing to decide. My wife—my dear friend—had been murdered. It seemed a no-brainer that her killer had to pay, either with the aid of the police and the courts, or through some more personal medium. Either way, the scales had to balance. I wouldn't leave it like this. *I* would not allow it.

So, yes, I would kill. If need be. If it came to that.

The how of killing someone, of finding that particular someone if, in thirty-six hours and counting, the cops couldn't ... that wasn't so clear-cut.

A car with Arkansas plates inched along Dauphine Street, the couple in the front seat ogling and pointing. The French Quarter is indeed something, visually striking, with its picturesque architecture, old Europe allure and quaintly crumbling ambience. But it was no good excuse for blocking traffic. A black and white United cab rolled up and quickly lay on its horn.

You could use some help. Maestro's words. I hadn't expected that, what was evidently an offer of help. I didn't know Maestro all that well. At least, I hadn't known him all that long. But I'd already started to think of him as a friend, something beyond the routine bar-chum. He had a good knowledge of film and a pleasing store of risqué humor. He was easygoing and easy to talk to. On some level below our surfaces, though, we seemed to have clicked. We recognized each other in some fundamental way that bypassed the two decades' age difference. I didn't know if I could quite define it.

It made a curious kind of sense that he was offering to help me ... help me to hunt someone, and help perhaps even to do the killing. I didn't know too much about his past—and Quarter etiquette deems it impolite to probe—but you don't get a nickname like "Maestro" from a reputation for sitting on your hands.

I bought my cigarettes. Inside the store the day crew and a few of the customers were, inevitably, talking about the fatal stabbing by the river last night. Lots of clucking about the homicide rate, the need for more police, and, of course, the inescapable undercurrent: *Did you know her, did you know her?*

My heart was beating heavy as I paused outside to light a smoke. My hand shook a bit as I snapped shut the lighter.

I'd had the radio on while I was making coffee, heard a newsbreak and knew the crime hadn't been tidily solved while I slept. *"Police are investigating, but have no suspects at this time."* I'd heard words like that often enough on local newscasts, was used to reading them in the paper. It was part of the tapestry of city living, nothing exclusive to New Orleans. (And once, crime and murder were a *much* worse problem here than they are today, I'm told.) But this was so absolutely personal, and every mention of Sunshine by strangers, by people who knew her only as a statistic, hit like a blow.

"Hey, Bone. What's shakin'?"

Big Tommy stuck out one beefy paw for a friendly clasp. Muscular and flabby all at once, like a bodybuilder going to seed, he looked a little like a mountain man, with a full black beard and a mop-top of curls that must have been hell in the summer.

"Tommy, how're things?"

"Fine, fine. Yourself?"

"They'll do."

Southern hospitality wasn't invented by some novelist or Hollywood screenwriter. It's the real deal. So, when your neighbor says hello, you stop and chat a moment.

"Where're you going with that?" I said, nodding to the rolled up futon mattress he was holding up atop one cannonball shoulder.

"Takin' it over to Greta's place. You know Greta, right? Works at the Clover, morning shift. She's just moved into a new place over on Dumaine. Left her bed behind in the old apartment. I told her I'd give her this"—Big Tommy shrugged the mattress awkwardly—"'til she got somethin' else. Greta bought me a cheeseburger once when I was broke." Sweat was bright on his forehead, dripped in his beard.

I wasn't being asked for anything. Despite which I said, "How about I give you a hand?"

Tommy grinned gratefully, and we lugged the damned mattress three and a half blocks and down a bricked cockroach-crawling entryway barely wider than Big Tommy's shoulders. I hadn't tied back my hair before coming out, and now it was plastered over my neck and shoulders. The day's humidity was merciless.

I shot the breeze a minute or two with Greta—I did know her, a heavyset blond, good waitress—begged off Tommy's repeated offers to buy me a beer, and skedaddled homeward. Going out for a cold one, though it was way to early for me, was nonetheless tempting. Tommy had lived half a block from me since I'd moved here. He was a good guy. His company would probably keep me distracted awhile. But I knew, I could *tell*, that I would be stepping aboard a merry-go-round while it was going—one round of beers at one bar and we'd bump into somebody we knew because that's inevitable and because everybody knows everybody. *"Hey, Bone, Tommy what's up? I was just on my way to such-and-where to see so-and-so who keeps asking 'bout you c'mon lemme get this round c'mon we'll shoot a coupl'a racks of pool I'm tired of beer I need a real drink ..."*

Hours would disappear as we whirled through the Quarter. No. *No.* I just wasn't in the mood. I love the Quarter and the sure sense of community here that I've never experienced anywhere else ... but not today.

I got back to Burgundy, and ran into Todd, one of my neighbors in the building, as he was leaving. I didn't know him well. He worked in one of the galleries on Royal, which made him a day person, so we seldom crossed paths. I waved to be neighborly and continued towards my apartment and blessed air-conditioning.

"Hey, Bone. What's going on?"

Something in his tone caught my attention. "Not much, why?"

"The cops were here, lookin' for you, 'bout a half hour ago. Is everything all right?"

My gut tightened and I felt chilled despite the heat. "Yeah everything's fine. Probably a mistake. Thanks, though." I forced a smile and walked woodenly back to my apartment.

The police! Maestro said they would probably want to talk to me. I guess I just hadn't taken it seriously, hadn't absorbed the reality of it. I took a deep breath. So what? I hadn't killed Sunshine. The sooner the cops got me off their list, the sooner they could look for the real killer. At least the fact they had been here meant they were doing *something*, however useless. I just needed to wait it out. I fought down the anger and frustration roiling just under the surface. *Wait.*

I looked at the videotape stack that Booboo had toppled. If I had to wait, hunkering down with a good movie seemed the best distraction. If the police came back, I would deal with them then.

I felt like something pleasantly grim and was weighing the merits of *Sweet Smell of Success* against those of *Serpico* when I noticed the light winking on the answering machine. I almost ignored it. But, with a sigh, I did go over to play the message. It was Alex. Forty seconds later, my boot heels pounded the stairs as I hit the street, running this time.

* * *

Excerpt from Bone's Movie Diary:

When life turns bleak, there is real comfort to be found in movies that are equally gloomy. Reality can be savagely dismal, but it can never match film's facility to dramatize. That is, truth is stranger than fiction, but it needs a serious rewrite. Following Nine-Eleven, during the just-after-the-car-crash shock/jitters of not knowing what was next, I deliberately switched off the news; didn't want to see & hear anymore, for a while, to take a break, so that I didn't see the Twin Towers coming down every time I blinked. To escape I plugged in a DVD of *Fail-Safe*. 1964, helmed by Sidney Lumet (my favorite director), the best of the Cold War disaster pictures, the opposite to not-really-that-funny *Dr. Strangelove*'s take on same subject by Stanley Kubrick (Kubrick is overrated; never topped *Paths of Glory* & *Eyes Wide Shut* is 2½ hrs. of my life I want back). *Fail-Safe* is tense, frighteningly believable (still) & superbly acted—including dramatic parts for Walter Matthau, Larry Hagman &, get this, Dom DeLuise. Let me just spoil the ending by saying it concludes with atomic bombs dropped on NY, the Empire State Building used for ground zero. I sat, I watched this terrific movie, I knocked back half a bottle of rum, I was able to locate and handle my emotions as I hadn't been able to since that Tues. morning ... & it was cathartic. I felt ready for reality once more. After all, how could it be more catastrophic than what I'd just experienced? Appraisal: *Fail-Safe* as movie * * * *; *Fail-Safe* as therapy ... priceless

Chapter 9

Maestro

I had insisted that Bone give the police forty-eight hours. I had no intention of doing the same. While I would avoid any direct in-volvement in the investigation, that didn't mean doing nothing. I needed informa-tion. I needed to find out what the police knew, and that meant finding a source.

But first, I needed knowledge of a different sort, something that the police weren't likely to have. That would require going out in the daytime. Not an easy thing for someone used to waking after sunset, but I figured the information would be worth the sacrifice. I dragged myself out of bed around three, dressed, and, after a moment's thought, grabbed an old cable box and an empty incense container and threw them in a bag. Thus prepared with props and an alibi, I stepped outside the cool darkness of my apartment—only to be blinded by the glare of the huge glowing disk in the sky. Oh, yeah ... it was the sun. It had been a while since I had seen it that high in the sky. I scrambled to pull my sun-glasses over my eyes while ducking back into the shaded alcove by my door. As I huddled in the shadows waiting for my eyes to adjust, I could not help but think of Bela Lugosi's Dracula, cowering beneath the deadly onslaught of daylight. It hadn't taken a vampire bite to turn me into a creature of the night—just a little time living in the French Quarter.

Once I could see again, I headed down Bourbon Street, toward St. Ann. This early in the day, Bourbon was still open to motorized vehicle traffic and the Quarter was an entirely different place. Instead of the wanton lady of the evening I knew so well, cloaked in darkness and adorned with garish neon and beads, the daytime Quarter was a quaint French Colonial Lady, showing her age in the cracks and crevices clearly visible in the unforgiving light. The smell of stale beer and puke, usually so prevalent on Bourbon, had given way to smells of café au lait and beignets, burgers, gumbo, and seafood, seasoned with hot asphalt.

I'm normally alert on the street, aware of those around me. In ten years down here, I haven't been successfully mugged. Today, though, I felt an extra wariness. I still had no idea who'd been walking Decatur last night looking for me. My subconscious hadn't conveniently matched the Bear's description with some hidden mental file while I'd slept.

I stopped in front of Marie Laveau's House of Voodoo. One of the older buildings in New Orleans, it had once been home to Marie Laveau II, one of fifteen children of the original voodoo Queen of New Orleans. Now it housed a shop catering to tourists and occult practitioners. The cracked paint and ancient timbers of the building added an air of authenticity that probably made it easier for tourists to believe they were in the presence of old magic. Above the door a hand-painted sign promised:

Special Exhibit
Strange Gods, Strange Altars

Inside the shadowy interior, the air was thick with the smell of incense and essential oils. Shelves lined the walls, overflowing with an eclectic combination of candles, fetishes, gris-gris, dolls, and potions, as well as statues of Catholic saints and rosary beads, statues of Marie Laveau. Altars for various religions and rituals were artistically scattered about the room. Gator skulls, carved masks, and chicken feet hung from the ceiling and off the shelves. One section of the building was set aside as a small voodoo museum. T-shirts, books, jewelry, and posters filled the remaining spaces. But I knew the front was mostly for the tourists. Anything serious took place beyond the beaded curtain separating the main store from the back room.

"Can I help you?"

The young man behind the counter wore a Voodoo Shop T-shirt and had spiked hair. I didn't know him. "Just came to get some incense," I said. "Is Mother Mystic around?"

"Is that Maestro?" The clipped contralto of her lilting, accented English echoed from somewhere in the back. A moment later Mother Mystic swept out through the beaded curtain, her arms open in greeting. A bright caftan draped her ample figure in colors that complemented her mahogany skin. "My dear Maestro, I have not seen you out my way much. At least, not in the daylight."

My patterns were getting much too predictable. I would have to do something about that.

"I was just out doing some daytime errands and decided to stop by." I grinned. She cocked an eyebrow at me as if she didn't entirely believe it. "I needed to pick up some more incense for my altar." I pulled out the empty box. Actually I had plenty of incense at home.

"Well, you know where to find it." She gestured towards the large display. "Let Mother know if you need anything special."

I made a show of examining the racks of incense.

"Did you hear about the murder last night? Down by the Brewery? I heard something about a voodoo ritual?"

When Mother Mystic didn't answer I glanced at her. Her face was stone.

"I heard it was Sunshine, the little blonde waitress," I continued.

"I do not think I knew her." She answered coldly.

"I remember her," the guy at the counter piped up. "She used to wait tables at Big Daddy's. She was hot."

"Did she ever come in here? Possibly show an interest in voodoo or anything?"

He shook his head. "No. Not that I know of."

"Why do you ask so many questions, Maestro?" Mother Mystic frowned at me, and at her clerk. "I've never taken you for the gossip type. What is this thing to you?"

I had planned to treat the whole thing as casual conversation and give a glib answer, but one look at her face convinced me that I needed to level with her if I wanted any real answers.

"She was a friend. I'm just trying to find out what happened to her."

Mystic looked at me for a long moment. "Come. Into the back."

I followed her through the beads into the "reading room" usually used for psychic and tarot readings. She gestured to one chair at the small table, taking the other for herself.

"Look," she half-whispered, "the police have already come here. I did not have anything to say to them, or to you. The girl and her fate were unknown to me until I hear of it this morning."

"But they say there was evidence of a voodoo ritual at the murder scene," I pressed.

She snorted in anger. "Yes. That is what they say. And it did not take but one whiff of that rumor to spread it all over the Quarter. The tourists are spooked. They do not come to Mother's shop today. They all want to play with the voodoo—right up until they think it might be real. Now folks are upset, they worry." She sat back in her chair, crossing her arms over her chest, "It is enough that sometimes a fool tries to get me to do a black magic curse for him! Now some nutcase kills a poor girl, tosses some tourist toys around, and everyone believes we are all murderers!"

She sighed, then she leaned in close, her eyes intensely bright. "I'll tell you this, because I think you of all people ought to know better. The *Vodun* is a religion. It is about connecting with the saints and with the gods. The *Vodun* we practice has more in common with the Catholics and their saints than anything else. It's not about murder."

"But aren't there ritual sacrifices?"

"Of course. The same sacrifices the farmer makes every time someone decides they want chicken for dinner. We kill animals in some of our rituals, but we do it more humanely than the slaughterhouses, and we cook them and eat them after. There is no part of *Vodun* that includes killing *people*. That only happens in the movies. Whoever did this is some kind of sick *bokor* want-to-be—knew just enough to think he could do a ritual. Either that or somebody out there has decided to practice the dark arts." Her eyes turned hard. "If that be the way of it, we're all in trouble. The *Vodun* is a respectable religion, of the light, and we do not need anyone perverting it with the darkness."

I thought for a moment, disturbed by that last possibility. "Just out of curiosity, how do you kill your animal sacrifices?"

She studied me for a moment, then said, "We slit their throats with a very sharp knife."

I thanked Mother Mystic for her time and headed out the door. I needed to find out exactly how Sunshine died. I still had no idea what the police had actually found at the crime scene.

In almost every detective novel I've read or movie I've ever seen, the hero has a contact with the police he or she can call on for information. It's a neat, handy way to get facts not readily available to the general public. Unfortunately, I've never been that fond of the police. I try to stay as far away from them as possible. This, of course, precludes having one of them as a first-name-basis friend. Still, it's the Quarter, and if you try hard enough you can find anything ... even a cop.

Sorry. That's an overly harsh exaggeration. In truth, the police make themselves easy to find in the Quarter, in their prowl cars, on foot, on horses, and even on bicycles and scooters. Tourists, who are responsible for a great deal of this city's income, can walk around in protected, well-lit comfort. That is, as long as they stay on ticky-tacky Bourbon Street and retreat to their hotels at a reasonable hour.

I wanted to find someone connected with the police to sit and talk to, and that was tricky. My solution was to stop at a cop bar. This, at least, is not a phenomenon peculiar to the Quarter. It's my impression that every large city has at least one cop bar per precinct, where the off-duty officers gather to drink and swap stories, both funny and horrifying, of their work. The one in the Quarter is a half block off Bourbon on Iberville, one block short of Canal Street.

It was approaching late afternoon, the optimal time to hit my target bar. Late evening it would be a bit too loud and raucous for conversation, and in the morning the odds of anyone being there who'd know anything were slim.

As it was, I got lucky and caught Sneaky Pete, the owner, behind the bar when I wandered in. He was yet another pool shooter, and got his nickname from using a "sneaky pete" pool cue. That's a custom cue that is deliberately crafted to look like an ordinary bar cue.

"Hey, Maestro," he said, straightening from reading the newspaper. He was shorter than me, with a lot of scalp showing through his thinning white hair these days. "What brings you up to this end of the Quarter?"

Objectively, the Quarter is small, some thirteen city blocks by seven. But within this curious neighborhood of ours there are inevitable subdivisions and regions. Denizens of the Quarter are creatures of habit, usually hanging out at specific bars at specific hours. Any deviation is unusual and therefore draws attention. Fortunately I was ready for Pete's question and had my excuse ready.

"I was just hiking up to Cox Cable to return my box," I said. I brandished the bag I carried. "They cut off my service a couple of months back and are trying to bill me three or four hundred for their equipment. It's worth the walk in the heat to get them off my back." As prepared as a Boy Scout, of course I actually *did* have the old cable box in the bag. I do have cable in my apartment, but frankly, I watch the Cartoon Network more than anything.

"Get you anything?" Sneaky Pete asked. We were the only two in the place.

"Yeah. I'll take a Bud draft."

I rarely drink beer. It's filling, it's fattening, and I don't need any more waistline than I've got. But it was in the high nineties outside and far too early to start in on my traditional Irish whiskey.

"You got it," he said, opening the tap to fill a large plastic go-cup—French Quarter crystal, we call it. "How's your team doing this session?"

"Struggling a bit, but we're still in the running."

Pete also shot on a league pool team, but I'd never really warmed to him or his compatriots. Though I still shot pool and was even co-captaining a team, it seemed I'd once had more enthusiasm for the game. I wondered in the back of my mind if this hobby would go the way of my sword-fighting club. Once, I'd been wildly enthused about that. But it had just sort of drifted away.

We chatted for a few minutes. Though I wasn't especially enamored of Pete, good manners are valued in the Quarter. Besides, it's good to collect as many familiar faces as you can, for those occasions when you might find yourself out of your normal prowl range. Sometimes people will come to your aid even if they only know you in passing. And you never know when trouble will come, or when you'll need that aid.

Eventually I tried to edge the conversation around to the subject on my mind.

"I suppose you've heard about Sunshine getting tagged behind the Brewery last night," I said, lightly, or as lightly as the statement could be made.

"Yeah. The guys were talking about it when they came off shift."

"Any word as to what it was all about? From what I've heard she didn't have an enemy in the world."

Instead of answering, Pete favored me with a long stare, then turned and poured himself a short beer.

"I dunno if I should say anything about that to you, Maestro."

I didn't have to fake being surprised.

"Whoa, Petey. You lost me there."

"If I recall, the last time you were asking about a case here in the Quarter, the perp turned up in the Charity ER about twenty-four hours later."

I blinked at him, genuinely trying to remember what he was talking about. Then it came back to me. It had happened six or seven months back.

The perp in question was one of those who made a habit of beating up his women. In the final round with his latest girlfriend/punching bag, he had smashed a vodka bottle over her head, coming within a fraction of an inch of taking out her left eye. The doctors at the emergency room convinced her to swear out a complaint against the boyfriend and he got picked up. The next day he was out on the streets again.

I remembered now asking Pete about the incident only because I knew the girl and was concerned, and because it was league night and we were shooting against Pete's team. I remembered Pete saying that the girl had dropped the charges.

The reason it had all slipped my mind was that I hadn't hunted the dude down. In fact, I almost wasn't involved at all. As it happened, I found myself sitting two stools down from the punk at Fahey's, late, the night after he'd got out of lockup. He started bragging about it—bragging loud, as drunks tend to do.

"Damn straight she dropped the charges!" He said this to nobody in particular, puffing up his scrawny chest like a bantam rooster. You could tell just by looking that he was a mean little shit, but not brawny enough to take on anyone even his own size. "The bitch knew what I'd do to her if it went to court. When I got home I slapped her 'round again anyway for talkin' to the cops at all. Reopened her stitches and she had to go back to Charity, but this time she's keepin' her mouth shut. I'll shut that mouth of hers for good if she tries any of that shit again."

It wasn't the sort of trash you normally hear anyone talk in Fahey's, but Milo was simply ignoring the guy, probably not wanting the headache of tossing him out. Listening to this crap was distasteful enough that I abandoned my seat and shot a couple of practice racks of pool instead. I could still hear him as I shot, though, and my irritation grew until I found I couldn't concentrate on my shooting anymore.

I gave it up, settled my tab, and hit the sandbox, figuring to call it a night. That probably would have been all there was to it. But as chance would have it, when I came out of the rest room, Bantam Boy—now very drunk—pushed off his stool and went staggering out of the bar, not ten feet ahead of me. I followed him out, but I didn't *follow* him, understand. I was just heading home, and he happened to be in front of me.

Even then, had there been anyone else out on the street, I probably would have let it go. As it happened, Toulouse was empty in both directions.

If fate intends something that adamantly, why fight it?

As usual, I was wearing "felon-fliers"—that's athletic shoes to the suburbanites. I like to move quietly, as it lets me hear what else is going on around me. In the shape he was in, though, I don't think he would have heard a brass band coming up behind him as he staggered and lurched his way down the sidewalk.

He certainly didn't hear little ol' me as I lengthened my stride and slid up close behind him. I took one last glance up and down the street, and then I raised my hand until it was floating just behind his shoulder blades. Then, when he was in mid-stride and off balance, I powered him forward with a full hip twist and all the strength of my arm and upper body. He would have plowed the pavement face first if a street sign hadn't been in the way. It made a vague, dull, but pleasing musical sound as he hit it and went down. I took the corner without breaking stride and never looked back.

It didn't even make the papers, being a fairly unremarkable incident. Rumor said that he had a broken nose and jaw plus multiple lacerations. Since he still had his money when he was scooped up, it was generally written off as a drunken tumble. He himself had no recollections of what happened. I'd heard his girlfriend—the one lucky to still have her left eye—left town before he got out of the hospital. He had since moved away, too. Good riddance.

I mentally shrugged it away and focused my eyes on Pete, opting for indignation over innocence.

"*What?* You're talking about whazizname? The rough-off artist? You think *I* did a number on him? Com'on, Pete. You've known me for ... what ... five years now? Have you ever known me to get into a fight? Even when the other guy was leaning real hard?"

He thought for a moment, shrugged.

"Yeah. You're right." He shook his head. "Sorry. Just wishful thinking on my part, I guess. When I heard he took a tumble, I didn't want it to be that easy. I wanted the son of a bitch to have gotten a bit of his own."

"It would have been nice," I agreed, "but we'll have to settle for what happened. Call it karma."

"I guess."

"As far as Sunshine goes, I was just curious is all. Everybody's tongue is wagging over the murder, naturally. Some are saying she was doped up when it happened, but some are saying she was straight. Since I was here, I thought I'd ask. No big deal."

"Somebody thinks it's a big deal," Pete insisted. "That's why I flinched when you asked. The boys are keeping real quiet on this one."

"Yeah?" I didn't press, just waited, hoping he had more to say.

He did. "They found some dead chickens and voodoo stuff around the body. You'd think that would be enough to set them on edge. But that's not what's bothering them." Pete leaned closer and dropped his voice, even though there was no one to hear. "The word is she got done with an ice pick, or something like one. Double punch to the heart."

I gave a low whistle. "No wonder they're edgy," I said. "Do me a favor. Forget I asked anything."

"You didn't ask. And I definitely didn't say anything."

"Yeah. Well, catch you later."

A lot of thoughts were churning in my head as I made my way down the street. Mostly, I was annoyed that Pete had connected me with that rough-off artist. Even if I had convinced him I had nothing to do with it, it would surface in his mind if anything else came up with my name on it. Repeated coincidences draw attention, and the last thing I wanted was attention. Once, hospitalizing people—or doing a bit more than that—was nothing extraordinary to me, but those days were pretty long ago.

Then, too, the fact that Sunshine had been killed with an ice pick bothered me. It bothered me a lot.

Chapter 10

Bone

Summer is considered, among most of the local service industry ilk, to be a lousy time to wait tables here. Louisiana's summers are brutal, heat and humidity spiking into the nineties. At the same time the hotel rates plunge, and the yokels and overseas tourists come. And they don't come with a lot of money, or they don't lay out decent tips when they do.

Summer ... and waiters and bartenders prone to panic *will* panic, and talk desperately about the *SEASON*. The *SEASON* starts in October or December or January—depending, naturally, on who you're talking to—and it means Mardi Gras and Jazz Fest, and if we can only hold on until the *SEASON*, the promised *SEASON*, we'll be *set*, rolling in tip money, and all our troubles will be over!

I don't subscribe to this faith. Granted, I work at what's very nearly a locals-only restaurant. I don't depend on influxing tourists, but that's not the point. If every day of the year was the *SEASON*, those wait-folk who bitch and panic the worst would *still* always be on the verge of financial tragedy. They'd be doing the headless chicken dance, wondering if the $27 check they just wrote Entergy would clear before the lights got turned off. They'd piss and moan about the night's cheap tips, even while they fed those aforementioned tips a bill at a time to the poker machines you'll find in nearly every bar in the Quarter.

In short, I don't have a whole lot of sympathy.

When Kirk, one of Pat O.'s green-jacketed waiters, started that familiar sullen gripe after I'd asked him about Alex, I wanted very much to snatch his tray out of his hands and bash his skull with it. But I wanted more to know where she was. Someone I didn't know—and who didn't know Alex's whereabouts when I'd asked—was currently guarding the gift shop's array of T-shirts, sweatshirts, champagne flutes with the Pat O.'s logo, and other souvenirs.

"I'm tellin' you, these tight-ass people coming over here from France an' It'ly an' shit ..." Kirk, who was young twenties and still going with his griping, I knew only slightly.

"*Kirk.*"

We were standing on the large, two-tiered, open-air rear patio. When Pat O.'s is busy, this area is mobbed. Right now, on this summer weekday with the sun still up, it was dead.

Kirk blinked and centered on me.

"Where is Alex," I said, steel in my voice, "the girl that's usually in the gift shop right around now?"

He glanced toward the bored girl sitting at Alex's usual post at the window. I started to push past this dumbfuck kid and go find a manager. Something in me was thrumming like a live wire.

"Bone!"

I turned, and there she was, coming off the stairs from the second level. Relief slapped me like a cold wave. Her message on the answering machine ...

"Oh Bone, I'm sorry." She took my hand, pulling me through the club's long brick archway. "I shouldn't have called. It's nothing—not what I guess I made it sound like, but I was really upset, and I just wanted to talk to someone ..."

We were out front now, on St. Peter, the Calf across the street, but hours before Padre and the regulars showed up.

"Alex, *what* happened?" I turned, squeezed her shoulders. Two doormen in those sad green jackets were sweating and standing by the club's entrance. I do despise my job, but I don't have to wear any uniform to it. Alex wears slacks and a white shirt.

She looked into my eyes. I could see she was a little frightened, still, though she forced a brave smile. "I thought you'd just phone me back," she said. "Honestly, I didn't expect you to come out all this—"

"Alex. *Please.*"

"First off, I'm all right."

I nodded. She picked a cigarette from her shirt pocket, and I lit it. "Second," I prompted, "you said someone threatened you. Who? And, how?" Just saying the words, entertaining the thought, I could feel the fury ... a waiting fury, but no less dangerous. I didn't stop to wonder why I felt so protective toward her. I hadn't been there for Sunshine. That wouldn't—couldn't—happen with Alex.

She took a deep drag off her cigarette, holding it for a long moment before blowing it out. "He ... this guy ... started out as just another customer. He came to the window, drunk of course—because all those *auslander* tourists come here and think all physical laws are suspended for them! They think they can drink *way* beyond their limits, or the limits even of those of us who are used to it." I could hear the anger building in her voice, but she caught herself and took a deep breath. "I deal with guys like him all the time. But he was more annoying than most. I tried to help him, but he got pushy—every time I brought him the cap or T-shirt he asked for, he demanded to see it in different colors and sizes."

She fortified herself with another quick puff. "He obviously had no intention of buying anything. He just wanted to make me run around the shop like a trained monkey." I recognized the bitterness in her voice. Such treatment was all just part of the occasionally foul task of serving the public. Alex knew it. I knew it too.

"Then he started making suggestive comments—trying to push my buttons, I guess. But they weren't even very imaginative—nothing out of the ordinary. I refused to rise to the bait, and remained polite. Apparently that pissed him off, so he got really crude, telling me, in detail, about all of the deviate sex acts he wanted me to do for him, and how all I needed was a real man, like him. I had had enough by that time. I just wanted to get back to my cross-stitch. I told him he would have to leave. I obviously didn't have what he wanted. When he refused I told him I was going to call security. He got really mad. And that's when he said it."

Alex's hands were shaking a little, but I couldn't tell whether it was from fear or fury.

"What did he say? Exactly?" Alex doesn't have my memory, but I knew she could come close.

"He said," she lowered her voice, attempting to approximate his vocal tone and style of speech, " 'Wanna gimme trouble, huh, d'yuh? Well, watchit or yer gonna end up like that bitch by the river las' night.' I yelled for security, at which point he apparently reached the limit of his drunken bravery and ran off."

Alex looked up at me. "He said, '... like that bitch by the river last night.' Bone, do you think he could be the one who got Sunshine? That's why I called you."

Not because some cretin had threatened to kill her, but because she thought I would want to know what he said about Sunshine. Brave, but ...

"So what does he look like?"

Alex has a natural eye for detail. She described him as mid-forties, a round face with a pudgy gut, and mud-colored hair cut short.

"He had a new T-shirt with a flashy black and red logo. I think it had the silhouette of a woman. I'm sorry, I can't remember what the logo said."

"It's okay. I'll figure it out." Alex couldn't remember what the logo said, but I quickly sorted through the images that matched her description, came up with a matching design and the name of the bar it had come from: *Sin City*.

Alex insisted on going back to the gift shop, calmer than when I arrived. We planned to meet at two tonight at the Calf, everything as usual. I marveled again at how tough she was for such a tiny thing.

My dash across the Quarter had winded me, but I didn't notice until I set out, walking now. I felt it now, the tightness in my smoker's lungs, calves a little rubbery, sore. More, though, I felt dogged purpose ... felt it cold and remorseless, even as the fury came with me while I walked.

It's better to fight cold than hot.

I mistook it for a movie quote for a second before I remembered Maestro saying the words to me at Fahey's. He was offering me his services—whatever those services might be—in finding Sunshine's killer. Fine. That was nice. I appreciated it.

This, though ... this was mine.

Sin City was on St. Philip, not far, and my breathing leveled—or at least no longer hurt me—by the time I arrived. I'd been in before. A good bar, with character, though that character was definitely on the scuzzy side. A long crypt of a place, with a pool table in back, but this wasn't one of those bars where the silly-ass pool league commandeered the joint once a week to shoot their oh-so-deadly-serious games. Maestro had made nudges at me about joining up. I love pool, hate organized anything, but especially organized sports. Want to know what one semester of high school basketball did to me? Tell you later.

So, I'd been here before, but not often. The bartender—husky biker type, tattooed shoulders—didn't know me, and I didn't immediately recognize any of the customers. There were only a few, but with my sunglasses still on, I gave each a good furtive looking at. None fit the description Alex had given me of the man who had threatened her life.

Objectively I could understand that "threatened her life" was stretching it. Drunken imbeciles will say atrocious things that don't, in the end, mean anything. But there are things that should not be said, by anyone, to anyone—and certainly, oh yes most *abso-fucking-lutely,* should never be said to **my girlfriend**.

The vehemence of the thought caught me by surprise.

I'd always thought of "girlfriend" as a kind of throw-away term, almost neutral. My feelings for Alex weren't neutral in the least. They weren't moderate. They were ...

No way. She was like my sister, *Sunshine's* sister, our very best friend, one of the family, but not ...

When the hell did this happen? How?

Impossible. Crazy, but there it was.

And ... it felt right. Did she feel ... no, there would be time later to find out how Alex felt. After ... after we'd dealt with Sunshine's murderer.

I ordered a rummincoke, even though I was still only just out of bed. I didn't want to be remembered for ordering soda or asking the burly bartender to make a pot of coffee. He looked like he was suffering with summer allergies. A number of people I've met who've never had allergies before become susceptible when they move down here. Christ knows what's in our air, but luckily, it's never caught up to me.

The shirts were here for sale, tacked up on the spotty glass behind the bar, obscuring old fliers and dusty semi-pornographic Polaroids from birthday bashes and Halloweens. They all bore the Sin City logo. The threatening man's shirt had been crisp and new. That he had been in here earlier—maybe earlier today—was no guarantee he'd be back, but this was the most logical place for a blind.

It was tempting, of course, to grill the bartender, to see if he'd sold a shirt to anyone matching the description, but I didn't know what was going to happen here, if anything, or what I might or meant to do. Calling the least attention to myself seemed right.

Sin City had a trivia machine at the end of the long bar top. It put me a long way down from the swinging French doors, but I could also study incoming patrons at my leisure before they realized I was watching.

I gave the trivia machine a few bucks, laid my smokes by my cocktail and settled in for an ambusher's wait. Naturally I played the movie category, and even with only one eye on the game, I put the previous high scores to great shame.

I drank slow but tipped well, the dirty panes of the French doors got dark, and I was long since trying to top my own scores. Sin City was close enough so I could hear the cathedral's bells toll the passing quarter hours. I also heard the heavy, low-level rumble of a freight train on the tracks that run alongside the Mississippi. A meal would be a good idea. Not that I was particularly hungry, of course, but I would need something eventually to counteract the booze. It could wait, however.

I watched people coming and going in the dimness. They were a youngish crowd, more punk than Goth or white trash. In my customary jeans and dark T-shirt, I wasn't conspicuous. I filled an ashtray with butts, didn't lose focus on what I was doing, and I didn't see the man I wanted.

And then, I did.

Okay, so I was reaching. No way—it was too much of a coincidence.

But what if he really *had* killed Sunshine, had evoked her to Alex as a way of bragging about the deed? Not that I needed any more motivation. Sunshine's death was too recent. Alex had been too close to her. Or maybe he'd just heard about the stabbing, thought it would be—what? Funny? Clever? Amusing to use it to threaten Alex? Maybe he was a murderer. Maybe he was a part of that disease that allows some people to mistreat others, to think that because we are the clerks in your shops and the cabbies in your taxis and the waiters in your restaurants that you can say or do what you like, that you're the masters and we're the vassals, and that there will be no repercussions.

He banged on the bar top until the bartender hulked over. He was already obviously loaded, but you have to be *damned* drunk before the typical Quarter bartender will cut you off. He got his drink, spent a moment disdainfully surveying his surroundings, and then wandered back to where I waited by the pool table. I had a quarter laid out on the table, a pool cue by my hand. I did my best to look bored.

Hair, weight, face—all just as Alex had said—and the T-shirt. He looked at the table, glanced up and noticed me.

"Hey, beanpole. I'll play yuh." He tossed another quarter onto the felt. "Rack 'em."

I left the bar top trivia machine to beep and chirp to itself and went to slot the quarters and rack the balls. The other customers were all up toward the front, drinking and talking and playing the juke.

One reason Sin City doesn't have a league team is that its table is a liability, with felt like corrugated cardboard from having drinks spilled on it, a serious table roll, and house cues straight as shepherd crooks.

"What's your name?" I asked, picking up the cue stick.

He sneered my way. "What's yours?"

"Alex."

He was no doubt much drunker than when he'd visited Pat O.'s gift shop. "Mitchell," he said as he stepped to the table. "Back off, I'm breaking, and yer 'bout to get yer ass whupped."

He had come deliberately to this locals' bar, instead of to the tourist clubs created for his kind, had bought a T-shirt as some symbol of solidarity ... which meant he was looking for a *real* New Orleans' experience. I knew his type. They want to know where it's really happening, where the scene is, want the insider's scoop, want to *be* inside, to be cool and hip. Some of these people are fun and worthwhile. Some are idiots. Some ... well, some are something else.

Mitchell played sloppy and loud and belligerent. I lost consistently and found him starved for companionship, which I provided. By the third game I knew just about all there was to know about him and his life back in New Jersey. He was a schnook, a shlub, and seemed nothing more. He was still drinking, past all safety limits now.

During our fourth pool game I asked, "You heard about the girl getting stabbed by the river last night?"

By now he didn't know if he was shooting solids or stripes, but he grunted, "Yeah."

He straightened after his shot, started chalking his cue tip with deliberate, exaggerated motions, but seemed more to be using the stick to keep himself upright.

"Where were you last night?" I asked, enunciating explicitly but not loud. But there was nobody there to hear the question but him. I was near him now, very near. "Midnight to 2 a.m.—where? Where were you?"

He blinked. It must have seemed a non sequitur to him. Blinked more, and said, "I was ... in Trenton. Did'n' ge' here 'til disssmornin' ..."

And he was crashing out, right there. He let go his cue and pitched toward the nearby men's room door. I took a fast look around—no one was looking back this way—and followed him in.

Mitchell was trying to use the urinal, but the necessary motor skills and rudimentary knowledge of aiming had fled. He stood, half-crumpled against the graffiti-rife wall, swaying, making a pathetic little whimper. And that was satisfying, it was. It was karmic ... but it wasn't quite karmic enough.

He seemed hazily aware that someone was behind him and awkwardly cranked his head around, round face bleary, eyes trying to focus.

I slammed him with everything I had, the heel of my right hand driving in between the bridge of his nose and his left eye. I hit him that hard because I was only giving myself the one shot, no more. His head whipped back the way it had come, and kept going, smacking the splintery wood wall. His hips turned, and his feet didn't follow, and down he went. He toppled, tangled, and managed to wedge his chubby body tight alongside the urinal, forehead touching the damp floor, ass high in the air. He stayed there.

On the way out I told the bartender he had a drunk passed out in the toilet.

* * *

Excerpt from Bone's Movie Diary:

Is there any more viscerally satisfying movie moment than when Charles Bronson makes his first kill in *Death Wish*? He's being mugged, & for that moment he is everyone who's ever found himself at gunpoint surrendering wallet or purse to some scumbag. (Virtually everyone I know has been mugged at least once in their lives; it being that common, is it a social condition we're supposed to just accept?) Instead, Bronson shoots the mugger, & however civilized we may think ourselves, it's a beautiful, bloody, righteous, *quenching* moment! Bronson's daughter is almost catatonic & his wife dead from a rape-assault. Nothing he can do will change what's happened. But it's that very helplessness, that powerless rage that we recognize & attach to. And so Bronson is out there getting even for all of us.

Chapter 11

Maestro

"I don't get it. What's so special about an ice pick?"

It was late night at the Calf again. Bone came in, asking if anybody had heard anything. He'd been keeping an eye on the news all day, but so far as he knew the cops didn't have anything on Sunshine's killing. I'd quietly corralled him and told him what I'd learned from Sneaky Pete that afternoon. He had blanched when I first told him how she'd been murdered.

"The fact that Sunshine wasn't on a direct route home," I said, "that she was deliberately off the beaten path and walking all the way out by the *river*. The Moonwalk doesn't actually go anywhere, at least not toward where any Quarterite lives. That makes it unlikely that it was an ordinary mugging gone bad. The fact that whoever it was used an ice pick cinches it."

"I'm still missing something here, Maestro," Bone said, frowning. "What's so significant about Sunshine being ... killed with an ice pick? And what about all the voodoo stuff?"

To be honest, I had half expected that he would have forgotten our conversation at Fahey's once last night's cocktails wore off. What surprised me was that I found I was sort of glad he hadn't. He was still focused on finding Sunshine's killer and avenging her death, presuming the police didn't come through. So far, twenty-four hours of the forty-eight had expired.

"Think about it, Bone," I said patiently. Bone is intelligent, and usually I have no trouble speaking with him as an equal, despite the two decades I have on him. Every so often, though, something pops up to remind me of how young he is, how lacking in the experiences I've had and taken for granted. Then, too, there are times when I wonder if I was ever that young.

"Okay. I'm thinking about it," he deadpanned. He was flexing his right hand. He'd been doing that off and on since we'd taken our stools.

"Our whole country is gun-happy," I said. "Hell, these days I think even petty criminals that break into parked cars for radios carry guns. Predators are almost always packing when they're out mugging. Why? Too many John and Jane Q. Citizens, paranoid about muggers and rapists and terrorists, are walking around armed too these days. So the predators *have* to pack heat. Otherwise, it's too big a risk. Sunshine, you'll note, was not shot."

"I note." He lit a cigarette. He was drinking a soda, but I didn't ask why. Quarterites don't have to drink liquor *every* night.

"As to the specifics of an ice pick ... do you carry a knife? Or have you ever?"

Bone shook his head.

"I do," I continued. "My favorite is a moderate-length folder knife with a lock blade. Easily hidden, and in a pinch I can possibly talk my way out of it if a cop tries to hassle me over having a concealed weapon."

I paused for a sip of my drink, which was my usual Irish whiskey.

"An ice pick is a different animal altogether. Like a rigid construction sheath knife, you have to deal with the extra length when you're carrying it. Speaking of sheaths, they don't make them for ice picks, so you either have to come up with a rig yourself or carry it with the point exposed or capped with a wine cork. The damning twist is that if you get caught with one, there's no way you can try to claim that it's just a pocket knife or that you use it at work."

"Which means—"

"Which means that whoever nailed Sunshine was going through a lot of extra inconvenience and risk just to carry his favorite killing tool. And that means she was being deliberately hunted. No accident or happenstance involved."

"And the voodoo shit?"

"Actually proves it. Someone went to the trouble to put that stuff in place. Whether they intended some kind of ritual or were just trying to make it look that way, they definitely intended Sunshine as the victim."

Bone nodded grimly. "Still ... what was she doing by the river in the first place? I keep thinking about that. Did this ice-picker chase her there from Jackson Square?

I paused to light a cigarette of my own, blowing out a long plume of smoke. It was good to see the kid thinking logically, even if I didn't have an answer to his question.

I hadn't yet told Bone about the message Sunshine had left on my machine two days before her murder, or the note. I don't give out my phone number willy-nilly, but I'd given it to her ... probably during my brief infatuation, in hopes of ... well, in hopes that didn't mean anything now. I had no idea what Sunshine might have wanted to talk to me about, and I didn't want to bother Bone with it. After all, we were still waiting for the cops to solve this.

"There's even more to the ice-pick thing, though," I said. "Ice-pick killings went out with Penny Dreadfuls. And they certainly have nothing to do with any version of the *Vodun* practiced here in the Quarter. That raises the question of who would prefer to use an ice pick instead of a more conventional blade weapon. I keep coming up with one answer. I think the hitter is an ex-con. Someone who is used to using a shank for quick kills."

"A jailhouse shank, you mean?"

"A homemade prison knife, yes. Convicts have a whole lot of time on their hands, and they've devised every way imaginable to make weapons while they're in stir. Classically, you take a spoon and grind the handle down to a point, either on the floor of your cell or on the sly in tool shop. The metal isn't good enough to hold an edge, so what you end up with is essentially a point weapon, like a foil or an epee ... or an ice pick. There's no squaring off for fights in lockup because of the guards. You've got to be quick and unseen. Basically you walk up on someone, preferably from behind, and slam-punch a couple of holes in him without breaking stride."

"Sounds like every prison film I've ever seen."

That unexpectedly annoyed me. "We're talking about the real world here, Bone," I said, just a bit sharply.

He didn't react to my tone. "Thanks, Maestro. I've been able to distinguish reality from fantasy for some time now."

I decided to chuckle quietly at that. But we still had serious things to discuss.

"Now, the way I see it," I said, leaning nearer his stool, "this very likely involves an ex-con. Possibly one who has an interest in the darker side of the occult. That's a nasty breed of creature, especially if he's made a habit of shanking people in the joint. The cops will smell the same sort of fish. They'll be looking for local parolees and whatnot. That means we back off an extra couple of days before we stick our heads up, give them time to—"

"Hold that right there."

I stopped. Bone had turned sharply on his stool and was staring at me intently. I automatically noted the tension in his thin wiry body.

"An extra couple of days?" He was speaking in that low growl I'd heard him use before.

"That's right," I answered blandly, waiting for him to say whatever was on his mind.

He seemed to be making an effort to rein himself in, as if he were on the verge of lashing out.

"I agreed, Maestro, to forty-eight hours," he finally spoke, his jaw tense. "I agreed to that because you said the cops might take care of this thing within that time. That made sense to me. I also agreed because you made some vague noises about helping out. I appreciated the offer of help. I still appreciate it. I consider you a friend, and I don't throw that term around indiscriminately. But, understand this. *You* dealt *yourself* in. I didn't ask for the help. And, I have to say ... I don't have any real idea at all what kind of help you could give me."

With that he got to his feet and marched out through the bar's rear, toward the rest rooms. It was still half an hour before Alex was off work, or I imagine he would have just left the Calf at that point.

I blinked. My first reaction was, I think understandably, of the *who-the-hell-do-you-think-you're-talking-to-kid* variety. I felt a strong surge of anger. But having had years of operating with my emotions, especially anger, carefully in check, I quickly centered myself. I imagined myself with a foil in hand, stepping onto the fencing strip, mind cool and clear.

Who the hell did Bone think he was talking to? The fact was, I realized calmly, he didn't know.

I was suddenly aware of Padre standing on the other side of the bar, eyeing me.

"Bone all right?" he asked. Like any good bartender, he could track multiple patrons at once.

"He went to powder his nose," I said. "Seems it's out of joint." I pushed my empty whiskey glass toward him.

Padre refilled it and got me another water back. "Bone is young, isn't he?" he observed.

"I understand it's a curable disease."

"Yes. It is," he agreed, as though my smartass comment had been serious. "He's young, but I'd say he's a good man. You always used to say good men were an endangered species and shouldn't be wasted."

It's a good thing, in its way, that I don't have many longtime friends. I hate it when they know me well enough to quote me at me.

Padre wandered off, and Bone came back. He regarded me from a few steps away, not retaking his barstool.

"Bone," I said, my tone level and reasonable. I stood up. "Let's take a walk."

He glanced at the clock on the wall. There was still time before Alex showed up.

"There are a few things I'd like to explain to you," I prodded him.

Finally he nodded. I dumped my fresh Irish in a go-cup, and we stepped outside.

* * *

We'd cut across the Square and come out now on Chartres Street, which was quiet this time of night, save for the occasional passing United cab. Bone wasn't being pouty or sullenly silent. He was just waiting for me to talk.

Yeah, talk, *but how to begin?* I've worked hard to keep my past just that—the past. In the Quarter, that's fairly easy. Usually, nobody asks. It was a new thing for me, an *unnatural* thing, trusting someone like Bone with even a part of the truth. Only Padre knew the whole story about me, and he only knew because he'd been the one who'd helped me set up my new identity ten years ago.

I wasn't sure how much I meant to tell Bone. Not all of it, of course, not yet, and probably not ever. Some of it, if he let it slip in the wrong place or to the wrong people, would land one or both of us in serious trouble.

"Do you remember—" I cut it short. Silly question, that. "Have you ever heard about the old *Mission Impossible* TV show?"

"Sure," Bone answered. "They've made two movies from the series. First one directed by Brian De Palma, second by John Woo—"

"Right," I cut him off. There had been nights he'd gotten so wound up talking about movie minutiae that I'd found myself wishing he had an "off" switch. "Anyway, in the show, the team gets a fifteen-second recording and a couple of photos, and then proceeds to pull off some *very* complicated scams and capers—you know what I'm talking about? Good. When I was younger, watching that show, I always wanted to see more about the unsung, unseen operators that put all that incredibly detailed information together for them. I mean, how do they know that the bad guy's desk is exactly eighteen inches from the north wall so they can drill into it from the basement? Or that the mistress of the general will take the right-hand elevator at exactly two twenty-five so they can kidnap her and ring in a substitute?"

Bone nodded. I took a sip from my plastic go-cup.

"Well, that's the kind of stuff I used to do. Only ... I worked for the Outfit."

We paused on a corner, and I automatically stepped out of the immediate circle of the streetlight. I hadn't heard anything more about the guy both Jet and the Bear had warned me about last night.

"The Outfit," Bone repeated. He looked me in the eye. "You're talking about organized crime. Right? Mafia? Cosa Nostra?"

"The Outfit," I insisted firmly, but I was pleased how fast he'd picked it up. "That's what we called it. As for it being 'organized crime,' once you've seen it up close, you realize it really isn't all that organized."

It was a joke from the old days, but Bone didn't crack a smile. We started walking again, making the long circle back to the Calf, like I had last night after Sunshine's murder.

"I was never into the heavy, rough-off stuff personally," I continued. "Didn't like doing it, and after a while I didn't get called on for it. I chose my own specialty, and I got good at it. I was a hunter/tracker. See, if someone skips on a debt to a loan shark, everyone can see the knee-cappers coming a mile away, and suddenly nobody knows anything about anyone. Me, I'm no one's idea of a goon. I don't look it, don't act it, don't give off the vibe. Purposefully. So I could nose around, find out if the debt-skipper was holed up with his uncle or an old school buddy, without setting off any alarms. Then I'd feed the information back up the pipeline, and the collection crew would know just where to go. It helps build the legend of an all-knowing, omnipresent organization, one that you can't escape if you commit a transgression against it. Myths like that are very valuable. They keep institutions like the Outfit operating on a paying basis."

I paused for another pull on my drink, but also to make sure I was still centered and clear. I hadn't spoken about any of this in a *long* time. I was surprised to find I felt slightly lightened. Of course, I had no intention of telling him what I did *before* I joined the Outfit.

Bone was still listening, eyes a little wide but otherwise expressionless.

"Anyway," I continued, "I would hang out with the crews that made use of the info I provided. I picked up a lot from them sitting over drinks. Knowledge your common citizen doesn't have. So, I know some stuff. Okay?"

We were swinging back toward St. Peter and the Calf. Bone stopped us before we got within range of the hubbub that overflowed off Bourbon. He hunted up a cigarette and a lighter. He was nodding while he thought.

Ahead of us and across the street, a predator who was wearing the latest in housing project reject wear slowed and checked us out. I stared back at him, and, I realized a second later, so did Bone. As if suddenly remembering a more pressing engagement, he broke eye contact and slid off. Apparently he didn't like what he saw. There were two of us, both reasonably fit and sober. Muggers are on the lookout for victims, not hassles. There is enough of a variety of easy marks wandering the Quarter that the predators are seldom desperate enough to try for healthy prey.

Bone turned toward me. "I take it you're retired from ... this Outfit?"

"Yep." How I came to be "retired" was a story unto itself, and he didn't need the extra information right now.

"And I'm guessing some of these skills you acquired, some of your 'non-citizen' knowledge ... all that'll help in hunting down Sunshine's killer."

"I'm confident it would." I felt more amused than annoyed now to find myself "applying for a job" with this kid. Then again, it *was* more his affair than mine. Sunshine had been his wife—or ex-wife, at least. And I was pretty sure he had never completely stopped loving her.

Bone smoked his cigarette down to the filter and pitched it. I finished off my cocktail.

He was flexing his right hand again, looking quietly pleased with himself for an instant. "I'm not exactly a helpless lamb myself, you understand."

"Never imagined you were."

"Last night you said you wanted to watch out for me," he said. "Because I reminded you of someone. That someone is yourself, of course."

"Of course."

"Okay, Maestro." He put out his hand. "But I promised forty-eight hours before moving on this, and that's still all I promise. If that's cool with you, come aboard. I'd welcome your help ... and your company."

We shook hands, but did it warrior style, clasping each other's wrists tightly. It's how blood oaths used to get sealed.

"Fine." I was unable to keep the warm smile off my face. I shook the ice in my empty cup. "Let's confirm our compact with a libation to the gods. I don't know about you, but I could use another of these. I'll buy the round."

Chapter 12

Bone

"Jesus! I swear I'm about to *lose* it, Bone. *Jesusjesusjesusjesus—*"

I may have done a disservice, painting the picture as strictly Us versus Them. You work in the service industry in a tourist town, it's easy to fall into generalizations. You band together with your fellow locals and pass your free hours carping over cocktails about the boneheaded out-of-towners that come into your restaurant or bar or hotel or that you see committing acts of touristy idiocy on the streets.

Fact is, of course, there are plenty of homegrown idiots. Some of them are your coworkers.

Judith was practically foaming at the mouth as she tried to work the espresso machine. She had two tables of customers—I had six going. She was at her professional capacity, and, yes, "professional" is very misplaced here.

We were getting a late pop at the restaurant, one of those unexplainable surges of customers, but not really unexplainable since these were locals, mostly Quarterites, and a lot lived night-is-day lives. I figured I would be out of here in an hour, hit the Calf, meet Alex there. This was her Friday. But I'd be going to the Calf also to find Maestro. By then the forty-eight hours I'd agreed to would have officially expired. Which meant we had work to do, or at least plans to make.

The radio and the paper still reported that the police had made no arrests in the riverside "Voodoo Murder" as they were calling it, but there were fresher stories now. From tomorrow on Sunshine's murder wouldn't be mentioned unless the crime was solved. I felt a pang that the media was moving past and leaving Sunshine's corpse in its wake. Forgetting her. Replacing her. It wasn't rational, but I let myself feel it anyway.

Clouds of coffee powder flew around the waiters' station, where I stood, grabbing a smoke and calmly keeping an eye on my tables.

"*I*—am—*going*—to—go—*out*—of—*myfuckingmind*! I swear to Jesus!"

I felt sorry for Judith's customers, though there wasn't really anything I could do. They would be getting their food late, probably wouldn't get their drinks at all, and would have to fire off a flare to get Judith's attention if they wanted their checks. Mostly, though, they had to suffer being served by someone frazzled, thoroughly self-absorbed, and on the verge of hysteria. It's difficult to enjoy a relaxing meal when your waitress is having a personal meltdown.

I hate my job. I think I've made that clear. But my customers do not suffer my bad moods, and my reputation as a waiter is actually a very good one.

Judith had been working here two months, and I dreaded when luck of the draw put us together on a shift. She was twenty-two, twenty-three, thereabouts, large-breasted, babydoll face ... I could only figure she was sleeping with the restaurant's owner. Incompetent workers turn up in every industry down here, but Judith was beyond the pale.

"I'm gonna go crazy, Bone! *Bone?*"

It was her high drama, you see, Judith's Coffee Crisis, and I was supposed to be playing along with it. Or at least paying attention.

I felt sorry for Judith's customers. Didn't give a rat's ass about Judith.

"Maybe you should look into committing yourself," I commented, sedately finishing my smoke and heading back out onto the floor.

The Quarter is many things to many different people. One of them is Bohemia. That means a population rife with young folk, lots of them transplants, since this is the place to be living doggedly "alternative" lifestyles. That further means a whole lot of leather jackets, nose rings, visible tattoos, dog collars, and guys wearing black lipstick. But those are symptoms. What it really means is that *everyone* down here is some kind of artist. Everybody is going to put a band together and sell a screenplay and become a famous standup comic and found a moneymaking website and write a best seller and get stinking, filthy, revoltingly rich designing interiors and silk-screening T-shirts and circulating mimeographed poetry newsletters—and those are the sensible schemes.

I know there are some very successful people who live in the French Quarter, at least part-time. That includes acclaimed actors, movie directors, TV personalities, novelists. For every success story, though, there are uncounted failures and wannabes and sad sacks.

In other words, a lot of people around here are full of shit.

I made my rounds, gathering dirty plates, refilling drinks, gabbing with my tables. Raindrops still lightly spattered the restaurant's front windows. Earlier, though, we'd gotten one of those slam-bang summer squalls—thick, sudden clouds, a Judgment Day lightning storm, and two inches of water dropping in half an hour. It had rolled in right above the rooftops, thunder punching loud enough to set off car alarms. We get real weather here, vastly different from the year-round fifty-five degree chill of San Francisco. Summer, in fact, is hurricane season, and one fine day—the natives say this with great foreboding, and perhaps, some secret, rueful pride—some big blow is going to come roaring up the Mississippi and wipe New Orleans off the map. I guess we'll see. When Sunshine and I left, San Francisco was still waiting for that killer earthquake that was going to dump it into the Pacific.

It belatedly occurred to me that the rain was probably responsible for this late influx of customers. Most of my parties were of the type I mentioned— poseurs, struggling artists. Some of them were no doubt worthwhile and the genuine article, but, *Christ*, you hear people talking the same shit over and over, it gets hard to believe anything.

Did I, for instance, believe what Maestro had told me about himself?

I had shot pool with the guy, occasionally seen dawn's light seeping through a bar's shutters with him. We were pals. He was some odd ethnic mix, like Indonesian-Scottish or something equally goofy, with a swarthy complexion, but not too dark. His hair was curly and very thick, and black where it didn't show grey. He probably could have stood to lose a few pounds, but he generally appeared fit for his age, early fifties—certainly healthier than most of the booze-bloated, on-their-last-legs, middle-aged barflies I see around.

Maestro looked and acted like a fairly ordinary Joe ... or as ordinary as the Quarter has to offer.

What he did *not* seem like was an extra from *GoodFellas*. A Mafioso. A made man. A mob warlord.

Okay, he hadn't claimed that. Still, it was a hell of a bombshell. Particularly because I believed him.

Judith shot me dagger looks as I fetched coffee for one of my three-tops. I sailed past, still not giving that rat's ass. Four of my six tables had checks on them now. Everybody was happy with the food, with my service. I hadn't even ball-parked the tips I'd already made. Probably I'd end up doing very well tonight. And for once I didn't feel overly soiled, degraded. It was, of course, because I had larger things on my mind.

Twenty more minutes, I figured, and I'd rendezvous with Maestro. And then we could start the wheels turning on avenging Sunshine.

I was ... looking forward to it. Excited by it. That realization, sudden and powerful, actually brought me to a standstill for a moment there in the middle of the dining room floor, coffeepot in hand, eyes centered intently on nothing.

I had enjoyed punching out that creep last night in Sin City's toilet. I didn't have any problem admitting that to myself. But—looking forward to hunting— to *killing*—Sunshine's murderer? Did I have the right to happily anticipate that? Where was my moral high ground?

Pushing myself back into motion, I let the questions hang. How I felt about what I meant to do wouldn't have any bearing on my actions, I decided, and rightfully. For instance, I could love being a waiter or hate it, but I still had to show up and do the job. I didn't have a choice.

The new waiter, Otto, had clocked in and come on, and he could have the graveyard shift. One of Judith's tables had walked out. Her other party was looking very pissed off. I collected my checks, delivered two more—my last two—and started sorting the contents of my apron pockets.

I recognized the detective when he came in because I'd known him before his promotion, had poured coffee for him here when he was still in a uniform. Zanders. Liked lots of Equal instead of sugar; cream; tipped well. So my brain automatically reported.

He was dressed in slacks and a lavender shirt, and crossing the floor, heading for me. He had an easy gait and looked very comfortable in his new rank. His auburn mustache had since grown handlebars, and his hairline had receded a bit further.

I nodded hello. "Detective Zanders. How're you tonight?"

"Fine, just fine. I'd like a word with you, okay? You got somewhere quiet here—office, something?"

He had a pistol holstered on his belt. I was suddenly very aware of that, of what it represented. Even when he'd been in uniform, this man had always just been one of my customers. Now, he was ... a cop. A cop who wanted to talk to me, privately.

I thought of Mitchell, the guy who'd threatened Alex, lying crumpled beside the urinal in the back of Sin City.

"Sure, Detective," I said with a shrug. "Right this way."

Phil, the shift manager was helping out the cooks—Werewolf and Firecracker—in the kitchen, so the little office next to the prep room was empty. We entered. Detective Zanders closed the door behind us.

"What can I do for you, Detective?" I propped a hip up on the edge of the desk in the center of the small room, pulled out my cigarettes and offered one to Zanders. Detective Zander waved it off, pulling out a little notebook and positioning himself comfortably between me and the door.

"I'm conducting an investigation into the murder of Peace S. Williams. Did you know her?"

Hearing someone official talk about Sunshine in the past tense like that made the truth of her death somehow more real, more raw. But I calmly lit my smoke, inhaling deeply, determined not to let it show.

"Yeah, I knew her." I exhaled smoke. "I was married to her." I certainly wasn't going to lie about it. As Maestro had pointed out, it was something he probably already knew.

"But you're not married now."

"No. We divorced last year."

"A messy divorce?"

"Not particularly. She just wanted her space. We stayed friends." Damn, saying that aloud made it sound trite.

"Really? What about Molly's Bar about ten days ago? I gotta say that the scene witnesses described to me sure didn't sound very friendly."

I felt anger build, even though I knew he had to ask—had known these questions would come. He was deliberately trying to pull my chain.

"Yeah, OK. We had a fight that night. I think if you ask your witnesses, you'll find that she came at me."

"So I'm asking you. Can you tell me exactly what happened?"

At Zanders' request I recounted the whole awful confrontation, including Sunshine's appearance and behavior when she came at me. " ... and even at that, it never got physical."

"Maybe not then."

"Not ever! Fact is, that was the last time I saw her alive. And just to clear the air and get this over with, I was here, working, when she ... died." I didn't quite glare at Zanders. He heard it in my voice, though, and gave me a sharp look.

He made a point of looking at his notebook. "Well, one of your co-workers, Judith I think, says you weren't here that night—says you clocked in and left."

"Judith!" I almost exploded off the desk, biting back a furious torrent of expletives. *That bitch!* I forced my anger down. It was just a cop interrogation method. He wanted to rattle me to see what popped out.

"First, if you check with anyone, you'll find that Judith wasn't here at all that night. So whatever she told you about anything is shit. Second, during that night's shift I served fifteen tables, ending with a four-top of tourists—the guy who paid was named Ned something—and a two-top with Boogie Joe and Lisa who work at the House of Blues." I proceeded to rattle off exactly what each diner had ordered just to make it clear that I could.

" ... and if you need more proof, check with Phil," I said and gestured toward the outer restaurant. "He's here tonight and he was shift manager that night." I took a deep breath, ground out the remains of my cigarette, and focused on Zanders. "Look, Detective Zanders, I know you're just trying to do your job—and you need to understand, that I really, really *want* you to do your job. But the fact that you are here questioning *me* means that you have no idea who really killed Sunshine, do you."

"I can't discuss the investigation with you."

"Right. Now if you don't mind, Detective, I've had a long day and would like to clock out now." He moved out of the way as I walked past and opened the door, gesturing for him to lead the way out.

"Just don't go too far, Bone. I may need to talk to you again."

"Well, you know where to find me, Detective Zanders. Always happy to help." I forced a smile and shook his hand as I escorted him out the door. I knew I was in the clear, there were just too many people who had seen me here that night. But it still felt disconcerting to think that the police might keep tabs on me—especially since it looked like we were going to have to do their job, after all.

* * *

Excerpt from Bone's Movie Diary:

> My personal favorite gotcha! movie moment occurs at the end of *The Mechanic*. Jan-Michael Vincent is the protégé & Charles Bronson (again Bronson; wood-enish actor but turned up in some good films) is the seasoned assassin. Fairly standard hit-man-in-training stuff. Eventually the "son" slays the "father," Greek tragedy-like, & Vincent is smugly victorious, about to inherit it all ... until he gets into Bronson's car, has just enough time to read the brief note waiting for him— then the bomb goes off. It's an effective twist, which I admit caught me flat-footed. Gotcha, Jan-Michael.

Chapter 13

Maestro

The rain almost caught me, but the Quarter is full of umbrellas. Lots of the older buildings are fronted with balconies—"galleries" is the local term—overhanging the sidewalk, usually made of decorative wrought iron, often filled with potted plants and sometimes patio furniture. When a sudden cloudburst comes along, you can still get around on foot by ducking under a gallery and hopping from one to another of these shelters.

Or you can just go into the nearest bar and wait it out.

I'm aware of other parts of the city, like Mid-City, the Garden District, the Ninth Ward, etc. I know they're real the same way I know Norway and Thailand are real. But *my* New Orleans is the Quarter, and so I confine my activities to it.

I had been purposely doing a high-visibility walkabout. I was out earlier than usual, by which I mean it was slightly before midnight. Still, it was plenty late enough for the locals to be stirring.

I didn't bother with Bourbon but strolled up and down the parallel and cross-streets at a leisurely pace. I was on alert, though, of course.

When I first relocated down here, a fellow displaced Northerner summed up what I could expect from the Quarter with one explanation: "Man, these folks down here have one solution to everything—let's party. Yuh got a new job? Let's party. Yuh lost yer job? Com'on, let's party. Y'er gettin' married? Hey! Let's party. Y'er gettin' a divorce? Screw the bitch, screw the bastard, let's party!"

New Orleaneans in general, and Quarterites specifically, will party down anytime for any reason. Birthday parties, wedding parties, anniversary parties, graduation parties, and leaving-town parties you can find in any city, but the Quarter doesn't stop there. We also have hurricane parties, bar-anniversary parties, raise-bail-money parties, not to mention holiday parties for every American holiday and several foreign ones I'd never heard of until I got here. Then you toss in a wide assortment of specialty theme parties—like classic toga parties, '60s retro parties, white-trash parties, barbecue parties, and high-heel pool tournament parties (don't ask)—that the bars host periodically just to keep things from getting too dull, and you might start to get a feel for what the "normal" nightlife in the Quarter is like.

I enjoy my whiskey, but I don't expect it to change or solve anything in my life. Drinking is more of a time-killer than anything ... like a lot of what I do these days, it seems. Also, in deference to my age and liver, I tend to go easy on the more hardcore bar celebrations.

Tonight, though, I had figured as a good night for "doing the rounds." First of all, it established among the sundry bar patrons that I was presently in an "up, party" mood. Second, roaming from bar to bar reestablished me at some of the places I hadn't hit for weeks or months, as well as let me update my mental files of who was still in the Quarter and where they currently worked.

It was elemental groundwork. I might not need any of it. This hunt that Bone had in mind for Sunshine's killer might come to nothing for any number of reasons. But if it actually happened, I didn't want anyone remembering me as brooding, maybe thinking dark vigilante thoughts about Sunshine's murderer. As for re-circulating my face ... you never know which contacts will do you good when. Use what resources are at hand. I had saved myself immeasurable hassle in my career days with the Outfit simply by making the right casual acquaintances.

While I was out and about, I was also accosted four different times in four different bars by acquaintances of varying familiarity who told me about somebody walking Decatur two nights earlier, looking for me. Nobody had a description as thorough as the one the Bear had given me, of course, but it was the same early thirties, clean-cut male. Nobody knew who he was. Nobody had told him anything. The Quarter's traditional conspiracy of silence was working in my favor.

To each of these four giving me the heads-up, I said casually, "Thanks, I know. I know the guy, but neither of us has a phone number or address for the other. If you see him, tell him I'm looking for him too."

It's never good to be the prey. As a former pro tracker, it seriously rankled me to think of someone hunting *me*. It wouldn't do. If this guy surfaced again asking questions, my message would very probably reach him, and might give him pause.

But more disturbing, I ran into Mother Mystic—or rather she found me—just outside of CC's coffee shop, which was closed for the night.

"Maestro! You are quite a hard man to find." She grabbed my arm and walked with me toward my next bar.

"Thank you. I'll take that as a compliment. Were you looking for me?" *Somebody else hunting me—great!* Only Mystic had found me. She asked if we could go somewhere to talk, so we stepped into the next available bar. After throwing a few hello's to those I recognized, we grabbed a table in the back corner. I ordered a coke and Mother Mystic had coffee. I sipped my coke and waited for her to speak.

"You remember the day you came to visit me? You ask about that girl—your friend—who was murdered? You asked about the *Vodun?*" She looked around nervously, leaning forward. "I did not say it then, but the night before she died, someone broke into the Voodoo Museum. They desecrated the shrine, and took some powerful *gris-gris*—the kind that could be used for evil purpose by those with dark hearts."

She took a deep breath. "But that is not why I looked for you, Maestro. When you came to me, I was angry. I had been asked to do black ritual by a man I didn't know. It happened days before the girl died. I refuse. Not unusual. The world is full of those who look to the dark rather than face their own faults. But ..." She looked around again and dropped her voice so low I had to strain to hear her, "I get a call today. This man speaks to me, that if I do not do his ritual, I end up like the girl by the river—and he will use my blood to feed the *Loa.*"

"What did he look like?"

She sat back in her chair. "I have never seen him. He has only used the phone and e-mail. I do not even know if he is in the Quarter."

I could tell she was upset. "What are you going to do?"

"I do not know. But the *Loa* will protect me. I will be fine. I just wanted you to know." She looked around again. "I must go." She got up and quickly left the bar. I waited a few minutes, long enough to socialize with the few folks I knew and to make certain no undo attention had been paid to my meeting with Mystic, then left. I had no idea if Mystic's mystery man was actually our murderer, but her story had certainly been disturbing.

I continued my rounds, even putting in appearances along Decatur, a track that is more for the younger crowd and not one I frequent regularly. It was too early for the Bear to be on at his joint, but I still made nods and hello's and *whatcha-been-up-to's* at several places. I caught up on a lot of unnecessary bar gossip, but never stayed around long enough to get totally sucked into anything.

Mind you, I was not, repeat *not*, having a cocktail every time I stopped. Had I been, experienced drinker or not, I'd have been flat on my face before long. It's usually not any big deal if you want to go out in the Quarter and not drink alcohol. You can sit with a soda, coffee, or a juice, and no one looks at you sideways. The fact that I was tipping for Cokes, even though I only drank one sip, kept the bartenders happy.

During my rounds, I even passed the restaurant where Bone worked, also on Decatur. I glanced in the tall front windows, but it looked busy so I walked on. Work is the curse of the working class. The last time I had a square job—my boyhood paper route—Eisenhower was president.

After sitting out the rain, I picked my way through the sidewalk puddles that were already being sucked back into the air. If this were the fall or spring, we'd probably be treated to a nice thick fog eddying in off the river. In the summer, though, all a heavy rain does is turn the night into a steam bath.

I swung back to my pad and shed one shirt for another. Sometimes I wondered why I bothered. Thirty seconds after stepping out of the shower down here in summer, you'll find yourself dripping with sweat. I don't wear eyeglasses, but up North your lenses fog up in the winter when you step from the icy outdoors to the cozy indoors. Here, in the summertime, they fog when you step *out* of the nippy air-conditioned bars into the sauna-like streets. It's just another little item of culture shock that after ten years doesn't seem so bizarre to me anymore.

No messages on my machine, but that was how it usually was. I loaded up with a fresh pack of cigarettes and headed out again. It was late enough that Bone ought to be off work and at the Calf.

The Two of Cups from Rose's tarot reading meant the appearance of a lover or partner. I felt quite safe that Bone wasn't the former, but he was certainly looking like the latter: a partner. Thing was, did I want a partner?

Evidently I did, I thought as I made my way toward St. Peter Street. I had invited myself into Bone's undertaking to find Sunshine's killer. Frankly, I wouldn't be tackling that venture on my own initiative. I liked Sunshine, but I'd never been in the revenge business ... not for personal reasons, anyway.

Bone apparently was, or at least he was looking to break into the field. His ex-wife had been murdered, and he had a real stake in seeing her avenged. And I had—what? A stake in not seeing him get himself into irreparable trouble, maybe get himself killed? He was going to be taking on a rough customer, an ex-con, one who'd punched an ice pick *twice* through his ex-wife's heart—one who might possibly be dabbling in the occult.

I still found it more amusing than irritating that I'd had to present Bone with my "credentials" to qualify to come on board this thing. But amusing or not, it showed me I was serious. Obviously I wasn't in the habit of revealing my past to people. Bone, then, was different.

When I entered the Calf, a nod Padre's way was all it took to get me my Irish. When he brought it over, I asked, "Has Bone been through already?"

"Nope."

I waited. The regulars popped up one by one or in pairs, but I didn't join in any of the conversation clusters, not even when they started casting a fictitious remake of *One Flew Over the Cuckoo's Nest*.

The night Sunshine had been murdered, Bone had gone off to Big Daddy's asking questions. Bad move. It was sticking his head up unnecessarily, letting people know he was interested in the killing. The only one who really knew I was interested was Mother Mystic, and I knew she was trustworthy. She had proven that by sharing her information tonight.

The clock was creeping up on two when I finally admitted I was worried. Bone still hadn't arrived. I had an ashtray full of butts in front of me, which Padre spotted and dumped.

"Another, Maestro?" He nodded at my rock glass.

Should I go out looking? Did I really want to partner with someone as frankly amateurish as Bone? If he got himself in dutch, was I going to get pulled down with him?

It was easier to answer Padre's question. "Yeah. Please."

A short while later, Alex showed up and spotted me. "Thank gods it's Friday," she said as she gave me a swift peck and hug. It was the end of her work-week. I slid a bill toward Padre to pay for her drink and smirked at her "thank gods" comment. It indicated she was of the neo-pagan persuasion, a vague amalgam of earthy, aboriginal worships that seems to be the dominant religion in the Quarter. (I've been in the Deep South ten years. It may be the Bible Belt, but I still don't personally know any Baptists.) I wondered fleetingly what beliefs Bone had, if any. I would have figured him for a devout atheist.

Alex looked around as she took the barstool next to mine. "Seen Bone around anywhere?"

I shrugged. "Must be running late." I made it sound casual.

She took a long pull on her cocktail. Obviously it had been a grueling week for her. She dug her cross-stitching out of her knapsack to show me her latest project, and I paid dutiful attention. And continued to wait.

Bone doesn't have much skin tone, even for a Caucasian, even for a Quarter night waiter. But he looked extra pale when he came through the Calf's door.

Alex hurtled off her stool faster than I guessed I could move even during swordplay. I hung back, waiting, very antsy now. Bone was quickly reassuring Alex, their voices below the level of the jukebox that someone had fed a few bucks.

Their body language—especially Bone's—told me that I was right in what I'd been thinking. Bone was starting to figure out how he felt about her.

Finally they came over together.

"Cops," Bone said to me. "Actually—cop. A detective. Guy I know who knew where I work. He wanted to talk to me ... about Sunshine. Thanks,

Padre." He picked up his glass, took a swallow. I noted that his hand wasn't shaky. Neither was he giving off a panicky vibe.

Whatever had happened, he'd kept his cool.

"Detective Zanders. He asked me my whereabouts. Lucky the night manager was there at the restaurant, and was there two nights ago too, when Sunshine ... well. You'll be happy to know I'm not a suspect in her murder."

He met my eyes. I nodded with a shallow dip of my chin.

Bone fished out a cigarette, but his lighter just threw sparks when he flicked it. "Dammit," he muttered as Alex lit it for him.

My gaze shot significantly at her as she leaned past me, then I threw a quick questioning look at Bone.

It was his turn to nod slyly. He put an arm around Alex's shoulders. "Alex," he said, "I'm pretty wound up from this. Plus it was a rough night at work. Would you mind if I didn't walk you home tonight? Let me call you a cab instead? I need to stay out a while ..."

I moved away to let them talk in private. Bone had always insisted he and Alex were just good friends, but to me, it looked like something more, even if he wasn't aware of it. He was very protective of her, and she always seemed to be there for him.

A few minutes later Padre phoned for a cab. A few minutes after that the United rolled up to the curb and Alex went out after kissing Bone on the cheek and waving a big, general goodbye. The building that housed both their apartments was somewhere on Burgundy, more toward the quiet residential end around Esplanade. Quiet, yes, but also where predators will most often sneak through on the off chance of catching someone alone on the sidewalks. Alex, in her black pants and white shirt, was wearing "target" clothes: standard wait-staff wear, even though she was only a clerk in a gift shop. Therefore, the cab—even though home was technically easy walking distance.

Bone sat down next to me with a grunt. "Christ ..."

"Have you told her anything about it?" I asked.

"About what?"

"*It.*"

"Oh." He took a swallow of his drink. "No. Nothing about going looking for Sunshine's killer. These last two days ... they haven't been fun. Alex and Sunshine were very close. They had this long-lost sister thing going. Before Sunshine ... well, *shit!* Before Sunshine started changing."

"Okay," I looked at him. "Are you planning on telling her?"

He regarded me flatly. "Yes. Of course. Among other things, she's got the right to know."

"You think so?"

"I definitely do. The three of us were like family ... once."

I've had relationships, mostly of the hello/goodbye variety, including several here in the Quarter, but I've never been married, never had a female best friend. I could understand Bone's loyalty to Alex because I was experienced and knowledgeable and full of aging wisdom—*ha!*—but I couldn't *really* understand, you know? It was guesswork on my part.

Even so, I'm pretty good at guesswork. I figured that Bone had come to a sudden, dim realization regarding his feelings toward Alex, but he was still too caught up in his memories of Sunshine and their three-way friendship to see what anyone else could plainly see about Alex. She was completely gone on him, probably had been all the while when he was married to Sunshine, but she was far too good of a person to ever let it show. And she'd been there for him ever since Sunshine left him, being the friend he needed instead of pushing him to notice her. Probably suffering a little guilt for what she felt for him, too, and maybe even some misplaced guilt for the breakup of his marriage.

A damned complicated situation, one mined with all kinds of potential emotional explosives. Would Bone's decision to include Alex affect what he and I meant to do? Would she get underfoot, become a distraction?

"So," Bone drained his glass. "When Detective Zanders came around tonight to question me he pretty much confirmed, without actually saying as much, that the police haven't made any arrests in Sunshine's case. In fact, it seems that by questioning me they're scraping the bottom of the suspect barrel. Which means they've got nothing, nada, nil. So ..." His eyes went to the clock on the wall. "Ding, ding. Time's up. Forty-eight hours, Maestro. What do you say?"

I sighed. "Sure you wouldn't rather talk movies, have another drink? We were remaking *One Flew Over the Cuckoo's Nest* earlier. How would you cast it?"

"*Cuckoo's Nest*," he said slowly.

It didn't seem credible he didn't know it. Actually it didn't seem likely there was a movie made he wasn't thoroughly familiar with. "Y'know, with Jack Nicholson ..."

"I know the film. Some things shouldn't be tampered with." He shook himself visibly. "Well, Maestro. We start this now, together—or we part company, now, over it."

I sat a moment, looking at him.

"You understand that if the killer's not in the Quarter we don't stand a chance of finding him. If he's split town, or even if he's gone to ground in New Orleans East, he's as good as on the moon."

Bone nodded. He was still waiting for my answer. But I'd already decided.

"Let's get to work," I said.

Chapter 14

Bone

A lot of Quarterites draw the line in the sand at noon and will not cross it. Daylight is meant to be slept through, or so say those that work the graveyard shifts, or those that *can't* stop drinking once they start and so do it until the sunrise tells them to go the hell home. The bohemians like this schedule because it further distances them from the bourgeois lifestyles they so loathe.

Myself, I don't like sleeping too, too late. It's a lousy thing to stir in the late afternoon, brush your teeth, grab your shoes, and go to work.

Even so, when I slipped out of bed shortly after 10 a.m.—having been out until the not-so-wee hours with Maestro—it was a shock to my system.

Alex's apartment had been dark when I'd come in last night, and there was no sign that she was stirring yet this morning. Hopefully she was still sleeping. Today was her day off. Which was why I was prowling out this early. I could take care of an item on the to-do list Maestro and I had concocted and be back about the time Alex normally got up. I had to talk to her. She had to know what was going on. That she had a right to know wasn't just something noble-sounding I'd said to Maestro. It was the plainest truth. She had been Sunshine's best friend, had been part of my family—while I'd had one. She didn't show her pain and fury the same way I did, but I knew it was there. And I needed her to know that someone—that I—was trying to find justice for Sunshine.

I threw on some clothes and started to make coffee only to discover I had run out. I grabbed my boots from the living room, where Booboo lay splayed comatose across the arm of the couch, no doubt dreaming she was a great leopard lolling on a tree branch on the Veldt. Her black, triangular ears abruptly perked up, reacting to some noise in her dream-hunt, her head lifted, rolled, and she promptly and gracelessly dumped herself to the floor. I pulled on my boots and got out of there so that her indignity wouldn't be compounded. I've no children and never will have, but Booboo satisfies whatever paternal itch I might be harboring. Doesn't matter that my child is a bit clumsy.

Queasy heat and daylight were waiting for me. I swayed, realized I'd damned well *better* get some coffee in me if I meant to function at all. I started out toward the river. I could swing back around after, hit my target and then head home.

Workmen were on several different surrounding rooftops above, yanking up old shingles, driving nails. That much nearer the murderous sun, and not a lick of cloud in the sky today, and doing manual labor ... dreadful. I could have a worse job than what I've got. I know that.

Some part of the Quarter is always under repair. I sometimes wonder if we're not the proverbial grandfather's axe. You know the one: the handle's been replaced four times and the blade-head three, but we still call it the original axe.

I scratched the stubble under my chin. I hadn't shaved yesterday or the day before, wouldn't bother today. I don't need to be unreasonably groomed for work.

It had been that unpleasant, cringe-inducing incident at Molly's on Toulouse—that and my ex-husband status was what had brought Detective Zanders around to see me. That very last time I had seen Sunshine alive, a week and a half ago now, and we'd ended up screaming at each other, squandering that last moment that wasn't going to come again. My fist bunched at my side as I slogged on. *Goddammit!* It was so hateful, so cruel. More than my ex-wife, she had been my dearest friend, and we didn't get our goodbyes in, didn't leave things on anything remotely resembling a kind note. It was, I knew, one of those ruthless little jokes of fate that would stay with me for the rest of my days.

Explaining the incident to Zanders, however, had meant recounting Sunshine's condition that night—her high-tension anger, her shrieky mind-altered behavior. There was no way to pretty it up, to paint her personality that night as anything except that of a raving maniac's ... and that hurt, describing her that way. It magnified how I already felt about the entire thing. It was like ... pissing on her grave.

Except, of course, she probably wasn't in the ground yet. There was a grisly thought. I knew she had family—a mother anyway—in Chicago and presumed the ... body ... would go there.

Is this how it goes? Sunshine stops being Sunshine, and becomes, instead, a body; from animate to inanimate in my thoughts. Next? Sunshine *was*, not Sunshine *is*.

These were inevitabilities, of course. That was how it went, and, more to the point, how it was supposed to go. Humans must process the deaths of those around them. Sunshine wasn't the first person I'd known who had died, though she was certainly the closest to me. She was also the only one I personally knew who had been murdered.

I generally frown on people that visit their places of work during their off-hours. *Don't you have anything better to do?* Yet here I was, blinking at the familiar yet strange dining room currently awash in stark daylight and populated by just a few occupied tables, and this the decidedly subdued breakfast crowd.

I went to sit at the L-shaped bar. A minute later P.J. came up to the other side.

"Bone. Out in the daytime. And you haven't burst into flames."

"Hilarious. Coffee, P.J. Please."

I'd always thought her a good waitress, too good to be wasting her time on this dead-ass shift. I dug out my smokes.

She set a hot cup in front of me. "Do you want some breakfast with that?"

I'd remembered to refill my lighter with fluid. I lit a cigarette. "This *is* breakfast," I assured her.

The coffee was good. I sipped, smoked and generally stayed hid behind my sunglasses. I thought about what I had planned for this morning. It was quite an itinerary we'd devised, Maestro and me, though—credit where credit's due—last night he had laid out the bulk of the scheme for locating Sunshine's killer. Actually, it was less than a scheme. Nothing flashy about it, just solid logical avenues to pursue. And he had rattled it off so easily and precisely, like he was reciting the rules to a board game. *We could try this, we could look into that.* We had such-and-such in our favor, but these factors were against us.

We had moved off to a back booth of the Calf, and Padre had somehow magically orchestrated the crowd so that we were left alone. There we'd hatched and outlined and polished.

There was in the end, of course, no presto-quickie formula for locating some-one the police were already actively hunting. Our man—and "man" we took on faith, owing to the murder method and to Mother Mystic's information—had eluded the cops long enough to outlast the immediate attention of the media, and thereby the public. That first go-for-broke frenzy would die down. This wasn't to say that the police would just drop it now, or that they were more inter-ested in good press than in actually catching the murderer. But—and Maestro had said it at the outset—they had limited manpower and resources, and other cases would be taking up their time by now.

P.J. reappeared to refill my coffee. I was feeling a lot less zombie-like now.

"Uh, Bone ..."

I glanced up. P.J. is my age or older, with that accompanying maturity that sets both of us apart from the world's twenty-somethings. She had a pageboy haircut, and her eyes were regarding me ... leerily, it seemed.

"What?"

"Did the cops really come by here last night and arrest you, or is that just crap?"

I suddenly felt my blood cooling. I would have just sat there staring at her from behind my shades, but luckily my smartass-retort chip activated. "Do I look terribly arrested this morning, P.J.?"

Behind P.J.'s left shoulder, back toward the waiters' station and the entry into the kitchens, I now noticed two heads peeking out. One was the dishwasher, a perpetually stoned gutter-punk-with-a-job; the other, one of the cooks. They were nudging each other with elbows, trading hushed, gleeful words, looking my way.

Oh, Christ. Like I needed this.

"You don't," PJ admitted, to my comeback. "Crap, then."

I pushed up from the stool, dealt two singles onto the bar top.

"Coffee's only a buck, Bone. And I'm not charging you for it."

"Then put it all in your pocket. If we don't take care of each other, who will?" And I was out of there, aware that yet another onlooker had come out from the kitchens, to ogle, aware of those eyes following me back out into the blast furnace morning.

I didn't appreciate being gossiped about, but there wasn't much I could do, and frankly, I should have seen it coming. The tale of Detective Zanders stopping by the restaurant to question me would, naturally, be passed on and embellished. You don't have to go into a bar to make contact with the local rumor mill, I reminded myself. Still, as one who doesn't listen to gossip, it irked me to be an *item* of gossip.

*   *   *

Sunshine, I knew, had moved sometime during the past two months from the apartment Alex had helped her find after our split. The second move had happened during that stretch when I was deliberately avoiding her. Changing addresses is nothing unusual here. Compared to the rest of the city—though certainly not to, say, oh, San Francisco—rents are steep in the Quarter. Your basic working class Quarterite might vacate his or her premises for a number of reasons. Landlords renovate buildings, raise rents, might even turn your place into condos. I had been lucky. Two years at the same apartment, still paying the same monthly rent.

Quarterites stop being Quarterites when they bail out to go live in the Marigny or Uptown or other neighborhoods where you can rent bigger places cheaper. I just don't get that. New Orleans is hardly an earthly paradise. If you're not going to live in the Quarter—which is undeniably exotic and interesting and unique—then you might as well be living in San Diego or Allentown or Knoxville.

I turned off Decatur at Barracks and started following it away from the river.

I didn't know why Sunshine had moved, and I wondered now, with that same squeamish feeling of betrayal I'd felt with Detective Zanders, if her drug usage had been wrecking her finances. I still didn't know how heavy she'd been into what. I knew she liked pot and painkillers, didn't know if there were other things. Despite an adulthood of boozing and cigarette smoking, I wasn't versed in the peculiarities of narcotics. They were expensive, you could get arrested for possessing them, and you had to associate with riffraff to keep yourself supplied with them. That much I figured I knew. I'd never been tempted to find out more firsthand.

Sunshine's place was in the eight ... no, nine hundred block of Barracks. I remembered pouring her into a cab one night, out of the Shim Sham club, hearing her garble her new address to the driver. I couldn't recall the exact number, but I was pretty sure I could find the place.

Barracks' nine hundred block had a park along one side of the street—the Cabrini Playground—though it had no actual playground toys. It was mostly a big open dog park surrounded by a tree-lined, open-work fence of wrought iron and brickwork. Inside the park dogs chased Frisbees and owners mingled and picked up after their pets. That made my job easier. I blended in as just one more Quarterite out for a stroll. I walked slow—not unusual since nobody hurries in the summer heat unless they're looking to keel over.

Along the side of the street opposite the park there was a dry cleaner's, a used bookstore that Alex—who reads at an inhuman speed—was keeping in business, and several residences. I eliminated those that appeared to be single-unit dwellings, which left a building that appeared to contain a number of apartments.

I paused on the sidewalk, taking my time getting out a cigarette and lighting it. Meanwhile, I eyed the place, memorizing details Maestro had said to look for. Four buzzers, that meant four units. A steel security gate over a wood interior door. You'd need two keys just to get to the foyer, another to get inside your apartment.

The building showed its age—and there are places still standing here that were put up well before the Civil War—crumbling around the edges. But it was that quaint French Quarter brand of decay. Very little in the Quarter looks trashy. Our neighborhood is a historical preserve.

I palmed moisture off my forehead, realizing I could probably wring a quart of sweat out of my T-shirt by now. A mule-driven carriage clattered by down

Barracks. The driver, wearing a top hat and ruffled white shirt, regaled his two tourist passengers with grand tales of the Quarter's yore, some of which might actually be true. It was a street scene out of another century.

I noticed the bicycle when the carriage had passed. Big front basket, chained to the lamppost in front of the building—a delivery bike. The building's interior door swung suddenly inward, and someone stepped out, unlatching the outer gate. I was moving, reacting fast, not rushing but crossing the street, fishing my keys out of my pocket, glancing up, "noticing" the delivery kid emerging. I caught the gate casually, stepped forward to block the swinging shut inner wood door with my foot—all like I belonged there, like the keys jingling in my hand opened these doors.

The delivery guy, a kid in a ragged denim vest, scowled past, paying me no mind, grumbling, "No-tippin' son of a bitch." He freed his bike and pedaled off.

My bluff had worked! I was unduly surprised by that, but lingering here slack-jawed wasn't bright. I let the security gate close and lock itself, stepped into the dim foyer as the old pressurized overhead arm squealed shut the interior door.

Breaking and entering? No, this was just trespassing. *Just?*

I'd meant to case this place, just take a look-see, as Maestro had recommended. Instead, I found myself driven to push ahead. Probably a dumb idea, but I wasn't going to stop to examine it now that I'd gained entry. Four apartments in here—one of them was Sunshine's last address. I might as well try to find out what I could. Why waste the opportunity?

I flipped my cigarette to the uncarpeted floor, ground it out and pocketed my sunglasses. It was shabby in here—water-stained ceiling, very old paint on the walls, the musty smell of old mold from years in the damp climate. Music thumped heavily from one of the units, obnoxiously loud, the bass cranked up.

My heart too, beat heavy and loud, but I could have my attack of nerves later. Still, how surreal this was—and, yes, a bit of a thrill too. Me, a waiter, an average guy in a lot of ways, never seriously transgressed the law before, and here I was, sleuthing around, slipping through the shadows ...

For Chrissake, Bone, have your heart attack later.

I saw an apartment door, a stairway, and further back the foyer looked like it led to rear units—probably the old slave quarters.

Four buzzers, four units.

The nearby apartment door sported a big "#1" drawn in black marker—very classy. I stepped up quietly to it, leaned my ear against the wood, had no idea what I was listening for, and heard nothing. If this was Sunshine's apartment, it would be unoccupied, wouldn't it? Did I want to look inside? Who knew what sorts of clues might be found in her old place?

I gingerly touched the knob. Locked. Break in? I didn't know how. Maestro, though, probably would. I wished briefly he were here. Then again, he probably would've told me not to do this, to be careful, play it safe. He was definitely protective of me ... and it belatedly occurred to me that might become a problem.

I would check the rear units last. Now I turned toward the stairway. I crept up, trying to be silent in my boots. The stairs hooked to the left, and the *thump-thump*ing music was coming from up here, from behind a single door at the top.

Three steps below the door I stopped, stared, and knew I had the right place.

Sunshine had a talent for sketching. People used to tell her she ought to go to college for it. That's what people say, and Sunshine knew what crap it was. She herself didn't take her art seriously. It was a minor kind of therapy, and I'd always understood that, as far back as when we first met. Still, I recognized the talent.

As I recognized, now, the sheet of drawing paper thumbtacked to the center of the apartment door at the top of the stairs.

Sunshine ...

I watched as my hand, almost as if had a will of its own, lifted and knocked on the door. This apartment was occupied, the source of the music I'd been hearing. What was I intending to do? I stood frozen, feeling the pounding bass reverberating through the door, proof that I knew even less about Sunshine's life than I thought. I didn't want to know about what lay behind that door—but I had to know.

The door opened, even though I hadn't touched it, and a head stuck itself into the dim stairway. "Dude, I already paid yuh. Whacha wan'?"

Here, then, was the delivery kid's "no-tippin' son of a bitch"—twenty-four or thereabouts, lean, head shaved up to the temples on both sides and dark sloppy hair where there wasn't scalp, earlobes pierced to within an inch of their lives, wispy hair on the upper lip, eyes like fried circuits.

"Is Sunshine here?" I asked, not missing a beat.

He wore camouflage cargo pants and a dirty white T-shirt with a red Japanese character on it. Behind him a stereo pounded. The air wafting out from the apartment smelled like a marijuana jungle might while it was being slashed and burned. He was holding a roast beef po'boy, still half in its butcher paper.

"Sun ... shine." He blinked his nobody-home eyes; then, rallying, said, "Naw."

"Shit. I was s'posed to come see her, y'know, come get somethin', y'know."

"Well ..." he started, then a light seemed to slowy come on in his head. "Yeah. You must be *that* dude." He shut the door. I heard him rummaging around for a moment, then he opened the door and shoved a stained manila envelope at me. Surprised, I took it. He started to close the door again.

"So when's she gonna be back, dude?" I pushed into the doorway. I figured the kid was too wasted to wonder how I'd gotten into the building.

"She ..." He took a bite from his sandwich and chewed, cow-like, while he thought. "Oh ... Sunshine's, like, not here."

Great. Inside, past him, the floor was scattered with clothes, magazines, plastic milk crates. Mardi Gras beads, a pile of souvenir tourist junk. A battered saxophone lay across a third-hand coffee table.

"She ain't here, right." I did my best to imitate his slacker-lax speech patterns, but he made Keanu Reeves sound like Olivier. "S'all right, y'know, maybe I could come in an' wait for her, dude?" A closer look at the apartment might be good.

He made no move out of the doorway. His stoner-red eyes narrowed, showing a first hint of suspicion. "Wai' ... who're you?"

"Name's Slim," I improvised, "friend of Sunshine's. Are you, y'know, like, her roomie?"

Something seemed to come alive in that doped-out head at that.

"Sunshine ain' here." He was enunciating carefully now. "She ain' gonna *be* here. She's dead. Yuh unnerstan'? Yuh geddit? An' I ain' her fuckin' *roomie*, a'ight? I'm her boyfriend."

This last he said proudly, defiantly.

Sunshine's romantic judgment had never, for as long as I'd known her, been especially astute. But I mean, come *on!* She must have scraped deep in a rank barrel to find this beauty.

For a moment, just a split second, I wanted to beat him to death for ever having touched her.

"Sunshine—dead?" I shook my head. "Aw, dude, no way—really? I can't believe ... shit. Wow. Hey, dude, I'm real sorry. Real sorry. I feel you. Hey, what's your name anyway?"

He seemed to like my show of grief, but it was and wasn't a show, and I hated, for Sunshine's sake, having to do it. "Dunk," he supplied.

"Short for Duncan?"

Those fried eyes narrowed again. "Hey ... whacha askin' me my name for? Huh?"

"Hey, I'm just a friend of Sunshine's."

"Yeah? Well. *Fuck off.*" He pushed me back, hard, slamming the door in my face.

I found myself standing outside the door, with an envelope in my hand. Someone had scrawled a capital M—or maybe a W—on it with a marker. Curious, I opened the battered envelope and looked inside. It held only a yellowed old photograph of a dark-haired man and a blond girl, probably in their late teens or early twenties, both wearing clothes that looked like something from the '60s. There was something familiar about both of them, but nothing I could pin down. I turned the photo over, but there was nothing written on the back. I had no idea what the photo had to do with Sunshine, but it had come out of her apartment, so I decided to keep it.

Who had Dunk thought I was when he'd handed it to me?

Replacing the photo in the envelope I looked up, and found myself looking at the big sheet of drawing paper again. It was yellowed, and taped at its upper right corner. Old ... how many years? Four, five? That was when I'd first seen it, both of us still back in San Francisco, Sunshine and me, still the tightest friends. This drawing ... this sweet, sad drawing of dancing dragons and a magic forest and that remarkable self-portrait, there—Sunshine herself, lying nude on a slab of rock, her then-dark hair spilling over the edge like a waterfall. The dragons danced around her, but it was ceremonial, not celebratory ... and she looked sad. And beautiful.

I remembered her showing me this, the sheet still in the oversized notebook.

I pried out the tacks with my thumbnail, rolled up the paper. Whatever else, this Dunk imbecile didn't deserve to inherit this. I went back down the stairs, the picture in one hand and the envelope tucked under my arm, trying mentally to put the ice pick in that waste-case's hand.

* * *

Excerpt from Bone's Movie Diary:

The stoner is that tried & true movie laugh-getter. Familiar from endless teen sex farces. We see Brad Pitt playing this character in *True Romance*—for once with a performance not beyond his range. Probably best embodied by Sean Penn in *Fast Times at Ridgemont High*. The stoner is funny in that same way that drunks were used for laughs in early films. Things change, not for the better. Who knows, 20, 30 yrs. from now maybe we'll all be laughing at pedophiles. The stoner archetype, however, got an unexpected flip-flop with *River's Edge* & Crispin Glover. It's one of those based-on-a-true-incident movies that is truly disturbing, & not just because I remember the incident in question, which took place in the Bay Area when I was younger. Glover plays a sort of demented tribal chieftain, presiding over a pack of doped-out teen metalheads, one of whom has strangled his girlfriend & then gone to school to brag about it. See? Disturbing. Glover's mesmerizingly tweaky perf. will seem exaggerated & absurd if you don't know and recognize this particular subculture. He is the lovably goofy stoner ... gone evil.

Chapter 15

Maestro

"Nice shot!"

"Hey, no trick shots allowed."

"Save some of that for league!"

I still had hopes the cops would turn up something on Sunshine's killing all by their lonesomes. No doubt they were aware of the ex-con angle, vis-à-vis the ice pick. Bone, though, wasn't going to wait any longer. Youth is always impatient and tends toward the frenetic even when standing still.

Even so, I recognized that determination to act. When I'd first gotten into the game—much younger than Bone—I had been a bit overeager about the work. It had taken me a while to learn not to operate hot. Anyway, by now I'd gotten used to seeing myself in the kid.

Last night we had stayed late at the Calf, compiling our "shopping list." I had laid out a somewhat watered-down version of the standard operating procedures for finding someone that didn't want to be found. I withheld some of the methods I know because Bone wasn't a professional. I had no intention of steering him into water that was over his head. Quite the contrary, I meant to see him safely through this thing.

We sat at Fahey's, having grabbed a small table beneath a stereo speaker. Milo was off tonight, and Debra the bartender was playing a rock CD, and the music blared loud enough that the extra ears in the place wouldn't hear us. It was a little after one o'clock. Bone had come out without Alex. He'd told me that he had given her the low-down about our hunt for Sunshine's killer. If I could trust Bone with the truth—some of it, anyway—of who I was, or had been, then I had to trust Alex. I hoped that trust wouldn't prove misplaced.

Bone finished telling me about his day's adventure. My first reaction wasn't to be impressed by how far he'd gotten in scoping out Sunshine's last residence. Instead, I bit down on my real response, which was to rebuke him for showing himself to this Dunk character ... that and the potential danger it represented.

"I'd say he qualifies as a suspect, wouldn't you?" Bone was drinking soda again tonight, instead of his normal rum.

"Yeah," I agreed. "Dunk is on the list." Bone could have his soda. I was drinking my habitual Irish, and took a slug of it now.

"That's progress, then." He sounded pleased. He hadn't worked at the restaurant tonight and so was in a better mood than usual.

"Sure."

I didn't point out that virtually everyone we came across at the outset of a hunt like this would be a suspect. The idea was to gather every possible candidate, fixing the odds that *someone* in the net was our man. Then we eliminated suspects as fast as we could, shrinking the field, until we could confidently pick out our friend with the ice pick. Still, there was no point in being sour. Bone *had* done well.

I had spent my day doing some of that mundane legwork that constitutes much of a hunt. That's the thing about my old trade. It is, for the most part, boring, or at least not exhilarating. I acknowledged that this search for Sunshine's killer was different from the jobs I used to do up North. In the old days, I would normally know exactly who I was looking for. My targets, of course, would often be using phony names and even disguises, but they were already identified. Here, neither Bone nor I knew whom we were after. So it wasn't just a search. We had to solve the crime as well.

"So, what'd you do today?" Bone asked.

There were matches going on both pool tables, and I was mentally playing along out of reflex.

"I listened to gossip," I said.

Bone regarded me for a beat. "Gossip?"

I nodded, lighting a cigarette. "Walked all around the Quarter, stuck my head in here and there. Coffee shops, art galleries, antique stores, grocers. Made a lot of chitchat with the Quarter's daytimers, people I wouldn't normally bump into in the bars. You've been living in the Quarter, what, two years? You know a whole lot of folks, right? Well, I've been here a decade. I know even more." I blew out a plume of smoke. "It doesn't take much to steer a conversation without seeming to, especially if it's toward something juicy. The newscasts might not be talking much about Sunshine's death anymore, but everybody else still is. Particularly Quarterites, who want their neighborhood safe, where they don't have to worry about somebody tagging them with a blade when they're walking home from work."

Bone nodded. "So, what do the gossips have to say?"

"Everything. Sunshine was picked off by some random predator from the projects. Sunshine is the victim of a serial killer that the cops are being hush-hush about. Sunshine was the victim of a voodoo cult. You think people only talk out of their asses in the bars? Wrong."

"You mean you collected a bunch of lame-brained theories as to who killed her? *That's* what you did today?" His eyes didn't exactly bug out, but he did look a bit dismayed.

"Yep."

"Why?"

"Because someone out there might be telling the truth, might even be confessing to the crime. I don't believe you can have too much info in something like this. I've always operated in a 'high-data' mode, and I don't see any reason to change now. The trick is not to let the material overwhelm you. The vast bulk of what you hear is, of course, bullshit. That may be true in all walks of life. Anyway, you listen, you file away, and sometimes your brain makes the connection for you. Sometimes the answer is right in front of you. You just have to get out of your own way to be able to see it."

I realized I was being somewhat verbose tonight. I also realized that I was enjoying this. It wasn't the "thrill of the hunt" or anything like that. I didn't miss my old life. What I was enjoying was being partnered up with Bone like this, engaging in something worthwhile with someone who was more than the usual bar chum. For the first time in quite a while, I was definitely doing something other than marking time.

"There is one thing, Bone."

He waited expectantly. I didn't figure he was going to like this.

"I should've said this last night, when we were at the Calf." I spoke firmly but still below the level of the music. "I want you to think about this carefully and get it set in your mind. This isn't a novel, and it's definitely not a movie. It's real life, and we're just a couple of guys who don't have a bunch of powerful connections or unlimited resources. If we find out that this is just the tip of something really big, if Sunshine got capped because she decided to blackmail someone high up in the local political structure or tried to get cute with the organized drug networks, we back away from it. There are adversaries out there that are simply too big for us to go to war with or even snipe at a little. Everybody with a brain knows Goliath squashed David like a bug, but David had the better press agent. We do *not* tackle any giants. It may not be heroic or dramatic, but survival seldom is. I want us to be in agreement on this before it goes any further, or I'll deal myself out right now. Do we understand each other?"

I knew Bone didn't respond well to reprimands or orders. Over the past weeks of hanging out with him, I'd gathered he had a serious anti-authority streak. But I had to communicate the gravity of this.

He pursed his lips and grimaced as he thought it over. It clearly wasn't making him happy. That was all right. I wasn't that happy with the idea myself. Still, reality is reality.

Finally he gave an abrupt nod. "Agreed."

I let out a breath. "Good." I was all speeched out for the time being, and also ready for a refill.

At that moment I realized that a good number of the patrons in Fahey's were suddenly putting their heads together in pairs and small groups and murmuring while looking at the same door. My line of sight was blocked by the cue lockers, but I leaned forward slightly to check out what had caught the bar's attention. I was, of course, still in alert mode for my mysterious, clean-cut, early-thirties guy wearing the silver crucifix. I could pretty much relax here in Fahey's, though. I knew virtually everyone here by name.

That people in the Quarter know each other is an axiom. It's also a given that Quarterites tend to cling to specific haunts. Sneaky Pete, the bartender from the cop bar I'd visited a couple of days ago, had just eased in through the side door and was shaking hands and joking with a couple of the regular pool shooters.

Normally, the only time Pete comes into Fahey's is when he has some hot stick in tow, trying to bait some of the young turks into a money game. Since it's rare that the Fahey's shooters will play for anything more than a drink, Pete's gambits are not particularly well received. He only does it once or twice a year, though, so it's politely tolerated.

Tonight he was by himself and wasn't carrying a cue. Within fifteen seconds, every shooter in the room, and most non-shooters as well, were aware of his presence and speculating on what he was doing here.

As I watched, he continued greeting people, but his eyes darted around the room even more intensely than his normal automatic "cop scan," a habit he'd no doubt picked up from his cop clientele. Pete had been on the force before owning his bar, but I understood he had been only a file clerk. I started to get a bad feeling.

"Bone," I muttered, leaning his way. "Do a fast fade. Wander over to the bar and don't let on you know me until I come over to you."

To his credit, he didn't ask any questions or show any outward reaction. He just stood from our table and glided off around the pool tables, observing the action and eventually wandering to the bar, where he grabbed a stool. The regulars here knew we knew each other but wouldn't think it terribly strange that we were sitting apart. Bone had also slipped away from the table before Pete had scanned this way. Whatever Pete was doing here, I could see no advantage to letting him spot Bone and figure out that we were hanging together.

Without looking around, I casually got up and made my way to the men's room.

When I emerged, Pete happened to be standing between me and my table. As I headed back that way, he made eye contact and moved toward me. Uh-huh.

"Hey, Maestro! What's happening?"

"Same old same old, Pete. What brings you to our end of the Quarter? Doing a little scouting?"

"Naw. I had to drop some stuff off for a buddy of mine down the block and just thought I'd stop in."

Sure. That was even lamer than the "cable box" jive I'd laid on him.

"Well, then, let me buy you one," I said with a smile. "I don't get to see you on this side of the bar very often."

If he wanted to play games, I could play too.

We brought our drinks over to the table under the speaker. Pete sat in the chair Bone had vacated. With Pete safely "chaperoned" by me, the rest of the bar ignored him and returned to business as usual.

We chitchatted about the slow business that comes with the summer, swapped comments on the shooters currently on the tables, and speculated on the sexual preferences of some of the ladies present. Then he bought me a round back. Uh-huh.

"Incidentally, Maestro," he said as he casually glanced around, "thought you might like to know. That case you were asking about—the Sunshine girl? Well, the boys say that they've had to file it and move on to other things."

I frowned and shook my head slightly.

"I missed something here, Pete. Why are you telling me this?"

"I just remembered you were interested is all." He shrugged. "Some of the boys were complaining about not being given more time on it. Nobody likes an unsolved murder. Especially cops."

"That's a shame. She was a nice kid."

"Yeah. Well, if you hear anything, would you pass it along? If the boys got a new lead they could maybe reopen the case."

"No problem, but I haven't heard anything yet, so I probably won't. You know the Quarter. Last week's news is an incarnation ago."

"You're right about that. It was just a thought."

I nodded casually toward the back table. "So, you want to shoot a couple racks? See that guy with the baseball cap and the tuxedo shirt? He shoots a pretty good stick." It was all still perfectly friendly chitchat.

"Naw," Pete said, getting to his feet. "I got to get back to my bar before they give the place away. Take care of yourself!"

"You too." I gave him a ta-ta wave as he made his way to the door and out.

I lit a smoke and nibbled at my drink, thinking hard. That hadn't been a chance encounter by any stretch of the imagination. He had been specifically looking for me here, at one of my regular hangouts. *Someone* else *looking for me*, I thought acridly. I had become uncomfortably popular of late.

"So what was that all about?" one of the shooters on the nearer table asked, wandering by. "I always get twitchy when ol' Pete shows up here."

"No big deal," I said. "He was asking if I knew anyone who wanted to stake serious money on this new stick he's found."

"Yeah, right." The shooter was Superboy, yet another Quarter waiter. He snorted. "Like everyone has *so* much extra cash, slow as this goddamn summer's been."

"That's what I told him." I smiled in easy agreement. "He's probably gotten the same answer all over. Cash must be pretty slim for him to be canvassing this far off his normal range."

Superboy nodded and went to take his next shot.

I drained my glass down to the ice, caught Bone's eye where he was sitting waiting at the bar, and made a small jerk with my head toward the door. He gave a slight nod.

We left the bar separately about two minutes apart and regrouped a block away. I was suddenly feeling *very* cautious.

"We may have a problem," I told him, aiming us toward the Calf. I wasn't ready to crash yet. In fact, I was feeling wound up.

"What's up?" asked Bone.

I gave him a quick briefing on what Pete had told me.

He thought about it for about half a block, then shook his head.

"I don't get it."

"I'm still trying to work it out myself," I admitted. "On the surface it looks like I'm being given an unofficial go-ahead from the cops to conduct my own investigation. Pete went out of his way to tell me the case was being back-burnered and that if I came up with anything on my own, I should pass it along."

After a moment Bone said, "That's one way to see it, I guess." He sounded dubious.

"Pete and me aren't buddies, Bone. He was delivering a message to me."

"I guess," Bone repeated, but now he seemed to be considering it seriously. "I didn't think the cops worked that way."

"New Orleans is a funny place," I explained. "It's not unheard of for the police to bend the rules or take some covert action to get things done. There's a long tradition of unorthodoxy here."

My steps slowed as we turned onto St. Peter Street, closing on the Calf.

"On the other hand, there's another possibility, too ..."

"What's that?" asked Bone.

"That there's someone high up on the force who's got a bee in their bonnet that I'm meddling in this Sunshine business, vigilante-wise. They might not look favorably on outside interference. It follows then that they might be slyly goading me into acting on this so that if I try something, they get the killer and me in the same net."

Chapter 16

Bone

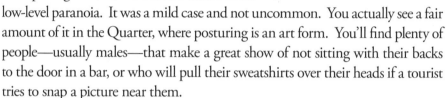

Tired fingers tied my apron's strings—tired, and the night hadn't even started.

So *sick* of this fucking job ...

In the short time that Maestro and I had been palling around, I'd become aware of his low-level paranoia. It was a mild case and not uncommon. You actually see a fair amount of it in the Quarter, where posturing is an art form. You'll find plenty of people—usually males—that make a great show of not sitting with their backs to the door in a bar, or who will pull their sweatshirts over their heads if a tourist tries to snap a picture near them.

Don't want nobody *seeing my face.*

This is said with great moment, with ominous tone, like a kind of reality-show bar drama. We're meant to buy tickets and keep the show rolling. Right, my friend, somebody's going to come through the door any minute, Wild West style, and plug you in the back the minute you let your guard down. And, oh yes, absolutely, a photograph of your face would be of inestimable value to the police, to the FBI, to the terrorist networks, or wherever your over-inflated sense of self-importance takes you.

It's usually people living humdrum, repetitious, everyday lives as desk clerks and carpenters and bar-backs that most need to pretend that they are important, extraordinary. The idea of being *wanted*, even in negative fashion, is quite appealing. If there's someone out there looking to harm or kill you, then you are made valuable and significant. If you can get your friends or acquaintances to go along with your sham, it reinforces it immensely.

True paranoiacs have a *They*, an intricately constructed and "logically" thought-out conspiracy where they themselves star as the persecuted individual. These are pitiable people, and they need treatment and care.

Everybody else that plays at paranoia by adopting the trappings is just talking shit.

Maestro's dose of this locally common disorder had never bothered me. He wasn't obnoxious about it. It had seemed less the macho shtick than it is with most guys—more a mild over-cautiousness, like someone who's been mugged once too often and is now apprehensive about walking the streets, day or night.

Of course, my diagnosis of Maestro had taken place before I learned he'd once worked for the Mob. Or ... what did he call it? *The Outfit?* Sounded like a sporting goods store. Still, it certainly gave his cagey manner some credence.

This thing about Sneaky Pete, though ... there I had to wonder.

Dallas was the restaurant's night manager, a former Navy serviceman and upright guy. He tapped my shoulder before I went out onto the floor. "Nicki's quit," he said.

The too-nice, too-sweet waitress who'd been hassled to tears by that eight-top of college boy mooks the night Sunshine died.

"How come?" I asked, pointlessly. Who needs an excuse to quit this line of work?

Dallas shrugged leanly muscled shoulders. "Dunno, Bone. She phoned it in yesterday, when you were off."

That was certainly decent behavior. When one quits a restaurant, it is almost conventional to go storming out in the middle of one's shift, preferably while the place is swamped and definitely while tempers are flaring. Big, spectacular, pyrotechnic exits—*that's* how you quit a restaurant.

But Nicki had been nice, apparently, right to the end. I had liked working with her and would miss her. But, hi-ho, people come and go, and how many coworkers had I known in my time? Hundreds? A solid thousand? Faces replacing faces. Interchangeable personalities. Names programmed to evaporate the minute the person drops out of view.

I hadn't even gotten a "So long" in, same as with Sunshine. Well ... not the *same.* Nicki wasn't dead, after all. Just gone.

Feeling another snit coming on, Bone? I hit the dining room floor—it was moderately busy—and my face, of course, betrayed nothing. Sometimes it was a fit of anger, impotent resentment that I had to do what I do for a living, anger against no one. Sometimes it *was* focused on somebody or something, usually of little or no consequence, blown all out of proportion. Sometimes, and here was my specialty, it was just a blue funk, that sadness ...

Whatever I felt, though, I'd had a lot of years now to learn not to ride those feelings like a passenger on a runaway train. I was capable of control.

So I waited my tables and fed my feeders and made my tips. It wore away the hours.

Maestro and Sneaky Pete ... the thought nagged. Maestro was theorizing that the NOPD, using Pete as a mouthpiece, might be setting him up. "Setting me up" is off of page one of the Paranoid's Bible, but Maestro wasn't a true paranoid. He didn't have a *They* that was out to get him. But he might have enemies from his past, might even have inadvertently stepped on some police toes during his decade in the Quarter. I didn't know why, after all, he had retired from the Mob—the *Outfit*, rather. Frankly I wasn't comfortable with the idea of grilling him on the subject. Maestro was my friend, yes, but Quarter etiquette about privacy is pretty severe.

Still, the cops setting up Maestro, giving him the green light to go hunt down Sunshine's killer, all so the police could then both bag her murderer *and* get Maestro for vigilantism ... sheesh! That presupposed a lot, not all of it terribly rational.

Then again, if I wanted to second-guess myself, what did I know? The biggest run-in with the law in my life had happened last night with Detective Zanders. I couldn't say, really, what the police were capable of.

Maestro gave off a general air of assurance. Whatever else he might be, he seemed sure of his own capabilities and judgment.

I'd made sure Maestro and I exchanged phone numbers last night. I had the feeling he didn't give his out casually. Before this Sunshine deal, we just used to run across each other, having learned one another's customary bar-routes. Now we were tied together into something serious and might need to make contact fast. Actually, cell phones would be even better, except I didn't own one, and I didn't think Maestro did either. I more or less detested the things, having learned to hate them from self-immersed jerkoffs that bring them into and use them in movie theatres. *Heretics in the temple.*

Maestro told me about the phone call he'd found on his answering machine from Sunshine, two days before the murder. I had found that ... troubling. No, to be honest, that actually hurt a bit. That Sunshine had phoned Maestro, not me. That, maybe, she had been in trouble and needed a hand and didn't call on me—me, who had once loved her as my wife, and, except for Alex, had known her longer than anyone in this whole city. I could even feel jealous.

What had that call been about? That was the question I ought to be thinking about. Had Sunshine seen trouble coming? Had she seen Maestro as someone who could get her out of a jam? Maestro had missed her call, hadn't hooked up with her, and two days later she was dead, killed. Could he—or I—have done anything to prevent it?

He didn't know. I didn't know. We were going to have to settle for revenge.

I'd told Alex about our plan. We were sitting on the couch in my apartment, where we often watched movies together. She listened quietly. Afterwards she nodded solemnly and said, "Okay."

Then she leaned over and kissed me.

And I let her. I kissed back. As for the question I was waiting to ask her untill after we'd gone wherever the trail of Sunshine's killer took us ... well, I had my answer without ever having to ask for it.

It was nice holding her in my arms.   She was completely different from Sunshine, but her body fit against mine in a way that made it seem almost as if I had found my other self—the female version. It felt so right that I completely forgot about the photograph from Sunshine's apartment. I had meant to show it to her to see if she knew anything about it.

"That all your tables, Bone?"

I blinked. I was sipping a stone cold cup of coffee and dragging languidly on a cigarette. Earlier, I had been rolling silver—that's wrapping individual settings of silverware up in napkins for the busboys to deliver to fresh tables—so the graveyard shift wouldn't have to bother. I looked now and saw the big wicker basket was full. I didn't have any customers left out on the floor. In fact, the place was just about dead.

"All done, Dallas."

Dallas cupped my shoulder briefly with a large strong hand. "Well, why don't you total your tickets and cash out, huh? You don't look so hot."

"I don't ..." Then I was nodding. "I think—I'm going to need a few days off."

He eyed me. "I can't really spare you on this shift, Bone."

And I couldn't afford to miss work, not really. I didn't live as close to disaster as some, but I brought in enough money to keep my apartment, pay bills, spend modestly, and not a whole lot more.

"Bring Conrad up from the lunch shift," I suggested. "He's always whining about not making enough tips."

"Conrad whines about bad tips because he's a lousy waiter. I put him in your slot, he'll just be making bad money at night, and this shift will suffer. Oh, screw it. You really need time? Okay, Bone. Take your days. Just so long as this isn't your way of quitting on me."

"Thanks, Dallas."

I tossed my coffee and my smoke and was picking at my apron strings, my fingers raw. I had been peripherally aware all night of the rest of the staff eyeing me, the nudging and nodding and murmuring. Yes, the gossip about Detective Zanders' visit was still going. There was no point in trying to explain the truth. It would only be fanning the flames. Fortunately, I was already too tired and out of it tonight to really care.

My hurt, sore fingers—sometimes they got banged and bumped hard enough to break the skin, and I wouldn't notice until the end of the night—froze in untying my short black apron. I hurried across the floor, my eyes tracking along the front windows.

I pulled open the restaurant's door, leaned out of the air-conditioned cool into a sultry night alive with music knocking from passing cars, roaches scuttling the sidewalks. I called out, "Piper! Hey!"

He was a little guy, as small as Alex, wearing a draping old raincoat that pretty much enveloped him. His steps were tiny, and he was that nebulous age of all gutter-punks—sixteen going on death. Sleeping bag in a dirty knapsack, unhealthy skin. "Dropped out," they might have said when I was a boy. Piper had definitely been dropped, and I doubted anybody wanted him back. And even so, he was among the less scummy of the homeless youths that we all share the Quarter with.

"Hi, Bone."

"Piper, we got a leftover sandwich. You want it?"

He grinned rotting teeth at me, and I ushered him inside, steering him toward the end of the L-shaped bar.

"One last customer, all right?" I told Dallas, who shrugged and went into the office, as I fetched Piper the sandwich. Employees at the restaurant were entitled to one free meal per shift. While I usually skip it, sometimes I'll box mine up to take home on the off chance I'll remember to eat it later.

I slapped the cold Italian salami and cheddar onto a plate and brought it out to Piper. He was so named for the penny whistle he sometimes blew in the Square as he begged for spare change. Others of his rather sorry breed panhandled, prostituted themselves, and committed petty crimes. Very lucky ones might hook up with a lover who had a job and an apartment.

Piper looked at the food with moon-eyed hunger.

"How about a beer?" I offered and didn't wait, pulled the tap and set the amber pint by the plate.

"I, um, well, y'know ... I don't got anything to spend."

"No worries, Piper."

"I can't think of anything I done to deserve this," he said, appearing genuinely confused.

"I'll give you the chance to deserve it."

His black fingernails drummed either edge of the plate a few seconds. Then, he said, "Okay."

I described Dunk to him in the same detail I'd given to Maestro, highlighting those same points he had told me to look for in any suspects I came across during this hunt.

"You know who I'm talking about?" There was nothing to see on Piper's pimply, dirty face, but I was quite sure on a gut level that he knew Dunk, the waste-case boyfriend I'd found living in Sunshine's apartment.

"See," I said, quietly, with a shade of sorrow, "I heard Dunk was going with Sunshine. The girl who was stabbed on the Moonwalk a few days back? She was my friend. Old friend, from back in the day. I just want to talk to someone else who knew her—really knew her. I ... I can't get her death straight in my head, y'know? I'd like to find Dunk. Any idea where he hangs, what he does?"

It wasn't a bad performance, I thought. But what I thought didn't matter much here. I waited on Piper. Piper was a gutter-punk. Dunk had certainly looked the part of that same subculture. It was reasonable they might know each other, considering the intimacy of that low circle. Also equally likely Piper would go mute rather than answer an outsider's questions. We "normal" Quarterites must seem like aliens to these kids, who would find running water and electricity awesome luxuries.

Outside the windows, on Decatur, some drunk nitwit was stumbling around in the intersection with Governor Nicholls Street, shouting some girl's name and, "I'm *sorry*, I'm *sorry!*" over and over. Car horns blared, and someone came out of one of the bars to pull him from the street.

Piper traced the brim of his beer glass with a grimy fingertip. He hadn't yet taken a sip.

"Yeah. I can tell you a thing or two about Dunk." He looked down at the plate, moon-eyed again. "Mind if I eat this first? I'm starvin'."

Probably not much of an exaggeration. I hung back and waited while Piper dug in.

* * *

Excerpt from Bone's Movie Diary:

> Roger Corman is a genius. Undisputed master of the low-budget schlock picture. Launched careers of a ridiculous number of now big-name directors, actors, and actresses. I greatly admire his work as producer/director, mostly because watching a Corman flick is to

experience & appreciate how a worthwhile film can be wrung from next to nothing. Super-cheapie sets, slap-dash scripts, one-take performances & *still* the vast percentage of his movies are enjoyable today. Watching a micro-budgeted film is to be in on the fun. Yes, that's a blatant cardboard wall, not the side of a castle; yes, the sound's noticeably off; yes, the story plays like it was knocked out by a screenwriter over a weekend binge of diet pills & Wild Turkey. So what? It's like seeing a play your friends are putting on in a warehouse basement. You're rooting for the film to succeed despite its handicaps, & you forgive a lot if it's making a sincere effort. I always root for Corman. Besides, the world would be a poorer place without *Death Race 2000, Rock 'n' Roll High School, Battle Beyond the Stars* and 1962's *The Intruder,* with William Shatner (yes, Shatner) giving a terrific performance. Another Corman-produced fave of mine is *Suburbia.* Not the ode-to-slackerdom pic. from '96, but the cult film about a tribe of street punks that band together for survival & companionship in the decaying suburbs. Fine movie. With no perceivable budget & a cast of virtual non-actors, it conveys the punk/squatter scene absolutely convincingly. Not glamorizing, not even angling for much sympathy, you nonetheless *do* sympathize with these kids who, in real life, you would probably dismiss as "scumbags." Appraisal: *Suburbia* * * *

Chapter 17

Maestro

Night was definitely going to be the better time for the fact-finding mission I had in mind. I habitually roll out of bed late, but today I was still left with a lot of daylight. Normally these are the hours for the mundane chores of living, like doing one's laundry, shopping for groceries (actually, the bizarre local expression is "making" groceries, don't ask me why), occasional banking, etc., etc.

Necessary chores or not, these are also ways of killing time. What was odd was that today I felt antsy, maybe even a little guilty, about wasting the hours. Bone was working at his restaurant tonight, would be tied up till late. That meant if I didn't do something, nothing was going to be happening with the hunt all day.

I automatically set about clearing my mind. Discipline is as important as every kung fu master in every martial art film tells his apprentice it is. I hadn't done this kind of work in a long time. I wasn't about to trip myself up at the start making beginner's mistakes.

So I took care of a few quick ordinary errands, then ducked back to my pad. Stepping out of the shower, I noticed a message on my answering machine. Isn't that always the way? Actually, I don't regularly pick up my phone when it rings. Like a lot of people, I use the message machine to screen my calls, since I don't have caller ID.

This one was from the Bear. He identified himself, then said, "I heard from a buddy of mine who's a bouncer on Rampart. He told me late last night a guy was in his joint nosin' 'round about you. Description matches, down to the silver crucifix. Same thing, him askin' for you by name. Lookit, I'm gonna set up a red-alert perimeter. Whoever this dude is, he's not goin' away. He's gonna pop up again an' when he does I wanna know it right when it happens. That way me or one of my buddies can nail this guy's feet to the floor 'til you can come check him out. I'm figurin' you'd like to ask him some questions. If you don't want me doin' anything, let me know. You might be handlin' this your own way. Later!"

My clean-cut early thirties guy again, and this time working Rampart Street trying to find me. Rampart bordered one of the long sides of the Quarter and was totally off my normal routes.

I understood what the Bear meant by "red-alert perimeter." Like all Quarter bartenders, the Bear knew other bartenders, especially those who worked the graveyard shift like he did. It's a very active network. Often it's used for silly purposes, like "phone shots," where one bartender calls another and they share a shot of Jack Daniel's or whatever over the line. Sometimes, though, the network is put to more serious use.

The Bear was going to put out an APB on my friend with the crucifix. If he showed up asking questions about me in any of the network bars, the bartenders, probably enlisting the aid of some of their regular customers, would hold him on the premises. Then I would be contacted. Chances were at that hour I would be out at one of these bars anyway, so I could be tracked down with a few fast phone calls.

It's good to have a support system. As far as I know, the Quarter's is unique.

I pulled out my big drawer and started looking over my short blade collection. Then I reconsidered, shut the drawer and dressed to go out. My stomach was rumbling. I knew Bone ate rarely and catch-as-catch-can, but I liked a regular eating schedule. It was time for dinner.

My dining choice was Poppy's, one of two '50s style greasy spoons in the Quarter that specialized in burgers and round-the-clock breakfasts. When you first visit New Orleans, it's almost mandatory that you try the gumbos and jambalayas and blackened whatevers that are as much a part of the atmosphere as the bars and the Mardi Gras beads the shops sell year-round. When you live here, however, particularly if you weren't born and raised here, you build a list of small, hole-in-the-wall restaurants and takeout places where you can get Chinese, pizza, gyros, or whatever else you were used to eating back in the World.

I sat at the counter with a paperback I'd brought along and was working my way through a waffle with a side of sausage when I felt a presence closing in. I had developed the "sixth sense" early on. In my line of work, I'd sort of *had* to develop it. What it is, of course, is simply perpetual watchfulness, using all of one's senses. Sometimes they deliver a warning from something you're not consciously aware of going on. I hadn't lost the ability after retiring and moving down here. It was probably because the Quarter, while not a war zone, explodes into random or aimed violence periodically and in isolated instances. My danger/warning instinct has saved my neck a couple of times, even if it was only by letting me get out of harm's way before things blew.

I was keenly alert for Mr. Silver Crucifix, ready for him to pop up anywhere, but I was not jumpy. My discipline stayed with me. Without raising my head,

I shifted my eyes to the long mirror and scanned the diner. "ESP" forewarnings are nice, but sometimes it gives you an edge if you don't telegraph that you're alert and have the antennae out. In cases like that, it can buy you an extra couple of seconds beyond what your reflexes can provide, and in a serious fight, a couple of seconds is a long time.

This time, however, it was easy to spot what I was picking up—Alex, making her way toward me, her face set and determined. I had a hunch I could almost write the script for what was coming, but since it was unlikely the situation would be physically dangerous, I dropped my eyes back to my reading and let the scene unfold at a normal pace.

"Hey. Maestro." She slid onto the stool beside me.

"Alex!" I said, faking a surprised tone. "How you doing? Join me for a bite or a cup?"

She was wearing snug black jeans and a yellow T-shirt. It wasn't often I got to see her in anything but her Pat O.'s uniform. For an almost scrawny girl, she had a very nicely proportioned figure.

"I want to talk to you for a few, if it's all right. Actually, even if it's not all right."

"No problem." I smiled easily, slipping my bookmark into the paperback. "Still, did you want a cup of coffee at least?"

"A coffee I'll take."

"And is this anything we want to share with the hoi polloi?" I figured it wasn't.

Alex's big eyes darted toward the counterman and the fry cook, both hovering in the near vicinity.

"Didn't think so. Scotty," I said and signaled the waiter, "bring a coffee to the back booth, won't you? Thanks a lot." I always tipped Scotty well, so he didn't give me any grief about relocating. I had always been a fairly conscientious tipper, but hanging out with Bone had driven home the "sacredness" of it. I understood he made good tips himself, but was a zealot when it came to tipping bartenders or other waiters.

I tucked my book in my back pocket, picked up my plate and my own coffee, and led the way to the diner's rearmost booth, safely insulated from eavesdroppers.

"So. What can I do for you?" I said, settling in. As I positioned my food and cutlery, I studied her at leisure.

She tossed a pack of cigarettes on the tabletop, dug one out, and pulled the ashtray to her. "Mind if I smoke while you nosh?"

I did, but said, "Not at all." Her short, dark hair formed a halo over her resolute face. Scotty came by with her coffee.

"Bone told me yesterday what you two are up to."

"He said he was going to." I shrugged. "He knows you better than I do, naturally, and if he thinks you can be trusted with the information, I've got no problem with that."

"Well, I do," she said, her lips flattened into a thin line. "What are you getting him into, Maestro?"

So much for eating. I sighed, leaned back and lit a smoke of my own before answering.

"First off, Alex," I said evenly, "I'm not getting him into anything. He was determined to do this thing before I even talked to him. My first and foremost concern in this is keeping him safe. Frankly, he's a lot better off with me on his side. If he went it alone—"

"For Chrissake, Maestro!" For a second she looked ready to launch into a real tirade, then leaned forward and pinned me with those large eyes. "I know Bone wants whoever killed Sunshine. *I* want her killer too. I want his fucking head on a stick. Understand? What I want to know is if what you told Bone about yourself—is any of that true? Do you have some actual experience in this stuff? You wouldn't be the only guy walking around the Quarter talking pure bullshit about himself to impress people."

I took a slow drag on my smoke, exhaled it, and stared at her through it. "Impugning my honesty, Alex?"

"Oh what, are you trying scare me?" she shot back immediately. She was obviously not one who could be easily intimidated. I'd never seen her in this mode. She was a firebrand. "I want my question answered, Maestro, and I'd god-damned well better like the answer. Are you who you said you are to Bone?"

Looking into her fierce eyes was like looking up into the heat and glare of the sun, but I didn't blink.

"I didn't lie to Bone," I said.

She slumped back at that, stirred some sugar into her coffee and took a sip.

"Okay," she finally said, dropping the challenging tone. "So you really are a pro at this?"

"A retired pro."

"Bone said that too. Okay. He'll be safer doing this thing with you. But 'safer' isn't 'safe,' of course."

I arched an eyebrow. "Both you and Bone would be 'safer' not living and working in the Quarter. You'd both be 'safer' living in Podunk, Idaho. We all make our choices, and sometimes we opt for a path that isn't as secure as an-other."

"I had a fortune cookie last night that said that," she murmured, her eyes wandering away.

I went on. "It was Bone's choice to get into this thing. I didn't talk him into it or con him at all. He feels it's something he has to do. And he's made it quite clear he'll do it with or without me."

"I'm not the worrywart girlfriend, Maestro," she said, her gaze centering on me again. "Bone's not so fragile that he needs to be kept in a box. I could object to this thing, if I wanted, if I thought he was doing something totally stupid. He respects me enough to listen to me. And he could veto me if things were re-versed. But I don't object. If the cops can't find Sunshine's killer, then somebody else should ... somebody else *has* to. Sunshine was my sister. We just didn't have the genes to prove it. I feel bad, real bad, that she drifted away from me and Bone toward the end."

There didn't seem to be anything for me to say to that, so I kept quiet. Alex had obviously wanted to talk to me privately. Bone was at work now. I wondered how long it had taken her to track me here to Poppy's.

I waited to see if she had anything more to say.

She did. At that moment her eyes grew slightly glassy. Her earlier hell-hath-no-fury manner vanished, and she suddenly looked uncertain and subdued.

"I was married once," she said softly. "It was an unholy disaster. When I climbed out of it, I thought, 'That's it. No more men.' Then I met Bone. He's the kindest, most caring man I've ever met—at least he's that way with me. He's also the bravest soul I know." She caught herself. "Don't misunderstand. I never got between Bone and Sunshine—never would have. But when she pulled away, he became my rock, my best friend. You know how into movies he is, right?"

I nodded. "He's mentioned it a time or two."

She sighed, let out a little laugh. "Yeah. I know. Sometimes you can't get him to stop talking about them. Bone and his movies. Did you know he keeps a kind of movie journal? No, you wouldn't know. He doesn't tell anyone. He writes in these spiral-bound notebooks, like from high school. Fills them up, one after the other. He's been doing it for years. And I mean *years*, like since he was 18. He's got boxes at his apartment, full of these notebooks."

I had no idea where she was going now, but I was intrigued. "Tell me, what exactly does one write in a 'movie journal'?"

"Bone writes down his own reviews of movies he rents or remembers see-ing as a kid. Sometimes he writes these sort of short philosophical essays about different aspects of films. Or he writes about specific actors or actresses, or pans famous movies or praises obscure ones. He's an encyclopedia. I love to watch movies with him. He enjoys them so much, it's infectious. He doesn't always show me what he writes, and he never tells anybody else about it. He's not looking to publish these notebooks or anything."

I nodded again. "Why are you telling me this, Alex?"

"Because you don't know Bone. You may have been hanging out with him at the bars for a few months, joking, having a good time. But there are things you don't know ..." Her eyes went glassy again; her pretty face deadened. She looked right through me, like she could see something I couldn't.

I ground out my cigarette in the ashtray. "You can tell me or not tell me," I said, very gently.

"When Bone was 16 he was hospitalized, for a full year. For ... depression. Serious. He was committed." A tear dropped from her left eye.

I found myself sitting very still.

"He worked hard to get himself together," she went on. "Then he got sucked into a bad marriage, and *Jesus*, that bitch tore him apart. Learned where he hurt and kept hitting there, over and over. But he pulled himself together. When everything went south with Sunshine, he survived that, too. And that's why I say he's the bravest person I know."

Her small hand came across the table and closed around mine. Her grip was like steel.

"Obviously, I don't go around telling people this stuff. But I want you to know. Not because I don't think Bone is capable of being your partner in this—what do you call it?—this hunt for Sunshine's killer. I know he's capable. But I want you to know about him ... because I want him returned to me in the same condition when this is done. That's on you. Clear?"

"In fact, it is," I said, and I couldn't hold back an awed little smile. Either they're making women different these days, tougher and smarter, or women are just starting to let it show. Either way, Bone had certainly picked himself a live one ... or vice versa.

Alex quickly wiped her eyes with a napkin and took a long slurp of coffee. She cleared her throat.

"I don't suppose I need to point out that if there's anything I can do to help in this hunt, let me know. And you will refrain from all macho bullshit about 'keeping the women out of the line of fire.'"

"I shall so refrain."

"Good." She took another swallow of coffee, and gathered herself up to leave. "I'm trusting you to use me if you need me. I'll be telling Bone this when I see him. I just wanted to make it clear with you first. The rest of our conversation here is between you and me, Maestro. Got it?"

"Deal," I solemnly agreed.

I was sitting with my back away from the door, of course, and watched her go out. Scotty eventually came and cleared my plate. I paid the check, but sat a little while longer, absorbing it all—or trying to, anyway. It was hard enough processing the information, much less figuring out how I felt about the news Alex had told me. It certainly cast Bone in a new light.

I got up and left. I focused instead on the fact-finding mission I had planned for tonight.

Chapter 18

Bone

"Where can I buy some drugs?"

I was clocked out. The graveyard shift was on, in the form of that young newish waiter— Otis. Piper had told me what he knew about Dunk, and was gone. I should have been gone too. Shift over. Hell, now I had days off ahead of me, days that Dallas had granted me, and it had been some long time since I'd last had an appreciable number of days off work all in a row.

Blitz was chewing gum, a big wad of it, chewing it loud. He was your typical Quarter dishwasher.

"Wuzzat yuh wan'? Drugs? Wha' the fuck's that s'posed to mean? Drugs?" He leaned a hip on his sink, which had mounds of suds in it. You couldn't just bang dishes straightaway into the dishwashing machines. They had to be scraped off and rinsed first, so that the melted cheese and other tenacious food residues wouldn't cling.

It was a job low on the totem pole. Dishwashers put in physically grueling days. There was the added fun of doing the job in summer—up to your elbows in hot water, your machines spitting steam at you. You would sweat your clothes soaked. You also got stuck with whatever shit jobs your higher-ups needed done. *Everybody* was your higher-up, even the busboys.

Finally, the job paid lousy, so of course the turnover was insane. It was no Quarter record to have five dishwashers come and go inside a week.

Which meant Blitz, a three-week employee—it's the *really* wretched ones that actually stay with the job—was shiftless, hostile, and had probably been hired straight out of one of Decatur Street's seediest bars.

"Where do you people go to buy your dope? Grass, coke, whatever. I know some of the bars along here are places where you can buy. Which ones?"

He snapped his gum, chewed, lifted his chin toward me. "Fuck yuh mean by 'you people'?" He weighted his tone heavy with threat.

I was standing in the entryway into the dank dishwashing nook. My earlier snit, the one that might have become anger or might have become melancholy, had sharpened into an impulse to act. I had gotten good information from Piper, and I had acted on my own initiative in questioning him, not on marching orders from Maestro. I was proud of myself. I wanted to do more.

I stayed where I was. "What I mean, you jelly-brained, knuckle-walking, houseplant-IQ idiot," I said coolly, "is that I want to know where around here you and your illiterate breed of troglodytes gets your pep pills and magic powders and wacky tabacky. You understand *that?*"

Most guys have heftier builds than me. Mine is a wiry thinness, and I'm capable of some fast physical action, but nonetheless I don't have that ready muscle to back up my opinions that others have. That, Blitz had. He was taller and larger. He wasn't someone that had to take any shit like this.

He also wasn't moving from his spot leaning on the sink.

I peeled a bill out of my pocket, held it up.

"See?" I said. His dull ox-eyes saw the ten dollars. He'd stopped chewing his gum.

"Now," I said. "Tell."

* * *

It was almost like something runaway ... but *not*. No, not that helplessness, that terrible sense of being borne along, hands folded leadenly in your lap, and all struggling pointless. This was different. I was not possessed. This was no snit—and there's a word, "snit," my word, my special soft word to cover what was harsh and powerful.

It wasn't my emotions, though, that were driving me. I wasn't going headlong. I was moving, but moving cold.

Maestro would take this thing slow, I realized. He would exercise caution and make sure I did the same. He would, if he could, call all the shots, and see to it that I drew the safe assignments in this hunt. I was him, after all, wasn't I—the younger him, giving off a vibe he recognized. And what was that exactly? I doubted very much we had led parallel lives. At some stage of his past, though, Maestro must have been a good deal less settled, less complacent, less assured. Maybe that was what looked familiar to him in me. So, what was he doing—rewriting his past by trying to keep me out of trouble?

I chuckled, lit a smoke, and pushed through into the bar. I wondered what Maestro would say about me psychoanalyzing him—particularly if I was right.

I was in boots, jeans, and T-shirt, and I was still several days unshaven. That was the right look, more or less, for this place. I had passed this bar any number of times going to and from work, had never once considered going in. Even from the outside it looked rank, oozing white-trashy sleaze. The inside didn't disappoint.

Dimly lit, but hiding things other dimly lit Quarter bars didn't need to hide—patrons even more riff-raffy than those I'd found at Sin City. I felt the check-out stares and glances, and I responded with a perfectly at-ease swagger, down along the bar, past the occupied stools, finding an empty at the end.

The bartender was another big guy. It you're going to sling booze in the Quarter, it pays to have some beef on you, or else to be an attractive female. Either can cancel out trouble.

"What can I getcha?" It was the same neutrally friendly tone I used on first-time customers at the restaurant. Everybody gets a fair shake before being judged, though, oh children, that judgment might be swift.

"Cap'n and Coke." I'd been drinking soda off and on in the bars for a little while, but here wasn't the place for it.

The big bartender—black beret, sandy hair past his shoulders—set down my rummincoke, and I paid and waved off the change. With that, I realized how much money I had just spent—on Blitz, on this cocktail—and that I had cut myself off from making tips for the next ... next ... how long? It was the right thing to do, though, I knew. I was on a hunt for Sunshine's killer. I couldn't do that effectively and try to hold on to my job at the same time.

I tapped an ash into the nearest ashtray. California's anti-smoking laws may have reached fascist extremes, but smoking is embedded deep in New Orleans culture, and you'll have a hard time finding a non-smoking anywhere here. Certainly not a bar.

The jukebox stopped playing a twangy, miserable country song, started playing a grungy, unintelligible heavy metal one. It was that kind of joint. No bar top trivia machines. Just pinball, a hulking old arcade video game, and a pool table awkwardly wedged into the rear of the bar. I'd never known about the table. Even had I known about it, it wouldn't have tempted me to come into this trailer park trash refuge.

It's easy to sit in a bar and be left alone—if you're a male anyway. You can sit on your barstool and stare at the rows of bottles and drink your drink slow and maybe nod along with the juke a little, and nobody will bother you. Just don't put out any energy.

If you want to mingle, though, you have to give of yourself a little.

I went and chalked my name on the cracked slate next to the cobwebby Budweiser sign, and waited and watched the current game. The guy holding the table was missing both canines. (Dental hygiene in this city is, beyond doubt, generally atrocious.) He was also in the habit of shouting *"mothafucka!"* after every shot, whether he sank something or not. A good player, one stripe left to his opponent's four solids.

"Mothafucka!" The thirteen plunked into a corner pocket, the cue rolled out and, there—a perfect shot waiting on the eight ball.

"Good leave," I said from where I was leaning, watching.

"Mothafucka! Thanks. That's yer ass, Billy. Who's up onna board? Who's Bone?"

"That's me." I've played pool since I was old enough to go into bars, but I've never owned a custom cue. Thus, I'm very good at picking out good or decent or the least decrepit bar cues. I picked one off the wall rack and slotted quarters into the table.

"I'm Brock. Wanna play fer who buys next round?"

"Sure," I said, racking. "What rules do you like to play? League?"

"Fuck that pussy shit," Brock said amiably. League rules were the next best thing to playing slop. "Call your shots."

Brock was a better shooter than me, though I'm not at all bad, even if I do play "side-arm." That is, I don't line my elbow with the rest of my arm, and it makes for erratic shots. Even so, Brock ended up buying me my next rummin-coke. No one else was interested in the table, though, so we just kept shooting—two games, three. As happens, we got to talking.

He had a bristly Vandyke that was entirely grey, and he had permanent pouches beneath his eyes. His nose was dark with ruptured blood vessels. I realized after a while that this guy was maybe four years older than me, and thought with some amazement what a killing machine the Quarter can be for some people—a climate designed to connect the individual with what will age or destroy him or her fastest. Most visible one here is alcohol.

But I'm not chasing booze tonight, I thought, sipping nonetheless on my drink. I was after drugs. Or, more to the point, after those who dealt drugs.

Specifically, I wanted very much to meet Sunshine's supplier. And Dunk's. He was a pothead, and Sunshine had been living with him, so they probably used the same pusher.

"Mothafucka! Aw, you in the shit now, Bone, *mon frère."*

I was indeed. Brock had neatly arranged a three-ball run for himself that the lamest shooter would have a hard time botching. I lolled against the wall's cracked plaster, planted my stick between my boot heels.

"Hey, you heard about that girl that got stabbed? By the river? Well, yeah, you must've, right?"

Brock was chalking his cue. "Sure."

"Did you know her?"

"Knew *of* her, y'know. Word gets around. I prob'ly even met her, if she'd been hanging in the Qwardah fer any amounta time."

"Well, I did know her. She worked over Big Daddy's. We—"

"Those chicks there are *fine.*"

"Yeah," I agreed because that's what guys do. "This—chick, though, we used to get stoned together. Sunshine was her name. And I'm telling you, she had the best weed. It was amazing. I'd sure as hell like to get my hands on some—*that* stuff, I mean. If I could just find out who was selling it to her ..."

Brock finished the slow deliberate chalking of his cue stick. He lined up for the start of his three-ball run.

"Well, there, Bone, I'm gonna finish kickin' yer ass here, yer gonna buy the round, an' then, well, maybe we'll talk some more 'bout what yer lookin' for." He wasn't looking at me, but I nodded anyway.

I waited until he put down the eight before I went to buy the new round.

* * *

Excerpt from Bone's Movie Diary:

> William Peter Blatty created a gem called *The Ninth Configuration*, where Stacy Keach presides over a military mental asylum & exhibits his own eccentric behavior. Eventually we learn that he too is nuts, & more, how he came to be the head psychiatrist. Breathlessly entertaining for the hilarious lightning-fast dialogue alone, but also intelligent & quite insightful. At that turning point, though, when we find out the truth about Keach's identity and past, it's a jolt. We backtrack over the movie & place all of his character's behavior in the new context, & suddenly his craziness makes "sense." We *understand* him, and we sympathize. Appraisal: one of a kind.

Chapter 19

Maestro

I took a bit of extra time gearing up.

On the one hand, pretty much anything goes for bar-hopping dress in the Quarter. T-shirt and jeans are the norm, but a sport coat, or a cloak for that matter, are common enough that they don't raise much of a stir. When I first relocated down here I was surprised at the number of men shooting pool or just hanging out while wearing tuxedo shirts and slacks, until I realized this was pretty much standard uniform for the waiters who work all those spiffy restaurants the tourists and upper-class locals support.

On the other hand, certain bars attract clientele of a particular look, so that if you wander in wearing apparel that goes against the trend, you're immediately marked as an outsider. The most obvious examples of this are the various Goth bars, where the kids who revere Anne Rice as a vampiric deity hang—and you can wear anything, as long as it's black.

The other thing to consider is that if you are too successful at matching the establishment's dress code, but are unknown to the regulars, it can easily be taken as an attempted infiltration. In layman's terms, you'll look like an undercover cop trying to blend with the locals. At the best of times, this can set you apart socially. At other times, like tonight maybe, it could border on suicide.

The place I was targeting normally was heavy on the "biker look" with a bit of "good ol' boy" thrown in: denims and leather, boots, flannel shirts, chains connecting one's belt to who knows what in their pockets. After a bit of thought I settled on a pair of black jeans that were a bit worn, and a pair of boots that were more so. I topped them with a khaki military-style shirt with epaulets and button-down flap pockets.

My goal was to capture the rough-and-tumble feel of the place without trying to pass myself off as one of the crew.

Then there was the matter of weaponry.

I pulled open the big drawer of my bureau for the second time tonight. I rarely carry a firearm. I've always felt that unless one is legitimately licensed to carry one, like a cop or a PI, it is apt to get you into more trouble than it gets you out of. Still, things can get rough enough out there that there's some question of being able to handle situations bare handed, so I normally opt for a knife. You can sometimes talk your way out of a concealed-weapon charge if all you have is a knife. If they catch you with a pistol, your lawyer will have to do the talking.

Guns have killed a lot of people on the streets of New Orleans, especially among the minority population that is really the majority. I'm not white, but my South Pacific blood doesn't make me black according to local standards.

There was no way that I'd walk into the bar I had in mind unarmed, so a knife was a gimme. The only question was: Which one? Or really, which *ones*?

My students, the ones who had hung the Maestro tag on me, never ceased to be impressed by my collection of swords, some of which are displayed on a wall in my front room. What few of my fledgling fencers had seen or were even aware of was my armory of knives. A saber is a fine weapon, but you can't carry it on the street unless you're on your way to a Renaissance Fair.

It was one of my old students, in fact, a guy who died in a freeway pileup a few years back, who asked (as he was helping me move into this place, the second apartment I've had here) how many knives I actually had. I had to answer him that I honestly didn't know. I've never actually stopped to count. I estimate the collection at somewhere between seventy-five and one hundred twenty-five. I've been using and collecting knives a *long* time, well before I ever even became involved in sport fencing.

I looked down into the big drawer.

Simple size eliminated a certain percentage right off the bat: the *kukris*, dress daggers, and bayonets were never meant for covert work, and I own them for the simple pleasure of having them. The fact that it was summer, and therefore hot and humid, reduced the selection even further. There are rigs for carrying a lot of the rigid blade styles that won't work without a coat or a sweater to cover them.

That pretty much brought it down to the folding blade knives. The switchblades and the Philippine *balisongs* (butterfly knives) were out, as they were immediately identifiable as "fighting knives," so getting caught with one would be almost the same as getting caught with a pistol. Of course, the idea was not to get caught at all, but prudence pays off.

I finally settled for an Al Mar Quicksilver for the hip pocket, held upright by my wallet; a SpyderCo with a non-serrated edge and drop point on it for my left pants pocket; and a small Puma Cub for my shirt pocket next to my cigarettes. They were all small, lock-bladed, razor-sharp, and easy to open one-handed.

All this might sound like a lot, but it let me get to at least one with either hand (even if I were perched on a barstool) without telegraphing what I was doing. With the crowd I would be in tonight, if anything went down, I'd only get one chance to handle it, if that.

Taking a deep, focusing breath, I decided that I was as ready as I would ever be, so I eased out into the night, locked the place behind me, and set a course for the night's target bar.

Before continuing, I think a clarification is in order. Specifically, regarding my attitude toward ex-cons.

There are, I'm sure, ex-cons who are relatively ordinary citizens who have erred once, gotten frisky and gotten caught, done their time or community service, and have rejoined society again without looking back. They're out there, but I haven't met them. That's not being snide, just honest. Simply put, they're holed up with their families leading normal lives, not hanging around the Quarter clubs whose customers make up my circle of acquaintances. If one pictures "normal life" as a path, they've strayed from it, but returned and gone on their way.

Then there are the ex-cons who are hardened, career criminals, for whom life in the World could be defined as brief spells between stretches in jail. Their lifestyle is fast and dangerous and also outside my normal sphere, particularly in this stage of my life when I am taking great pains to avoid notice from those on either side of the law-enforcement game. They live separately from the citizens, encountering them only when they pick them off the "normal" path, like lions stalking a herd of herbivores. Those types would never dream of trying to pass themselves off as citizens, except, perhaps, under oath.

The ex-cons that tend to hang in the Quarter are an entirely different breed of cat from the first two types. For the most part, they are petty criminals, brawlers who are heavy-handed enough to have it come up as "assault," and sneak thieves. A lot of them are also low-level dealers, and while I don't do drugs myself and avoid them as much as possible, I've been around enough to know there's a marked difference between "dealers" and "pushers." The people who fall into this class of ex-cons often have regular jobs as bartenders, waiters, or bouncers, and in general consider themselves to be just like anyone else.

So why was I gearing up so carefully for this fact-finding mission? Because, in my opinion, the Quarter ex-cons are dangerous.

The physical builds and personalities may vary from individual to individual, but they have one thing in common: an extremely casual attitude toward the law in general and violence in particular. I really don't know if specific character types are drawn to the outlaw life, or if the life itself brings it out in everyone who partakes, but the common denominator is there. If this is hard for your average suburbanite citizen to grasp, simply imagine a life where going to the cops or the courts for help is not an option. If someone shorts you on a drug deal or the split from a job, you can't sue them. You settle it yourself. If you have a record, are on parole, or engaged in some quasi-legal activity, and a fight breaks out, you don't call a cop. You settle it yourself and settle it hard.

It's an addictive mind frame that's easy to slip into, especially if you're surrounded by people who think the same way.

Not all of them are bad people. The cross section of personalities is roughly the same as you'd find in any group. Some are nice people, some are schmucks. Some are loyal and generous; others will freeload and mooch you to death, financially and emotionally, if you let them.

Still, the Quarter's breed of ex-con is different from the normal citizenry, the way a lynx is different from a house cat. Example: the time I mentioned to a guy on one of the pool teams that I was short on walking cash because someone hadn't paid me back on a loan. His immediate reaction was to offer to "rough the guy up a little, maybe break his arm" for me, as sincerely and casually as a "citizen" friend would offer to spot me twenty dollars to tide me over. They're different, and the difference can be scary. (Truth is, I never hurt for money, but mentioning things like that "loan" makes people think I'm workaday ordinary.)

Perhaps what scares me most is how little it would take for me to slip into that mind frame myself. My days with the Outfit were rather long ago, but not, in the end, *that* long ago.

Like the off-duty cops, there are a couple of bars in the Quarter where the ex-cons tend to hang out. Quarterites know where these bars are, even if the info doesn't show up in the guidebooks.

The place was about a third full when I breezed in. Most had the look of hardcore regulars, but there were a few gutter-punks scattered through the place. I made a point of not checking the crowd out in great detail, but even though only a few heads turned my way, there was no doubt in my mind that everyone in the place had noted my entrance and mentally logged me in.

"*Maestro!* Hey, how you doin', Bro?"

The Bear broke off his conversation with a sweet young thing and strode down the bar to greet me, grabbing my wrist in the "warrior's handshake" he reserved for a chosen few. The rest of the crowd relaxed visibly.

"Pretty good, Bear," I said, grasping his wrist in return. "It's been a while."

The Bear was among those very few people I called a friend, not an acquaintance. Though we'd spoken on the phone recently, I realized a little guiltily that it had been over a month since I'd actually seen him.

"Too long," he said, unintentionally rubbing it in. "Can I get you one? It'll have to be Jameson. We don't have Tullamore Dew here."

Your typical bartender may forget your name, but if you have a "usual" they'll often remember it.

"That's fine." Jameson was my normal default Irish whiskey anyway, when Tully wasn't available.

The Bear tossed a few ice cubes into a squat tumbler, filled it to the brim, and set the drink in front of me, pushing my five back across the bar with his other hand.

"This is on me," he said. "You know your money's no good when I'm workin', Maestro."

Once, years ago now, the Bear had needed a place to hide out. Literally. Someone from his military past was in the city and wanted to see him. The Bear didn't want to see this person. I was under the impression this visitor quite seriously meant to kill him. The Bear was in my sword club at the time, probably my best student, very disciplined. He solemnly asked me, his *sensei*, for asylum. I gave it. (Like I said, the Bear's a *friend*, not an acquaintance.) So he hid out for six days. This was at my old apartment, when I lived on Conti. I had a room with no windows where I put him. I cooked the meals. I brought him his cigarettes. I asked no details, and six days later he left, everything normal, the threat passed.

Ever since, as part of his "paying me back," he pours me free drinks on his shift at every bar he's worked since then. It's the main reason I don't hang at his bars very often. Too much like taking advantage of him. Besides, if my own past ever catches up with me, it would be nice if the Bear still felt he owed me.

"I got that perimeter set up, like I was talkin' 'bout," he said, serious and low. "Tank an' Jane an' Condor, Paulie at the Abbey, Apache at Shim Sham, y'know, like that. If your nosy friend comes up for air, we're gonna know."

"I appreciate that."

"So how's the team doin' this session?"

"On again, off again," I said, taking a deep sip of my drink. "We're in first place in nine ball and sixth at eight ball. Go figure."

"Padre still on your team?"

"Uh-huh. Co-captains both teams."

"Man, he was in here a couple'a nights ago an' kicked my butt all over the table."

"His game's gotten deadly lately," I confirmed. "Don't really know why. As near as I can tell he's practicing less than he did last session."

We chatted a bit more, then he had to wander down the bar to serve the other customers. I figured it was about time to ease into my specific questions.

When he came back, though, he leaned in close and dropped his husky voice, "Say, Maestro, do you know that dude on the table? Skinny guy with the dark hair in the ponytail?"

I did the mirror trick to check it out without turning my head, carefully keeping my face expressionless. It was a good thing I went poker-face before I looked. Bone was there, stick in hand, apparently talking intently with his opponent.

"Seen him around the upper Quarter a couple of times," I kept my voice as low as the Bear's. "Shoots a pretty decent stick. Why?"

"He's been tryin' to talk Brock back there into a dope deal for 'bout twenty minutes."

"Selling?" My tone remained admirably steady.

"Buyin'. When Brock came up for the last round he asked me an' some of the regulars if we knew him. Nobody does, so Brock's prob'ly not gonna sell."

I didn't remark on the Bear's rather casual attitude about drugs moving in his bar. It wasn't any of my business.

"I didn't know you needed credentials to buy dope," I said.

"Nobody likes a strange face."

"Well, as far as I know he's not law." I shrugged. "Think he's a waiter someplace."

I took another sip of my drink, tracking the level carefully. If it got too low, the Bear would have it filled again before I could say anything.

"Speaking of the law," I said, leaning even closer to him, "do you know of anybody in trouble with the parole board? Someone out fairly recently?"

"Why? What's up?"

The Bear was all attention now. I noticed he hadn't answered my question.

"I was in Fahey's a couple'a nights ago, and there was some guy in there asking around trying to locate someone."

"Lotta that goin' around, seems."

"One of the Cajun Cabin crew was shooting a rack and said the same guy had been in there asking around as well." I took another sip. "To my eye, he had 'parole officer' written all over him. Thought I'd pass the word. If you know who he's after, you might want to tell him to check in or lay low for a while."

That was the story I had settled on after considerable thought. It let me fish for the information I wanted without having to come right out and ask. The Bear was a friend, but the fewer people who knew I was operating, the better.

"What's the description of the guy your parole officer's lookin' for?" he asked.

"White male, late twenties, athletic build, close-cropped blond hair, a swastika prison tat. He prettied it up, but that's the bare bones I got."

Like the story, the description was fabricated. Plausible, but it didn't fit any of the Quarter regulars.

"Doesn't ring any bells," the Bear said with a frown. "I'll pass it along, though."

"Nobody I recognize either. That's why I thought it might be somebody fresh out."

"Only recent arrival I can think of even close is a dude called Juggernaut, and that's only 'cause he's white and male. Man, this guy's so big he makes *me* look runty. Mean as a fuckin' snake, and he's been havin' problems with his love life that haven't made him any sweeter."

That got my attention.

"Girlfriend troubles?"

"Not Jugger." The Bear rumbled a laugh from his big midsection. "He's only into guys. *Young* guys. Seems that when he got back out, his boy toy had hooked up with someone else."

"And you say he's the only white guy?" I tried to steer the conversation back to the original point.

"That's right. There are two black dudes just out of OPP, and one Hispanic guy, but Juggernaut's the only new white one."

OPP is Orleans Parish Prison. "Parish" down here in Louisiana means county, an example of the Deep South's cultural religiosity, I guess.

"Wait a minute," I said. "Back up. You said Hispanic. That wouldn't be Hector, would it? I thought he was up in Angola with at least another year to go."

I was pretty sure it wasn't Hector. Both the Bear and I knew him from when we'd all been on the same pool team before he got sent up, and if it had been Hector, the Bear would have mentioned him by name.

"Far as I know, Hector's still in. Man, I really miss that little guy. 'Member that thing he could do with his thumbs? Always busted me up. No, this one's name is Jo-Jo. Mid-thirties. Mexican. Bit of a pretty boy. The ladies love him, though. Hangs at the Stage Door. I think he's started workin' at the Court of Two Sisters. He's also got this thing about voodoo—keeps one o' them protection spells on him all the time."

I let the conversation drift on to other subjects after that. It *was* good seeing the Bear, but my mind stayed preoccupied. This Jo-Jo character interested me, but I didn't want to show it by asking more. Both the Court of Two Sisters and the Stage Door were within a couple of blocks of Big Daddy's, where Sunshine had worked. And he was into voodoo. Very interesting.

The Bear went off to open a couple of beers. At that second Bone went past my stool in the dimness, apparently not seeing me as he headed for the door. He looked annoyed. Back at the pool table the scruffy guy he'd been playing looked pissed. There was a cue lying across the table, apparently dropped there unceremoniously. I guess he'd decided not to sell Bone any dope after all.

Out the door he went, turning down Decatur in the CBD direction.

Bone had once sworn to me, when it came up in casual conversation, that he didn't do drugs. What the hell was *this* about then?

While I was wondering that, three gutter-punks who had been slouching near the pool table suddenly went sliding toward the door, moving with uncharacteristic haste. Somehow I wasn't surprised when, after a quick glance up and down the street, they turned and headed in the same direction Bone had gone.

I gave the place a quick visual sweep using the mirror behind the bar again. Nobody else seemed to have noticed the mini-parade heading out the door. It wasn't a Carnival parade after all, where they throw beads and baubles into the crowd and girls flash their boobs. More important, no one appeared to be watching me to see if I had noticed.

I stood from my stool.

"Gotta roll, Bear," I said as he came back to my end of the bar. The sweet young thing he'd been talking to when I came in was starting to look pouty, but still hanging around. "Let me have a bottle of water, will you?"

"Sure thing." He fished one out of the cooler. Bottled water is very popular in the Quarter, since most people don't trust what comes out of the taps.

"Come by Fahey's some night," I said as I clasped his wrist in another handshake. I was in a serious hurry now to get going, but not showing it.

He nodded. "We'll shoot a couple'a racks. It's been too long since I kicked your butt."

"Sounds good, Bear. Later!"

When he turned his back, I quickly dropped a ten on the bar for him. It was a fifty-fifty chance that someone would pick it up before he noticed it, but I had to make the gesture. Then too, he was the Bear. If he weren't, I would have made his chances one in ten of ever seeing the tip.

I stepped out onto Decatur, my full plastic bottle of water in hand, ready for the trouble I knew was brewing.

Chapter 20

Bone

I had company. When I managed, a block down Ursulines, to get a glimpse behind, knew it wasn't company I wanted.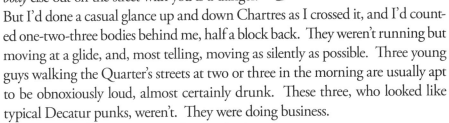

Of course, late at night, you presume *anybody* else out on the street with you is a danger. But I'd done a casual glance up and down Chartres as I crossed it, and I'd counted one-two-three bodies behind me, half a block back. They weren't running but moving at a glide, and, most telling, moving as silently as possible. Three young guys walking the Quarter's streets at two or three in the morning are usually apt to be obnoxiously loud, almost certainly drunk. These three, who looked like typical Decatur punks, weren't. They were doing business.

Apparently, *I* was going to be that business.

My heart kicked hard in my chest, but the rummincokes I'd had back at that rathole bar counteracted the adrenaline rush. I kept a sharp eye out for a squad car or cab, but nothing moved for as far as I could see.

Of course—this being the residential end of the Quarter—the homes and apartments I passed were occupied. A number of them still had lights burning in their windows, and those people in there had telephones that could reach the police. I could raise a fuss out here, start yelling and hollering, and no doubt someone *would* ring the cops. But would they do it in time? My three trailers might bolt the minute I started my hullabaloo, or they might decide to take me right then—jump me, beat me, hell, maybe knife me for pulling the stunt.

I kept a good pace, staying on the "open" sidewalk. The Quarter's streets are narrow and all one-way. It can make for a hell of a maze if you're driving and don't know the pattern. There is only room for parking on one side of every street, though, so you can walk along behind the parked cars or out in the clear. I stayed as visible as possible. My trio already had me spotted, but maybe some insomniac in one of these overlooking windows would see me and the punks and ring the police without any prompting.

I wasn't holding my breath.

Ursulines would lead eventually to Burgundy Street, and near that intersection was my apartment, where Alex waited for me, probably wondering where the hell I was and why I hadn't called her. Since I'd told her about the plan, she'd insisted I keep in touch. I'm normally conscientious about that stuff, particularly since Alex never nags. I'd just been all charged up after successfully squeezing info about Dunk out of Piper. I had wanted to keep it going, the energy of the hunt, so I'd gone out trying to ferret out Sunshine's drug dealer—presuming she'd had somebody who was her regular supplier. Not an idiotic plan. In fact, it was a potential avenue Maestro had put on our hunt's to-do list. I doubted seriously he would have wanted *me* pursuing it—too hazardous—but that was too bad.

It was also too bad that that guy, Brock, who looked like he'd had a bit role in *Deliverance*, had just been jerking my chain about a dope deal. That had pissed me off enough that I'd stalked out of there. Or maybe he'd just been sniffing me out in prelude to selling to me, and didn't like my scent.

Another thing that was *very* too bad were the three gutter-punks who'd apparently followed me out of that seedy hillbilly bar.

I got to Royal and turned. If I went right and sprinted, I could maybe reach the 24-hour deli on the next corner. There would be people and a phone. But, again, the punks might overtake me. Petty thieves aren't professional thieves, and they don't operate cool. More often, they tend to be self-styled cowboy bad-asses with a lot to prove. The three grungy bastards behind me would probably enjoy rumbling me just for the kick of it.

So I went left, and from the corner of my eye I saw them—apparently still unaware I was on to them—hurrying to the intersection so as not to lose me. If I was going to run, now was the time. But I knew my smoker's lung capacity would weigh against me. I was thirty-one, and the kids behind me were, well, *kids*—fast, energetic, veins probably throbbing with adrenaline. I had about fifty bucks left in my jeans after the night's expenditures. I didn't want to part with it, but I would, of course, to buy myself out of harm's way. However, gutter-punks who do muggings usually want your money *and* your hide.

I didn't run, but kept that same steady pace. I've got a fairly long stride, though, so I cover ground quicker than I seem to. Even so, it was a long stretch down Royal Street to the zone of the Quarter that was still buzzing at this hour. Here, Royal was twin rows of dark antique shops and clothiers.

Shit.

My breath was growing tight in my chest. I knew without turning that they were moving, for real now, breaking loose toward me. I could hear feet pounding pavement, the trio pouncing, and I had better do—

BOOM!

Like when you don't notice the car idling at the curb and it backfires just as you're walking past; like the pickup truck that rear-ends the car next to you at the stoplight; like the nearby gunshot you hear just as you're drifting off to sleep—and in New Orleans you learn that sound, if at no other time, then on New Year's Eve when yahoos like to fire their guns in the air.

Like any sudden, loud, unexpected surprise-shock incident that makes you jump out of your skin.

In this case, like the thick storefront window that had just shattered thirty feet behind me.

I don't usually jump at big, unexpected sounds. I tend to go stock-still, every muscle tensed. Here, though, I deliberately spun around, ready to do whatever it was I could to defend myself. This situation would be decidedly different from when I'd punched out that guy in Sin City's men's room.

The store's alarm rang out, blisteringly loud in the night, a heartbeat after the window exploded. The window—broken—why? It made no sense. And there were the punks—all three—yanked to a halt in mid-stride—panicking. Why would they break a window? They scrambled away suddenly—not at me—hightailing it in the opposite direction back down Royal.

It was all herky-jerky, very *cinéma vérité*.

I did not understand what had just happened, but saw absolutely no percentage in hanging around to wonder about it.

My would-be muggers had gone their way. I went mine. I was, of course, innocent of whatever had just occurred, but did I want to explain that to the police when they arrived? Lights were coming on all along the street. I set off at a good run, and yes, my lungs did burn after about ten strides. I didn't head for home. Didn't want to lead anybody there, even if that was Maestro-esque pseudo-paranoia. Instead, I ducked swiftly down to Bourbon. As a local I'm privileged to revile Bourbon Street and its chintz and touristy tawdriness, but now I grabbed at it like a lifeline. Here there were people and noise, and I could blend, slowing from my run, forcing myself to step casually but not too casually. I wanted to look like I was going somewhere, not just loitering.

So I decided to go somewhere. I headed for St. Peter Street and the Calf. I heard sirens well before I got there.

* * *

Excerpt from Bone's Movie Diary:

Superman is, of, course, one of those franchises on a sharply descending quality curve. (Other obvious ones being *Jaws*, *Rocky*, *Batman*—though that last one didn't have that far to fall.) A single sequel is dicey enough, but making a cycle of films from a single successful movie is a recipe for disaster. No two directors see the main characters/atmosphere/objective of the enterprise the same way. Throw in four different screenwriters hacking at the script, & you've got ... well, a summer blockbuster. But—*Superman*. 1978, with Christopher Reeve a convincing Man of Steel & Gene Hackman blasély brilliant as Lex Luthor. Great fun through & through. That rescue of Margot Kidder, though, early on, with the helicopter spilling off the top of a skyscraper & Superman flying up from the street like a rocket to catch Lois Lane as she freefalls—I've always got to laugh at that. Normally I forgive a lot in movies, like audible laser blasts in space and wineglasses that mysteriously empty and fill during a scene. But come *on*. Lois falling into Superman's arms at the speed she was dropping would be no different from her hitting the sidewalk. Ker-*splat*. If I'm ever rescued, I hope it's by somebody with a better grasp of physics.

Chapter 21

Maestro

When I strolled into the Calf, five minutes behind Bone, Padre said he was out
back on the pay phone. Since Padre will let
just about any regular use the bar phone, I figured Bone had marched straight
through. I also guessed he was phoning Alex, not the cops.

Padre held up a glass and threw me a questioning look.

"Yeah, I'll take one," I said with feeling, and Padre put the Irish in front of
the stool I grabbed.

Five minutes was pushing my luck, a little too close to make my "bumping into" Bone here a likely coincidence. I was sure he hadn't spotted me at the
Bear's bar, or seen me stalking his stalkers out on the streets. I was doubly sure
he'd missed it when I crept up behind a parked car and threw that bottle of water
across the street and through the antique store's window. At that moment the
three gutter-punks had been making their move on Bone, and I'd *had* to act.

Citizens don't run in the Quarter unless they're jogging, and they usually
do that up along the Moonwalk while the sun's up. Someone in normal street
clothes running is usually either running away from something or after someone.
I'd done a discreet float back behind the punks, a "late for work or a date" stride.
Walk fast, break into a lope for about four steps, drop back to a hurried stride,
glance at your watch and run for another six steps.

Of course, I was doing it silently in my usual soft-soled felon-fliers. The act
was just in case someone was watching the parade as it went down Ursulines and
onto Royal. While the neighborhood watches aren't all that effective, they will
make note of the time and description of anyone they see running without the
identifying shorts and sweats of a jogger, particularly at night.

Bone was either oblivious to the rat-bag gutter-punks a half block behind
him, or he was playing it cool. I hoped for the latter.

I suppose I should be more sympathetic toward the nomadic tribes of lost
kids that pass through and occasionally colonize the Quarter. From what I hear,
a lot of them have tragic histories of abusive homes that they've run away from,
preferring to beg for pocket change or rummage through restaurant Dumpsters
for food. Once, when a delivery guy on a bike stopped me and asked if I wanted

to buy a pizza for three dollars because he was stuck with a bunch on a false delivery call, I gave him a twenty for all four that he had, walked them over to the Square, and gave them to the packs of kids that always seem to hang out there. I'm not totally lacking in the charitable department.

On the other hand, they're scavengers. Their solution to the dangers of their lifestyle, chosen or otherwise, is to band together in groups. Well and good, but in a group they inevitably discover they can take a more aggressive role, and often do, being verbally abusive to anonymous passersby as a partial payback for what life has dealt them. Sometimes it's much heavier than that.

Kids or not, I see this breed as being as dangerous as a sackful of rattlesnakes with their rattles removed. One night, ten o'clock, on Toulouse Street fifteen feet off Bourbon, a couple of them were panhandling and begging cigarettes in front of a bar. One of the Quarter regulars was having a bad night and instead of ignoring them or simply shaking his head, turned around and mouthed off at them. They both swung on him with knives and ran. One of the blades nicked his jugular and he bled to death long before 911 responded. That was less than a year ago.

Just kids down on their luck. Yeah. I'll still watch my back around the little bastards.

I took a swallow of my whiskey. It was late, but not too late for me to be showing up at the Calf. There was a thin layer of regulars and two drunk but cheerful tourist couples. I sat and waited for Bone to emerge from the back.

To gutter-punks, twenty dollars is a small fortune. If Bone had been in the Bear's bar trying to make a drug buy, it was easily assumed that he had money in his pocket. Probably more than twenty dollars. Skinny guy, traveling alone. Worth following to see if he ended up on a dark, empty street.

I had learned the "full plastic water bottle" trick from a lover a few years back, who'd never had to use it herself. She routinely walked a short stretch of Dauphine after work in the wee small hours. She refused to take a cab for four blocks, and wouldn't let me gallantly escort her night after night. So she packed a folding Buck knife (women who dig knives are an old weakness of mine) and a bottled water. One of those liter bottles makes a nice weight. Throw one of those through a window and you'll suddenly have a lot of attention focusing on you. Probably more than enough to scare off a would-be mugger.

It had been lucky, if that's the word, that Bone had led his stalkers onto Royal Street, which is lined with numerous small businesses, all of which have alarmed windows.

After I'd hurled my plastic missile through the storefront, about six feet behind the punks, I'd stayed ducked behind the parked car long enough to make sure they and Bone scattered in different directions. Then I quickly got myself the hell out of there.

I did a fast swing over Chartres and came down St. Ann. I gathered my weaponry in one hand, ready to ditch it under a car in case the cops beat all records in responding to the alarm. They didn't.

When I hit Bourbon, I saw Bone yet again, and again wasn't seen by him. He was a block ahead, walking at a calm pace, and had also had the smarts to come to Bourbon, not try to duck home through the empty streets. I hung back, watched him turn onto St. Peter, gave him five minutes, and followed him into the Calf.

I threw him a wave when he came back into the bar from out back. Feigning surprise at seeing him wouldn't make sense, since Padre would have told me he was here. I didn't want Bone knowing I'd shadowed him all the way from Decatur.

He didn't look pale like when he'd come in after being interrogated by the police detective. Neither did he look too surprised to see me, returning my wave and coming over. His T-shirt collar and the edges of his hair were wet, like he'd splashed water on his face. He looked composed.

"I got one for you, Maestro." He took the neighboring barstool. "Who's the latter-day Spencer Tracy?"

"I give."

"Gene Hackman. Think about it. Both have an ease on the screen that's very similar. Neither's an over-the-top emoter. In fact, it's tough to actually *catch* them at acting. They're both character actors, even though they've usually played lead roles. Both are two-time Oscar winners."

"Sensible," I said, but I didn't want to talk movies right now. Casually I said, "What're you doing out so late tonight? Don't you usually go straight home from work on Alex's days off? Hey, let me get you one. Padre—"

"Just a soda," Bone said as he pulled his cigarettes out. "Believe me, I've already had enough." He lit a smoke. "Anyway, I went out doing a little operating ... or trying to. First, though, let me tell you what I did that *worked* ..."

I suggested we relocate to the back booth, out of any immediate earshot. There Bone told me he was going to take a leave of absence from his restaurant gig, at least for a few days, in order to concentrate on the hunt.

"Makes sense," I said, checking my line of sight to the Calf's front door. "Can you afford time off work, though?"

"I'll scrape by."

"I could front you some scratch if it's tight."

It was the first time I'd ever offered him a loan. I knew some people could get weirdly offended about such things.

Bone thought about it a few seconds, then shook his head. "Not now. Maybe later. Thanks, though. Anyway, what I was saying. I bribed this kid named Piper with a sandwich and a beer and got him to tell me about Dunk— that scumbag I found in Sunshine's apartment? Said he was her boyfriend? Well, I found out he's a serious doper, but he's also a musician, a sax player."

Calling yourself a "musician" in the Quarter is easy as saying you're a "novelist." It's all horseshit until you're getting paid for it.

Bone continued. "Dunk's got a gig at Check Point Charlie's this weekend. He plays in a quasi-punk band called Clamjaphry. I figured to check out the show, get a longer look at him. Maybe find a way to question him. What do you think?"

I realized Bone wasn't asking my permission. How much more comfortable I would have felt about this whole thing if he were acting strictly on my orders. I was the experienced party, after all. Bone, though, had the driving motive to see this hunt through to the end. Immovable object meets irresistible force? Maybe.

"Sounds good," I agreed. "You'd blend in better with Check Point's crowd anyway, at least at a rock gig. Watch how you handle it if you start asking Dunk questions, though. Try not to sound like you're a cop or a reporter. Okay, that was the part of your night that 'worked.' How about the rest of it?" My tone didn't change.

He told me what he had been doing at the Bear's place, about Brock and the aborted dope deal. He mentioned nothing about the adventure I knew he'd had on the way here, with the three gutter punks. I wondered silently what he thought about that window shattering to save his skin. Oh well, if he wanted to believe in guardian angels, that was up to him.

On one hand, I felt relief. He hadn't been trying to buy drugs for himself at the bar—or so he said, and I believed him. On the other hand, he'd been tackling a dangerous assignment from our "shopping list." Too dangerous. I had figured on taking that one for myself, though obtaining an inventory of recent ex-cons in the Quarter was more of a priority. I had done that.

I told Bone about it.

"'Juggernaut,'" he muttered, dragging on a fresh cigarette. "Jesus Christ, *he* sounds like fun, doesn't he?"

"My contact said he's strictly into guys." I'd said nothing to Bone about the Bear being my contact or where I'd been tonight. If I told him we'd been at the same bar, he might think I was spying on him. "Juggernaut stays on the suspect list, of course, but we'll probably eliminate him."

"What motive could he have to kill Sunshine—that's what you mean?"

"Right. Considering Sunshine's tendency toward screwed-up relationships, I'd guess jealousy figured in it somewhere. But, who knows? We'll keep an open mind." I sipped a little more whiskey. "Did Sunshine date across racial lines? Did you personally ever know her to go around with blacks, Hispanics, or Orientals?"

He gave me an odd look, then he started chuckling.

"What'd I miss?" I asked.

Bone shook his head, still amused. "Sunshine and me were both living in San Francisco, Maestro, remember? Aw, maybe you wouldn't understand. You don't say 'Hispanic' out West. The word is 'Latino.' And it's horribly politically incorrect to ask about dating across racial lines. You have to be very, very careful in SF whenever the issue of race comes up. People back there love to get offended about things."

"None of which answers my questions," I said flatly.

"Guess you had to be there," he said with a shrug. "Sunshine dated two Latinos that I knew of and had a Japanese boyfriend for about three weeks, which was almost a record for her."

"Nobody black?"

"Nope. Not for as long as I knew her." Suddenly he was shaking his head again, all the amusement drained from his thin face. "Sunshine ... still hard really believing she's dead."

I nodded solemnly. I found myself studying Bone closely.

Clinical depression, which Alex told me Bone suffered as a teenager, was a serious condition. It went way beyond having the blues or the blahs, or feeling listless or gloomy. From what I gathered, it was like dragging around a battleship anchor. It put one in a permanent state of despair and dejection, where everything felt hopeless and pointless all the time.

Well ... I guess not *permanent*. Not in Bone's case, anyway. Alex had said he'd been hospitalized for a year. If he were committed, presumably by his parents, then he must have had a bad case. It was also safe to assume he had recovered. After all, he'd been released. Even so, here I was sitting across from him in the booth, furtively *studying* him, maybe even looking askance. Was I searching for some telltale hint of his past condition? That made me a little uncomfortable. I had a past that was no doubt more unconventional than Bone's, and he was still treating me as a friend, without reservation.

"So is that it?" he asked. "Business-wise, I mean."

"I think we've both done enough for one night, don't you?" I stifled a yawn, realizing this cocktail on top of everything else tonight was putting me to sleep. I was tired from the hunt, I thought with a little dismay. It had been quite a long time. Yet I still felt good about what Bone and I were doing. Hunting Sunshine's killer was a positive deed.

"Can I ask you something?" Bone pushed aside his soda.

I gave him the standard Quarter answer: "Well, you can ask."

He'd heard it before, and chuckled again. "How did you come to retire from ... your previous line of work?"

I went immediately into hyper-wary mode, but it was just reflex. I was already trusting Bone with a lot of crucial info about me. Glancing around, I saw that the drunk tourist couples had gone, and there were just two regulars left, down at the far end of the bar. They stumbled out as I watched, both looking loaded enough that I hoped they were heading home in cabs.

Padre came around from behind the bar. "I'm going to lock it up, guys. If you want to stay that's fine, but I've had enough of everybody else." He went to pull the shutters over the door and turn the key. He switched off the juke and it was suddenly very quiet in the Calf.

Bone waited, not impatiently. I gazed back at him an extra moment, then turned to Padre who was starting in on the cleaning and restocking that usually takes him half an hour at the end of his shifts.

"Padre, Bone here wants to know how I came to be retired. From the Outfit."

Padre straightened slowly from wiping down the bar top. He measured both me and Bone from behind his eyeglasses.

"And how, pray tell, Maestro, does Bone know what you used to do for a living?"

"I told him. I told him because Bone and I are on a hunt. For whoever killed Sunshine."

My words hung there, and Padre continued to stare. Padre was my oldest friend in the Quarter. Hell, my oldest friend anywhere, since I'd necessarily severed all ties when I'd bugged out of Detroit.

I went on. "He might even enjoy hearing the story of how I came to relocate down here. What do you think?"

Bone wasn't saying a word throughout this, still just waiting and watching.

"A *hunt* ..." Padre murmured, like he couldn't quite grasp that. "Wow. Never thought I'd hear you saying this."

He reached into the cooler and twisted the cap off a beer. He came over to the booth and sat next to me so we were both facing Bone.

"Go ahead," Padre said. He took a big swallow of beer. "Tell him."

I leaned slightly forward, toward Bone. "Remember when I told you I wasn't into the rough-off work when I was in the business? True, but that doesn't mean I couldn't handle myself. It comes in handy if you slip up and someone you're hunting turns on you. I learned some fighting techniques formally, when I first was getting into fencing. Some, like down and dirty bar fighting, my buddies taught me. I mean, most self-defense classes don't get into how to handle someone coming at you with a straight razor or a broken bottle."

Bone nodded, following. I'd decided not to tell him about my time in the military before I'd joined the Outfit.

"One night," I continued, "I was asking what I thought were some low-key questions in a bar. Bars are gold mines for info everywhere, not just down here. Anyway, some guy I didn't know suddenly started to draw down on me. I'm not good enough to play around with disarms when the other guy is waving heat. So I killed him."

I paused to pull on my Irish, to let Bone absorb that. Actually, to be honest, I just wanted the drink at that point.

"I didn't like doing it, but I figured I didn't have a choice and that my connections would cover for me."

Nobody in the booth mistook my humorless grunt for a laugh.

"As it turned out, the joke was on me. It seems the guy I dropped was the vacationing nephew of some out-of-town higher-up in the business. When I found that out, I knew the next step would be for my bosses to offer me up as a sacrificial apology to keep the peace. Didn't matter one whit that the nephew was a notorious cowboy and borderline psycho who'd probably drawn on me just for giggles. Didn't matter the years I'd put in. I was a foot soldier, totally expendable."

I drained my tumbler to the ice and pushed it aside.

"Needless to say, I didn't care much for the idea. I decided to implement my own Witness Protection Program and got the hell out of Dodge. Problem was, of course, my people were going to be sending out some other hunter/tracker to find me. Probably more than one. It would be important for my bosses to make that gesture, to appease the other gang." I fished out my smokes. "Granted, I had the advantage of a head start, plus the knowledge of what sorts of trails my hunters would be likely to try to follow. I discovered I was *very* good at covering my own tracks. This may be the information age and the time of Big Brother, but a man can still slip through the cracks with enough determination."

I lit my smoke. Bone's eyes had gotten a bit wide.

"At this point," I exhaled smoke, "Padre comes into the picture. You want to tell the rest of it?" I eyed my friend sidelong, giving him another chance to put the kibosh on the whole thing.

He swallowed more beer. "Naw, you finish it, Maestro. You've got such a lovely speaking voice."

I couldn't quite join in the wise-ass jocularity.

"I knew Padre by professional reputation," I continued. "Before he retired, he was making a hell of a name for himself in the business."

Bone's palm suddenly slapped the tabletop. "Hold on! Is *everybody* I know an ex-mobster? You've got to be shitting me!"

Padre was snickering. "Didn't Maestro tell you, Bone? 'Mob' is such an ugly word. He prefers 'the Outfit.'"

I ignored him, wanting to get this finished.

"No, Bone," I said. "Padre wasn't in *my* business. He was a free-lance identity specialist. He had a lot of status among my circle of hunter/trackers. He did identity theft—that's stealing another person's official records, IDs, credit card numbers. It's all done by computer—"

"I know what it is," Bone retorted.

Right. Bone might not have had my background, but I wasn't talking to a preschooler.

"This was ten, fifteen years ago, though," Padre put in with a kind of casual pride. "I was very avant-garde."

I nodded agreement, "Padre's other gig was setting people up with false identities, ones that had never existed before. He would build fake pasts, from birth certificates to credit histories. He was indeed an *artiste.*"

Next to me, Padre bowed his head, grinning.

"I contacted him. It cost a pretty penny, but he set me up. All he had to know was where I wanted to be so he could doctor up the appropriate state ID and whatnot. I told him New Orleans."

"Any particular reason?"

"I'd visited once or twice. Liked the place." I shrugged. "Besides, people down here keep the same vampire hours I was used to. Reinventing myself in Bumblefuck, Missouri, might have been lower profile, but I'd go nuts inside of a week. Why bother to stay alive if you're only going to bore yourself to death? Besides, you know the Quarter. Once you're established here, nobody will give the time of day to an outsider if they come asking around about you."

That was certainly proving true in the case of my inquisitive friend with the silver crucifix.

"As it happened," Padre said with a grin, "New Orleans was where I based. I started out in Texas, but that's another story."

"So you met Maestro when you supplied him with his new identity?" Bone leaned toward Padre, taking in every word.

"Yep," I answered. "We got to be friends after that. Kindred spirits."

"Maestro said you were retired," Bone continued, still talking to Padre. "Why's that?"

I lifted a hand. "Now, Bone, too many questions can—"

"I believe the young gentleman was addressing me," Padre cut me off. "It happened like this, Bone. Some people showed up at my house one day, tied me up with duct tape, beat me to a bloody pulp, and trashed the place top to bottom. I thought they were going to set fire to it as well, but they didn't. While I was in the hospital, I decided to retire. I had no idea who had assaulted me. They never said a word to me. That's the scariest thing, actually—that kind of out-of-the-blue, could-happen-any-minute type violence—particularly when it's directed at you. After that, I went back to tending bar, like in my college days. It's a slightly less hazardous profession."

He snickered again, and I had to admire somebody who could laugh at something like that. I certainly didn't get a lot of chuckles out of my own past.

"I see what you mean by 'kindred spirits.'" Bone looked back and forth between us. Then he shook his head sharply. "This has been fascinating, Maestro, really, but I'm going home. I called Alex to tell her I'm on the way. I'd better make good on that. Padre, think you can ring me a cab?"

For a second there I thought I saw Bone eyeing Padre in that odd, leery manner. He was getting the idea that, in the end, it may be that no one in the Quarter is who he first appears to be.

Maybe he was right. I rubbed my eyes. I was tired.

Padre unlocked the door for Bone when his cab rolled up and honked. He hopped in and was gone. I made to go too. Padre tapped my shoulder.

"Needless to say, Maestro, if there's anything I can do to help out in this hunt, just let me know."

It was virtually what Alex had said to me last evening. Did the whole world want in on this?

"Thanks, Padre. I may be missing some pool games for a little while."

"That's what co-captains are for."

We shook hands and I went home.

Chapter 22

Bone

It all came out, the night's events, full
disclosure, and Alex made herself *very* clear.
I had told her about the hunt the day before.
Now she was telling me.

"In on it?"

She nodded slowly, her eyes pinned to mine.

We were sitting on the couch. I'd come out of the cab, up the stairs, and
found her waiting in my apartment—she'd had a key since Sunshine and I had
taken her in. Booboo was waiting, too, looking at me intently with green eyes.
She wanted mostly to sniff at the boots I'd pulled off my sore feet.

Booboo hadn't liked Alex's sharp tone. Neither had I, since I wasn't giving
her an argument; saw no basis for one. Hell, I agreed with her.

"You want in on it?" I repeated. "Good. I'd like that."

"Not going to get all *boys' club* on me?"

My eyebrows went up. "Where the hell are you getting *that* from?" Sexist
is one of the last adjectives that could be applied to me.

"Nowhere," she muttered, eyes going someplace else.

"Are you thinking Maestro might object?"

"Might he? I mean, to working with another nonprofessional."

I sagged back on the couch. The air-conditioner, a window unit, was going, though I can't afford to run it constantly like some people do in summer,
those people who also get themselves outrageous electric bills. Above, the ceiling
fan—there's one in every room of my apartment—whirled. Like other features
of life in the Big Easy, these are exotic at first, right out of *Casablanca*; then, later,
they're practical. I remembered Sunshine stepping through the door when we
first rented the place, into this very room with me, both of us filled with hopes
for some sort of better life. I remember her eyes, long, natural lashes fluttering
as they rose, seeing that same fan that wasn't turning then, and even so her lips
forming to make a delighted, childlike *ooooohhh*.

I shook myself.

"Maestro?" I said, looking for the thread of what I was saying. "Maestro ...
well, he's been retired ten years, hasn't he? I'd say he's lost his pro status as well.
And ..." My turn now to trail off uncertainly.

Alex cupped my knee, squeezed.

I sighed. "Well, you heard what I was saying, what he told me tonight at the Calf. I believe him, by the way. Same as I believe the rest of it. If he's delusional, he's got people—not just me—going along with him, and he's portraying himself without a hitch. No." I laid my hand over hers. "What I said—ten years. Killing this mafioso nephew ... hey, at least he didn't say the guy's name was Vinnie. Then I *would* say delusional, no doubt. But think about it. Maestro retired—deserted the Outfit, came down here from up North, got himself an entirely different identity to live under ... *ten years ago.*"

Alex nodded, but it was a "go on" nod.

"Does he still seriously think he's being hunted?" I asked softly.

That got her looking suddenly thoughtful.

"Ten years is a long time for anybody to be looking for anybody," I continued. "Even if the object of the search is revenge. Even if it's the Mob that's looking for that revenge. From what Maestro says they couldn't even have any leads to his whereabouts. The only lead is Padre." Alex had shown something of my same shocked incredulity when I'd told her about Padre's past. "If Maestro's old cronies tracked him to Padre—bammo. Hunt's over. So he's still completely in the clear. And has been for a decade."

"Sounds like you're thinking delusional after all." Alex rocked back into the cushions.

"No. No, not quite. But ... I've spent a fair amount of time with him, especially these last couple of days. I've watched. Just about everything Maestro does is colored by the assumption that he's in constant mortal jeopardy."

She shrugged. She was wearing a formfitting white T-shirt that had a wolf baying at a full moon printed on it. She looked good in it. "In a larger sense," she said, "we all are."

"Not the sense I mean here, okay?" I wanted to convey my point, or maybe just to listen to my own words, like a bystander. "How he walks on the street, how he checks out a barroom coming back from the toilet. How he stands when he talks to you. How his eyes move when his head doesn't."

"Street smarts?" suggested Alex.

"Oh, he's got those. To be sure. But it's like he's *always* got them revved up. Even when he's relaxing, when we're two rounds past when we should've stopped drinking, and we're jabbering about movies or pool or bullshit, and he's having a good time, a genuine good time—hell, even then he's waiting for it."

"It?"

"The end. The other shoe to drop. It!"

She frowned. "Waiting ... like, not complacently?"

"Hell, no. He's going to put up a hell of a fight! He's got ten pent-up years of guard-duty nerves. But, see—is it justified? Is anyone still actually, truly after him after all these years? *Could* anyone still be hunting him?"

Booboo was presently trying to insert her entire black body into my left boot where it lay on the floor.

I let out another longer sigh. "How did I get talking about this?"

"I think maybe you've had a cocktail or two tonight, unless I miss my guess." Alex's lips curled drolly.

"Well, I'll be slashing my booze budget now," I said. I'd told her also about asking for some time off work. She offered to help out from her own paycheck if I needed it. I blinked, tired now. "You were wondering if Maestro would object to you coming on board the hunt, right? That was it. Answer: he doesn't *get* to object."

Her laugh was soft, warm. So was she for that matter, as she edged nearer me on the couch. I put an arm around her.

"I'll feel better about this if I'm involved, too," she snuggled in closer.

"So will I."

"I ..." She breathed out, and it warmed my neck. "I want Sunshine's murderer. I want him to die. I really do, and that doesn't bother me, on any moral level. Isn't that interesting? How about you?"

"I don't think it bothers me either," I said honestly. "Don't *think*, but don't *know*. You can only be so sure about your own feelings. Regardless ... " I shrugged, and we pressed nearer still. "I will kill whoever was holding onto that ice pick if I get the chance."

"So will I." Words I'd just said, but she said them with different meaning, weight, depth.

I helped Booboo extract herself from the boot, and Alex took me down the hall, to the bedroom. I didn't question it, just followed, grateful for her companionship.

* * *

Awake. *Awake!*

Like that, slam-crash, and I knew it was hours later, knew I was up out of bed ... knew the company I'd just been keeping. But at the moment I was frozen through, every muscle locked, tense, as if my body had turned to stone. My eyes were pried painfully wide, sweat above them, maybe tears below.

I had woken stock-still and on my feet, naked, body caught in a paralyzed scream that had never emerged.

Hands closed, gentle but firm, around my upper arms from behind, and that didn't startle me. Alex had followed me. I had left the bedroom, come down the hall, come in here—the smaller room off the front room, where the television set lived, and more importantly the VCR and DVD player that were hooked to it. The movie room. It was as rumpled and slovenly as the rest of the apartment, but how comfortable it was to huddle in here, to play tapes from my collection that had been accumulating for years.

On a wall, painted that generic apartment white, I had reverently tacked up the old sheet of Sunshine's drawing paper that I'd stolen off her apartment door. Here were the dancing dragons, so detailed, down to the textured scales; and the magical forest, each branch and leaf so distinct. Meticulous penciling, very talented. Sunshine lay on her slab of rock. The dragons danced, forepaw-in-forepaw, around her, ritualistically. Sunshine's hair was very long and dark, like it had been back when she'd drawn this. One knee was raised, one arm flung across the stone. She was looking wistfully up into the sky, and whatever she was looking for up there, it was plain she couldn't find it.

Alex had never seen the drawing before I brought it home yesterday after the visit to Sunshine's apartment and Dunk. I'd shown it to her, and she'd stared, stunned. It had that effect. After, I'd told her about the hunt; it had seemed the right way and time to tell her.

Now I was standing there, directly in front of the patch of wall in the movie room where I'd tacked up the yellowing sheet of drawing paper. Alex stood behind, holding me.

The scream I hadn't let loose stayed in me. The first of my muscles started to relax. Gently I let go of the fiercely-held breath in my lungs.

"Bone?"

"I'm okay," I breathed.

Alex touched her forehead between my shoulder blades. "Was that sleep-walking?"

"Yes." I swallowed. "But I remember it all. Is that how it's supposed to be?"

"I don't know."

"I was asleep and walking," I said slowly, studying the words as they came, "and dreaming. I dreamed Sunshine came into the bedroom and beckoned me up—"

"Bone."

"—and led me here and gestured at this drawing. There was ... an urgency. It mattered that I saw this. And you were behind me. You heard me get up, asked me if I was okay. I didn't answer, and you followed."

Finally, I turned to her. The room was dim. The lamp we always leave on in the front room softened some of the shadows on Alex's face.

"Then I woke up. It was the urgency of it all, the importance. It was too much. I was going to scream. I didn't understand what Sunshine was trying to communicate, and it frustrated and scared me. But I woke up." I ran my palms over my face. They came away wet.

Alex was biting her lip, looking up into my eyes. I smiled.

"I'm okay now."

"Sleepwalking?" She sounded unsure.

"And some very vivid dreaming." Now that my body had unlocked, I felt a tingling flow in all my limbs. It felt good.

"You're sure it wasn't her ... well, her spirit?"

I put my hands on her bare shoulders.

"Don't you think that makes sense?" she pressed. "Can't you imagine that making sense—even a little bit?"

We hadn't argued the matter before. Our friendship included very few actual disagreements, but we did disagree, here, on this, on the subject that was now waiting to hatch.

"Did you see her?" I asked, not sarcastic, not smarmy. "You were right behind me, right? I saw Sunshine two steps ahead, gesturing me forward. Did you ... see that?"

"No," she admitted. "Not really the point. If she were to visit someone in this apartment, best bet is it would be you."

"Wouldn't she want to visit somebody who would believe in her manifestation?" I squeezed Alex's shoulders. Sunshine had been very vivid in my dream, yes, but she was also fading, fast and absolute the way dreams do. The emotions that had prompted my near-scream were all but evaporated. I was suddenly and hugely tired.

I made to steer Alex back to the bedroom.

She put a hand to my lean chest. "Dream, visitation—whatever. But maybe something or someone is trying to tell you something. Maybe *you're* trying to tell you something. Your unconscious. Something about Sunshine. Think about it."

I smiled again. "I'll sleep on it."

I followed Alex back to the bedroom and lay there, unable to get back to sleep. I listened to Alex's breathing become slow and even. After a few minutes I got up again, walked back to the front room, and stared at the drawing. Could Sunshine really be trying to tell me something? Or, more likely, was it my own subconscious mind trying to send me a message?

I started to give up and go back to bed when I caught sight of the battered manila envelope lying where I had tossed it on top of the VCR. That envelope, the one Dunk had given me because he'd thought I was ... whoever. I had put it there the other day, then I'd forgotten about it. I picked it up, turned on the small lamp by the video cabinet and pulled the photo out. Staring at it in the lamplight, I suddenly realized what was so familiar about the photograph.

* * *

Excerpt from Bone's Movie Diary:

There's nothing quite like a good ghost story. On screen they are distinctly different from other horror films. Think *Poltergeist* v. *Rosemary's Baby* or *Dracula*. Two I saw as a kid—8 or 9 yrs. old—that scared me half to death were *The Uninvited* and 1963's *The Haunting*. Both old, black & white, bloodless, maintaining a level of suspense & dread that mega-budgeted special effects can't match without a good story & sincere effort. But, to show I'm not a classic movie snob, let me say I rank M. Night Shyamalan's *The Sixth Sense* from 1999 among the best of the sub-genre. Frightening, suspenseful, eventually quite touching. I was, first time I saw it, struck by all these emotional effects ... & one more. Pity. I felt tremendously sorry for the ghosts in the movie—not because of whatever horrible ways their earthly lives had ended & not because many were seeking belated justice for what they suffered as mortals. Instead, I felt sorry that they were trapped between the worlds, without the benefits of being either living or dead, caught in dismal repetitious cycles. How tiring it must be, I thought. How useless to be a ghost. Myself, I intend to cut my ties immediately. Whenever death finally overtakes me, I shall go forward toward ... toward ... well, whatever/wherever. What I *won't* do is loiter around holding grudges about meaningless mortal matters. Let the living live, I'm *outta* here. Appraisals: *Sixth Sense/ Uninvited* * * * ½; *Haunting* * * * *

Chapter 23

Maestro

The Stage Door is on the corner of Toulouse and Chartres, four blocks closer to the river than my more normal hangout of Fahey's. The distance between the clientele of the two bars, however, was much more pronounced.

I had dressed myself only slightly less grubby than when I'd visited the Bear's Decatur Street bar last night—old blue jeans and a faded red T-shirt. I was also out much earlier. There was still fading daylight in the sky. The Bear had mentioned the Stage Door as Jo-Jo's hangout. Jo-Jo he'd described as a Mexican ladies' man—but of course the fact that he was also a recently released ex-con had me particularly interested.

Like I've said, everybody's a suspect at the start of a hunt. However, Jo-Jo had a little more going for him. If he was in fact a vain pretty boy who dated or slept around a lot, then he might just be the type of ready-made trouble Sunshine always picked for her boyfriends. Also, Bone had said Sunshine had dated Hispanics—excuse me, Latinos—in the past, and he apparently had an interest in voodoo.

There are lots of reasons to kill people. Actually, "motives" is the word I'm looking for. Jealousy is a good motive. I'd mentioned it to Bone last night because I wanted him to keep the possibilities in mind. He'd been at the Bear's bar trying to track down whoever dealt Sunshine whatever dope she did. (I wondered if Bone understood how insular and cagey the drug-dealing world is.) It would be good if we could find that specific dealer, presuming there was one. Sunshine's murder might have just been a drug buy gone bad ... though it didn't make much sense that she'd be doing it on the Moonwalk in the middle of the night. I know how casually drugs move in some Quarter bars.

Even so, Bone had to keep an open mind. So did I. Jealousy, blackmail, drugs—there were lots of motives that could lead to someone to do murder.

With Jo-Jo, though, I was definitely figuring along the lines of a love affair gone awry. I would have liked to have milked the Bear for more on him, but I'd gone to some trouble to get the info I had without drawing attention. I didn't want to spoil that.

For instance, it would have been nice to know at what time of day or night Jo-Jo did his usual hanging at the Stage Door. The Bear had said he thought Jo-Jo was working at the nearby Court of Two Sisters, on Royal. I didn't want to go snooping around his work, though, not yet. Two Sisters is a classy joint. It's a lot easier to finesse information in a rough-and-tumble bar. However, I knew that some of the Two Sisters' employees hit the Stage Door regularly. I might be able to pick up some solid facts about Jo-Jo just by eavesdropping.

Another thing I wouldn't have minded knowing was what kind of crime our Mexican friend had been in stir for.

Fahey's is a service industry hangout. Lots of waiters, busboys, and cooks show up. The Stage Door is the same, drawing in workers from a different set of restaurants. That's where the similarity ends. Fahey's is a spacious, low-key place that leans toward the Beatles on their sound system. The pool games there, as I've said, are mostly clean, and the people who drink there are educated, or at least well-mannered and passingly intelligent.

The Stage Door, on the other hand, is cramped, and the heavy metal or rap blasting from the speakers makes it seem even smaller. The place has a shady, blue-collar vibe coming off even those wearing their natty restaurant black-and-whites. This is particularly apparent around the single pool table. Money games are often shot there, and from around one o'clock in the morning on, the stakes can get high. The woofing and trash-talking that goes on is loud and forceful enough so that, to the uninitiated, it often seems like a fight is about to break out any second.

That was pretty much the scene I found wandering in off Toulouse's sidewalk. I figured if I didn't find Jo-Jo on this run, I'd hit here again after one or two o'clock. By then a new bartender would be on and if anybody else was still hanging, they'd no doubt be too owl-eyed to remember my face.

It would have been tight enough inside even if it hadn't been crowded. I had to wait until a huge guy at the table took his shot, then edged past him to an open seat at the bar. German Caroline was bartending, and came over as soon as she saw me. The "German" was to distinguish her from British Caroline and Tennessee Caroline, also Quarterites.

I said a lot of people use nicknames down here. I didn't say they were all clever.

"Hey, Herr *Dirigent*!" Caroline called out. "You shooting or scouting to-night?"

"Just watching," I said with a smile. German Caroline has been around the scene awhile. I've always hoped that that "Dirigent" she calls me translates as

"Maestro," and not something else entirely. "I heard the Hanoi Hangovers have a couple of new sticks on their team and I thought I'd try to scope them out before we shoot against them in a couple of weeks."

Perfectly reasonable. The Hangovers shot out of here, a good team but notorious for disputing shots, most often when they stood to lose a rack. If I were a lesser man, I'd say they were all a bunch of pussies. Good thing I'm not a lesser man.

"How're you doing this session?" Caroline doesn't speak with much of an accent.

"The Snake Plisskens or me, personally?" Our team name comes from how so many of our players are transplants who've "escaped" New York. It helps to keep the mood light.

"Both," she smiled.

"Team's good." I rattled off our stats. "Padre especially. Me, I'm shooting so-so, but I still have my good nights."

"Sounds like a personal problem, Herr Dirigent. Take it up with the Chaplain."

I chuckled.

"*Gott in Himmel,*" she said suddenly, exaggerating her accent. "You must be dying of thirst. Are you still drinking Tullamore Dew?"

I nodded and tossed a fiver on the bar.

Caroline set down my Irish and scooped up the money. "Well, good to see you. You should come around more often. Okay?"

I blew her a kiss and she wandered off down the bar. While big money rolls through the bars during Mardi Gras and Jazz Fest, most Quarter bars live and die on the local business that tides them through the dry spells. Bartenders are often hired because of their "cult" followings, and there is an ongoing low-key competition among them for the limited pool of regulars. Even so, somebody that drinks at Molly's—the one on Decatur, not Toulouse—isn't likely to start making O'Flaherty's, for instance, his regular hangout, no matter who's bartending.

After ten years in the Quarter I've seen a lot of bars change ownership and names. Longtime Quarterites will sometimes continue to refer to a bar by its old name, even if that name is obsolete by two incarnations. The Calf/Yo Mama's thing is a perfect example.

I took my drink in my hand and pivoted around to face the pool table, my elbows resting on the bar behind me. While seeming to watch the action of the game, I made a leisurely scan to see who all was in the Stage Door.

The Court of Two Sisters waiters and busboys were easy to spot, their bright green jackets hung over the backs of their chairs as they gathered around a circular table near the back. A few faces I didn't recognize, and those I did were mostly nodding acquaintances. But nobody among them fit the description of Jo-Jo I had gotten from the Bear. Still I kept an ear cocked in their direction, listening to hear if the name popped up in conversation.

The huge guy at the table was wearing big, stomping boots, and a pair of overalls that had enough fabric to cover a good-sized Volkswagen. His head was shaved. He wasn't all flab, not by any means. A lot of his enormous weight looked like muscle. Something that looked like a dried bird claw on a leather thong dangled from his massive neck.

The other shooter was some skinny kid who wore a blue baseball cap pulled low. The big man would have dwarfed anybody in the bar, but he looked big enough to carry his opponent in his pocket.

I watched the kid make a precise short-rail shot, easing the cue ball off the rail around the six to tap the eight into the corner. It's satisfying to win a game on a well-executed tough shot.

"I don't think so," his mountain of an opponent spoke. Biting through the almost indistinguishable Cajun inflection in his low, deep voice, he made each word a snarl.

"Whatcha mean, man? That was a beautiful shot!"

"You came off the six. That's a foul. So puttin' down the eight means you lose."

The kid looked ready to argue more, for a second there. Then I guess his instinct for self-preservation kicked in. He laid his stick on the table.

"Hey, man. You don't want to pay me, no problem. I don't want no hard feelings."

It was an old scene I'd watched before. Someone makes a bet on a game, then tries to argue his way out of it when he loses. Surprisingly enough, contrary to the big bad image of the Quarter, it rarely goes to a fight. Like the kid was doing now, the winner usually just waives the bet. Of course, if the loser tries the same stunt too often, he suddenly has a hard time finding anyone who'll shoot him for money.

Then again, why on earth would the skinny kid want to fight *this* guy? He was doing the smart thing.

"That's bullshit! It was a foul. You lost. You owe me five!" The big man wasn't about to let it go.

The even smarter thing now for the kid would be to bolt out the doors and not look back. No doubt he could outrun his opponent. It would only cost him his dignity. I didn't think that was too unreasonable a price. Obviously, the kid didn't want to fight the big guy, but he couldn't stomach turning tail. Paying out five dollars for a game he'd won was simply out of the question. He looked around the bar, appealing for help. People watched, but no one stepped forward to interfere.

His eyes settled on me.

"Maestro! You were watching. Was that a clean shot or not?"

I was startled but hid it. I hadn't recognized Willie under the baseball cap. He had shaved off the neat beard he usually sported, probably unable to stand it anymore in the summer heat. He worked at Ralph & Kacoo's, just up the block.

"This isn't league, Willie," I said. "I'm not in a game, I keep my mouth off it."

Suddenly, the lights went dim. The big guy stood in front of me, blotting out the rest of the room. I noted he was balanced on the balls of his feet like a fighter. I didn't move from my elbows-behind-on-the-bar slouch, though to all appearances it left me wide open. My SpyderCo was a heartbeat from my right hand.

"He asked you a question, fella!" he said. "Tell him he ticked the fuckin' six."

From being the unnoticed observer, I had suddenly become the focal point of the entire bar. I didn't particularly like that.

You've heard about how the martial arts let a small man beat a big man. That's basically bullshit. It works nicely when the little guy knows how to fight and the big man doesn't. Then the little guy takes the big man like a LAWS rocket takes a tank. Unfortunately, if the big man knows how to fight as well, the little guy loses.

It was weird thinking of myself as the "little guy," but the evidence loomed hugely over me.

This scenario illustrates perfectly why I like knives. The knife was the great equalizer long before the Colt revolver came along. I shifted ever so slightly on my stool, so that my right hand was now only *half* a heartbeat from the SpyderCo.

To my surprise, the big guy caught the "casual" move and took a step back.

Uh-oh. He was a knife-fighter too and recognized the move. We had both just identified each other. That put the ball in my court.

I didn't let it become a standoff, aware of the audience watching the scene. I tilted my head a few degrees so I could see past the big guy. Willie was holding his ground.

"You both agree to go along with what I say?" I said evenly. I looked directly at the giant in the overalls. "Even knowing that I know Willie there?"

"That's right. Call it."

I shifted again on my barstool, getting my feet under me.

"In that case, I was looking right at it and it was a clean shot."

The big guy stared at me hard. I got ready to make my move, being careful to avoid twitching a muscle. Then, slowly, he nodded his head.

"All right," he rumbled. "I'll take that as honest. Otherwise you would've called it against him just to keep from lookin' like you were throwing the game to him."

He fished a five out of his pocket and handed it to the kid. Willie took it and faded fast, dignity intact, but he didn't even bother to return his cue to the wall rack. He left it on the table and hit the sidewalk.

The crowd turned back to their drinks, the collective tension draining from the room, everybody glad the confrontation was over.

I should have been so lucky.

"How about you and me shooting the next rack?" The big guy was smiling, but still wary. It was a very creepy look, mostly because he seemed to be trying to be genuinely friendly. His eyes, sunk deep beneath his heavy brow, glittered a bright, strange neon blue. But that *smile*. His mouth looked like it could swallow the average human head.

"Thanks, but I'll pass," I said, managing to smile back. All I wanted from this man was distance. "I've seen your game, and mine's not good enough to shoot money with you."

Sometimes a little flattery is enough to make any problem go away. Sometimes it isn't.

"Com'on," he insisted, like a child that was going to ask and insist until he got his way—a 350-pound child. "That kid called you 'Maestro.' I figure anyone with a handle like that knows which end of a cue stick to point downrange."

"You'd think so," I agreed, looking to keep things amiable and still brush him off. "But I got that name from teaching people to handle an epee, not a stick." I was vaguely hoping I could lose his interest with an unfamiliar word or two.

"No shit. I haven't picked up a foil since I was eighteen."

You never can tell, especially in the Quarter.

He was smiling even broader now, and it was twice as disturbing. He was looking at me closer, appraising me anew. He was *warming* to me. The thought wasn't terribly pleasant.

"Lemme buy you a drink and we'll shoot a couple'a racks for fun."

I was already in too deep. If I refused a drink now with this short-fused monster, I'd run the risk of offending him. I was supposed to be doing a quiet lookout for Jo-Jo. I calculated that I could still do that and shoot a rack or two. I signaled to German Caroline for another Irish.

"Appreciate the gesture," I toasted him with the drink as he started racking. "By the way, didn't catch your name." I offered my hand. Sometimes you just have to go with the flow.

He took a step toward me in his stomping boots, and folded one enormous, callused mitt over my hand so that it disappeared. He didn't squeeze hard but I got a quick idea of how solid and strong he was.

"I'm called Jugger," he said in his low rumbling voice. "Short for Juggernaut."

Suddenly, the evening got a lot more interesting.

Chapter 24

Bone

"Bone!"

My accumulating stubble had finally started itching bad enough for me to shave. I'd also showered, put on clean clothes, after spending the daylight doing the few domestic chores that ever get done in my apartment. I did the dishes, which mostly consisted of washing out coffee mugs, took out the trash. One of the privileges of Quarter living is that we get garbage pickups every day except Sundays. Garbage is important in New Orleans. During Mardi Gras we determine the tonnage of the trash that is collected from our streets, and that's how we measure the success or failure of any given year's Carnival. *The first full day of my leave of absence,* I thought with some dismay, *and I've turned into a housefrau.* Oh, well. Wasn't so bad, really.

Alex was back at work after her weekend. It had been particularly nice waking up next to her, and I decided I could get used to that. I hadn't slept with anyone since Sunshine left. It seemed wrong. But somehow, I knew this time Sunshine wouldn't mind.

"Bone."

I could hear the sneer in the voice—female, familiar. I was walking along Dauphine, and the voice snapped from behind. I considered just walking on but, instead, stopped and turned.

Judith, the hysteria-prone waitress from work, stood with one curvy hip shot outward, her fist resting on it, chest thrust forward. A very deliberate pose of sexuality as aggression—and entirely wasted on me. Besides, the look of naked scorn on her kewpie doll face made her decidedly unattractive.

She stood outside the corner grocery where I go for cigarettes. She was still obviously upset that I'd dared to ignore her a few nights back during her Great Coffee Drama with the espresso machine.

"Judith," I said with the same neutral affability I use on my tourist feeders.

She sashayed a step nearer, cocked her hip in the other direction. "I heard about you and the cops. I heard you were in some *seeer*-ious shit." The grin she offered wasn't friendly.

No thanks to you! I thought, rolling my eyes. Detective Zanders' visit to the restaurant continued to have repercussions. It annoyed me to be the subject of gossip, doubly so hearing this bimbo chickiepoo talk about it.

Argue with her? Screw that. Indifference, I knew, was my best weapon against Judith. I turned away. It was nearing midnight, but it was still hot because night means nothing to the summer heat. Although it had rained briefly and heavily in the afternoon, the temperature dropped a few degrees only for the length of the downpour.

"I heard the cops think you're the one that stabbed that girl at the river."

Stopping this time, I felt something that was either very hot or very cold in the pit of my stomach. I turned back, slowly.

Judith's grin had gained a few more teeth.

"Heard? Who from?" I realized as I said it that it was a pointless question. One rumormonger is as good as the next. And now I was buying into Judith's game.

"Ohhhhh," she teased, "just around."

Of course, she might be making it all up. I couldn't decide if that would make me angrier; and I *was* feeling anger.

"That ... *girl* ... was a very good friend of mine," I said, gritting out the words. I flexed my right hand.

"Of course she was. Bone's good friend. That's why you had that big fight at Molly's. Remember? A week or two back? Screaming and clawing at each other so the bartender had to pull you two apart. Sound familiar?"

Exaggerated, of course, like any rumor; but hearing it tightened my hand into a fist that went white. It hurt to even think about that night ... that last, awful night of seeing Sunshine alive. But to hear it from this—this—

"Go to hell," I spat. There was no point in prolonging this. I turned away, walking on, leaving her on the corner. My gut burned hotter/colder.

Behind me, Judith let loose a hyena's laugh, and there wasn't anything I could do.

* * *

I dialed the direct line straight into Pat O.'s gift shop and told Alex where to meet me after work. Some asking around had confirmed some things I already suspected.

The staff of my restaurant routinely did their drinking at the Abbey, a grunge bar a short, convenient stumble along Decatur. When bartenders at the Abbey ordered food from us, one of the busboys would usually run it down there, and more often than not the portions would be much bigger than the regular public ever sees. When the restaurant crew showed up at the bar after shift, they could expect their drinks strong, and even the occasional free round. It wasn't my kind of bar, but at thirty-one, I was in a different age and taste bracket from most of my slacker coworkers.

The staff of Big Daddy's had staked out Molly's on Toulouse as their turf.

I went there, feeling like I was returning to the scene of a crime. I would have felt like that anyway, but bumping into Judith, that dig she'd gotten in— and good—made it acute. I sidled in the door, tense, expecting ... I didn't know. Maybe for every head to turn, every finger to lift and point. I could still see it— Sunshine and me yelling at each other, so hateful and ugly, so far away from the closeness we'd once had.

That incident had made enough of an impact, I thought bitterly, that it had alerted the NOPD to my existence and still proved popular gossip. And now, it was a knife Judith had just used to get under my hide.

I edged to the bar as if I walked across broken glass, barefoot. There were a few people in the place, and a few of the heads did turn, but it was the normal bar check-out. I made a conscious effort to relax my posture, saunter the last few steps.

The bartender wasn't the same gal who had been on duty *that* night. I ordered a soda and lit a cigarette, glanced down into the emptying pack.

For budgetary reasons, I wasn't drinking. No big deal. If I wasn't living in a community where the social scene was based in its bars, I no doubt wouldn't drink nearly what I do, and sometimes I drink soda anyway when I'm out. Without the tips coming in for the next few days or however long, though, I couldn't justify laying out much money for booze. But if I had to give up my smokes as well, God help everyone. It was too bad, I couldn't help thinking, that nobody was *paying* me to do this hunt.

Quarters I could spare, though, so I slotted them into the table and killed the next half hour with some solo practice pool. I thought about seeing if I could get a money game going with someone, maybe pick up a couple bucks, but Molly's wasn't that kind of bar. Anyway, I certainly wasn't going to solve my financial troubles on a pool table. I wasn't a good enough player, and didn't have the necessary diligence to hunt down the number of low-level cash games I'd need to make any difference in my finances. And I didn't have the time. I had much more important things to attend to.

I knocked off, waited for Alex, stood up from my barstool when she came in with her knapsack over her shoulder, and kissed her and ushered her onto the adjacent stool.

"How was work?" I asked.

"Ugh." She ordered a rummincoke. Decompressing, she gave me a familiar run-down of her evening, with the usual incidents involving drunk/rude tourists, and drunk/horny college boys, and waiters and bartenders whining about how they'd never survive on these crappy tips, never make it till the *SEASON*.

I listened and smiled and watched the door.

I lit another smoke and, lowering my head slightly, whispered, "Target's here."

"You mean Chanel?" Alex arched an eyebrow. "Where'd you pick up the James Bond lingo?"

Too much hanging around Maestro, I thought with a little wince. Molly's had filled up with a decently sized crowd since I'd walked in. Using the mirror, I pointed out Chanel to Alex, making sure I wasn't seen. Then I backed off my stool, retreated to the back of the bar and fed dollars I couldn't really afford into one of the poker machines. "Video crack," the locals call these monsters. And, yes, 24-hour drinking and legalized gambling make New Orleans a veritable nest of vice. The fact that these machines are as prevalent in Quarter bars as ATMs means that weak-willed service industry folk lose a good chunk of their overall tips to these beeping, winking, highly addictive contraptions.

I can understand the draw, same way I understand why people jump out of perfectly good airplanes and call it skydiving, but it doesn't grab me, that gambling rush. Still, in the abstract it would be a fine thing to hit the jackpot for $500 right about now. In reality, however, I fed the machine my money slowly, betting only one credit a toss, and remained sharply aware of Alex moving toward the barstool where Chanel had settled.

Chanel was wearing civvies, like last time I'd seen her outside Big Daddy's on Bourbon after she'd got off work—the night of Sunshine's murder. I remembered that hadn't gone so good. I'd wanted info about Sunshine, but had been a little clumsy, a little heavy-handed. That, I realized with a mild sense of historical importance, had actually marked the start of the hunt—my asking those questions, acting on my desire to know *who* had killed Sunshine, so I could *do* something about it.

Now, the hunt was even more serious. I was partnered with Maestro, who had demonstrated he had some know-how in these matters.

I had also welcomed Alex in on the hunt. I'd been very sincere when I said I was glad to have her with us. I most certainly meant to keep her from any harm, a bit like—but even more earnestly—what Maestro wanted for me.

Here, though, was something Alex could definitely help in, and which didn't have a risk factor. Alex is generally warmer than I am—friendlier, easier with people, able to break ice like she doesn't even know what ice is. I'm not socially incompetent by any means, but Alex could charm a person out of catalepsy.

She'd been immediately game when I told her what I had planned. Happy about it too. I wondered if maybe she thought I'd been shining her on when I'd told her she could come on board. Probably not, probably just enthused, the same way I was eager to move this forward, to put us all nearer to identifying and locating Sunshine's killer.

I gave Alex her time. My credits dipped and rose around the three-dollar mark, and I glanced back periodically to see how things were going. Alex and Chanel were talking. In no time they'd probably be yammering like old friends. Alex had a knack that, frankly, I could only admire.

When it was time, I wandered across the bar, pretending to notice Chanel for the first time.

I threw her a casual nod. "How's it going?" I slid an arm around Alex. "No luck on poker tonight, honey." Then, ran my gaze back and forth between the two women. "Hey, I didn't know you two knew each other."

"Didn't," Alex said, with a fetching grin. "Do now."

"Bone," Chanel said, just getting around to responding to my greeting. She was a little off, wanting to be aloof with me, but now I was attached to the person she'd just been chatting so friendly with. What to do?

"I'm getting this round," Alex said as she slapped down a bill, effectively nailing Chanel to her barstool.

My manner stayed perfectly at ease, as if Chanel and I hadn't had short words the last time I'd seen her. It would make her start to think she was blowing the incident out of proportion. I figured with a few more rounds, and Alex's fun friendly presence, Chanel might be susceptible to some questions—if they were presented just right.

As it was, she saved us all the bother.

"Bone ... hey ... have you heard anything about Sunshine's funeral?"

I paused. "Funeral wouldn't be here, Chanel. Sunshine had some family in Chicago. I'm sure her body's gone there."

"Her body ..." she repeated, examining the term and shuddering. Her spiked red hair was shoved under her cap. She'd traded her Big Daddy's T-shirt for a loose plaid shirt that didn't over-accentuate her breasts. "Dammit," she sighed. "Chicago. Was she from there? I never even knew. Never knew any-thing about her, really. Never bothered. *Dammit.*"

Alex put a hand on Chanel's wrist and squeezed. "Hey, nobody saw this coming."

"Actually," I interjected, "*some*body did. Whoever it was who killed her."

Chanel chugged a big swallow of her cocktail. "I keep wondering, keep thinking, what if it was me? What if some fucker decided to stab me? Kill me?

Who would know I was born in Columbus? That I met Joni Mitchell when I was five years old? That I've driven on the Autobahn at 130-miles-per-hour, that—that—that I want to live in Hawaii someday when I'm old and be the old smiling lady that little kids wave to on her front porch and—and—fuck fuck fuck ..." Her voice cracked. She knocked back the rest of her drink, slammed it on the bar top. "Are the cops *ever* going to catch this son of a bitch? Are they even trying?"

"What would you be doing that the cops aren't?" I threw the question out almost rhetorically, but I watched her closely, waiting.

"I'd collar that punk prick bastard of a boyfriend, stick him in a dark wet room and beat him with a hose, just for starters!" Chanel waved for and got a fast reload on her cocktail—a regular's treatment from the bartender.

Alex's hand was still on Chanel's wrist. "Sunshine had a boyfriend?" she asked gently. Of course, I didn't point out that Chanel had more or less claimed ignorance on the subject when I'd talked to her before. Quarterites may love to gossip, but they apparently don't take well to being questioned outright.

"Arrogant little faggot." Her hand shook a little getting a cigarette to her lips. Still standing behind the stools, arm folded around Alex, I lit it for her.

I've never liked "faggot" as a catchall insult. It doesn't have the ring or persuasiveness of "jerkoff" or "nimrod." Besides, having grown up in San Francisco and worked in Quarter restaurants the past two years, I normally reacted to "faggot" the same way right-thinking white people respond to hearing "nigger."

Now, though, I didn't react. I just listened.

"Name's Dunk. He came by the club a few times starting a month or two back. Scuzzy. Looked like one of those dirt-bag kids that panhandle and peddle their asses around the Quarter. He talked some *shit*. How Sunshine was totally devoted to him, how he was going to be big someday, y'know, just like everybody talks that same crap. He said Sunshine was lucky—*lucky*—to be supporting his freeloading punk ass now, because of course he was going to be some famous hot-shit musician someday." Chanel shook her head sharply, warming to the subject, getting angry.

Which was where I wanted her, if it would loosen more info out of her. "You can't mean Sunshine was supporting this kid financially?"

"Rent, roof over his head, bills, the works. 'Course, every dollar he could get his grubby hands on he blew on dope."

My arm tensed slightly around Alex.

"I knew Sunshine used to be into coke," Alex said, thoughtfully, before I could think of a way to pry slyly into the subject, "but I thought she'd quit, years ago. Was she back on it? Doing it with this Dunk guy?"

Chanel blinked at Alex. I waited for a glimmer of distrust, and like that, the whole thing would be off, but Alex had done her work well. "Don't know nothing about coke," Chanel said. "Sunshine's thing was crystal meth, far as I knew. She was cool with it, though. Dunk was just a stupid pothead."

Chanel turned, something deliberate in her expression now, and looked directly at me.

"So, to answer your question, Bone," she enunciated, the way you do when the booze gets its first real grip on you, "if I were the cops, I'd grab Dunk and get him to talk and hurt him a whole lot because for my money he's the one that killed Sunshine, and even if he's not ... it would be a hell of a lot of fun to make him bleed. The little faggot."

I hadn't grilled Chanel. I hadn't asked direct, leading, earnest questions. I had bumped into her; we'd made chitchat; she'd spouted off about Sunshine's murder and might've mentioned something about Sunshine's last boyfriend. No big deal.

I gave Alex's shoulder a squeeze.

"Well, I've got to go home, get out of this monkey suit." Alex smiled at Chanel, indicating her black-and-whites. "It was nice meeting you."

Chanel smiled, because Alex is easy to smile at. She turned to me, and the smile didn't completely cool. She nodded. I returned it.

I shouldered Alex's knapsack, and we got out of there.

* * *

Excerpt from Bone's Movie Diary:

> Movie interrogation scenes are usually pepped up with a little torture, be it cops, criminals, soldiers, or tribesmen doing the questioning. Torture makes me distinctly uncomfortable. It's not the pain inflicted or the clever intricacies of the methods—it's the helplessness of the victim. *That* affects me, & I have been known to squirm. Nonetheless everything must be rated, so I name the interrogation scene in *Nineteen Eighty-Four*, released in the titular year, as the best. John Hurt—stunningly gifted actor—is being tortured by Richard Burton in his final performance. (Burton's death was another huge personal loss.) It's a grim, relentless sequence—gorgeous in its ghastliness. Not

interrogation per se, but brainwashing; still, the effect is the same. I'm always made most uncomfortable, though, when Hurt, after some serious measures by Burton, starts cooperating in his own persecution. It's diabolical, & what's worse, is that Burton remains utterly reasonable throughout, even during the bit with the face-eating rats in the cage. By the end you almost think he's in the right.

Chapter 25

Maestro

Ever have a really big dog try to follow you home?

I stayed awhile at the Stage Door, keeping an eye out for Jo-Jo. He didn't show. I didn't want to stay too long, since I meant to make another pass through here sometime around two o'clock. I eavesdropped on the Court of Two Sisters crew still sitting at their table, but didn't hear his name come up.

Meanwhile, I shot racks with the Juggernaut. It got old fast.

He was getting chummier with me. We carried on a "conversation" where I put in the occasional grunt or "uh-huh" and Jugger babbled about everything that came into his big, shaved head. He was a good stick, and I tried giving him a good game. My custom cue was in its locker at Fahey's, though, and the Stage Door's bar cues were pretty typical of bar cues everywhere. Mostly, though, it was the Juggernaut's nonstop chatter that was throwing me.

I made some I-should-be-going noises, and the Jugger immediately invited himself along. "Where we goin'?"

Uh-oh.

I quickly backed off the idea, and we shot another rack. The huge man in the overalls was putting away draft beers one after the other. I waited for them to take effect—not getting him drunk, but sending him to the sandbox so I could duck out. Since, however, I was more or less stuck for the moment, I made use of my time and Jugger's loose tongue.

He liked to talk a lot about fighting. Hardly pausing to take a breath, he told me about some of his triumphs: guys he had sucker-punched, people who had tried to back out of a confrontation but who he'd hospitalized anyway, the guy who sent him up and so had it coming in a big way. Fascinating stuff like that.

It was inevitable he would get around to the fight that had most recently landed him in the clink. By now, I figured assault as the odds-on favorite for reasons he would have been in jail.

I figured right.

"Fella was messin' with my bitch. You don't do that. You don't mess with a real man's bitch. You mess with *mine*, and you can expect to be taken apart." He finished guzzling another beer.

There was a simple carom shot sitting there on the table, staring at me. I tried a thin cut shot to a side pocket instead and made a show of grimacing when it missed. I was giving the Juggernaut a good game, not my best game. Why show him everything I had?

I had to do some translating on what he'd said. The Bear had assured me the Jugger was strictly into males. That made "bitch" something other than the normal derogatory term. It was of course also a prison expression, one he probably knew very well. I've never done time and never intend to. However, I know that on the Inside even a lot of completely straight men will turn to homosexual acts just to keep themselves sane. The bigger and tougher you are, the easier it is to procure yourself a steady "bitch," who is usually somebody smaller, weaker, and willing to submit to your needs. I wouldn't imagine the Juggernaut having much trouble intimidating some kid into being his plaything.

If, however, the Bear was right and Jugger was normally homosexual, inside or out in the World, then I pitied anybody coming between him and whoever his "bitch" was.

I took some personal comfort in that the Bear had said Jugger was only into young guys. At fifty-plus, I wouldn't be his cup of tea. *Hopefully.* His buddy-buddy manner with me, though, was bad enough. He slapped me on the shoulder when I took the eight neatly between the two and the five and into the corner to win the rack. I almost reacted reflexively when he touched me. It took me a few seconds of deliberate effort to relax my stance.

"Great shot, Maestro!" he congratulated me.

No quibbles about winning shots now, not with me. I was his new pal.

"I gotta piss," he said as he headed for the sandbox. "Be right back."

Needless to say, I did my quickest fade.

* * *

I had coordinated with Bone earlier over the phone. We were set to rendezvous at the Calf late. He was going to Molly's, planning to use Alex to try to finagle information out of a Big Daddy's waitress who had worked with Sunshine. That meant Alex was now definitely in on the action, though from the sound of it, Bone meant to keep her away from the rough stuff.

I didn't want Bone putting his foot in quicksand either. He'd shown some smarts so far, but that didn't make him an experienced professional.

Even so, as it crept up on two o'clock, I almost wished I could tell him to come join me on this particular operation tonight. I was a bit loath to return to the Stage Door, leery of finding the Juggernaut still there. If I could send Bone in instead, keep a watch on him from the street, then he could do the second lookout for Jo-Jo. I shook my head and had a private laugh. Bone wasn't something I could attach to the end of a fishing line and cast in the water. He was my partner.

The idea of being able to get in touch with him, though, struck me. Sure, we each had the other's home phone number. But, what if I absolutely had to reach him right now? It was something to think about.

After ducking out from the Stage Door, I passed a couple of hours doing some secondary look-overs. These were much easier than tracking down new faces. Jo-Jo and Jugger were new ex-con arrivals in the Quarter, but there was already an established population of Quarterites who'd done time and now worked jobs as bouncers, bartenders, etc. Even in the unique melting pot that makes up the Quarter, these particular people were easy to find.

Mostly, my look-overs consisted of stopping in casually here and there. Often I didn't even need to buy a drink or spend more than a minute or two. It was a list of some two or three dozen, and I didn't intend to question these people—not now anyway. I only wanted to see that they were still around, that they hadn't suddenly ditched their jobs and gone AWOL.

"Hey Iggy, how's it going?"

"It's cool, Maestro."

It was like that. If the ex-con I wanted happened to be working back in a restaurant kitchen, or someplace else I couldn't just wander into, I needed only say a casual hello to the doorman, then add, "Hey, tell Max I said, 'hi.' He's still working here, right?"

In this way I confirmed by sight or reliable word that the Quarter's normal ex-con population was accounted for.

I had taken particular interest in the new arrivals for a good reason. An ice-pick murder definitely suggested an ex-con's involvement. It was somebody newly released, though, that would be most likely to use the weapon. He'd have had less time to readjust to society and to break the incriminating habit. Someone who'd been back in the World a while was more likely to know better. Even if he couldn't stop himself from committing a killing, he'd probably use a gun, or at least a knife that didn't scream "prison yard shank."

I stopped home briefly to swap my red T-shirt for a faded green one, keeping the old blue jeans.

I was dawdling, putting off heading back to the Stage Door. I did a long loop and came back along Chartres. I would at least scope the place through the side window first. The Juggernaut would be easy to spot.

I didn't see him. I kept moving, around the corner to the Toulouse side doors, petted the friendly, somewhat bedraggled, stray dog that hung by the door looking for handouts. I have to admit, I much prefer the furry kind of stray to the human kind.

I wandered in. German Caroline was off and there was nobody else in the bar from before. There was also no one who could be Jo-Jo. A new pair of Court of Two Sisters waiters sat at the back table now, green jackets over their chairbacks. I picked a stool within earshot and ordered a Coke. If I wanted to still be on my feet to rendezvous with Bone I'd have to take it easy with the Irish.

That unpleasant mix of rap and heavy metal boomed from the speakers, but I could still hear the waiters' conversation. It helped that they were loudly decompressing from their shift.

It was a brand of dialogue you can find in virtually any bar in the Quarter. The main topic is complaining about management, your customers, even your coworkers. No insult is too low. The two waiters were letting loose with their opinions. They were both in their young twenties, so their speech was peppered with "like," "y'know," and "dude." I shouldn't be too judgmental, I suppose. When I was a kid, we were ruining the English language forever with "daddy-o," and later, "groovy."

I of course stayed alert for the Juggernaut or anybody wearing a silver crucifix around his neck. If the Jugger confronted me, asking why I'd ditched him, I would explain that I had gotten an urgent page. I didn't have a pager on me— or even own one—to support that, but I figured I could still make it believable enough.

If silver crucifix man showed up, I would respond however the situation demanded. I wondered idly if the Bear's red alert perimeter would actually bag this mystery character. That would be nice. I didn't like him hanging over my head, particularly not now. I was on my first tracking job in ten years, and didn't need any distractions.

"—Jo-Jo—"

My ears went up. I sipped my Coke and blocked out all other sound in the bar, focusing a tight beam of attention on the waiters' table.

"Man, he is, like, so full of himself!" one said.

"God's gift to women, dude," said the other.

"Not to hear it from Yolanda! Man, she told Jo-Jo's ass *off*!"

"I never seen anybody spend so much time, y'know, like, looking in the mirror, dude."

"Not a guy anyway."

Both waiters laughed at that. Then, summing up Jo-Jo in succinct terms, the skinnier of the two said, "Dumb-ass method Mexican."

I puzzled over that as they moved on to their next victim. I must have misheard over the blare of the music. Picking through the syllables, I still couldn't come up with anything, and it wasn't like I could go over and ask them to run it again.

I sighed silently. A few minutes later, the waiters split. At least I'd confirmed that Jo-Jo was working at the Two Sisters. I couldn't see anything else I could accomplish tonight at the Stage Door, and decided it was about time to start rolling toward the Calf. I didn't want to be bumping into the Jugger again tonight, though it was good I now had an idea where I might find him if I wanted to.

Dumb-ass method Mexican?

I shrugged. Like, y'know, dude, who knows?

Chapter 26

Bone

St. Peter Street, late because I'd insisted on stopping by my apartment, Alex and I walked out in the street between the rank of show-room motorcycles that always crowd the front of Johnny White's and the line of Uniteds cruising for late drunk fares out of Pat O.'s. We cut around a gaggle of young *gangsta-from-da-hood* types standing on the sidewalk. They would scoot—and rightly so—at the first sign of police. Alex's hand tightened in mine as I kept the kids in the corner of my eye—not worried, too open out here for anybody to start anything, but you don't totally trust your assumptions.

Christ ... was this *Maestro's* thinking turning up in my head?

"Oh ..." I heard Alex say, a little worried. The shutters were pulled over the Calf's door. We had been at Molly's fairly late, but had expected to catch the Calf just before Padre closed it. I was scheduled to see Maestro, compare notes. Alex was looking forward to it. She was proud of herself, deservedly so, over how she'd handled Chanel. I could not have accomplished that little ploy without her.

We went up to the door anyway. I tried peeking through the slats, and Alex rapped on the jamb. From across the street, one of the Pat O.'s doormen hollered a hello. She turned, waved, and then the Calf's door unlocked.

Padre opened the shutters and ushered us inside, something like a smirk on his face. He threw a glance down the sidewalk at the pseudo-gangsta kids. If they hung around long enough, someone would ring the police house on Royal. Soon enough after, a squad car would do a slow roll down St. Peter, and the kids would scamper back to their normal stomping grounds. We've got our troubles in the Quarter. Gang violence isn't one of them. City Hall and the NOPD won't let it put down the tiniest root.

The juke was silent, the lights turned up slightly, and Maestro waited, sitting back in what was becoming our booth. The booths are usually for diners since the Calf serves burgers and baked potatoes and whatnot. The grill, which operates out of the back, was being thoroughly renovated, though, so nobody was eating. Maestro had a cigarette going and a whiskey in front of him. Once again we had the joint to ourselves.

"Does this mean I can't get a drinkie-poo?" Alex asked Padre with a coyness that would have been nauseating from anybody else.

"Madam shall have as madam wishes," Padre pronounced, definitely pleased with himself about something. "Go sit. I'll bring you your drinkie-poo. Bone?"

"I'm good." I walked past the row of empty stools, set down Alex's knapsack of knitting and reading, and took a seat on the booth's bench opposite Maestro.

"Greetings," he nodded, his somewhat lined, swarthy face, set in its usual, casually neutral cast. He wore an almost threadbare green T-shirt, and—were those blue jeans? Come to think of it, he'd been dressed rather out of the normal last night, too, when I'd bumped into him after that episode with the gutter-punks and the broken window.

"Howdy," I returned. I picked a smoke out of my pack, near the end of my supply.

Alex paused to give Maestro the once-over. "Slumming it tonight, sweetie?" she asked, eyeing his ensemble. She leaned over, gave him an arms-around-the-neck hug. He smiled and returned the hug.

Padre appeared with Alex's rummincoke.

"I got it." Maestro quick-drew a five and slid it over. For an older guy he had fast moves. The T-shirt he wore also betrayed rather solid-looking biceps and chest. They weren't a weight-lifter's muscles—more like a dancer's.

"Did you shut down early so we could have privacy?" I asked Padre.

The innocent blue eyes behind his old-fashioned, wire-rimmed spectacles blinked at me. "As the night bartender, Bone, I can close at two a.m., I can close at six. It's up to me. It's a sacred trust."

I chuckled, blowing out smoke. Well, as long as Franklyn, the owner, didn't catch wind of it. Then again, Padre *was* the Calf, as far as a good many of his spending regulars were concerned.

"Okay," Maestro began as Padre went back behind the bar, tending to the restocking and cleaning up. "What have we accomplished tonight?"

I told him what we'd gotten off Chanel at Molly's: Sunshine's preferred drug was crystal methamphetamine—something new for her, as far as I knew—and she had definitely been supporting Dunk, her live-in boyfriend. I made sure Alex got her credit. Maestro nodded a solemn bow her way, not being a smartass, just commending her.

"So—" Maestro tapped a finger on the brim of his rock glass. "Dunk smokes grass, but Sunshine was into this other stuff ..."

"Crystal meth," Alex supplied. "Speed in crystal form."

"Gives you a big rush," I added, seeing Maestro's brow furrow slightly. "Makes you manic. You end up scrubbing your bathroom floor tiles for hours."

"Sounds like fun," Maestro observed dryly, sipping from his cocktail. *Ah, alcohol, blessed depressant.*

"Chanel made it sound like Sunshine had a hold of the habit," I said, "not the other way around."

Maestro looked at me. "Did she do speed back in San Francisco?"

"Might have tried it. I think she probably tried a little bit of everything at one time or another—just sampling." I shook my head. "But not when we were together. All she did routinely was pop prescription pain pills when she could find them, and smoke pot. As far as drug usage ... I always thought it was pretty harmless."

"How common is this crystal meth in the Quarter?"

I turned to Alex. We shrugged at each other. I said, "Common as anything else, I guess."

"Is there a particular group, like a subculture, that's especially into it?"

"Ravers?" I put out.

Alex shook her head, "Ecstasy, more that crowd. Crystal meth doesn't exclusively *belong* to anyone, I think. But at least we know what Sunshine's thing was now. If we find someone that deals a lot of crystal in the Quarter, we may have her dealer."

She said it simply, clinically, and I felt a chill I couldn't help. Alex had done good tonight at Molly's. But ... hunting down drug dealers? I didn't want her in danger, but I wasn't sure that what I wanted had any bearing on reality.

Across the table Maestro's dark brown eyes had gone still. Nothing of it showed on his face, but I felt he was sharing my thoughts. He brushed back a lock of his thick, black hair.

"Then there's Dunk," I threw out to break the pause.

"This Chanel said he'd been on the scene with Sunshine how long?"

"A month or two." Alex sipped her drink.

"It occurs to me," I took a deep pull on my cigarette, "that Dunk's status as a freeloading barnacle attached to Sunshine definitely lessens the possibility of his having killed her. Sunshine was his meal ticket. Why cut his own lifeline?"

"Logic and murder don't always go hand in hand," Maestro said, "but that's still good thinking. Do we know how Dunk met Sunshine, what he did before meeting her?"

"Piper, the kid I bribed with a sandwich, told me he was just another gutter-punk not too long back. He'd be around, doing the panhandling and the rest of it. But he had a saxophone and could play it. Sometimes he'd blow it for spare change up by ... the ... river."

Maestro's gaze sharpened slightly. Alex turned.

I shook myself. "Hey, c'mon. Kids use the Moonwalk as a hangout. There are street musicians up there all the time. Just because Sunshine ..." *Got killed there.* Something unpleasant rolled over in my guts. My brain replayed the scene in Dunk's apartment ...

"Ahh—I think that Dunk had one of those voodoo dolls, the junk kind that they sell to the tourists. It was lying on a pile of Mardi Gras beads on the coffee table. Could be nothing, but ... "

Maestro nodded. "You're right. It may not mean anything. I think finding out how Sunshine and Dunk got together, though, might be useful."

"Dunk's gig at Check Point Charlie's is tomorrow night," I said. "I'll be there. I'll see what I can find out."

"I'd like to go too," Alex said, taking a sip of her drink.

"Somebody ought to keep a job, Alex. One of us sacrificing a paycheck for this is bad enough. You shouldn't have to do it, too. Besides, I may need you to rescue me if I run out of money for smokes." I gave her a smile that I had to prop up slightly. Who knew what would happen at Check Point's? The truth was that I didn't want her exposed to that risk factor.

"*Bone* ..."

"Well, here's what I did tonight," Maestro interrupted before Alex could continue. He ticked off the events, detailing everything neatly.

"Nobody's MIA among the usual Quarter ex-cons?" I asked when he finished.

"Not as far as I could tell."

"Which doesn't mean one of them isn't our killer."

"Of course it doesn't. Every last one of them's a suspect." Maestro ground one of his narrow black cigarettes into the ashtray. "Questioning each of them on their whereabouts on the night of Sunshine's killing, or even establishing those whereabouts independently through our asking coworkers and such, that would be very tricky. Also time-consuming."

"And we might as well be waving a red flag announcing that we're hunting her murderer," I muttered.

"Exactly." He set his elbows on the table, steepled two fingers. "Of course, the cops know the ex-cons in the Quarter too, and they don't need any pretext to interrogate someone. Investigating murders is part of their job, after all. They would've already questioned these guys. That no one among them has been hauled in means everybody's already established their alibis."

"Christ," I with a sigh, "you'd think being a vigilante and operating outside the law would make things measurably easier."

Maestro shrugged. "Yes and no. It's not like there are *no* rules—just different ones."

I paused a moment, feeling it wash over me suddenly. And I marveled, uneasy and pleased in the same instant. *Vigilante.* I'd just used the word casually, applying it to myself. *Operating outside the law.* This was real. We were actually doing something about Sunshine's death. I wasn't sitting back, taking it, swallowing it ...

I shook myself again. I could get philosophical about this later.

"You got any thoughts on this Juggernaut guy?" I asked.

Maestro pursed his lips a moment. "Big and dangerous. I can't see any possible way of linking him to Sunshine—romantically, that is. Remember, that's still probably our best bet, Sunshine having been killed by someone she was involved with. A lover, an ex-lover. Jugger's homosexual."

"Um, Maestro," Alex said, gently, "did it occur to you Juggernaut might be bi?"

Maestro blinked, once, twice. "Frankly, no."

"You're sure he's gay, exclusively?"

"I've got a source, Bone. That's what he says."

I nodded. "Well, you've sort of made friends with this guy, right? You can keep an eye on him. Probably wheedle him for more info."

"Probably. He's definitely a talker."

Dipping into my diminishing reserves, I lit another smoke. "And you've got a line on this Jo-Jo character too? Ladies' man, works at the Two Sisters?"

"Supposedly hangs at the Stage Door. But I didn't see him at any point tonight. I'd rather scope him out there than try to stop in at his job. He's still our number one candidate, even without a tie to Sunshine. 'God's gift to women' a 'dumb-ass, method Mexican'—that's what those two waiters called him. He's sounds like a prize. Sunshine's cup of tea, wouldn't you say?"

I had to nod sad agreement. "What was that last bit, though?"

"Huh?" Maestro was nearing the bottom of his Irish.

"'Something-something Mexican'—what those waiters were saying?"

"Oh. I misheard 'dumb-ass method Mexican.' Don't ask me what it means. Maybe it's something the kids say nowadays."

"Method?" I frowned. "What—method actor ... ?"

Maestro regarded me flatly. "Right, Bone. They were denigrating his thespian abilities."

Alex's cocktail glass came down with a sudden bang. I turned, saw her large eyes light up, her lips quirk.

Enunciating carefully, she said, "Dumb-ass, *meth-head*, Mexican." At Maestro's raised eyebrow she continued excitedly, "Don't you see? Jo-Jo does meth. Enough of it that his coworkers know about it."

Alex had been proud of herself earlier. For this she could strut like a peacock if she felt so inclined. Neither I, nor Maestro, would stop her.

"I'd call that a potential link to Sunshine," I said. I grinned at Alex.

"So would I." Maestro raised his glass in salute. "Outstanding."

"Just paying back the drink you bought," Alex said, raising her glass in return and grinning even wider.

Having no drink I reached for my dwindling pack of smokes, then I remembered the envelope. We were late because I had stopped by the apartment to pick it up. I retrieved it now from Alex's bag.

"One more thing. I don't think this is related to the murder, but I thought you might find it interesting." I pulled the yellowed photo out of the envelope and pushed it in front of Maestro. "Doesn't this guy in the picture sort of look like you? Maybe twenty-five or thirty years ago?"

Despite his dark skin, Maestro turned pale. "Where did you get this?"

"It came from Sunshine's apartment. Dunk sort of 'gave' it to me—when he thought I was someone else. I forgot about it until last night. Is that you in the picture, Maestro?"

Maestro said nothing, just continued to stare at the photograph, not touching it.

"May I see?" Alex reached for the photo. Maestro let her take it.

"I didn't recognize you at first," I said, "so young and with that haircut. But last night something made me look again. I don't know the woman, though she looks a little familiar, too. Who is she?"

Maestro started to answer, but Alex spoke first. "That's Hope. Sunshine's mom."

Maestro and I both stared at Alex.

"Sunshine once showed me other pictures of her from around this time. But I've never seen this one."

Now I knew why the girl in the photo looked familiar. She had Sunshine's eyes, her smile. I'd never met my mother-in-law—Sunshine had cut all ties with her family—but I knew Alex was right.

Maestro drained his glass in one quick motion. "Hope is Sunshine's mother?" He looked like he was about to go into shock.

"So you knew her? Hope, I mean?"

"Yeah. We were close. I met her ..." He hesitated for a moment, and when he did speak, it was as if each word hurt him. "I met her after the ... shortly after

I joined the Outfit." He shook his head. "I was a young punk back then. Had a lot of girlfriends. But she was … special. I lost track of her when she moved away from Detroit."

"Did you sleep with her?" Alex asked.

Maestro gave her that hairy eyeball look.

"Oh." Alex got quiet.

"So Sunshine could be … ah, could have been …" I couldn't finish the sentence, couldn't wrap my mind around it.

"Not terribly likely," Maestro said. "I was young, but I was neither stupid nor callous—at least, not in that way."

"But Sunshine might have thought it was possible," Alex suggested. "That might be why she was trying to reach you. She told me she never really knew who her real father was. Her mom was a free spirit, met and married her step-dad after she was born."

"That's right," I said as I struggled to come to terms with … what? The sheer Dickensian coincidence of it? People said that strange things happened in New Orleans, in the Quarter. I guess this was proof.

"Sunshine never said anything about this to you?" Alex asked. "She never mentioned it?"

Maestro shook his head, and the look on his face told me that he might need some time to himself to deal with what he'd just learned.

Alex handed the photo back to Maestro.

"May I keep this?" he asked. He had to clear his throat to speak.

"Sure," I said. "She probably would have wanted you to have it. I think maybe she meant for you to have it." I gave him the envelope. He looked at the "M" scrawled on the outside, nodded once, and then carefully put the photo away.

I turned, looked at the clock on the wall.

"Yes, time for all good children to be in bed," Maestro said. He flicked a fingernail against his empty glass and pocketed his cigarettes.

"I'll call you before I head out to Dunk's gig tomorrow evening," I said. "Shall we do another late meet here?"

"We'll talk about it." He moved to slide himself from the booth.

Abruptly Padre was standing next to the table. With that odd smirk still on his face, he laid two objects on the tabletop. Small, oblong, faux walnut housing—matching cell phones.

We all looked up at him.

"Speed-dialers preprogrammed," he said as he pointed proudly at the phones. "Hit 1 and it rings the other phone. There're enough minutes on both you don't have to worry about it. Use them till this thing's done, then ditch them—preferably in the river."

"Padre ..." Maestro started.

"Hey, thanks," I said.

"Bone, Alex—I've called your cab. Maestro, let me know if you two are going to want to rendezvous here tomorrow night. And a pleasant evening to you all."

We all exchanged silent glances and decided to let him have the last word. Alex kissed Padre soundly on the cheek on the way out.

* * *

Excerpt from Bone's Movie Diary:

> Ian Fleming was a hack novelist, & James Bond as *the* movie franchise hasn't aged especially gracefully. The superspy-in-Cold-War milieu doesn't have modern relevance. The world's current villains are bargain basement thugs without any daunting resources but the willingness to surrender their own lives. Doesn't fit, really, with the glamour & panache of a typical 007 baddie. Do I still like the series? Of course. Bond is great fun. I won't enter into the Connery v. Moore v. Brosnan debate. Honestly, does the role require much from an actor? I often find myself more interested in the secondary characters anyway. The late Desmond Llewelyn, as Q, was my fave. He was the gadget supplier—dry wit, breezily good cameos in the vast number of the films. I mean, what would 007 be without his gizmos but an effete, martini-swilling, sex-addicted ninny? Appraisals: *On Her Majesty's Secret Service* as best Bond film (no, not *Goldfinger* & no, I don't care about George Lazenby in the part); Paul McCartney gets best title song for *Live and Let Die*. No arguments.

Chapter 27

Maestro

The Two of Cups usually indicated lovers or partners. What about both? Was it even remotely possible that Sunshine could have been my daughter? I didn't think so. While not impossible, it was seriously unlikely. Sunshine had nothing of my skin coloring, no trace of my distinctive features. Besides, Hope would have told me about her. It was the free-love '60s, but we had been more than just lovers. We had been friends. We'd respected each other.

But she had also been a genuine free spirit. While she didn't know anything about my growing connection to the Outfit, she could sense, even then, that I was getting into dangerous territory. She wanted no part of it. We split as friends, intending to keep in touch. But, in some twisted, gallant attempt to protect her from the possible consequences of my work, I never really made the effort.

Did it really matter? At the very least Sunshine had been Hope's daughter, if not mine. That meant my own stake in our little operation had just seriously escalated. I had come on board as the "experienced expert" to keep things on track and hopefully keep Bone safe. But now it was personal. By the time I made it back to my apartment from the Calf I knew one thing: failure was no longer optional. I would *get* Sunshine's killer.

* * *

Today's was a daylight operation. I picked out casual-dressy khaki pants, a short-sleeved cotton shirt with a collar, and loafers. My hair is long enough to put into a ponytail, but I went to the bother of digging out an old can of hair spray. After a little work, I had my mop swept back and styled. Checking myself in the mirror, I decided I looked like a citizen. By sliding a folding knife into my right front and back left pants pocket, though, I became a *well-armed* citizen. That I could live with. I also took along my new cellular phone.

"Use, don't rely," is a good adage for information. That is, gather what you can from where you can, and act on it as fit, but don't think everything is gospel. As a tracker, info had been gold to me, and reliable info platinum.

I had every reason to trust the Bear's information. For one, he had proven himself a friend over the years. He was long since out of the military but still lived by an almost samurai code of honor. He was one of those rare people that didn't promise things—he gave his *word*.

For another, owing to the company he kept and where he worked, he was in the pipeline as far as news on the ex-con scene went. Still it made sense that I should check an alternative source for anything he might have missed.

I was frankly tempted to bring the Bear in on things. I knew I could tell him outright about the hunt and had no doubts at all he would hop eagerly on board, bringing a lot of valuable resources and skills he'd accumulated in his Special Forces days. But with myself, Bone, Alex, and now Padre sticking his toe in the edge of the pool, things were getting crowded. These people knew who I was, and I could trust them. Any more, though, and it would feel like my years with the Outfit were common knowledge. That made me uneasy. So did my near-revelation of my military past, which was something that wouldn't have happened had I been thinking clearly.

Of course, the Bear didn't have to know any of that ...

I put the thought aside and focused on today's contact.

Lynch J. Morise had been a successful local PI in his heyday. That he'd retired twenty-five years ago and yet remained a Quarterite was a reflection of his deep affection for the neighborhood. That at age 85-plus he still made the rounds might give you some idea what a tough old cuss he was.

The Royal Sonesta Hotel's lobby bar, called the Mystic Den, was a class act all the way. Air-conditioned and fitted with plush furnishings, it was open to the public, but the staff nonetheless didn't let just anybody wander in. If you tried to catch a snooze in one of their chairs or looked like you were there to pick pockets, you got shown the door. It was one of my getaways. There are places I turned up regularly—the Calf, Fahey's, etc., etc. I am guaranteed to run into people I know at all these places, and that's part of my reason for going.

I like being a part of this strange community—it seems normal now, after ten years. But sometimes change is good. Once in a while I like to spruce up a bit and stop in at the Sonesta's bar, though not so often to be considered a regular by any means. Even so, my good tipping habits usually assured that at least someone on the staff remembered me.

Thing was, I rarely bumped into anybody at all from my normal bar scene. Sometimes I struck up conversations with guests of the hotel who'd had enough of Bourbon Street. Sometimes I'd meet fellow Quarterites that simply traveled in completely different circles from mine. I'd met attorneys, a taxidermist, a retired playwright who'd seen her work produced on Broadway, doctors from various hospitals and research facilities in the city, and so on. Generally, they were a different brand of people from those I usually mingled with. It was a fun game to play, even though in the end it was just another time-killer.

It was there, of course, that I'd made the acquaintance of Lynch J. Morise.

I wore a wristwatch today, and checked it as I came in off Bourbon, leaving behind the clutter of delivery trucks and of young children who glued bottle caps to the soles of their sneakers so they could tap dance for spare change. I breezed into the lobby bar, quietly relieved to see the old man in his chair. At four o'clock each and every day but Sunday, Lynch J. Morise could be counted on to be there, having his "high tea." That's an extra spicy Bloody Mary to you and me.

He was one of those indestructible old-timers you'll find around the Quarter. They are our royalty—kings emeritus and grand dames.

"It's Maestro!" he called out, spotting me instantly. "Com'ere, kiddo. You can keep me company."

The handsome black woman behind the bar recognized me. I gave her a smile and a healthy tip, and took my drink over to join Lynch. I was relieved to see him because, heck, at his age, his not showing up might be real cause for worry.

We shook hands. He had a bony but firm grip. He wore a beige suit. His hair was pure white, and his skin was like papyrus.

"Good to see you, Lynch."

"'Course it is, Maestro. I make you feel like a kid by comparison!" He cackled.

I didn't argue with him, but truth was, the fierce old man had a more energetic vibe than most people I knew. More impressive, perhaps, his mind was still razor-sharp. Several decades as a private investigator had exercised his mental faculties. Since retirement, he had kept himself purposefully busy. I admired—and even keenly envied—that on a personal level.

"How's that pool-playing team of yours?" he asked.

Some topics you can't escape. Dutifully, I told him where the Snake Plisskens were in the standings. I was struck, though, as always, by how different the atmosphere was in the Mystic Den. Carpet underfoot, no rock music blasting, no loud talk, just a comfortable hush in the lightly scented air. It was virtual tranquility. There was no one within earshot of us.

Lynch, even at his advanced age, didn't wear glasses or contact lenses. From the chair opposite, he regarded me with his sharp eyes.

When I first met Lynch a few years back and learned he was a PI, retired or not, I went instantly into alert mode. Someone who had made at least part of his living finding people who didn't want to be found wasn't someone I wanted to associate with. He was, however, an undeniably fascinating man who had an anecdote for every occasion. He was tremendously intelligent, also quite charming.

In a way, I realized, he might be Sneaky Pete's opposite number. Pete, an ex-cop clerk, was something of a contact with the local police. Lynch, though, represented the private sector. He had contacts and maybe even influence, but it was all unofficial. As an active PI, local legend had it, he had often found himself at odds with the authorities. I had no worries about *anything* I said to him being passed on to the NOPD.

"What's on your mind, Maestro?"

"What makes you think there's something on my mind?" I retorted blandly, but it was a fairly useless feint.

I couldn't run the same sham on him I'd used with the Bear. Lynch was a Quarterite, but there is every level of society represented in the Quarter. With Lynch, I needed a different class of pretense if I wanted information. I'd given my play a good deal of thought. It was almost toying with fire, but I was determined to go through with it.

"Come, come, Maestro. I've always smelled something about you that's not quite cop, not quite criminal. You keep your cards close to your vest, and I like that in a person, and I'd never try to peek at your hand ... but I *know* you're not a civilian. 'Least, I wouldn't rate you as one."

See why I immediately went on alert when I met him?

"Maybe you should be reading cards on the Square, Lynch."

He cackled again.

I hunched forward in my chair, setting my drink on the low table between us. "It's about that recent murder on the Moonwalk."

The old man shook his head grimly.

"Ugly business that. Hate seeing anything like it in the Quarter."

"I agree," I nodded. "So does everybody I know—so much so that a few people are talking about taking things into their own hands."

"Not surprising. It would be a fine thing if the police could solve every crime, if they had no limit to their time and means and attention. 'Course, that wouldn't have left me much of a career, would it?" He took a thoughtful swallow from his tall Bloody Mary glass. "Are you saying there's a hanging posse gathering?"

I was aware of the eggshells I was walking on. Lynch was astute, but I believed I could outmaneuver him, simply by hiding in plain sight.

"Nothing quite that drastic. Not yet. But the police haven't come through on this thing. That girl who was killed, she had friends. I've heard a lot of secondhand talk. I wouldn't normally give it much credit. But the buzz is that some parties in the Quarter—I don't know who—are getting serious about acting. I'm starting to worry that somebody might try something dangerous and foolish. I'm trying to be the voice of reason."

"How sage-like of you, kiddo."

Apparently, you're never too old for smartass banter in the Quarter.

"Lynch, I'm serious." I put on a worried face. "I don't want anybody going off half-cocked and getting themselves hurt, or worse. The girl's murder was bad enough. I don't want to see it lead to more tragedy."

He was nodding. He was a Quarterite, and he knew how talk in a bar could lead to unfortunate events.

"It's admirable of you, Maestro. Is there some way you can cool these people down?"

I took a breath.

"There's a rumor flying. You know how that goes in the Quarter, right? But I've heard that these people have got hold of it, and they're taking it for fact."

"And the rumor is?" He had dropped his joking manner, and was listening earnestly.

"That there's someone in the Quarter just out of jail that recently finished a stretch for murder. A stabbing murder."

"And this gang wants to find this person, put him on trial, judge, and execute him. Is that about the thrust of it?"

"That's what the hotter heads are supposedly talking about doing." I made an exasperated grunt. "If I could kill the rumor, they might back off this. As is, I'm afraid they'll pick the wrong guy. You know, some brand-new parolee trying to put his life back together."

"I understand."

Lynch extracted a cigarillo from his suit jacket. I leaned forward and lit it for him.

"What you want from me, Maestro, is to know if the rumor has any truth to it, right?"

"You're a well-informed man, Lynch. That's no secret. You're also not the police. I couldn't go to the cops with this. I want facts to disprove the rumor. If I can put the truth out on the grapevine for these people to hear, it might defuse the bomb before it explodes." Even to my own cynical ears, I sounded convincingly sincere.

The old man blew out a plume of blue smoke.

"I do get a lot of information passed my way. My old PI office still uses me as an unofficial consultant sometimes." He nodded. "Sure, Maestro, I'll give you the skinny. There are four men who've been let out in the past month who had French Quarter addresses when they went in. Presumably, they've returned here."

That matched what the Bear had told me—the Juggernaut, Jo-Jo, and two unspecified black guys.

Lynch ticked them off on his skeletal fingers. "One did a sentence for grand theft auto, one for check fraud, one for assault ..."

That one could be Jugger, I thought.

"... and, I'm afraid, one for murder."

I didn't have to fake my surprised look.

"I'm sorry, but the gossips are right on this one, kiddo. The guy stabbed his girlfriend with a kitchen knife. She tried to kill him with it first, though. There were two witnesses."

"Jesus wept," I muttered, but I was thinking hard and fast. "Maybe you ought to send word to this guy ..."

"And tell him there's a band of vigilantes after him? I don't think so, Maestro. Sounds like there's some rough stuff brewing, and I'm too old to get in the middle of it. You want this guy warned, *you* do it. Maybe he can get out of the Quarter. He's—let's see ..."

I watched files being mentally shuffled behind those sharp eyes.

"Munoz. That's the name. José Munoz."

I felt my stomach suddenly shrink.

Jo-Jo.

"I hope you find him before someone else does." Lynch stared into his glass for a moment. "There are a lot of guilty people walking the streets free, Maestro. But it's when someone innocent goes to jail, or gets offed for no good reason ... those are the troubling moral things that stay with us to the grave." I had a feeling he was speaking from personal experience.

"Thanks," I rose to leave. He stood with me shaking my hand again, his grip even firmer than before.

"Good luck."

Chapter 28

Bone

Esplanade Avenue divides us from the Faubourg Marigny, which is a neighborhood much quieter and gentler than ours. It has its bars, restaurants, shops, its own scene and culture and flavor. It's not the Quarter, and doesn't try or want to be. I know people in the Marigny. I have visited the Marigny. We are both a part of the city of New Orleans. Yet, in a real sense, we're separate states.

Maestro had speed-dialed me earlier to test our new cell phones. The ringing had startled me. I was having a last cup of coffee at the apartment before heading out on tonight's job when I heard the weird chirping and put the lightweight, tiny phone to my ear.

Despite its size, it had good sound quality. Maestro told me what he'd learned that afternoon about Jo-Jo. My blood went a touch cold. It certainly seemed the evidence was piling up on our Latino suspect. Maestro hoped to find him sometime tonight. I wished him luck.

I didn't ask Maestro about the source of his information, and he didn't volunteer to reveal it. We were partners, yes, but I understood he had his reservations, myself being the amateur, understood his nagging desire to keep me away from all potential danger. He would probably—consciously or otherwise—continue to try to marginalize me in this hunt, especially now that he had his own reasons for being involved. My thought? He could try. I had my bead on Dunk, and I had tracked him down without Maestro's help. Whatever else happened, Dunk was *mine*.

Check Point Charlie's squatted on the corner of Esplanade and Decatur. I hiked over at about ten-thirty, experiencing that common Quarterite vertigo when encountering two lanes of traffic after days or weeks or months of dealing only with the Quarter's narrow one-ways. I don't drive, and so never have to worry about negotiating anything except foot traffic. Still, it can be a powerful moment of culture shock. Esplanade was a border street, wide, split by a tree-lined median, fronted by large old homes. Cars rolled up and down it.

I don't feel guilty for the amount of time I spend in the Quarter, the degree to which I ignore the rest of our city. Home, job, friends, recreation—all are found in the Quarter. The rest of it ... the downtown, the old walled cemeteries where tour groups go, the plantation estates, the parks, the outlying suburbs, Lake Pontchartrain ... I'm content where I am. I'm happy. *Or as happy as I can be.* For once in my life, I thoroughly belong.

In spite of the heat, I had let my dark hair out of its ponytail, hadn't combed it. The high humidity made it stick to the back of my neck. It flowed disheveled around my lean shoulders. I wore my boots, black jeans, a T-shirt. Slacker neutral. Shouldn't call a lick of attention to myself.

There was heat lightning across the river, lighting the sky above the West Bank that's—I think—actually *east* from here. We don't use a North-South-East-West compass in the Quarter. Instead, you refer directions by adjacent districts or border streets or the Mississippi. The wide sheets of lightning were accompanied by no thunder, but flashed spooky, ghostly. A freight train grumbled and squealed along the tracks beyond the levee wall and parking lot. I heard a boat blast its horn on the river.

There were a few people standing around outside Check Point's, just that corner hang thing, checking out the scene without having to go in and buy a drink. Kids—I was immediately bummed for a smoke, gave it over, said to the next mendicant, "One's the limit on my charity." He shrugged, shuffled off.

I lit a cigarette for myself, having bought a pack on the way here with money I was now conserving. I hated waiting tables, but I was already missing those tips. That's the ugly dichotomy of my—or anybody else's—job.

I took a minute to study the phone pole on the corner, stapled endlessly with intact and tearing fliers, with the corners of old ones. Rusty staples ran up it from a point below my knees to well above my head. Handbills for guitar lessons, computer troubleshooting, lost dogs, garage sales. Lots of fliers for local bands that hadn't existed two months ago and wouldn't two months hence—Woad, Big Giant Jenny, $s & ¢s, the Garfunkels, Scurvy Mervy Is a Pervy. Some of the names were pop culture references, some were just weird for the sake of weird. They'll never stop saying New Orleans is the birthplace of jazz, and there is indeed a fine local music scene and a *lot* of homegrown talent. But c'mon, this is the Quarter. Every success—every artist who's been shrewd and smart and dedicated and lucky—could have his or her own personal entourage of loser wannabes that will nonetheless continue to talk shit about how true and righteous *they* are, and how if you make it you're a sellout, and you sure you can't spare 'nother smoke dude?

Alex had been upset about my going alone. Last night I'd done what I could to assure her that I would be fine. Would I take unnecessary risks? Of course not. Would I take *any* risks? Of course ... though I didn't know what kind of danger I might find tonight, couldn't even really speculate. I meant to gather some info on Dunk. Maestro had laid out a number of elementary pointers for fact-finding at the start of this hunt, and I'd done quite well—no small thanks to the way Alex had handled Chanel at Molly's.

Was tonight's job genuinely dangerous? I didn't know, presumed so, and walked into the club.

Check Point Charlie's has a feature that sets it apart from other local bar/music venues: it's also a laundromat. When I first heard about this place, I was struck by the perverse hilarity of it. How typically New Orleans, how decadent, that people drink so much here they need booze at their *laundromat*? But, eventually, I understood. Check Point's is a 24-hour joint. Few Quarterites live a nine-to-five, Monday-through-Friday kind of life. We do laundry whenever. Why not at four a.m., maybe the only free time you have for chores? You want to sit in a sterile laundromat at four in the morning watching your underthings go round and round? Probably not. Who else is open at that hour anyway? At Check Point's you can dump your stuff in a machine, have a beer, shoot some pool, flirt with whoever happens to be around, and you don't have to worry about the place being held up. Bar robberies in the Quarter are about as rare as murders. They happen, but they're virtually freak occurrences.

They happen ...

It didn't matter to Sunshine that as a crime statistic she was a severe anomaly.

The earlier band scurried around the stage breaking down its gear. A typical "Decatur style" crowd milled around—i.e., service industry and semi-trash—though the club is several rungs up the respectability ladder from, say, Sin City. Check Point's has a raised level at the rear where there are a pair of pool tables, and from up there I heard the comforting *clack-clack*, which reminded me of a few dollar games I'd shot up there. Check Point's washers and dryers were in an alcove at the opposite end of the bar.

I ordered a bottled beer at the bar. I'm not a beer drinker, but didn't want to be the exception, sipping a soda all night. Besides, the dark bottle hid the level inside. I could nurse this thing awhile.

I caught a few familiar faces, but faces only, couldn't come up with names—probably customers from the restaurant, not familiar enough to do anything but throw a nod. I mostly blended with the dark wood and brick decor, and watched the stage, and waited.

A group I assumed to be Clamjaphry started assembling on the stage. They had that serious, self-important manner of a band playing its first paying gig. The drum kit went up, amps were hauled onto the stage, jacks plugged into them. Somebody tapped on a microphone with a fingernail, and a young twenty-something girl with eye-watering scarlet hair, sunglasses, and a very lithesome figure, started getting a level, saying, *"One-two, one-two ..."*

Outside, overhead, I heard a helicopter pass low. Sometimes they're police choppers, sometimes news. Those circle longer. This one faded quickly.

I counted four band members.

"That's Clamjaphry?" I casually asked a guy I'd seen leading around one of the Quarter's haunted house tours from time to time.

"That's them." He nodded and wandered off.

There was a drummer, a long-limbed bass player, a white guy with dreadlocks with a guitar, and the girl was apparently the lead singer.

Where the hell was Dunk?

Piper had named names for me when I'd plied him with that sandwich and beer, and I'd believed him. Should I have trusted him? How were you supposed to know what sources of info you could rely on? I felt annoyance, some self-directed anger and a bit of mild dread that I might have wasted my time coming here, that Dunk—*my* Dunk—was going to slip out of my fingers.

There were some tables in front of the stage, but I kept to the back, standing, sipping minutely from my beer. Guitar strings twanged. Feedback whined. A drumstick tapped experimentally. The girl with the scarlet hair growled something—first to the bass player, who just shook his head, then at somebody off-stage. I couldn't get a line of sight through the intervening bodies. Then someone moved, and I saw a Check Point staff member. More people filled the club.

I checked the time. It was getting past even the normal delayed start of any live music show. I could hear the growing restlessness of the crowd. I could see the members of Clamjaphry on the stage start to jitter, their serious manner turning to worry. The dreadlocked guitarist turned to huddle urgently with the lead singer, who was spitting angry words and gesturing with growing violence.

Something was wrong, and the crowd sensed that and seized on it. Someone started the classic foot-stomping chorus of "we-want-the-show," probably just for fun, and it got quickly taken up. The crowd raised a whole lot of noise, and the band looked out on their audience for whom they hadn't yet played a note, and looked more worried now, getting frantic. Another of Check Point's staff members came up to the front of the stage, and the scarlet-haired girl started explaining something desperately.

At that moment a lean and mangy figure came bounding up from the crowd, the heels of his combat boots coming down on the stage with a loud crack. Then, swiveling about, he bowed deeply, theatrically and insincerely, first to his band mates, then around at the now-jeering crowd, arms outspread with a flourish, saxophone held high in one hand.

Dunk soaked up the catcalls with obvious relish. He sported the same camouflage pants and dirty white T-shirt I'd seen him wearing at Sunshine's apartment. Tonight being an occasion, though, he wore a baseball cap over his sloppy sides-shaved hair. Emblazoned across the front was FUCK Y'ALL.

Charming.

Her hand over the microphone, the lead singer spat what were probably some choice words. Dunk leered back and gave her a good long look at his middle finger.

She gave it up—all of Clamjaphry were visibly annoyed and irate at their late-coming band member—and cued the drummer.

The sticks came down.

It was that brand of D.I.Y. pseudo-punk that garage bands have been playing twenty, twenty-five years: fast, intentionally ugly, nihilistic. Even still, they were tight. It was a runaway dump truck sort of music, pounding and rattling, and I couldn't understand a single lyric the scarlet-haired girl sprayed into the mike. She had a curiously angelic voice, though—robust, almost operatic, borne along by rapid-fire guitar, drums, bass.

Dunk, for his part, stood loftily apart, tapping his foot purposely against the rhythm, a sneer on his face. It was clear that he thought that all this fuss and bother was just the groundwork for *him*. He drummed fingers against his saxophone, bored, disdainful, impatient.

The song hit its bridge and Dunk strutted to the fore of the stage. Up swung the sax, out blew a fantastic tangle of notes. The saxophone is not my favorite instrument. It's got a shrillness I find grating. But ... the sound Dunk coaxed from his horn echoed with layers, nuanced and forceful. He commanded it. His notes hopped and hurtled among the music. And as competent and sincere as the music was, as much effort and conviction as the rest of Clamjaphry put into that music, Dunk's wailing wiped them all into the background. *He* had the touch. *He* had the singular spark that separates expertise from capability, good intentions from genius.

The crowd heard it, understood it, and let loose a wave of cheers and applause. Dunk turned his back when his solo was finished. The band carried on, making their competent music. But from that first number, Dunk's sax became the centerpiece, and the cheers were for him. He knew it. He swaggered about, blew his notes in fabulous, effortless combinations. His band mates paid the price for him. He stood taller atop their crushed egos, and knew that too.

He strode off the stage during the number that finished the set—his last solo done, so why hang around? He dropped into the crowd, marched toward the bar, absorbing the enthusiastic congratulations. On stage, Clamjaphry-minus-one rolled through the finale. The singer said something that got lost in a blare of feedback, and it was over. They started meekly disassembling their equipment.

Was this why Sunshine had hooked up with this dirt-ball? Sunshine had always opted for lousy boyfriends, but Dunk was more rancid and repulsive than the worst choices I'd ever known her to make. The draw, the lure—Dunk's very evident musical gifts—had that proved the seduction that drew her into the relationship?

Dunk leaned against the bar, letting people buy him beers. I edged a hesitant step towards the crowd, but I soon realized I wouldn't be able to get a word in, much less get near him. Dunk shed his arrogance on all around him, and some of the crowd actually got a kick out of it, buying him more beers, lauding him as a celebrity. Girls pressed in around him and he preened for them. He seemed particularly interested in one slender blond who had long hair that hung to her waist. The girl hovered near him, one bare shoulder peeking out from an artistically tattered red T-shirt. I was surprised to find myself fascinated with her bare shoulder and tight jeans. Something about her looked familiar, but I couldn't place it.

Not until she turned around. She wasn't just familiar—she was Alex, disguised in a blond wig, extra makeup, and very tight jeans.

I barely stopped myself from yelling her name, from lunging forward into the crowd to get to her. What was she doing here? I was terrified and furious, all at the same time. She turned, saw me, and winked. Then she turned back to hanging on Dunk's every word.

I gritted my teeth and waited. After far too long she left the crowd at the bar and wandered out the door. I wanted to go after her, but I knew that the moment I did it could compromise both of us, and I might lose my chance at Dunk. *What did she think she was doing?*

Dunk continued to hold court at the bar. I continued to wait—and to fume.

Eventually all those free drinks caught up with him, and he broke for the rest room, carrying his sax with him in a dirty pillowcase.

I followed in after, and in the interval Dunk already had a joint lit. He leaned back into the corner, the pillow case between his booted feet, holding the smoke in his lungs—this after guzzling four or five large draft beers bought by his adoring fans. His eyes opened, dreamily, and still he managed to sneer.

"That was a hell of a performance," I said.

He blew the smoke from his lungs.

"Suck my dick."

"You should get yourself a record contract. You deserve one."

"Yuh gahdamn right I do." He took another toke. We were the only two in the bathroom. A urinal gurgled. He exhaled again. "So, suck my dick."

"I think you played ..."

I let it go, seeing what he meant. His dirty-nailed free hand had dipped into his roomy cargo pants. He pulled his half-hard cock into the pale light. He leaned his shoulders harder into the corner behind him, then thrust his hips forward.

I wanted a conversation with this loathsome gutter-punk, wanted to coax information from him, but I certainly didn't want to deal with *this*.

I started shaking my head, turning away.

He said, "Wai', *you*. Yeah, dude ... yuh were at ... I saw ..."

I watched him put it together, thinking, *Shit*.

"... that picture ... Su'shine's drawing. Offa the door. You took it! Di'n'cha? *Di'n'cha, motherfucker!*"

He didn't make for an especially threatening figure, his cock still hanging out, the joint still pinched between thumb and finger. I remembered—briefly—Mitchell in Sin City's toilet, and didn't dwell on it. KO-ing Dunk wasn't going to accomplish anything. It might spoil things later on, and I couldn't risk it.

Still, I wasn't going to get anything I wanted now.

"You've got the wrong guy," I raised my hands, turning again, exiting, hoping the beer and pot would muddle his head, wipe out the memory, give me the chance to approach him some other time, some other place. Which meant tonight was a bust. *Dammit*.

I slid out through the bar, heading for the door, ticking grimly over whatever other useful ways I could spend the night, unwilling to waste time that might get me closer to the identity of Sunshine's killer. I wondered if I was leaving him behind, here—*Dunk* ...

"Bone. Thought dat was you."

I recognized Werewolf, recognized Firecracker to the left, slightly behind. Cooks from the restaurant, I'd worked with them fairly often, always as a set. They were good workers. Whenever, on those busy swamping shifts that sometimes came up, they stayed on top of it and got the waiters their orders, and treated me particularly well, I always passed them a part of my tips—money I wouldn't have made without the speed and efficiency with which they banged out those plates.

It was Werewolf—solid shoulders, strong limbs—who'd addressed me. It would have to be, since Firecracker—a wisp by contrast, taciturn, mildly albino flesh—rarely made the effort to overcome his speech impediment for more than a word or two. Nevertheless, he grinned a timid hello at me.

"Guys," I waved. "What're you doing here?"

"Came see de show," Werewolf said. His West Indies' heritage gave him his accent and his flesh a pleasant, creamed-coffee hue. "You?"

My head lifted slightly, but sharply. "I came out looking for some crystal meth. You know anybody selling it?"

Good cooks, friendly guys, and we had a good professional relationship, but I'd never seen them outside work. They weren't of that same low caste as Blitz, our dishwasher. I couldn't coerce anything from them under any circumstances.

Werewolf's dark eyes stared a moment into mine, then shifted to Firecracker's pink ones and stayed there. The two seemed to commune. I waited.

Firecracker's thin, whitish lips twitched into a grin once more.

" ... yi-yi-yeah," he said.

* * *

Excerpt from Bone's Movie Diary:

> The single most depressing movie I've ever seen is *Slacker*. Director Richard Linklater's 1991 queasy voyeuristic glimpse into the go-nowhere, do-nothing, smugly aimless world of slacker youth leaves one in a kind of lethargic shock thinking how it will be when these kids are running things. It's a low budget indie & very effective in its way, but I would rather eat a plate of spoiled shrimp than ever have to see it again.

Chapter 29

Maestro

There was nothing to be done about showing up two nights running at the Stage Door, which wasn't my normal prowl. Last time, I'd hit around eight in the evening, then again at about two o'clock. I was of course hoping to stumble on Jo-Jo—or should I say, José Munoz?

I'd ordered my dinner in tonight, Chinese food that I ate with chopsticks while I listened to some Shostakovich violin concertos. Then I spent a little while limbering up in an exercise not unlike the one I used to teach my sword students to use in warming up for a match. At the height of my club's enrollment, I'd had twelve pupils. It had remained an informal thing for the years I'd kept it active.

It was a healthier social alternative to the bar scene. I never charged fees for my lessons, but I passed the hat whenever we rented equipment or fencing space. Mostly, we banged steel on various back patios around the Quarter, I imparted my knowledge of the sport as art, and we generally had a fun time.

Yet I'd shut the club down. I'd backed a step further into a kind of self-imposed state of inactivity. Why was that?

The limbering and breathing exercises, of course, helped to center my mind. When I was ready I put on some appropriate clothes, a comfortable amount of weaponry, and headed out. It was before midnight, a time of night I hadn't yet tried the Stage Door. Maybe I could find out Jo-Jo's work schedule at least, and thereby figure out when he was mostly likely to show.

Who did I find when I got there? Guessed it in one.

"Maestro!" the Juggernaut called out, coming toward me from the pool table. For one awful second I thought he was going to hug me, but he settled for shaking my hand with his giant paw.

I'd scoped him from the street but had come in anyway. He was definitely a nuisance, but he was still technically on our suspects' list. I would suffer his company if it meant I could establish for sure he hadn't killed Sunshine.

"Jugger," I said with a seriously fake smile, "good to see you."

He liked that. "Let me buy you one!"

It was the least he could do. I sighed, resigning myself to hanging out with the big man for a while. I'd already done my visual sweep, and Jo-Jo wasn't among the patrons. There was only one Court of Two Sisters waiter, and he sat at the bar talking eagerly to a redheaded tourist girl who'd wandered in off Bourbon. I didn't know the bartender.

"Sorry I had to split last time," I showed him my cell phone. "Got an urgent call, and I had to go."

Jugger handed me my Irish. "That's okay. What do you do anyway? For a living."

"Free-lance accountant. Good job, but it keeps me on call a lot."

I didn't have a job and didn't need one, but that wasn't common knowledge around the Quarter. If Jugger started asking around, people would probably say something like, "Is *that* what he does? Free-lance accountant? Sounds right to me. I always thought he was fast with numbers."

He nodded his big shaved head. "Hey, how about a game?"

"Sure." It beat sitting at a table with him.

He gruffly shooed away the guy he'd been playing when I came in, and started re-racking the balls.

I didn't really understand why Jugger was so determined to be my buddy. Maybe I'd impressed him by making that fair call on the game he'd shot with Willie last night. He probably didn't get a lot of people contradicting or standing up to him. Whatever, tonight he was treating me like his lifelong pal.

I broke, and nothing dropped. He picked a tough carom with the seven and the four that would have left him near perfect to run the table if he made it. He didn't. I decided on solids, and started putting them down, though I still wasn't giving him my best game. With his temper, who knew how he would take to being drubbed too badly?

He regaled me with more of his delightful stories about the mayhem he'd inflicted, both on the Inside and out in the World. He was nothing but proud of the things he'd done. Every ass he had kicked, every face he'd bashed in, each bone he'd broken, belonged to some guy who "had it coming." No exceptions. He told me yet again about the poor dude who had "messed with his bitch." I nodded along to it all, shooting my game, keeping one eye on the doors.

"Only reason I got bagged this time was 'cause a guy ratted on me to the cops. They were doing their extra patrols for New Year's and he sent them after me. I hadn't had time to wash off my hands, and they stopped me on the street and backtracked to where I'd left that sumbitch. I guess it's a good thing after all I didn't kill him."

"Yeah. Good thing."

If the assault had been around this New Year's Eve, then the Juggernaut had served roughly six months. That sounded like a reasonable sentence.

"My little bitch kept begging me not to kill him." Jugger laughed, sinking the nine, then the fifteen. He lined up on the eight. "If'n he hadn't I probably would've broke that guy's neck."

He put the eight ball into the corner pocket.

If *he* hadn't ... referring to his "little bitch." Well, that certainly settled the Juggernaut's sexual preference ... or did it? Alex had suggested that Jugger might be bisexual, something that simply had never crossed my mind. One of the lingering handicaps of being hopelessly heterosexual, I guess. Even so it meant Jugger was definitely at least half gay.

"As it is, that snitch is definitely gonna pay. Too bad he ain't 'round here. Got some gris-gris with his name on it." He laughed again, obviously taken with the great comedy of it.

The Bear had told me about Jugger being into guys, but confirmed information is always better than just information. It was why I'd done that hopefully sly consult with Lynch in the Mystic Den earlier. That visit had turned Jo-Jo from hot suspect into red-hot suspect. I now also knew that the two recent black ex-cons the Bear had mentioned only in passing had done time for check fraud and grand-theft auto. Those weren't inherently violent crimes, so it lessened the chance that either of them had tagged Sunshine.

I racked for another game.

That was when the circus blew in.

I had Jo-Jo spotted even before the bartender hailed him by name. He was with two guys who were still wearing their green Two Sisters jackets, and he had a leggy, curvy blond wired to his arm. She nuzzled his shoulder and stared at him adoringly. With a complexion even more olive than mine, short curly black hair, and soft matinee idol features, I could see why he wouldn't be hard on any woman's eyes.

He had apparently already changed out of his work getup, was sporting slacks and a stylish shirt. His grin was bright and confident. It was almost as if the blond was simply part of his ensemble.

The group gathered up some beers at the bar and retired to an empty table toward the back of the place.

"Your shot, Maestro." Jugger had broken the rack, power-slamming his cue and scattering the balls everywhere. It was just one of those freak things that nothing had dropped.

I focused quickly on the table, kicking myself a bit for having been so obviously distracted.

I'd gotten a good study on Jo-Jo in those seconds I'd watched him cross the bar. I'd seen his type before and wasn't fooled by the pretty boy facade. He smelled like hard streets and jail smarts. Slender and graceful, he'd be fast as lightning in a fight. I could get a *very* good idea how someone would handle himself, simply by observing his gait. Jo-Jo had played rough games all his life. That he had survived to what I guessed were his mid-thirties meant he'd learned how to take his opponents down quick. He didn't have the body bulk to stand up in a prolonged brawl.

After my initial lapse, I refused to let myself even glance at Jo-Jo's table for at least four innings. (For you pool neophytes, an inning is how long a player holds the table before missing a shot, or winning or losing the rack.) At this point in the hunt I didn't want anyone to notice that I had more than a passing, casual interest in the man. As for Jugger, I figured any outside observer would realize *he* was the one interested in *me*.

As it turned out, I needn't have worried about scoping Jo-Jo too hard.

When the chunky brunette came charging in off Toulouse, every head turned. I cranked around and focused. She was in a huge huff, heaving big breaths that lifted her ample breasts. Her fingernails were out like claws, and her teeth were bared. Every Quarterite has seen this woman in one form or another, and every Quarterite would know what was coming.

"Jo-Jo! You fucking motherfucker cheating *bastard*!"

Jugger straightened up from his shot, leaned a big hip against the table and watched.

The brunette went straight for Jo-Jo's table like a locomotive. The blond was instantly on her feet, stepping forward. The two guys in the green jackets wisely pushed back in their chairs, knowing that a "cat fight," if not bloodier than a brawl between men, is still usually nastier.

As for Jo-Jo ... he sat there and let the blond intercept the brunette. He looked rather put-upon and saddened by the spectacle, though. Being fought over by two women might appeal to the male fantasy mentality, but the reality is unpleasant.

The jukebox was playing its normal rowdy music, but I had no trouble hearing the two women.

"Bitch! Getcher hands off my man!"

"He ain't your fuckin' man, bitch!"

There was a lot of that, plus a lot of arm-waving and confrontational body language. In the end, it really didn't look much different from a man-to-man fracas. Guys did exactly the same thing ... at least, until somebody finally threw a punch. I waited along with the rest of the bar to see if this would go that far. Even the bartender was obviously reluctant to intervene.

Abruptly Jo-Jo stood, marched past both women without looking or saying a word, and walked out the doors.

The brunette spun, went after him, and a few seconds later we could all hear the screech of her voice receding as she followed him down Toulouse Street. The blond, her teeth bared, visibly shaking, sat back down and glared at Jo-Jo's empty chair.

End of round one.

The Juggernaut laughed almost as hard as when he'd talked about his New Year's assault, then went back to the game. He was shooting a good game, but had his two wedged in behind the eight, so I knew I'd get another shot this rack. Even though the rest of the bar had now turned its attention back to whatever they were doing before, they were actively seeming not to eavesdrop on the quarrel. There was a very good chance it wasn't over yet. We'd all seen variations on this waltz too many times before. This was why I'd felt no burning need to go shadowing after Jo-Jo when he did his walkout.

Sure enough, our Latin lover came back in alone about five minutes later and made a beeline for the blond. Bending over the table, he leaned in close to say something into her ear. Before he had a chance to say more than a few words, the blond popped up and did her own march-out, her shapely legs stiff, her red-lipsticked mouth set in a tight line.

Jo-Jo watched her go, then sat down looking tired and vaguely disgusted. He picked up the beer he had abandoned earlier and took a long swallow. His two green-jacketed friends had since migrated over to the bar.

Round two.

Jugger started telling me about a guy a few years earlier who had tried passing an IOU at a card game he sat in on. I had the sneaking feeling I knew how the story came out. He interrupted himself when the brunette came back in, face stony, mascara running down from her eyes. She walked up to the table and stared at Jo-Jo without saying anything. He looked back at her but, probably wisely, didn't offer any words.

She drew herself up with barely-contained, furious dignity, spat noisily on the table in front of him, then turned and swept out of the Stage Door, her head held high.

Round three.

Jo-Jo sat quietly, staring at nothing in particular. With slow, careful motions he drank down the rest of his beer.

He was going to head out, having absorbed all the public humiliation one man could reasonably stand. I wanted to follow. If he went on tonight to get himself good and plastered, as seemed likely, he might be susceptible to a little friendly bar chatter from a stranger.

"Bitches," the Juggernaut growled. We were on a new rack. He slammed a shot into a corner pocket so hard the ball rattled and popped back out onto the table. "They'll always mess you up. Punk shouldn't have let them get away with that shit." He sneered in Jo-Jo's direction.

"I don't think he had much choice," I pointed out. Jo-Jo was standing now, and I thought urgently about the best, fastest way to extricate myself from the Juggernaut's company. "The Quarter crowd usually stays neutral in spats like that, but if he had started trying to slap them around someone would have felt obligated to step in."

Jo-Jo, head hung, walked toward the doors.

"I'm not talking about slapping them around," Jugger growled. "I'll tell you, Maestro, the last bitch that tried to get in my face like that didn't walk away from it. Know what I mean?"

I nodded vaguely at what promised to be yet another patented kicked-some-guy's-ass-ain't-I-cool story. I saw which way down Toulouse Jo-Jo was now heading, and mentally noted the bars along that track.

I *had* to get out of here.

Right then the cell phone rang in my pocket. One of those improbable instances where the gods grant you a favor even before you send up a prayer. I shrugged at Jugger, turned away, and put the phone to my ear, plugging the other with a finger so I could hear over the juke.

Seconds later, not giving a damn about niceties now, I tossed my cue onto the table. "I got to go." Jugger said something at my back but I was already gone, moving at a jog, not in the direction Jo-Jo had gone. My heart was thumping hard in my chest.

It had been Bone, of course. His brief message had ended with: *"I'm in trouble."*

Chapter 30

Bone

Alcohol is blunt and, for me, uncomplicated. I don't get violent or euphoric—I get grounded. While it may not be so to others, to me, that's an appealing state. Drugs, on the other hand, can fly you in an almost infinite number of directions. Those possibilities have their appeal—to others, not to me.

As I've said, my only serious objection to illegal narcotics—another reason why I place booze above them as a social and recreational outlet—is this: in the drug culture, you must deal with the scum of the earth. Alcohol, whatever you want to say about it, is legal. You can buy it over the counter, you can order it in a bar, and on New Orleans' streets you can drink it in the open for all to see. Drugs, you have to go a different route. Hell, just *getting* your drugs entails a lifestyle all its own, never mind actually using the stuff.

If you don't like the ambience of one bar, go to another. In the Quarter you'll have to walk about five feet. If you don't like drinking with anyone at all, uncork a bottle at home—a bottle you can purchase at the corner food mart, along with your toilet paper, beef jerky, and a copy of *Swank*, and nobody will say, "Boo."

But now, I had intentionally entered, for the first time in my life, that sleazy, scummy, seedy underworld of illegal street drugs. I had known it was a bothersome, complicated society. I'd also known it was a dangerous one.

But, foreknown or not, I had misstepped. And now I was in the shit.

We were in an apartment on Dumaine Street, a place I'd passed in the daylight many times and thought nothing of it because it was just a typical Quarter place: green-painted shutters over French doors that opened right onto the sidewalk, a faux gas lamp burning an electric bulb, stucco front crumbling a bit. Only a few weeks back I'd stopped in after my shift at Harry's Corner, half a block up, a usually blissfully quiet place. I had decompressed and chatted and bantered with the bartender, who had pointed this place out to me through the windows. I'd watched with her as cars rolled up and stopped at a time of night when only Uniteds and some of the other fleet cabs were moving. Watched people come and go out of the apartment's open doors, watched as one kid ran out and around to the driver's side windows, carhop style. It was all very busy. I wondered why the neighbors didn't buzz the cops.

The bartender shrugged her shoulders and said, "Maybe they've got the police paid off." I didn't give it much thought after that.

Werewolf and Firecracker had led me here, walked me in, and now were trying to verbally dissuade the leader of this pack of drug-dealing kids from *bustin' a cap in my ass*—his words. Spoken with all the exaggerated, urban-modern, gangland caricature-ness of a bad Tarantino rip-off. That was what this was, of course. Drug-dealing kids *acting* like dealers, this ridiculous, overstated punk who'd seen *Scarface* and *King of New York* a dozen times too many, who was burying himself in the part. You had to laugh.

But I wasn't laughing. As phony as this all might be on one level, the pistol that he waved around the room was very goddamned real.

"I tol' you tuh *sit*, boy. Yo. Huh? Fuck you be thinkin', motherfucker? Fuckin' think this a fuckin' game, homie? Fuck your shit right up, a'rite? Dig?"

It was an automatic, not a revolver, and he was rolling his wrist, pointing the big gun carelessly all over the place, even at his underlings, who didn't appear bothered by it. He paced the front room, waving the gun. There were four of the kids here, plus Werewolf and Firecracker, and myself. And *this* bozo. Blond hair buzzed down to fuzz, two gold front teeth. He was white and acting out the worst possible black stereotype. He wore the gangsta clothes, talked the gangsta talk, was plainly impressed by his own mock-up.

He'd told me to sit. I did not sit. A break for the front doors might very well be fatal, but I wanted the option, wanted to be on my feet, facing this. I didn't flinch when he stopped pacing and swung the pistol towards me.

"Lester ... be cool dere," Werewolf said in the kind of soothing tones one might use on a rabid dog, holding his hands out in a calming gesture. Firecracker's pink eyes were wide and following the pistol, but neither of the cooks looked panicky.

I could feel adrenaline in my veins, but my head was clear. In fact, the scene had an almost surreal clarity to it. There were four colored paper clips scattered across the coffee table. One of the couch's casters was missing. The kid standing by the front doors had wide red laces in his sneakers.

The shutters that would seal the front doors were opened, and the top halves of those doors were glass panes. Dumaine was quiet out there. Would someone in a passing car—even a cop—glance in here, see the pistol, and act? Help or do something? Did I want to be here if the police came? Me, who had come here to buy a dime bag of crystal meth?

I'd had my chance to call for help, and I had made my choice. I'd rung Maestro, not the cops, told him the address I'd noted on the way in, told him I was in trouble. No time for anything else. I had gone in to use the bathroom. Really, I had wanted that quick moment to hit the speed-dialer, wanted the flush of the toilet to cover those few words to Maestro. When I came out, I came face to weapon with this white "homeboy" impressionist—Lester—holding a pistol.

"Yo, I ain't fuckin' happy wit'chu neither, a'rite." Lester kept the automatic aimed at my face but turned to glower at Werewolf. "You duh one brought this motherfucker here intuh my crib, yo. Shit ain't cool. I might be fuckin' this fucker up *good.*" He turned back toward me.

It was, I guess, my cue to start begging for my life. The bore of the barrel looked as big as I've always heard it does when you have a gun pointed at you. I blinked at it. It wasn't fear I felt. Fear was on hold. I would get to it later maybe, when it wouldn't interfere with me getting out of this room alive.

Lester had my dime bag of meth in his other hand. He fidgeted with it, bouncing it about. It was a plastic baggie with a twist-tie, and there was what I thought was an unjustly small amount of granules inside. Ten bucks for this? There's another argument for sticking to alcohol. Cost-effectiveness. One of the kids had fetched the bag from a back bedroom at Lester's command. Lester was maybe twenty-seven, twenty-eight. The four kids didn't look old enough to drink.

"What you say now, fucker? Wanta ask me some more questions? Huh? Punk-ass motherfucker?"

"Lester, mon ..."

"Maybe you and Firecracker ought to split," I said, not turning Werewolf's way. With his husky solid physique and brawny arms he was far and away the biggest one in the room. But Lester was the best armed.

"*Don't* you be tellin' nobody what tuh do! *Don't* you be sayin' shit, boy!"

"We not going no place." Werewolf said it to me, not Lester. I was aware of Firecracker stealthily clocking everyone's place in the room. The four kids looked almost bored. One wore a Walkman, lips moving, now and then uttering some obscene lyric out loud.

We had walked here from Check Point Charlie's. Neither Werewolf nor Firecracker expected anything from me—no finder's fee for hooking me up with a crystal meth connection. It was, to them, a comradely gesture. I was a co-worker they respected, so they were helping me out.

One of the kids had opened the French doors, apparently recognizing Werewolf. Then we got shown in. Lester appeared, and I looked him over and wondered if Sunshine had been getting her meth from him. Wondered how professional this joker in the ludicrous hip-hop clothes might be? Was he the sort that might panic or overreact or be careless? How good was he with an ice pick?

Werewolf introduced me, and I told Lester what I wanted.

"Yo yo, homie! Chill. Wuzza rush, huh?"

He wanted to talk, maybe wanted to look me over first, like Brock at that Decatur bar. Maybe just wanted to bask in his inflated drug lord image, which, after all, meant nothing if no one was there to see it. These four dull-eyed kids didn't seem terribly impressed.

So we had talked, and I managed to understand just enough of his self-crippled English, and seemed after a few minutes to convince him I was "cool." But I hadn't gone to this trouble to make friends or to obtain the crystal meth-amphetamine I was going to fork out ten precious dollars for. I was here for info. So I slid in a question, then another. Did he have a regular supply of meth, so I wouldn't get stuck out? Had he been operating long enough that he was dependable?

"Know about that girl who was killed along the river? She had hold of this *tasty* crystal ..."

I had seen Lester's eyes narrow suddenly. He flicked a small gesture, and one of his kids got up and went to stand by the doors.

I pretended not to notice anything, said casually I needed to pee and walked into the bathroom I'd spotted when we arrived. Made my call on the cell phone, heard a quick ruckus outside the bathroom door, and came out to find everybody on their feet and Lester holding the automatic.

"Ho got iced at the river? Whachu askin' for? Whachu wanta know, huh? *Cops* ask questions 'bout that shit."

"Lester, he wait tables." Werewolf was still arguing for reason.

"Yo, motherfucker! That it? You some fuckin' undercover cop punk thinks he can fuck wi' me? Huh? Yo?" He now put the heavy, slightly cool barrel against my forehead where it pressed my flesh against my skull in a way that would probably leave a ring.

I blinked and blinked, then held my eyes wide, and for that instant the room was very, very still.

"Holy shit!"

My eyes, not my head, shifted sharply. I saw flames.

Lester turned, and the pressure of the bore eased off a bit.

Werewolf and Firecracker moved.

It looked like a couch cushion on fire. The flaming cushion burned from squarely atop the roof of the blue four-door that was parked immediately outside and visible through the front doors' glass. Yellow flame took hold of it, jumping higher and higher as the intensity of the fire increased.

I dropped as Werewolf's big arm swept upward and caught Lester's between the wrist and elbow. The pistol went up, flew out of his grip.

Firecracker's sleek body slammed into the kid standing at the doors who'd called out the alarm and now stood gaping at the fire. The kid rebounded off the doorjamb, blood flecking from his forehead as he started to crumple. The doors flew open under Firecracker's weight.

I did a fast twirl, had my feet under me, heard the automatic thump heavily on the floor behind me as I ran for the exit. I passed the kid wearing the Walkman on my way to the front doors. His lips were still moving, his eyes were watching the scene as dully as they would a Nintendo screen.

My boots hit the sidewalk as the big cushion flared up, burning brighter, smoking and stinking. Behind I heard voices, one of them Lester's ... but no gunshots, and I was very thankful for that. *Very thankful.*

Werewolf and Firecracker ran for Royal. Werewolf's steps hit heavy, hard; Firecracker's thin albino body moved lithely. Running en masse wasn't smart under the circumstances, though, so I turned toward Chartres, toward the river, legs pumping, head low ... my head, that Lester had held a gun to ...

My eyes were wide and looking. Maestro stepped slightly out from the corner. I ran, he caught my pace, and we flew like the wind.

* * *

Excerpt from Bone's Movie Diary:

Who is the more profoundly frightening movie archetype—the homicidal psychopath or the cold-blooded killer? We get all sorts of deranged murderers, from Richard Widmark's pushing-old-wheelchaired-lady-down-the-stairs psycho in 1947's *Kiss of Death*, through Andy Robinson in the original (& only worthwhile) *Dirty Harry*, to Michael Rooker's sickeningly creepy nutcase in *Henry: Portrait of a Serial Killer*, which is so effective it's nearly unwatchable; & stopping at all points along the way. At the spectrum's other end we find Max von Sydow as the morally neutral assassin in *3 Days of the Condor*, Michael Beach's entrancingly calm performance in *One False Move*, Rutger Hauer's sinister & efficient terrorist in *Nighthawks*, etc. To kill in anger, in a fit of passion or just to appease the voices in one's head ... is that more, or less, comforting than those movie villains who go about the business of taking human life without a ripple of emotion, without ego, strictly professional about the matter? I am still contemplating this one.

Chapter 31

Maestro

I did a fast risk-calculation and decided to duck into my place. Bone and I had run along Chartres for half a block, turned onto Madison which is a short, quiet street, then came out on Decatur where we had to slow. We were too visible, what with Café du Monde across the street and the security guards that wandered up and down around the levee wall. We did a brisk pace along Decatur. I didn't have to tell Bone not to look around, to appear casual. I didn't hear any sirens, which meant the fire I'd lit had already been put out. Any fire in the Quarter is treated like a four-alarmer, since the Quarter is a tinderbox waiting for a light. It has already burned twice in its long history and is probably due. Sometimes the age of the buildings here makes me think of the whole place as little more than decorative, aged firewood.

I wanted both of us off the street entirely, which was why I decided to go to my place instead of slipping into a bar. I didn't want the cops or Bone's new playmates dropping in.

Swinging away from the river, I stayed in hyper-alert mode until my gate locked shut behind us and I'd led Bone to my back patio apartment. The smell of jasmine from the bushes hung thick on the hot night air. The lights were out in the building that overlooks my smaller unit. I ushered Bone inside.

I felt a kind of territorial discomfort, realizing it had been a while since I'd had a guest. Bone stood looking at the swords mounted on the front room wall. He looked like he could use a drink, but I don't keep liquor in the place. Drinking at home or alone is too close to an alcoholic's shtick for me. Bone looked like somebody waiting to get the shakes.

"Want a cup of coffee, or some milk?" I asked, playing the host.

"Got any tea—herb tea, no caffeine?"

"Sure." I snapped on the air-conditioning, put on water in my small kitchen, and picked out the most soothing tea I could find. Bone had been through a lot tonight, experiences I'd wager he'd never had before. He seemed to be handling it better than your average citizen would, though.

I changed out of my shirt, wringing wet from our brief run. My heart still pounded in my chest, and I realized I wasn't in the same shape as when I'd taught epée fencing two days a week.

Bone sat on the sofa blinking at nothing. I brought him his tea and took a chair.

"Feel up to telling me all the details?" I sat back and lit a smoke.

He seemed to take that as a cue and lit one of his own. He turned his gaze on me.

"Thanks for getting me out of there," he said heavily.

"I just made the diversion. *You* got you out of there."

"I had help."

"Those two guys who ran out with you?" I asked. "The big black fellow and the guy with the weird white hair?"

"He's an albino. That's Firecracker. Werewolf's a West Indian. They're both cooks where I work."

"Werewolf" and "Firecracker"? And I sometimes thought "Maestro" was a strange handle.

Bone sipped at his tea and told me what had happened. I made sure he didn't see my fingers digging deeper and deeper into the arm of my chair as he explained the heavy risks he'd run tonight. When he was done talking, he ground out his cigarette and sighed.

"That was genius, you know. Setting that cushion or whatever on fire right outside the door. It was the perfect distraction."

Genius, I thought, was stretching it. I had jogged along Chartres and through Jackson Square as fast as I dared, the address Bone had given me during his quick SOS on the cell phone burned into my brain. I didn't have any intel on what I was heading into, and I seriously didn't like that. But Bone in trouble was a drop-everything situation.

I had done a fast shadow pass down Dumaine, had seen Bone and the kid with the gun through the door, and I knew whatever I was going to do had to be now. I couldn't storm the place, not unless I wanted to virtually guarantee Bone a bullet in the face. Then, like *that*, it came together. It was one of those weird preternatural moments where you suddenly know the universe is cooperating with you. I spotted a dirty cushion in the gutter, something the garbage men had missed. I grabbed it, snuck up along behind the parked cars, used my lighter, and hung back. As a bonus from the gods, the cushion was soaked with cheap alcohol and lit up nicely.

Bone yawned, maybe the ginseng taking effect. Maybe he was just coming down off the mortal-jeopardy rush. I had experienced it a few times—well, more than a few. It was powerful and could affect a person in many different ways.

"So I guess this puts Lester on our list," he said. "He certainly didn't seem like the most stable of personalities."

From what Bone had told me, I figured Lester as mostly bluff, and the gun his way of getting people to take him seriously.

"People in the drug trade sometimes get into their own product," I said. I took a last pull on my own cigarette and tossed it in the ashtray. "He might just be paranoid from using too much of it."

"The way Sunshine was killed," Bone said, "was calculated, like you said. Not random. I don't know if this Lester nimrod could get it together enough to carry off anything that premeditated. If he was going to kill somebody, I think it would be spur of the moment."

I nodded. He was actually thinking smart. Maybe some of me was rubbing off on him. I hoped to hell it was enough to keep him from diving into something foolishly dangerous again.

"How about you?" he asked. "What did you do tonight besides saving my bacon?"

I told him what had gone down at the Stage Door. I didn't add that his emergency phone call had interrupted my tailing Jo-Jo to someplace where I might have plied him with a few useful questions. Bone's welfare naturally took precedent, but now that the crisis was over, I permitted myself a little annoyance that I'd lost a valuable trail.

"What do you think about that?" Bone asked. "Makes Jo-Jo look the part of the ladies' man all right."

I pursed my lips. "But being publicly embarrassed by not just one but two women didn't set him off. He looked kind of sad and disgusted by what was happening, but he didn't show any signs of violence at all. That doesn't exactly fit the profile of some guy who would decide to knife Sunshine over a love affair gone bad."

"I guess that's true." Bone shrugged. "Except we know he's already stabbed one woman."

"From what I understand, it was more or less self-defense." Lynch J. Morise had said the girl Jo-Jo had killed with a kitchen knife had tried to stab him with it first.

"Maybe he does all his angry stuff on the inside and lets it out later," Bone suggested.

It was possible. Then again we were faced with a whole lot of "possibles." Way too many for my taste. I very much wanted to winnow out our suspect list.

"Jesus," Bone muttered, shaking his head now. "I keep wondering, what if Sunshine's killer isn't in the Quarter anywhere? What if he's blown town?"

"Then he's out of our range," I said firmly. "We can affect things here, Bone, in the Quarter. It's our turf and we have a special understanding of it. We maybe have some influence and the ability to do something worthwhile. But only here. Only here."

It had come out more wise-old-man-on-the-mountaintop than I'd meant, and Bone looked for a moment as if he were ready to disagree. Then he nodded and said, "Okay, Maestro. I get it. I'm the junior partner, I understand that, but I'm not a kid. I'm not going to lose it if we hit a dead end."

I stood from the chair and crossed the front room to the wide, double-doored closet in which my small altar stands. I didn't know where the sudden impulse to share this rather personal facet of my life had come from, but I went with it. Bone was my friend, my partner in this hunt. He needed to know that he could trust me.

"Bone," I said.

He cocked his head, gave me a funny look. "Yeah?"

"I trust you," I said. I kicked off my shoes, unlocked and then pulled back the sliding doors. I heard Bone's sharp intake of breath behind me as I adjusted the carved fossil-coral statue of Kali on the altar, lit two small candles and a stick of incense. I went to my knees, then bowed down and touched my head to the floor. I rose, straightened back up, and arranged my stiff legs to sit cross-legged before the altar. I took in a deep breath and then let it out slowly. "With our eyes on the horizon," I said, "we do not see what lies at our feet."

The candlelight revealed my treasures: the prayers inscribed on the hanging silk; the laquered *katanakake* stand that held the three sheathed blades; the *tachi* stand that held the long blade upright beside the altar; the crossed, polished staffs behind it; the two stone fu dogs; and the altar itself, with its carefully arranged bits of coral, crystal, silk, wood, and feathers.

"Wow!" Bone's quiet exclamation of wonder didn't surprise me. "Is that ... are *those* what I think they are? Samurai swords? Real ones?"

"Yes," I said. "They're real, and they're old." I touched in turn the blue silk that wrapped each of the rayskin grips (*tsukas*) in the traditional diamond patterns. "This is the *tanto*, the dagger, sometimes used for *seppuku* but also a combat blade. This is the *wakizashi*, the middle-length fighting blade. This is the *katana*, the longer fighting blade. And this," I said as I reached out to touch the last blade, which stood on its own, "is the *tachi*, the cavalry longsword."

I gestured at the staffs that stood crossed over the prayer scroll. "Those are the *baston* and *olisi*, sticks used in the Filipino *eskrima* fighting style. One is made of rattan, the other from a resilient wood known as *kamagong*. The hanging prayer scroll is caligraphed in Tibetian. The statue represents Kali, the Hindu goddess of both death and destruction, as well as creation and rebirth—or, as I like to call her, the four-armed dealer. The incense I get from Mother Mystic's shop, and as for the rest, well, you might just call me a pantheist or an ecumenical. Or maybe I'm just hedging my bets. I've been around a bit and seen a few things, and I've picked up the occasional *objet de arte* along the way. I guess you could look at all this as a kind of a road map."

"Wow," Bone said again. "And you are ... where did you ... what ..." He shook his head as if to clear it. "Maestro, just *who* the hell *are* you?"

I didn't get up, just scooted around to face him, grinned, and said, "Me? I'm just a retired bloodhound who's held onto some of his old tricks." Bone's return smile was forced, but after a moment he nodded his understanding. One didn't normally ask that kind of question of another Quarterite, not even of a friend—not even of a partner.

And what he'd asked—*What and who are you?* That was a good question— too good, because I didn't really have a straight answer. I've followed the path of contemplation—that's Zen Buddhism, to the unenlightened—ever since ... well, for a long time. The old samurai meditation techniques served me well in my old life and my old line of work. The Zen discipline had worked even better in allowing me to accept the life I'd made for myself afterwards—a life lived in a kind of permanent impermanence. Zen, at least for me, has never been about finding the answer or the question, but about the satisfaction offered by the search. Lately, though, the search—if not the hunt—had become no longer enough to satisfy. I needed to find the real question, at least, if not the whole answer.

I'd learned a bit about paganism in the 'Nam, but it was coming to New Orleans that had stirred my interest in it. Or maybe it was my age. Maybe it was the growing vacuum I seemed to find myself living within. Whatever, it seemed to make more and more sense to me to acknowledge the world's basic energies, to recognize the old gods that were so much easier to digest than the modern one. Earth, soil, rock, animals ... that all these things and more had spirits was something I was starting to take for granted.

Or maybe, just maybe, I was once again tracking the wrong prey down a blind alley. So be it—the search goes on, and sometime, someday, the hunter doesn't come home from the hill.

A little bashfully—a strange feeling for me—I looked back at Bone, who still sat on the sofa. "I was going to say a prayer for our success," I said. "Care to join me?"

He looked at the altar then, at the polished pebbles, feathers, and bits of bones. He regarded me for a few seconds, and then he dug into a pocket of his jeans and pulled out a string of beads that had a little wooden cross attached to it.

"I'm afraid you're barking up the wrong faith with me, Maestro." He smiled gently and put away his rosary.

The kid was full of surprises, I thought with mild dismay, and even some amusement.

"Can I ask you a question?" he said.

"You can always ask. It's the answer I don't guarantee."

He was staring at me. Okay. It was going to be one of those questions.

"I don't know quite how to say this, but ..." He frowned, then gave a small shake of his head. "All this." He gestured at my shrine, at the swords on the katanakake and the blades on the walls, but he seemed to mean more than that. "The way you live. It's ... it's all focused on this defense/offense hang-up you have. Almost to the exclusion of everything else. Is it worth it? I mean, is it really necessary?"

I stared back a moment. He almost winced, as if he regretted asking, but had to anyway. I looked away, thinking, then grimaced.

"Okay, Bone," I said finally. "That's an honest question. It deserves an honest answer. Just give me a second."

I got up, extinguished the incense, and closed the closet doors, then sat down in the chair across from him. I lit another cigarette and tried to organize my thoughts into words. A lot of the things I say I say often, like bar chitchat, which is almost like playing back a recording. For this, I wanted to make sure what I said wouldn't be incoherent, repetitive babble.

"Hang with me on this," I said, "'cause it's going to sound like the long way around the brier patch."

I took another drag on my cigarette and blew out the smoke.

"One of my deeply felt, seldom-stated beliefs is that there's a trend, a plague, loose in this country. It might be worldwide, but I haven't traveled that much ... recently ... and I can only speak for here. I think of it as a creeping loss of self-worth. More and more, the individual feels insignificant and impotent. That whatever he does, it doesn't make a difference. That's one of the reasons why people don't vote, and why they dog it at their jobs. Who cares? What difference does it make? It's a poison, and it's spreading."

I looked him in the eye.

"To be honest with you, you may be dead-on right. I could be living my life dodging shadows. Preparing for battle against enemies who could really give a rat's ass about me, who forgot about me a long time ago. Exaggerating my own importance in the real scheme of things."

I showed him my teeth.

"But if I accept that, if *we* accept that, then what are we? I'm a paranoid idiot with delusions of grandeur, and you're a waiter, and neither of us make any difference at all."

I let the smile drop.

Bone stared at me for a long, thoughtful moment, then drained his tea mug and set it down decisively on the table beside him. He nodded, just once.

Bone was yawning, looking beat, as I walked him to the door. I watched as he caught a cab back to his apartment.

I checked the clock. I wasn't ready to call it a night just yet.

* * *

As it turned out, I probably should have. I slid around the corner where the Stage Door is, creeping like a U-boat avoiding a big mine, but didn't see the Juggernaut inside, or Jo-Jo, though the stray dog was back, begging for scraps. I followed the now very cold trail as best I could. I hit some of Bourbon Street's tourist trap clubs, thinking here were fresh women, something Jo-Jo might be actively seeking right now. They had a drink minimum to keep out the pickpockets and the people who just wanted to use the rest rooms. I ended up having about one too many, and saw nothing of Jo-Jo. Neither did I spy anybody who could be the crucifix-wearing early thirty-something guy I was now always automatically on the lookout for.

After the pounding noise of the clubs and the ready displays of drunk college-kid idiocy, I figured I could use one more than one too many. I hit the Calf and found the place nearly empty. Padre arched an eyebrow at me as he delivered my Irish.

"You going to need the place tonight?" he asked quietly. "Where's Bone?"

"Home." I took a swallow. "I'm just going to have this and stagger home myself. It's been a ... long night."

"You and your new friend have fun?"

I looked at him blankly.

Padre chuckled. "Tucson Tony saw you and the big bald guy shooting stick at the Stage Door. Said you were both there together yesterday too."

I sighed darkly. "You know how it is, Padre. The only thing worse than dealing with a big, ugly, biker-type ex-con named Bubba is dealing with a big, ugly, biker-type ex-con named Bubba who *really* likes you!"

"I thought he was called Juggernaut."

"Six of one ..." I didn't like people connecting me up with Jugger, but I supposed it was inevitable.

The last few customers shuffled out and Padre started to lock up. I took a final hefty swallow of whiskey and stood. "You'll be happy to know," I said, "that those phones of yours have already come in handy."

"Glad to hear it." He looked very pleased by that. "If there's anything I can do ... "

"... I'll let you know," I finished, shook his hand, and went home to lie down before I fell down.

On the way there I met up with the police.

Chapter 32

Bone

Alex was waiting for me at my apartment. She'd removed the blond wig, which had left her own short, dark hair flattened, but she still wore the tattered tee-shirt and tight jeans.

"Bone, I thought you'd be in earlier. Are you okay?" She moved to hold me.

"No, I'm not okay," I snapped. "I spent part of the evening with a fucking *pistol* pointed at my *forehead!*" I proceeded to relay, in detail the events of my evening, not softening anything. I think I wanted her to understand how very dangerous our little endeavor could be. I wanted to scare her.

"Bone! Mixing with drug dealers isn't safe! You could have been killed!" She gripped my hands tightly enough to cut off circulation.

"And what about you?" I said, pulling my hands away. "What were you doing at Check Point Charlie's? Like that was safe?"

"I was doing the same thing you were," she snapped back. "Getting information. I figured if he liked Sunshine, he'd like me. I figured I could get closer than you could."

I didn't tell her how unpleasantly intimate it had gotten between Dunk and me in that grubby toilet. I said, "I thought we agreed you were going to go to work tonight while I handled this."

I felt the tension, and I didn't like it, not at all. Booboo peeked into the living room, her green eyes ticking back and forth between us, looking for all the world like a child watching her parents argue. It wasn't really a fight, though. Alex and I didn't have any fight in us for each other. And, I realized with the sort of philosophical clarity that usually comes to me at odd moments, we never would.

"*We* didn't agree to anything." Her eyes glowed fiercely. "Besides, what have you got from 'handling this' besides nearly getting killed?"

She waited, glaring, while I fumbled for some gem of progress I could parade before her. But the only really positive event of the evening had been my talk with Maestro—not something I could share.

"Well," she said, her frown turning into a grin, "I got this!" She triumphantly flashed a napkin with something scrawled on it. "Dunk's address— which we already knew—complete with an invitation to a hook-up at his favorite bar."

It was meaningful. There was no denying it. But something must have shown in my face at the thought of her going anywhere close to him again. "Alex ..."

"Oh, Bone!" She wrapped her arms around me, snuggled in close to me. My lips brushed her forehead. "I was perfectly safe," she said. "I knew you were there."

I stood in her arms, still worried—but feeling quite a bit of pride as well. She had done well. But I realized it was going to be harder having her in on the hunt than I had suspected. I could handle risking myself. But could I handle risking Alex? As I held her, burying my face in her hair, I understood that the choice wasn't mine to make.

"Well, before we make use of that invitation, let me see what I can get, OK?" I told her what I had in mind for our next move. We talked about it, picking back and forth over it. Eventually she agreed, pulling me into bed and ending the discussion with her mouth on mine. Eventually, we slept.

She wanted in on it, and I wanted and needed her help, but I didn't need it for the next phase. Tonight's job I could handle. What might—*might*—follow later on, *that* I could not do alone. It was wait and see, one event dependent on the outcome of the previous one, the dominos going down in order or not at all.

The hunt. This was what it was, and I thought I was truly beginning to understand it. It wasn't an escapade. It wasn't thrilling in the sustained, glamorous Hollywood meaning of the word. This, then, was work. Dogged and sometimes pointless, with as many dead-ends as dangers. I had started it in a state of furious vengefulness, indignant that my Sunshine had been killed and unable—absolutely unable—to swallow the shock and horror of that. Did I still feel that thirst for revenge? Most certainly. But it had cooled and hardened into something more enduring.

Later, before she left, Alex stopped at the doorway, grabbed a handful of my hair, pulled my head down, and kissed me hard. "Be careful."

"I will," I promised. I hated having to lie to her.

"Call me if you need me." She shouldered her knapsack, her eyes boring into mine. She turned and started down the stairs, tossing back, "Call me if anything goes wrong!" She reached the bottom and went out the gate into the early evening.

I got ready, and there wasn't much to that. I had made a composed space in my mind—had made it long ago, actually, when I'd probably needed it most. I entered it deliberately now, sinking, going cold as I sank. It was probably something like the "cold/fight" state Maestro had mentioned several times, usually referring to that sword-fighting group of his. But it had other applications. I imagined he had often adopted this mental state back in his working days with the Outfit ... or whatever else he'd done before that. I could see how it would be helpful.

When the sun finally faded, I made sure Booboo's bowls were full before I headed out. I wore my black jeans and a long-sleeved dark cotton shirt. I didn't have far to walk. I stayed on Burgundy, aware of each passing car, seeing the sidewalks deserted ahead and hoping that would hold, just another minute, at least until I reached Cabrini Playground.

At the park fence I slowed, did a casual sweep-around, then did a more thorough one. I moved a few steps further along, out of the worst glare of the nearest streetlight. Then, gathered and focused, I grabbed the ironwork bars between the pillars, stepped up on the brick footing, and silently heaved myself at the top rail. I kicked air at one misstep, gripped and pulled and was up, across the top, and risked the muffled sound of my dropping to the ground on the other side. I froze where I landed, huddled low and still—listening. Eventually, I allowed myself to move.

Naturally, I stayed to the shadows, and naturally, I headed toward the best cover, a vantage I had already reconnoitered. While most of the park is wide open and grassy for the dogs whose owners bring them here to run and romp, it does have a small sort of gazebo and a few trees. I picked a tree in deep shadow not too far off Barracks Street, leaned myself comfortably against the trunk, and waited. And watched. Because *this* was what a hunt was like.

I was effectively invisible in my dark clothes, shadowed from the street. I had a good line of sight across Barracks to the front of Sunshine's old apartment building, the place where Dunk had lived with her, now without her. I presumed the rent was paid to the end of the month. After that, Dunk, the freeloading scuzz-bag, would have to come up with the bread or vacate.

I settled in even further, in the night, hearing birds rustling above me in the branches, the occasional vehicle passing. I remained calm and composed, and even went without the cigarette my system was telling me it desperately needed. Waited. Watched.

The vigil would last however long it lasted.

* * *

Which turned out to be something like an hour and a half. Ever stand and do nothing but watch a door for an hour and a half? Is it boring? Sure. But I

didn't get bored. It wasn't a matter of concentrating. I was, after all, merely waiting to see if and when Dunk emerged. That didn't take a lot of mental diligence.
Stand, stare. I was in the zone, though. I shifted my stance every so often, felt
blood flow to one leg or the other. I wiped the sweat that accumulated in my
eyebrows. I picked an ant off my neck.

I could have, I think, done that for hours on end, without flagging, because
in a very odd and unfamiliar way it was fun. I was accomplishing something
and knew it. Even if Dunk never appeared, even if he was already gone from the
apartment and I was completely wasting my time, I was still doing the right, logical, practical thing. Holding up my end of the hunt. Maestro might be working
with a nonprofessional, but he could bank on my persistence, commitment, and
stamina. I wondered if he knew that.

Fortunately, Dunk did appear after that hour and a half, stepping out onto
Barracks wearing those same big camouflage pants and this time a dirty yellow
T-shirt instead of a dirty white one. He started strolling toward the river.

I crossed the grass fast, low and quiet. Dunk crossed Dauphine, staying on
Barracks. I froze, waited for a cab to pass, then went over the fence. He was half
a block ahead and didn't turn as my boots touched the sidewalk. I slipped across
the street, following him from the other side.

I kept it very casual, like when Maestro and I had walked Decatur last
night, after I'd escaped Lester's place. I called no attention to myself, did nothing
suspicious. I lit a cigarette, and that was truly wonderful.

Dunk stayed on Barracks all the way to Decatur, and I kept the same distance and kept him in sight. Accosting him on the street wasn't the way to go, I
knew. If he went in a bar somewhere, then I might have a chance at approaching
him yet again, with the memories of our encounters at the apartment door and
Check Point's hopefully erased by pot and alcohol. I realized that by now he
might recognize me no matter what. By tailing him, I still might learn something. There was no telling. But I couldn't afford to leave any stones unturned.
I was, after all, trying to solve a murder case that the police had not. That was an
ambitious undertaking for someone who was "just a waiter." And I didn't want
Alex to meet with him if I could prevent it by gaining the information on my
own.

He turned onto Decatur, and I hurried to catch up. I eased up at the corner,
worrying Dunk had been aware of me all the way from the park, hadn't let on,
was waiting around that corner with a bottle he meant to smash over my head.

But he was heading in the direction of the Square. Decatur Street was its
usual lively, scummy self. Still half a block ahead, Dunk waved a few hellos to

the beer-swilling urchins and wandering hustlers that the street has in abundance. I had to make a quick greeting or two myself. I ducked casually to the other side of the street once more, kept pace.

Dunk did go in somewhere, finally, when he reached the next intersection. He entered the restaurant where I work.

I slowed, stopped. I lit another smoke to ease off my nicotine fit and leaned back against a dented drainpipe, trying to look—and probably succeeding, since it's not that difficult—like a typical Decatur loiterer.

Kitty-cornered across the intersection I looked in on the restaurant's interior through the big front windows. It was strange to find myself looking *in*, but I didn't dwell on it. It wasn't like I missed the fucking job. Judith was in there, and I didn't need a close-up view to see she was in her normal about-to-go-nova hysterical work state. I didn't recognize the other waiter—blond, young. Maybe Nicki's replacement.

This being a weekend night, the shift included a bartender. I spotted red-haired Randy behind the restaurant's L-shaped bar, wearing his Irish ancestry for all to see. One of our better bartenders, he took very little shit from anybody. Dunk grabbed a stool, and Randy delivered him a draft beer a minute later. Dunk paid, probably didn't tip.

I shifted a few feet down from the drainpipe for a better line of sight. Randy leaned his arms on the bar in a way that squared his already fairly-sizable shoulders. I couldn't make out his face. Dunk was talking to him. Something in the way Randy had his head slightly cocked told me he was running low on patience. What could Dunk be saying to him? Well, from what I'd seen of Dunk at Check Point Charlie's, it wouldn't take much for the grubby little shit to annoy or offend anybody.

It took Dunk about thirty more seconds. Abruptly, Randy snatched away his pint glass, poured the beer into a go-cup, plonked it on the bar top and pointed at the door. I had seen Randy bodily throw people out on three different occasions. He had a flair for it.

Dunk, demonstrating wisdom or cowardice, didn't appear to give Randy any sass about it. He took his plastic cup and amscrayed.

I turned away, pretended to be fumbling in my pockets for something, and watched him from the corner of my eye. He stood a moment, looked up and down Decatur, then shrugged and started walking again. He had a lazy sort of walk, loose-limbed.

He headed back the way he'd come. I stayed on his tail, giving him almost a full block lead this time. Back down Barracks. He finished his beer and tossed the go-cup over his shoulder. A little further on he kicked at a cat that was sniffing around the sidewalk. It hissed hard at him, then scurried away through an alley gate.

What had Chanel said at Molly's? Something to the effect that even if Dunk hadn't killed Sunshine, he would still be worth hurting for the greater good. It was tough to find an argument against that.

I stayed on the other side of Dauphine and watched him reenter his apartment building. I'd been hoping for more. I had lurked in that adjacent park an hour and a half with thoughts of tracking Dunk someplace where I could approach him and squeeze him somehow for info, to fix for sure whether or not he was responsible for Sunshine's killing. At the least I had hoped I might manage to put myself where I could eavesdrop on him, maybe pick up something revealing, incriminating, or even exonerating. Instead, he'd just gone out for a beer.

And that, of course, didn't make sense in and of itself. Why go all the way up to a Decatur Street eatery for a single beer, particularly when Decatur has so many bars? If he wanted a beer, he could pick up a six-pack closer at Verti Mart, the corner deli on Royal.

My choices were to go back up Decatur to the restaurant to find out what Dunk had been doing there, or to resume my lookout in the park, hoping he would come out again tonight.

Investigation seemed better than surveillance, more expedient, certainly more active.

I went up Governor Nicholls, and it was odd to walk into the place, not there to punch the clock and tie on my apron. I'd been off—what? Two days, three? My third day, and I felt like a stranger here, like I wasn't a waiter anymore. Christ, didn't I wish.

Judith had feta cheese salad dressing sprayed across the front of her black blouse and looked like she could use a healthy dose of Thorazine, but she found time to glare malevolently at me anyway. I went to the bar, where only a few people were sitting, and took the same stool Dunk had occupied.

"Bone ..." Randy came over immediately. "Well, here's some synchronicity. What can I get you?"

"Coffee, please."

I lit a smoke and pulled over an ashtray, realizing I was yet again running out of cigarettes. Much more of this, I thought grimly, and I would have to dip into the bank account for money I shouldn't be spending.

When Randy came back with my cup, I asked, "What did you mean?"

"There was this guy—some punk kid—sitting right where you're sitting as a matter of fact—he was just in here, like ten, fifteen minutes ago. He was asking about you."

The coffee cup stopped on the way to my lips. "Asking how?"

"By name. Bone. 'Does a dude named Bone work here?' And he described you."

I set the cup back on its saucer. "What did you tell him?" My voice sounded leaden to me.

Randy shrugged. "Asked him why he wanted to know. Y'know, I'm not going to go talking to anybody about people I know without finding out what's what first. You know how we do things in the Quarter."

"I do."

"This punk started getting lippy." Randy shook his red-haired head. "Uh-uh. Not on my watch. I gave him one more chance to be nice. He wanted to know if you worked here, where you lived. That was that. He was also being a pushy little prick about it, so that was *really* that. I almost wish he'd tried something after that. I would've enjoyed breaking his jaw."

Yep, that was Dunk. A tireless ray of sunshine.

Sunshine ...

I squelched the thought.

"Well, I appreciate you giving him the blow-off." I lifted my cup to Randy, finally took a swallow of coffee, my brain chugging overtime.

"No worries, Bone. Any ideas who the punk is?"

"None." I gestured casually. "Hell, whatever. It's not going to keep me awake."

Randy smiled and nodded. He had large teeth and anachronistically long sideburns that nonetheless looked good on him.

"Hey, is it true you're taking some time off work?"

"Yeah. In fact," I glanced around, "I want to get out of here before Dallas spots me."

"Don't worry, he's in the kitchen tonight."

"Werewolf and Firecracker on?" I wanted to see the pair, wanted to seriously thank them for helping me get out of that drug dealers' den on Dumaine alive. They had led me there, but it was my own fault that things had taken a nasty turn after that with that Lester character.

"No. Spike and whuzizname—Carl. They're cooking, so naturally everything's been fucked up all night. Why you taking time off? Everything okay?"

I took another swallow of coffee. It was a fresh pot, tasty. "Everything's fine. I was just due for a breather."

"Shit. Ain't we all? Too bad I can't afford one ..."

I dropped two singles on the bar top and made to climb off my barstool.

Randy put his elbows on the counter, leaned toward me, face serious. "I do want you to know, though, Bone, that I don't believe a fucking word they're saying. About you."

"Which fucking word would that be?" I was already busy trying to absorb the implications of Dunk's coming here, to my place of work, and asking for me, *by name*. What was Randy talking about? Like I needed any more worries.

His voice lowered. "That shit some of the morons are mouthing ... that you, y'know, had something to do with that girl getting stabbed last week or sometime. I know crap when I hear it, and whenever somebody starts up with it, I tell 'em they're talking out their ass."

"I appreciate that too," I said. I wanted to scream out: *She was my wife! My best friend! How could I ever hurt her?* But they didn't know—as if knowing would change anything. And I did have something to do with her death. I brought her here, to New Orleans. And I didn't stop her from self-destructing once she got here.

Behind me, suddenly, a plate hit the floor. The diners, like they do everywhere because they think it's clever and funny, broke into a round of applause. I didn't need to look to know it was Judith.

"That dumb bitch," Randy muttered, confirming it.

I hit the street, reaching for the cell phone as if I had always carried one. I had to talk to Maestro. This was bad.

* * *

Excerpt from Bone's Movie Diary:

> *The French Connection*—a Best Picture winner for 1971 that deserved it. In fact, the Oscars got it right a lot in the '70s, a tremendous era of filmmaking that isn't exaggerated in hindsight. A large percentage of the best movies ever made came out of that decade. *French Connection* is a near-perfect example of that peculiar grainy grittiness of a good '70s flick. The grimness, the realism—these combine to seize the viewer, & in the better, darker films the experience can be harrowing. In *French Connection* we are subjected to the obsessive police hunt—by Gene Hackman (also

Oscar winner) and Roy Scheider—of drug smugglers in a grimy, trashy, indifferent New York City. What's amazing is that the picture sustains intense interest even during the workaday, lackluster business of stake-outs and tailing. Granted, there's that spectacular car chase, but even that is intrinsically 1970ish. It's spare, it's believable, & it's totally exhilarating. (If this movie were made today—probably as a so-called summer "blockbuster"—that car chase would no doubt provoke enough explosions & destruction of property to make 9-11 seem tame.) That one can watch Hackman stand in a cold doorway while the man he's following eats in a restaurant & *still* be gripped, is testimony to the film's power. Appraisals: *French Connection* * * *; the 1970s as a filmmaking era ... we'll never see the like again.

Chapter 33

Maestro

For the first time, I wondered if I was getting too old to be doing this.

That was an ugly thought, particularly since I'd woken up with a touch of the "French Quarter flu." I may drink on a regular basis, but I hardly ever drink so much I feel it the next day. Doing my usual afternoon roll-out today, though, I'd found myself a bit woozy, and the room wobbled some. My own fault. I *had* had that one too many last night. Or was it two ... ?

I didn't let myself wallow. I took a cold wake-up shower, popped a handful of vitamins, and drank down half a carton of orange juice. I started to feel human. Even so, I still felt the lingering urge to kick myself over last night. That had been some true adrenaline-pumping action, effecting that rescue of Bone from that drug-dealer apartment on Dumaine. Maybe I'd needed those extra drinks. I shook my head, dismissing that as lame. Needing drinks was bad. If I couldn't handle the world without alcohol, I was in trouble, and would do something about it—dry out, take a long sabbatical from the bars. If I couldn't handle this hunt without alcohol, I was in *serious* trouble.

I had to keep sharp. It wasn't just my life at risk. It was Bone's, too. I had to be there to back him up, watch his back, and whatever else I could do to keep him safe.

But ... was I too old for this?

Overindulging the booze was bad enough. Letting myself get stopped by the cops, though, that was almost disgraceful.

I'd left the Fatted Calf last night and had cut across Royal, toward my apartment. I could feel each of the drinks I'd had, and was now only looking forward to falling into my bed. As it turned out, I was doing a bit of a stumble-stagger. That's bad for several reasons. One, it clues the predators you're at least a little toasty. Muggers are opportunists, and one of the best mugging opportunities in the Quarter is the lone, wandering drunk.

It also provides an open invitation to the cops, if they're looking to kill some time on their shift by processing a "drunk in public" back at the station house.

I must have been just bobbing along in my muzzy little world, not paying any real attention to my surroundings. That was pretty disturbing right there. Being alert in general, and on the street in specific, is a practice I take very seriously.

I was completely unaware of the car cruising alongside me until the moment the side-spot lit up in my face. Let me tell you, something like that will sober you up fast! I went very still, turning just enough to see the police cruiser and the two cops inside. I consciously relaxed my posture. My hands were at my sides and I left them there, loose. I turned toward the blinding light and the grim-faced cop shining it in my face.

"What're you up to tonight?" he asked.

"I'm going home."

"Where d'you live?"

I told him. There was nothing in my stance, or the tone of my voice, or any muscle in my face that was in any way insolent, sassy, or belligerent. You don't talk to law enforcement folk like that anywhere, definitely not in the Quarter. Alcohol makes idiots feel invincible, and when they mouth off to the NOPD they can very easily find themselves guests at OPP.

Naturally, I prefer not to talk to cops at all. This was the first time since I had relocated to the Quarter from Detroit that the police had stopped me on the street. This was the end of a ten-year winning streak. *Damn.*

I had very definitely *not* forgotten about my last encounter with Sneaky Pete, and how the cops, through him, might have been setting me up just to take me down. Exaggerated misgiving or not, it was on my mind now.

The other cop got out of the cruiser on the passenger side, and walked around to me. From the way he moved, he obviously wasn't expecting trouble from me, but was also ready for anything.

"Let's see the ID," he said.

I produced it. Another first I wasn't happy about. I showed my false ID to virtually no one. Though Padre wasn't in the business anymore, he was still able to manufacture the fake Louisiana state identity cards whenever I needed a "renewal." Since he'd already worked all that computer voodoo that had made him famous in his peculiar trade, my false but convincing records were still in all the official systems.

The cop returned to the cruiser to run my name. He certainly wasn't going to find any outstanding warrants. The one behind the spotlight looked like he was thinking idly about frisking me. I wasn't carrying any of my true "fighting knives" but still had enough bladed weaponry on me to do real mayhem. These two officers might not appreciate that.

I blinked in the spotlight's glare and waited. Finally, the light went out, and he waved me over to the cruiser. His partner passed him the ID, and he held it out to me.

"Get home safe now, hear," he said.

"I will. Thank you, officer."

After that, I walked with absolute precision to my gate, with nary a stumble or a hitch. Once safe inside, I crawled into bed and pulled the sheet over my head.

Waking up, I really felt too old. If I hadn't killed that nephew in that bar, and was still in the Outfit, would I be too old to be doing the work? I didn't think so. Guys that work for my old "company" don't usually retire. They're made of tough, nasty stuff. I'd known knee-cappers and strongarm types that were still active into their sixties.

Just out of practice, that's all, I decided. I'd made one slip-up. It wasn't good, but it wasn't the end of the world either. Spending the day tut-tutting at myself wouldn't help.

That evening I went out to dinner. I put on duds even nattier than those I had worn to the Royal Sonesta's bar. I needed to be a bit dressed up for the Court of Two Sisters. It's a smart, swank place, but while being shown to a table for one, I recognized two people on the staff from the Quarter's various pool teams.

I hadn't wanted to come here, or at least it hadn't been my first choice of actions. I had hoped to corral Jo-Jo over drinks somewhere, but I was already starting to feel that this job had gone on too long. Maybe Bone's eagerness was affecting me. That would be funny. *I* was supposed to be the one influencing *him.*

It was Sunday but the restaurant had only a sparse crowd. They were society folk and the few high-class tourists we see in the summer months. I brought along a book to read, an Updike novel just so I would blend. I forewent a pre-dinner cocktail, opting for more orange juice. Slowly turning pages, I watched the room ... until Jo-Jo appeared.

He looked smart in the green jacket, white shirt, and black slacks—that's the same color-schemed getups that Pat O.'s waiters wear. His dark, curly hair was precisely styled, and he moved with that ballet-like grace that could so easily translate into fighting skills.

I ordered light. I put in my bookmark when my waiter brought out my meal. I'd recognized him on the way in but had waited till now to make my play.

"Excuse me ... didn't you used to shoot on the Silencers?"

He was in his late twenties, a little on the plump side, his bearing precise and formal. "Why yes I did. Sir ... ?"

"It's me—Maestro," I said, offering him a chummy smile. "From the Snake Plisskens. You clobbered us two sessions back in nine ball during the playoffs. You're Vincent, right?"

His starched manner relaxed visibly. "Maestro! Oh yeah. I remember that. We got knocked out of the running right after you, though."

"Them's the breaks. I haven't seen you on the tables in a while. How come?"

Vincent shrugged. "I got married. My wife—she doesn't like me 'wasting my time on kids' games' when I could be accomplishing something worthwhile. Damned if I know what *that* is, though."

That sounded like a pretty much pre-doomed marriage, but I of course didn't say so.

"Too bad," I sympathized. "I'm scouting hard for next session. I've got three shooters dropping out. You know how that always happens in bunches. You sure I couldn't interest you in a slot? You always had a good stick as I recall." From what he had just said about his new bride, I wasn't worried about him taking up my offer.

"Can't, Maestro," Vincent said, not looking happy about it.

"How about him?" I nodded across the plush dining room to where Jo-Jo was hovering over another table. This one was full of middle-aged women who were giggling like schoolgirls while Jo-Jo practically pranced and preened for them. You use what you've got to juice up your tips, I guess. "I've heard talk out of the Stage Door that he's a wicked stick."

Vincent turned and glanced. "I don't know about that. He's sure supposed to be a 'wicked stick' in other departments, though. 'Least that's what I've heard from a waitress or two around here."

I chuckled. "Think I could talk to him? The team's hurting."

He shrugged. "I guess."

I stood. "I'll meet him back by the rest room. Don't want your manager thinking he's hustling one of your tables."

I crossed the dining room and waited a moment by the sandbox door, lighting a cigarette. Jo-Jo appeared a minute later.

He blinked a little confusedly at me. "'Maestro,' is it?"

I smiled. "Yes. I'm sorry to bug you while you're working. I'll make it very fast. How would you like to shoot on a French Quarter league pool team? Namely mine."

His handsome, olive-toned face looked even more confused.

I explained, "I heard at the Stage Door you know the business end of cue. A couple of people said you hang out there a lot." I wasn't surprised he didn't remember seeing me there the other night. I'd done nothing to stand out, and he'd had his hands full with women problems.

"Well, I do," he admitted, "but I haven't been shooting lately. I've been ... out of town awhile. I used to be a hell of a stick, though, even if I do say so."

I nodded. Fact was, just about every shooter in the Quarter would describe him or herself that way.

"Well, our team has official practice every Sunday night, down at Fahey's. It starts at midnight. First, can you make it on Sundays?" I took a drag on my cigarette, and held the smoke, waiting.

Jo-Jo shook his head. "Sundays I'm tending bar from midnight to eight at Flanagan's."

I blew out a plume. "Every Sunday?"

"For a month now. Look, I appreciate you thinking of me for your team— Maestro, was it? But I don't really have time for pool."

"No harm, no foul. Sorry to trouble you. Thanks for hearing me out."

He nodded and went into the back. I ditched the cigarette, returned to the dining room, ate, paid, and headed out. Vincent said he'd throw any good shooters he knew my way.

Back at home, I opened the phone book. I knew the guy who managed Flanagan's on St. Philip. He was there. I gave him a song and dance, saying how I thought I had seen Hector behind the bar when I was passing by in a cab last Sunday at around midnight. Boris, the manager, told me I'd seen Jo-Jo, who he had hired a month ago and was working out well. Hector, so far as Boris knew, was still up in Angola. I thanked him, promised to stop by sometime soon, and hung up.

That put a big fat black line through Jo-Jo's name.

Sunshine's murder had taken place last Sunday. She'd come by the Calf around ten-thirty or eleven. Her body had been discovered a little before two o'clock in the morning. She couldn't have been lying there very long.

Damn. Jo-Jo had been prime suspect material. I sighed. Maybe I'd let my inclinations toward nailing the murder to him affect my judgment.

I changed clothes to more common Quarter apparel and went back out. Night had fallen. I went by the Stage Door, but the Juggernaut wasn't there. The stray dog was, though. That figured. Now that I'd lost my best suspect, I couldn't find the secondary one that usually clung to me like a leech. Rather than get into a funk about it, though, I fed the stray some leftovers I'd brought from my dinner at Two Sisters for that purpose—I'm a pushover for homeless critters, they're so much more grateful for handouts than people are—and focused my head. The

Stage Door had a certain rough quality about it. Probably Jugger was drawn to that, since it more or less matched his own coarse character. There are all sorts of bars in the Quarter, of course, but only a few that cater specifically toward the type of clientele among which the Juggernaut might be included.

I headed off toward the nearest one. This was how a hunt was supposed to go, I reminded myself doggedly. Gather all possible suspects, eliminate them as quickly as you can, examine those you've got left. We were doing that, Bone and I. Even so, I had the creeping sense that time was running out. Every day that we didn't bag Sunshine's killer was one more day he might disappear from the Quarter, from the city ... if he weren't long gone already. That feeling, coupled with my uneasy doubts from earlier about my age and abilities, left me almost queasy.

After a half hour of making the rounds, I was back at square one. I hadn't had to go in anyplace, since the Juggernaut stood out in any crowd and I had only to glance in a bar's door from the street to see he wasn't in any of the places I'd looked.

By now, a drink was starting to sound good, despite last night's overindulgence. I knew I wouldn't be doing *that* again soon, though. I was a stone's throw from the Stage Door, thought what the hell, and went in.

There was Jugger. That figured too.

He gave me the usual "hi-ho-good-to-see-you" treatment. He held a partially eaten Lucky Dog in one hand and a pool cue in the other. He wore those same overalls, head-stomping boots, and funky necklace. I offered to buy him a drink this time. It was time I got down to business with Jugger. By hook or by crook, I wanted to know if this big, violent, annoying guy was a viable suspect or not.

I handed him his beer and lifted my Irish, tried to think of an appropriate toast, then decided to do without one.

Jugger smacked his lips, "Aahhh! Thanks, Maestro. How about we rack 'em?"

"Mind if we sit and talk a minute? I just woke up. Still waiting for the head to clear."

He shrugged gigantic shoulders and we grabbed a table. Before I could say another word, he said, "Say, Maestro, do you know anybody named 'Bone'? Skinny guy, long hair? You seen him around maybe?" His big chunky face was set in neutral.

For those few seconds, I waited for him to move, and was ready to draw a blade on him. But he just sat there across the small circular table from me, waiting for my answer.

Meanwhile, the bar phone had rung, and the bartender—a guy named Daniel—called to me, "Hey, Maestro! Someone on the phone for you, man."

"Excuse me," I said to Jugger. It wouldn't be Bone. He would have used the cellular phone. As I stood up from the table the realization struck me cold: I'd left my own cell phone back at the apartment! I had probably simply forgotten it when I'd changed clothes. Careful not to let anything show on my face, I walked over to the bar.

Daniel passed me the receiver over the bar top. "Thanks. Hello?"

"Maestro!" said a gruff rumbling voice. "The red alert perimeter's been tripped. Your friend just turned up at Cosimo's—silver crucifix an' all. Yankee an' a couple of his pals are holdin' the guy there. I told the network to call me if he turned up, an' I've been callin' 'round lookin' for you. You interested in askin' him some questions?"

"You bet I am, Bear."

"Good. I'll be meetin' you there."

I turned back to the table where the Juggernaut was still waiting for an answer to his question: *Do you know anybody named "Bone"?*

Chapter 34

Bone

"No, I haven't seen him." Over the phone I could hear juke and rattling glasses behind Padre's voice. "But I know where he's heading, if he's not already there—Cosimo's."

I knew the place; had never been in. "What's he doing there?"

Padre told me.

Maestro hadn't picked up. I'd speed-dialed twice, listening to successive chirping rings; then punched his regular home phone, got his answering machine. I left a *where are you?* message, and he didn't pick up while I was leaving it. It seemed crucial I report to Maestro that Dunk was now apparently hunting *me*. It might somehow figure in with his own dealings with Jo-Jo or the Juggernaut. Anyway, he liked to operate with a lot of info. This was info, and important. Dunk tracking me meant—had to mean—that Dunk was onto me. That put a kind of dizzy thrill of fear into me, a quality of emotion I couldn't recall feeling before. It was entirely within the realm of possibility that Dunk's intent was to kill me. That was an awesome, dreadful, staggering thought.

Now, what Padre was telling me about Maestro ...

Somebody was hunting him, too? And why in hell hadn't he told me?

I kept the cell phone to my ear, listening intently. I'd stepped around the corner, off Decatur, for privacy.

"So ... you were part of this 'red alert perimeter'?"

"Yep. Ah ... hold on a minute, Bone. Yes, that's three seventy-five, sweetie, thanks." I had dialed the Calf's number from memory, had caught Padre in the middle of his shift. Addressing me again, he said, "The Bear set it up. Do you know the Bear? It's a bartender thing, Bone. People coming into our sanctuaries, asking unwarranted questions about someone like Maestro—someone well-respected, liked? No way. I admit I would've thought he'd tell you about it, though."

Probably figured I had enough on my mind, I thought. And yet, that just served to piss me off. Now I was worried about him. Was this how he felt about me?

"If I wasn't on shift," he went on, "I'd be hightailing for Cosimo's right now."

"But you don't know if this Bear guy's tracked him down yet, right? I mean, he was still looking for Maestro when he rang you?"

"That's right." Someone in the background was saying something loudly about either Manhattan or *a* Manhattan.

"Well, thanks for the update, Padre. It's so nice to be in the loop."

"Look, Bone, if you're heading down there, please be careful. And help out Maestro if he needs it. We want him back in one piece. That was the whole point of this lookout thing."

I said solemnly, "I'll do whatever I can."

I clicked the phone dead.

"*Yo!*" About two paces behind me ...

I was about a quarter of the way down the block from Decatur. On Decatur there were places still open, cars still passing, people, and more light than there was here. Was this all it took? You step ten yards off the beaten path and you're fair game for the muggers? What right did New Orleans have calling itself a modern city? Maybe it was *too* modern was the problem ...

Footsteps now, coming up fast. I stayed still that extra half-heartbeat, then tried to turn. I was caught by fingers gripping around the back of my neck, another hand grabbing the wrist of my hand that held the phone, and I was being pushed, up against someone's wrought-iron alleyway gate, further out of the light.

Goddamnit! I didn't have time for this shit!

I put up my shoulder so that my head didn't hit the bars. Whoever was on me wasn't that strong. He'd caught me off balance enough to move me. I moved slightly, experimentally, and discovered he wouldn't be able to hold my arm still.

"*Yo*, get dude's phone!" It was the voice of that initial "Yo," meaning the one holding my neck was a second person.

For some reason, in this moment, under these circumstances, *that* pissed me off more than anything. Two against one. Not a rational thought, but powerful.

The cell phone with the faux walnut housing, a gift from Padre, was torn out of my right hand, which consequently freed my arm completely.

"*Yo*, see what dude's got in his pockets!"

That was the mastermind of the caper again. His enforcer started patting at my jeans pockets. I was carrying three dollars after shelling out two singles for the coffee Randy had poured me. He found it.

I was still facing away from the pair, pressed against the gate. Behind, they were conferring, and the grip on my neck eased a little; and unfortunately I had no clue what these two were packing—knives, heat? It wouldn't do to pivot suddenly around, drive the squared tip of my boot up into the balls of one, dig my fingers into the eyes of the other. No, wouldn't do at all. Way too reckless. *Goddamnit.*

"*Yo*, where's the resta it?" asked Yo, and his confederate patted me down again from behind, found something of interest in the high pocket of the dark blue long-sleeved shirt I was wearing.

My left hand came up without any order from the reasonable part of my mind, and closed over those searching fingers, squeezing, grinding the knuckles together.

"You're not getting my smokes."

It wasn't my voice, but it had come from my mouth. I turned, pushing off from the gate's bars, but I did it slowly, ominously. The other hand didn't stay on my neck as I rounded, a look of I-don't-know-what on my face. I held on to the hand that had been going for my cigarettes.

I had had it.

Two white kids, looking at me wide-eyed. I wasn't behaving in any of the expected or endorsed manners: I wasn't cooperating; I wasn't pulling a weapon; I wasn't showing them my best kung fu moves from a self-defense class. I was calling the game. It was over.

Given the situation and a purely impartial view, I was very likely demonstrating the behavior most conducive toward getting myself seriously injured or killed.

It had nothing to do with my cigarettes, understand.

Neither kid had a knife or gun in hand. They were dressed in those over-elaborate, mass-manufactured "street" clothes—fashions that maybe had come out of authentic American ghettos once upon a time, but that had since been inevitably co-opted, absorbed into the vast money-making industry and sold to the kids that knew less about "street" life than I did. And ... something familiar about these two ...

"*Yo,*" said Yo, a look of stunned surprised on his young mook face, "it's *dude!*"

Last time I had seen him he'd been wearing a Walkman, lips moving to rap lyrics. The kid whose fingers I was still squeezing—and who was starting to looked pained by it—was one of the other background extras from Lester's apartment on Dumaine Street. Maybe this was what they did on their nights off from dealing drugs.

I tightened my grip, the bones crushing nicely together.

"*Yo*, we should, like, take him back with us. The boss'll wanta ..."

And that got me laughing. It wasn't my laugh. It was what you might hear atop a carnival haunted house coming from a painted clown with a wide mouth, filled with teeth.

"The 'boss'?" I said eventually. They were actually backing up a step, the kid whose fingers I gripped stretching out his arm. It was—to me, in that almost unearthly moment—immeasurably funny. "The *boss?*" What did they think this was? Some old-time gangster flick? Did they think Cagney or Edward G. Robinson was waiting for them back at the "hideout," as in: *Gee, bawhz, we brung yuh back dis mug with us 'cause we figured youse would wanta see him.*

They wouldn't understand the joke. They hadn't laughed along with me. In fact, they looked quite spooked.

"Not me," I told them. "Not tonight."

I let go of the kid's fingers, and stood there, and waited, and they turned and did a fast jog up to Decatur, turning, and gone. I hadn't tried to get the cell phone or my three bucks back. I had already pushed my luck so far beyond the pale it was preposterous.

I had done something stupid—and immensely satisfying.

I paused to light a cigarette, take one deep drag, and then I headed fast for Cosimo's.

* * *

Excerpt from Bone's Movie Diary:

Westerns are all we've got that are ours. As a genre they are peculiarly American, because it is a culturally idiosyncratic historical age that these films are ostensibly chronicling. & hell, who doesn't love a gunslinging Western? From the rousing—*Rio Bravo, Magnificent Seven*—to the intensely thoughtful—*High Noon*, John Wayne's last bow *The Shootist* (& if you think the Duke couldn't act, sit your ass down & watch this one). Naturally many Westerns are derivative, ripping off Kurosawa flicks, each other & any other available source. But that doesn't diminish their strength and worthiness. Where would we be without *My Darling Clementine, The Man Who Shot Liberty Valance* & *Red River*? I don't want to know. We don't get many good

ones anymore, sadly. Westerns have gone the way of
the musical. I confess an admiration for the truly surreal *The Quick & the Dead* from 1995, but of course it's
Clint Eastwood's somber *Unforgiven* that garners the
most modern attention. A good picture & one of the
few Best Picture Oscar winners from the 1990s that
one can actually stomach. [Note to self: must evis-
cerate the Academy's choices from the '90s. *Dances
With Wolves* over *GoodFellas*? *Forrest Gump* over *Quiz
Show* & *Pulp Fiction*—and *Ed Wood* for that matter?]
Anyway, *Unforgiven* has several extraordinary, elevat-
ing moments. One of them is near the film's end where
Eastwood is holding a gun on a saloon full of armed
men. He's one against I don't know how many. Any
one of his opponents could draw on him & objectively
have a fighting chance. 2, 3 or all, & Clint is a bullet-
riddled corpse. Yet Eastwood, demonstrating intense
cool & homicidal toughness, holds everyone at bay
with his single weapon. The tension is terrific. The
scene works, however, because it remains thoroughly
believable. Appraisal: *Unforgiven* * * * ½

Chapter 35

Maestro

To my horror, I found the Juggernaut was going to come along, and he wasn't going to take no for an answer.

I had already ditched him twice in our budding "relationship"—once when I'd snuck out when he was in the sandbox, and again on the night Bone had called in his SOS. He wasn't going to let it happen a third time, and had that "stubborn child" manner about him again. I told him I had a date waiting for me, but even that didn't deflect him. Stuffing the remains of his Lucky Dog into one of his pockets, he chugged the remains of his beer and invited himself along. I didn't have time to argue. My mysterious stalker was waiting for me at Cosimo's. People had gone to trouble on my behalf, especially the Bear, and it wouldn't be right to leave them hanging.

To Jugger's earlier question about my knowing anybody named "Bone" I finally said, with a casual shrug, "Never heard the name. But there's lots of weird handles around."

If I hadn't forgotten my goddamn cell phone, I thought darkly, I could step into the rest room for a minute of privacy and buzz Bone. That Jugger was looking for him by name had me very worried. I couldn't duck back to my place and grab it, though, since I couldn't have Jugger following me to my address.

So we set out on foot for Cosimo's, me and my "buddy."

As we left the Stage Door, the stray dog immediately tagged along, probably smelling the food in Jugger's pocket. Jugger slowed, trying to shoo the dog away, but I kept a steady pace, not looking back, hoping he might actually stop to feed the dog so I could lose him.

Behind me I heard the dog bark once, followed by a series of very loud "yi-yi-yi" yelps that ended abruptly. I spun around in time to see Jugger holding the dog by the throat, its body hanging like a limp rag from his massive fist. Stunned, I watched him shake it once, then toss the lifeless body to the side of the street. Brushing his hands on his overalls he hurried to catch up. I had to turn away quickly to keep him from seeing the horror on my face, while trying not to be sick. Any doubts that this man might be capable of murder had just been erased. It took all my concentration to keep walking, pretending that nothing unusual had happened, that we were still pals. Silently, I said a small prayer for the dog while Jugger kept up a steady spiel. I had to listen still one more time to the story about the guy he'd beaten that had "messed with his bitch," and how he was going to take care of the guy who sold him out, once and for all. At this point I could hum the tune by heart. The walk seemed to take forever.

Cosimo's is nice and out of the way. It's on Burgundy and Governor Nicholls, one of the quietest intersections in the Quarter. By the time we got there I decided it might actually be good that the Juggernaut was with me. Here at least he wouldn't be asking around about Bone. Whatever that was about, it couldn't be anything good. I would find out tonight the things I needed to know about Jugger. I *would*.

As we turned down Governor Nicholls Street I saw the Bear's old rusty Impala parked out in front of the corner bar. We crossed the street and went inside.

There was no music playing. What looked to be a couple of regulars sat on stools at the bar, folks who would mind their own business. Yankee stood behind the bar. He was an oak pillar of a man, tall and muscular with long hair.

"Maestro," he waved, "glad you made it." His eyes flicked slightly to the Juggernaut coming in behind me.

"He's with me," I said, then rolled my eyes to show what I really meant.

Yankee—what he was doing with that nickname in the South I didn't know—nodded, understanding I had someone in tow I couldn't shake for some reason.

"Where's our friend?" I asked quietly, but none of the regulars were even glancing my way. Even Jugger's presence didn't faze them.

"'Round back," Yankee indicated with a tilt of his head. "You want a Tully Dew?"

"Pass," I said. "He'll take a draft."

Jugger with his beer in hand followed me around to the bar's rear. It's a clean, comfortable space with armchairs, a couch, and a pool table too poor for any league team to use.

The Bear stepped forward, doing the same eye-flick at Jugger. Behind him two beefy types were standing on either side of a clean-cut guy in his early thirties. He wore a neat but cheap collared shirt, and where the collar was open a silver crucifix hung on a chain. His eyes were wide and he looked plenty scared and confused.

I studied him for almost a full silent minute. I didn't recognize him.

"He came in here askin' for you," the Bear said.

"This is your 'date'?" Jugger's voice rumbled behind me. I'd almost forgotten about him.

I glanced back. "Just some business I've got to take care of." I definitely didn't want him around for whatever this was going to turn out to be, but I couldn't see any way out of it.

"Maestro ... ?" the clean-cut guy asked hesitantly.

A while back I'd sent this anonymous person a message through the grapevine, to the effect that *I* was looking for *him*. I had hoped that would scare him off. It hadn't.

"Okay," I looked him over. "Who are you?"

He blinked, looking startled. "It's me, Maestro. Me! Barracuda!"

My turn to blink and look confused. The name registered, and I dug in mental files for info. Then I had it and I took a harder, closer look at him.

"It's been a while, kiddo. What've you been up to?"

At a silent wave from the Bear, the two beefy guys were no longer sandwiching him. "Been a while" was understating it, I thought. I hadn't seen Barracuda in six or seven years, and hadn't known him particularly well. Back then, he'd been just another twenty-something hanging around the Quarter bars. I couldn't even remember what he'd done for a living.

He smiled now, modestly. In the old days Barracuda had had blue, shoulder-length hair and a huge assortment of earrings in his ears. He'd worn a black leather jacket and drank like a fish.

"Well, I was in Ohio for quite a while," he said in that same shy tone of voice. "I ... did time. I did a whole lot of stupid things, and I got caught. I deserved to get caught."

"What does this have to do with me?" I asked. *Barracuda?* What the hell was going on? Whatever it was, I wanted it done with. I didn't need any distractions right now.

He smiled again. "I wanted to thank you."

"For?"

"You don't remember?"

"Evidently not," I said.

"There was this one night. It was a typical night for me, drinking and debauchery. I started a bar fight over a woman. *You* stepped in. You grabbed me, marched me into the bathroom, and stuck my head in a sink of cold water. Then you talked to me. You told me to straighten up, clean up my act. If I didn't, you said, I was going to end up in jail or dead."

I fished for the memory but it simply wasn't there. I could imagine it happening, though, easily. I confess to a weakness for trying to steer the younger generation away from trouble. It hardly ever works.

Barracuda went on, "You were right, of course. I left New Orleans and went up to Ohio, but my corrupt behavior didn't change. I got myself sent to jail."

I frowned. "And you came all the way back down here to thank me? For what? I gave you a talking to and it didn't take."

"But you *tried*. I wanted to say 'thank you.' And I didn't come all the way back here just for you. I'm on my way to Orlando, Florida. I'm taking the bus. I've got a job waiting for me. I've been in town for this past week, staying with a family Uptown. I'm leaving soon, so it's wonderful that I got to see you. I didn't know if you still went to the bars, and I couldn't remember which ones were yours, but I tried different ones when I could make it down to the French Quarter."

The Bear glanced at me, and there was laughter in his eyes. I understood his amusement. After all the bother of his red alert perimeter, to find out it had all started over something this harmless.

I sagged slightly.

"So," I said, conversationally now, "you've got your life back together. That's nice." And it was.

He smiled with a little more confidence. "Yes, through the kindness of my fellow man—men like you, Maestro, and the Bible network family I've been staying with—and through the guidance of my Savior, the Lord Jesus Christ, I am now fit to live among good people."

He put his hand out. I shook it.

"Thank you, Maestro."

"You're welcome, Barracuda."

"It's Michael Francis Norton now."

"You're welcome, Michael Francis Norton."

With that, he walked away.

The Bear finally chuckled out loud. The Juggernaut stepped forward. He had drained his beer. "That was weird, huh? Hey, look, they got a table here. Maestro, I'll rack."

At that moment I spotted Bone coming around from the front of the bar. I didn't bother wondering what he was doing here. As Jugger moved to slot quarters into the table, I waved Bone curtly to a halt. He hitched up, frowning, opening his mouth to say something. Urgently I mouthed the word "Calf" at him, and waved him away desperately, before Jugger saw him.

Bone hesitated, only a second.

"Hey, Bone!" one of the guys at the bar called out. "How's it going?" It figured that one of the regulars knew him.

"Bone?" Jugger repeated in a low threatening growl that rumbled through his entire body. He straightened, turned, and spotted Bone. Bone's eyes got very big as the man-mountain started for him. He immediately did his own about-face, racing for the door.

Juggernaut moved surprisingly fast for his size. I had to stop him, but he was across the room—too far away for me to reach in time.

The Bear had seen my pantomime and realized something was going on. I never saw him move, but a cue stick appeared in his hands and somehow managed to end up between Jugger's feet. Tangled in the three-and-a-half foot stick, the giant's feet stopped moving forward, but his upper body continued until he toppled onto the floor like a felled redwood.

Bear and I immediately rushed to his side, "helping" him up while making certain he stayed down. I glanced at the door to be sure Bone had managed his escape. Jugger finally managed to untangle himself from the now-shattered cue stick and regain his footing, despite our assistance. He rushed for the front door and hesitated. I joined him there, relieved that I could see no sign of Bone.

"Which way did he go?" Jugger growled.

"The skinny guy? I think he went that way." I helpfully pointed the opposite direction from the way Bone had run.

"I gotta go, Maestro. Rain check for that game?"

"Sure. Tell you what, I'll meet you at the Stage Door tomorrow night. How's ten sound? I'll buy the first round." I smiled.

He smiled back in that gruesome way of his.

"That sounds great, Maestro. Gotta go." Jugger turned and lumbered off down the street in the wrong direction.

I had to find out if Bone had any idea why Jugger was hunting him. I didn't. At least Bone was safe—for the moment. I exited Cosimo's, shaking hands with Yankee on the way out. The Bear stood out front, smoking a cigarette.

"Nice work with the cue-stick."

"Not really. I only sank the eight-ball." Bear dropped his cigarette to the sidewalk, grinding it under his heel. "Can I drop you somewhere, Maestro?"

"I'm heading for the Calf."

He nodded at the rusty Impala. "Hop in."

Before I did, I looked square at the Bear. "I suppose you're wondering about it—what I'm doing hanging out with the Juggernaut."

He spread his hands. "Ain't none of my never-mind."

I took a breath, deciding. "There's something going on, Bear. I'd like your help. How about you come on to the Calf with me?"

He met my eyes. "You bet, Maestro. Let's get goin'."

Chapter 36

Bone

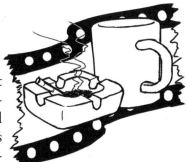

I made it to the Calf, out of breath, but without any unwanted company. Padre spotted me a rummincoke, even though I'd said it wasn't necessary. I had learned that it was best to accept Padre's kindnesses without argument. He had seen me arrive and, without question, delivered up the drink along with his no-nonsense attitude. I needed that drink.

Still breathing hard, I tossed my fought-for smokes onto the booth's Formica tabletop and was digging one out when Maestro entered. He had the sandy-haired fellow wearing the black beret in tow. I remembered seeing him before, bartending at that Decatur joint where I'd met Brock. I was much more concerned about the titan in the denim overalls. The image of that creature—large shaven head, thick neck, massive body of menacing muscle—coming after me was burned into my brain. Him, I was *very* curious about—especially how he knew my name and why he had come after me.

The bartender accompanying Maestro knew Padre, and they did that wrist-on-wrist handshake over the bar top. Then Maestro procured cocktails, and they came my way.

I'd taken the side of the booth facing the Calf's front door, and I admit to a mild enjoyment at seeing Maestro hesitate, then slide a bit uneasily onto the opposite bench. The guy in the beret remained standing, waiting with an air I can't quite name—cool vigilance maybe. Whatever, I had the odd impression he was aware of where *every*one was in the bar.

I blew out smoke.

"Bone, this is the Bear. Bear, Bone."

We shook, and it was a simple howdy handshake—but Maestro obviously had a reason for introducing him, for inviting him to the table. The Bear sat, apparently not sharing Maestro's discomfort about an exposed back.

"The Bear's coming in on the hunt, Bone." Maestro took a pull on his drink.

"Really now?"

"Trust me on it."

The Bear's drink was Jack Daniel's and water.

"I do trust you, Maestro." I clicked my gaze over to him. "Do you trust *me?*"

He tried for that blank, bland stare, but he seemed slightly flustered at the moment, and his annoyance came across. "What's that supposed to mean?"

"Red alert perimeter. I understand you set that up, Bear. You've had somebody out looking for you, Maestro—maybe *hunting* you—for a *week*? You don't tell me. You're just going to take care of it, you and some friends—"

"Look, I'm sorry if you feel left out ..."

"—and not worry that what affects you might affect me. Think about what we're doing, Maestro, what we're involved in. You could call these combat conditions, even. If there's something way out of the ordinary happening in your life, doesn't it occur that it might just have something to do with the out-of-the-ordinary activities we're engaged in?"

The Bear took a studied sip of his cocktail. Maestro let out what sounded like a beleaguered sigh.

"Okay, all right—you've got a point." He got one of his thin black cigarettes going. "As it turns out, though, it's nothing. Pure red herring. Some kid who's suddenly found Jesus and thought I'd done him a good turn once. It had nothing at all to do with the hunt."

"That's good news, anyway," I said. I knew, truly, that the better part of my anger was coming from worrying about Maestro's safety, and that anger was drying up, fast. "It wasn't that behemoth with the shaved scalp, was it?"

"No," Maestro said pointedly. "That, my friend, was the Juggernaut."

"He must have weighed a lot as a baby for his mother to know to name him that."

The Bear showed his teeth in a chuckle at that. It was a low, rich sound.

"I'd say Jugger moves into our number one slot for suspects," Maestro said, blowing smoke, "now that Jo-Jo's been scratched."

We were all speaking at low volume. It wasn't yet midnight, early, and the customers in the Calf were mostly tourists, but far enough from our booth.

"Jo-Jo? Why?"

He explained. I nodded, admiring his fancy footwork in shaking out the information at the Court of Two Sisters.

"I probably should've rung you with it earlier, but I, ah, left my phone at home." He looked embarrassed and pissed off at once; and tried to hide both reactions.

It explained why I hadn't been able to reach him earlier. "No worries there," I said, and told him about losing my own phone.

"Shit," he muttered.

"Yes. Hell of a night, isn't it?"

"Not over yet," the Bear put in.

"And we still don't know who the fuck we're after," I said, the anger flaring again, for a different, better reason.

Padre, seeing to his customers, had come down to the end of the bar. He threw a bartender's questioning look our way. Since I was facing, I shook my head. We were all okay on our drinks. I took a good swallow of mine now. Padre had made it strong.

"Well," Maestro said, "it's also the matter of who's after *us*. Okay, tonight we found out my guy's nothing. But why is the Juggernaut interested in you?"

"Hell if I know. I was hoping you could tell me."

He related how the Juggernaut asked him about me by name, hunting me right up until I almost conveniently delivered myself to him.

Something cold and oily closed around my heart.

"Well ..."

And I told Maestro about Dunk showing up at my restaurant, also asking questions. His cigarette froze halfway to his lips.

"This isn't good," he said stonily. "This isn't good."

"Are they ..."

"Working together? I don't know. How do we write it off as coincidence? How do we connect those two up if we don't?" Maestro ground out the cigarette, hard, stabbing, rattling the ashtray. "Dunk and the Juggernaut together? How does that make sense?"

"Bone," the Bear said as he leaned slightly toward me, "any ideas how Dunk might've made you? How he might know that you've been on him?"

I laid out what I'd done in the way of tailing and investigating Dunk over the past few days. Maybe this Bear would have some insight. He certainly came across as sharp enough. I realized I wasn't truly put out about Maestro bringing him on board without telling me ahead of time. Hell, the more the merrier. And the more—hopefully—the sooner we'd be at the end of the hunt. The end. Where we would find Sunshine's killer ... or when the hunt was done, and we had failed.

When I got to the part about Dunk offering to let me suck his cock in Check Point's toilet, Maestro actually looked aghast.

I shrugged. "I've had stranger things happen to me in French Quarter rest rooms."

From his leery expression I figured he didn't want to hear what that might be.

I finished up. "So, see, Dunk's actually laid eyes on me twice. And the second time, he remembered the first."

"He's askin' for you by name, though," the Bear said thoughtfully over the brim of his Jack Daniel's. "He knows where you work. Wants to know more—where you live. He's tryin' to zero in. Any ideas how he got your name?"

"Could've asked around at Check Point's after I left."

"Do you hang there a lot?" asked Maestro. "Lot of people there that know you?"

I shrugged again. "It's not a regular stop for me, no. But I only work a couple of blocks away, serve a lot of Decatur regulars. If Dunk went to the trouble of asking ... eventually, probably, he could find out my name from somebody. I mean, c'mon—it's the *Quarter.*"

Which was supposed to be our turf, and it was, but that wasn't supposed to work against us. I didn't voice the gloomy thought. I wished suddenly that Alex were here at the table, next to me. We could use her viewpoint, her quick thinking. I could use her hand in mine, soft and strong and steadfast. I took another big belt off my rummincoke.

The three of us sat there quiet a moment. You couldn't hear the thoughts, but the outflow of mental energy was palpable—minds ticking over the events, the facts, the details, the guesses. What was going through my head was starting to feel overheated, the thoughts like machine parts that might get dangerously warm soon.

I'm being hunted. I thought about rebuking myself for tipping my hand, for letting that slimy shit Dunk get wind of me, but I didn't see the point. I hadn't fucked up in any serious way. In fact, for an amateur, for a waiter playing at being a hunter and a vigilante, I'd done good enough to be proud. It was, of course, just a gosh-darned shame that nothing had come of it.

As to how the Juggernaut—who I'd now seen for myself, and who looked more like a Ray Harryhausen special effects monstrosity than a human—had learned my name, I had no clue.

Connect up Dunk and Juggernaut, as Maestro had said: How?

Good fucking question.

"Jesus wept."

I focused in on Maestro. Across from me his features—normally rigidly managed—had gone slack.

"What've you got?" I asked. The Bear had turned to look.

"I think ... I've got him." Maestro drew himself together, and for once it was a visible process. His emotions were churning nearer the surface tonight than I had ever seen them do. "Dig this: Jugger—I've been hanging with him a couple of days now, right? We're *pals.* He thinks so anyway. He's told me a few times now about the assault that put him behind bars. He says he beat the piss out of some guy around New Year's because the guy was 'messing with his bitch'!" He caught himself as his voice rose, did a quick furtive look-around. No one but Padre seemed aware we were in the bar.

The Bear nodded. "Right. His boy toy was hooked up with somebody else when he got back out. That's what makes him so unpleasant to be 'round. *One of the things*, anyway." He eyed Maestro closely. "You came reconnin' me for intelligence 'bout recent ex-cons. I told you all this the other night. You coulda just asked, y'know."

"I know. Didn't want to go bringing in anybody unnecessarily." Maestro was eager to get on with it. "*Listen.* What if *Dunk* is Jugger's 'bitch'?"

That brought a heavy beat of silence to the table.

"Bone, it was what Alex said." He said to Bear, "A close friend of Bone and Sunshine—she suggested a few days ago that maybe the Juggernaut was bisexual. We were trying to link him up to Sunshine in some sort of love affair gone bad. Knowing Sunshine, it was the most workable theory."

I felt a far distant pang. The hurt was still there, waiting for me.

"What if, though—like you said, Bear—the Jugger's strictly into guys, and it's Dunk who's bisexual?" Maestro looked back at us expectantly.

"Boy toy." My face felt numb, but I felt my lips moving. "Boy toy ... hooked up with someone else ... maybe *moved in* with someone else. While Juggernaut was locked up. Moved in ... with Sunshine. Dunk was living with her."

"And Jugger'd gone in for an assault rap for poundin' some guy who was messin' with his boyfriend—and you think the boyfriend was this Dunk character?" The Bear tilted his bereted head.

Dunk, bisexual? He would hardly be the only individual in the Quarter that swung both ways. And there was that little scene in Check Point's rest room. And ...

"Chanel," I said suddenly. "Sunshine's coworker. She knew Dunk. She kept referring to him as a 'little faggot.' I thought ... but—"

Maestro's palm slapped the table, jumping the ashtray. This time a head or two turned, saw nothing interesting in our booth, turned away.

Maestro's breathing got loud and even for a moment.

"I've got him. *We've* got him. I really think we've got him."

I realized my palms were damp.

"At the Stage Door," Maestro said, "after that deal with Jo-Jo and the two girls, Jugger said, let me see ..." His eyes wandered up toward the ceiling. "Something like, 'I wouldn't take shit like that from any woman.' Then it was,

'The last bitch that got in my face didn't walk away from it.' Something very much like that. Jugger likes to talk about his old fights, and I'd pretty much tuned him out. I thought ... I thought 'bitch' meant one of his boyfriends. I wasn't listening close. There's only so much of his crap you can listen to."

The last bitch ...

His eyes came down from the ceiling, met mine, and the moment went still.

"He meant Sunshine."

It took me a few seconds to realize Maestro had said it, not me.

There it was.

"How should we confirm it?" the Bear asked quietly.

* * *

We were parked midway between Dauphine and Bourbon, Barracks Street laid out mostly quiet ahead. The interior of the Bear's white-being-eaten-by-rust Impala smelled like cigarette smoke and old upholstery. I was in back, and we were all slung low in our seats, just dark, unmoving lumps to anybody passing. The Bear had produced a pair of binoculars from the glove compartment. They sat on the dash, which had lots of old-style dials and knobs. The car was a relic.

An hour went by, then two, then three. By the time the sky started turning pale, we were fairly certain we'd struck out. Just before we decided to call it, Dunk showed up, coming up from Burgundy. He was alone. We waited until he let himself in.

"Dunk must have gone over to Jugger's place." Maestro whispered. "And we don't know where he lives."

I groaned. "Which means that we're no closer to the end of this. We still can't be sure of the connection, and they're still hunting me."

We waited two or three minutes, then the Bear hit the ignition. We all needed to be somewhere where we could talk—all of us. Me, Maestro, Alex, the Bear, and even Padre. We had decisions and plans to make.

And even though I despised the idea, Alex was going to get her date with Dunk.

* * *

Excerpt from Bone's Movie Diary:

> The top 5 all-time great screen villains in descend-
> ing order are as follows. 5) The shark in *Jaws*. Yes,

that rubbery, often laughably fake-looking mechanical beastie that terrorizes first a New England beach town, then Richard Dreyfuss, Roy Scheider & Robert Shaw (brilliant) on a boat. Why? Because that shark is rarely seen, but is *always* there, hunting, mindless/ cunning, hungry/murderous. Terrifying. 4) Dennis Hopper in *Blue Velvet*. An obvious pick, & Hopper plays homicidal madman at the drop of a hat. So, why? As Frank Booth, Hopper is a sicko's sicko—depraved, sadistic, drug-addicted. But he's frightening in the role because all his degenerate emotions are there on his face for everyone to see. He hides nothing at all. He is nakedly insane & lethally dangerous. [Note: nothing else about this movie stands out. It's dead in the water until Hopper shows up. David Lynch has done much better.] 3) The leader of the Blue Meanies in *Yellow Submarine*. A cartoon character? Why? Listen to that overstrung, quivery, edge-of-psychotic-episode voice—ranging from an eerily gentle cooing to seething shrieking. He so plainly *enjoys* being evil, is aware of his nature & revels in it. 2) Robert Mitchum in the original *Cape Fear*. (Some might argue for Mitchum in *Night of the Hunter*. Good picture, but he hams up his part.) In *Cape Fear* (don't even get me started on Scorsese's 1991 remake & Robert De Niro's overwrought performance in taking on the Mitchum role) he's an ex-con out for revenge against Gregory Peck, the lawyer who "betrayed" him. Why is Mitchum frightening? Because he's like a force of nature. He can't be reasoned with or bought off or made to show mercy. He's like that schoolyard bully that's going to pound you come recess, & there's not a damn thing you can do about it, except fight back on his terms ... & the odds aren't good. 1) ... drum roll ... Margaret Hamilton in *Wizard of Oz*. Why? Please. Is there *any* movie character more deliciously petrifying than the Wicked Witch of the West? You see this film as a kid, & it sticks with you for the rest of your life. That witchy cackle, the green skin, the pointed hat & nose ... chills, absolute chills.

Chapter 37

Maestro

The next day I awoke early, well before my usual in-the-afternoon roll-out. Not surprising. My nerves are steadier than most, but I'm not immune to them.

I headed out into the unaccustomed glare and took a casual stroll along the streets surrounding the Stage Door. Everything looked clean. By which I mean no streets closed for some sewer or construction project hitherto unknown. That's the kind of unexpected complication that can screw up a perfectly good setup job. From now until I decided the operation was a go or no go, we would all maintain full readiness. Once we knew for certain that our suspects were guilty—or innocent—one call would either put the plan in action, or call it off.

Make no mistake in this. What I had in mind was nothing like a fair showdown. I had no intention of facing the Juggernaut in an "honorable" duel. I wanted better odds than that, *much* better. This wasn't chivalry. This was a hit.

I had a lot in my favor, not the least of which was that Jugger thought I was on his side. If Jugger proved to be guilty, I'd be happy to do a double-cross. Being Jugger's "friend" these past couple of days had been a soiling experience. It would be gratifying to use that friendship as the means of his destruction.

I was slated to meet Jugger at ten tonight at the Stage Door. But before that, Alex planned to use her invitation to meet with Dunk. Since Dunk knew Bone, but had never met me, I would be Alex's back-up. None of this seemed to sit well with Bone, but he realized we had no better options. Alex and Bone seemed certain they could get Dunk to admit his relationship with Jugger. After that, Dunk was Bone's project.

Since I was out, I swung through a deli and bought a ham sandwich. Then I stopped by one of the Quarter's New Age shops, one where I didn't know the owners or any of the counter help, to buy a brand new deck of Waite tarot cards, probably the most commonly used deck today.

"Are you Maestro?" the woman at the counter asked casually as she rang up my purchase.

Her question stopped me in my tracks. I knew I had never been in her store before, and I had certainly never met her.

"Why?"

"Well, if you are him, I'm supposed to give you a message." She blinked and gave me a big-eyed, questioning look.

"Which is?" I still didn't volunteer anything.

"Which is that Mother Mystic needs to speak with you right away. She says it's really important."

"So how did she know I would come here?" I felt very uncomfortable with the thought that my "anonymous" purchase could be tracked even before I made it.

"She didn't," she said with a grin. "She's good, but not that good. All of us—tarot readers, new age shops, occult stores, psychics—were asked to watch for you and give you the word if we saw you. It's kind of a network we have."

It made sense. If the bartenders had their network, why not the new age folk as well? I looked at the cards I had just purchased, wondering if I should put them back and start over.

As if reading my mind, the girl said, "All purchases are confidential. And I can never remember anybody who comes in my store." She winked, bagged the cards and handed them to me. "Just in case it matters."

I left with the cards, wondering how psychic some of these folks really were. It didn't take me long to duck up Bourbon to Marie Laveau's House of Voodoo. I found Mother Mystic there, in the back room, waiting for me.

"Maestro! My message reached you." She gestured for me to sit and gathered the large folds of her caftan into her lap.

"It did."

"That person—the one I mentioned to you who wanted me to do black magic for him? He called again. He insists we do the ritual tonight. Demanded it. Tonight, or I might not make it to tomorrow. His language was foul, and he promised I would envy one of my chickens if I did not do as he wished."

Mystic leaned toward me. "I tried to discourage him. I told him that such a ritual is too risky and usually fails. When done wrong it can come back on you with horrible consequences. It will only work if it is done on the exact spot where someone has died a recent and violent death. I told him the *loa* need to drink the blood of such past violence for the power he requires. This is not true, of course," she said and waved her hand dismissively, "but I think to myself, this will end it. I know of no such place in the Quarter."

She leaned back and sighed. "But it did not stop this man. He said to me ..." she dropped her voice low, mimicking a deep male baritone, "'No problem. I have the perfect spot. Less than a week old, too.' Then he ordered me to meet him there, tonight."

That was disturbing news. "Sounds like a real nut case, definitely someone you should avoid. So why are you telling me?"

"Because his 'perfect spot' is on the north end of the Moonwalk."

I went cold.

"Is that not where your friend died?"

I nodded. Even I didn't know the exact spot where Sunshine had died. Only the police would know that—and her murderer.

"That is what I feared. How could he know that spot, unless he knew of your friend's murder? That is why I sent for you."

How indeed. "Did you tell the cops?"

Mother Mystic shrugged. "They will do nothing until there is proof. All I have is a voice on the phone. Until I meet him, there is no proof."

"Meet him!" I slapped the table. "You're honestly not thinking of keeping this appointment?"

She patted my hand, her eyes sad. "There is no choice in this for me. Last night, a voodoo doll from the Museum appeared on my door, pinned with an ice-pick. He knows where I live. He knows what I look like. I only know his voice. I have to face him. End this now."

"So you're going to do his ritual?"

"No. He wants someone to die, someone he cannot reach. I will die before I sully myself with such an abomination." She made a hand gesture, a sign of protection, and her eyes sparkled with ferocity. "But I will not die helpless in the dark. I will make him face me, and make him face the wrath of the *loa* if he takes my life."

"When are you supposed to meet him?"

"Around ten-thirty tonight."

Suddenly the evening was getting very complicated. I tried to talk Mystic out of going, pointed out the stupidity of meeting a man she already knew to be a psycho, and possibly a killer. But she proved determined. I almost told her about our plans, but stopped. Involving her would only endanger her further, and I had no proof that her psycho and our killer were linked. I wanted to promise her that I would protect her—that I would get this guy for her. But I knew I couldn't make a promise I might not be able to keep.

On the way out of the House of Voodoo, I noticed some very familiar necklaces hanging from the shelves. They looked exactly like the bird claw Jugger always wore around his neck.

"Mystic, just out of curiosity, what kind of necklace is that?" I pointed to one of the claws.

"Oh, those are dried chicken feet. They are considered good for luck and protection by those who follow *Vodun*."

That solved the question of Jugger knowing anything about voodoo. The deck continued to stack against him. But I needed to be sure. I needed to see who came to the Moonwalk tonight. I was supposed to meet Jugger at the same time at the Stage Door. If he weren't Mystic's stalker, he would probably wait for me at the bar. Even if he were, it wouldn't prove him guilty of the murder, but it would definitely prove he knew way too much to be a casual bystander.

I took all my goodies home, ate my sandwich, and called the Bear and Bone to warn them of the latest developments. I wanted them ready if we needed to move tonight. I knew the Bear was reliable. I also knew he would have preferred more of a starring role in the operation. But, fact was, I had helped start this whole thing originally, along with Bone. It was basically our fight. I wouldn't expose the Bear, who was my friend, to more danger than I could rightfully deal out to him. He was already out on a limb as it was.

I told Bone that he would have to take over backup for Alex in order for me to cover both the Moonwalk and the meet with Jugger. Since Dunk knew Bone by sight, this would be a challenge. He would have to stay low and take precautions. He agreed.

Then I got down to work.

First, I opened up the deck of tarot cards, spread them out, and, using a pair of tweezers, selected one and eased it into an envelope. The rest of the deck, along with the box and receipt, went into the trash for later disposal.

Then I went once more to my bureau drawer and my knife collection.

Selection didn't take long this time, as I had already mentally reviewed my choices last night while I was waiting to fall asleep, and had decided what I wanted to use. There was an old straight razor I had picked up almost as a novelty item years ago at a flea market. The Solingen steel blade was too nicked and pitted to actually be used for shaving, but it would be just fine for my purpose. I had gotten it for less than five dollars. I also picked out my trusty Al Mar Quicksilver.

I also fished out the oiled stones and the water stones and spent the next hour honing the blade to ... well, to a razor's edge. The repetitious movements and sounds of steel against the stones were quite soothing. I devoted another half hour to practice, palming it out and opening it into the three preferred grips for using it. I had the moves cold after ten minutes, but kept it up for the full half hour just to be sure I could do it without thinking.

It's like riding a bike. You never completely forget.

The practice also helped me focus. I wasn't nervous, not in that normal, anxious, "Dear me" way that civilians get when they think the IRS is going to audit them, or their spouse is going to find out about that "someone else" they're

seeing on the side, or any of those nice, safe "terrors" that people face. I was preparing myself, on every level, for what might happen tonight.

And then, I spent another half hour before my altar, contemplating … or
trying to. Too many distractions, too many variables. The four-armed dealer
had been busy. Which way would Kali's cards fall tonight? I prayed they would
land in our favor.

By then, it was getting on toward six o'clock. I went out to the walkway
that leads from my rear apartment to the gate, and listened for the garbage truck.
Hearing it, I took my trash out to the curb when they were only three doors away.
Daily trash collection in the Quarter is very handy for disposing of incriminating
items. I stood in the doorway and watched while my trash bag got tossed into
the scoop with a couple of dozen others. The tarot deck with one card missing
was now history.

I set out my clothes for the night, and then I made myself a cup of herb
tea.

Satisfied I was ready, I took my tea, put on some music, and centered myself,
pushing all the possible complications out of my mind until nothing remained
but my breathing and the music. Calm and centered, I settled into a comfy chair
and drank my tea. I was where I needed to be, though not in combat mode—
not yet.

Eventually, evening came and I started getting dressed. Black Levi's jeans
and a belt with a modest, non-shiny buckle. A pair of black soccer shoes with
thin, light soles. I love these things. I wear them out quickly, but they're the closest I've found to black fencing shoes for street use.

I chose a shirt ideal for night work. Forget what you've seen about Ninja
outfits. Pure black only works in very dark situations, not in urban areas with
assorted lights and backdrops. If you walk past a concrete wall in a black outfit,
you stand out like a silhouette on a firing range. Charcoal grey is better, since
it looks dark in the dark and light in the semi-light. The shirt I picked was a
short-sleeved charcoal, red and purple paisley number. In the shadows it serves
like military camouflage to break up your outline, but if you wear it into a bar
or a party, it's so colorful no one would suspect you were using it for clandestine
operations. The reds in the pattern also help to cover any random splatters of
blood you might acquire while you're working.

Happy with my outfit, I loaded my pockets as any gentleman does when he
heads out for the evening. Wallet, money clip, handkerchief, and keys. No loose
change. The envelope with the tarot card went into my left hip pocket next to
my wallet. I put the razor and the Quicksilver where they were most comfortable.

Then I went to a movie. Sort of.

I hiked up to Canal Place, a medium-sized shopping center at a corner of the Quarter, and rode the escalators up to the four-screen movie complex on the third floor. At nine-fifteen I bought a ticket for the nine forty-five showing of a film I'd caught two weeks earlier. I went into the lobby, killed a bit of time in the john, then emerged and exited, joining the crowd that was exiting from another feature.

This is called establishing one's own alibi. I planned to attend movies every evening until we either got our killer or called off the hunt. Fortunately, since I am known as a serious movie buff, no one would find that unusual.

I now had a ticket stub for the nine forty-five show, with the proper sequence numbers on it if anyone wanted to check that closely. Leaving with the crowd meant that none of the ushers or the kids at the concession stand would remember me exiting partway through a movie. Even if someone wanted to quiz me on the movie's content, I was covered.

Then I lit out, following the train tracks behind the levee wall to Toulouse, and cut straight down until I got to Keuffer's, a bar kitty-cornered from the Stage Door. Keuffer's was a clean, easygoing sort of bar where I was unlikely to be recognized. I ordered an Irish and grabbed a seat that allowed me a good view of the Stage Door. Jugger wasn't there. My seat gave me good lines of sight down both Toulouse and Chartres. If he came on foot, he would use one or the other street.

Someone had left a newspaper, and I casually pretended to read the front page. I didn't taste my drink as I sipped it.

Ten o'clock came and went, with no sign of the Juggernaut. At ten-twenty I left Keuffer's and hurried back to the levee wall. Staying to the shadows I made my way north, toward the far end of the Moonwalk, scanning the area as I went. It was still early, a number of people strolled along the walkway by the river, enjoying the slight breeze off the water.

Almost to the French Market, I climbed up the stairs near the end of the Moonwalk. I found a shadowed spot and scanned the area. After a moment, I spotted Mystic's flowing caftan. She was alone, a cage with a live chicken in one hand and a bundle in the other. If I were wrong, I could be missing Jugger at the Stage Door.

But I wasn't. A moment later a familiar hulking form stepped out of the brush, coming up from near the river. There couldn't be two people that big and that ugly in the Quarter. It had to be Juggernaut. That confirmed half the puzzle. He knew where Sunshine had died, that proved he had been involved. If Alex could confirm Jugger's relationship with Dunk, that would cinch it for me.

I watched the Juggernaut gesture to Mother Mystic to follow him. She looked at him, looked towards the water, dropped the cage and bundle, and crossed her arms in defiance. He gestured again, more forcefully. She didn't budge. I wished once again that she had listened and simply stayed away. As it was, now I had to figure out how to get her away from Jugger without blowing the whole plan. I watched Jugger move forward and grab the cage with the chicken, forcing Mystic a step back. I could hear him yelling, though I couldn't make out his words. No one else was close enough to see or hear anything.

Just pretend to do what he wants!

I knew she wouldn't.

Juggernaut reached out his free hand and grabbed Mystic, his huge hand engulfing most of her upper arm. He started dragging her toward the river as if she were little more than a toy.

I sighed, put on my happy face, and stepped forward to intervene before they could disappear down into the bushes.

"Hey, Jugger!" I called brightly, bouncing down the slope towards him as if I had just come off the Moonwalk. "Where've you been? I've been looking everywhere for you. We were supposed to meet for a game. Did you forget? Jimmy thought he saw you come this way—and here you are!" Jimmy didn't exist, but Jugger wouldn't know that.

Jugger released Mystic—who immediately scrambled out of reach—and turned to face me. I prayed he would take my ploy at face value. I really didn't want to have to deal with him here and now, out in the open.

"Oh, yeah. Sorry, Maestro. I had to deal with this bitch first. Ya know how it is. I'll be along in a while."

No way I was leaving without either Jugger or Mystic. "So what seems to be the problem? This bitch bothering you?" I didn't look to see Mystic's reaction to my language.

"Bitch broke her deal." He sounded like a petulant child. "I'm payin' for a service, and I fuckin' well 'spect her to do the job. I got someone has it comin' real nasty, an' that's what her mojo shit is for. Now the bitch is too good for it!"

Mystic started to say something but I raised my hand and silenced her with a look. In the dark, Jugger didn't catch it. "Let me handle it. I know this bitch, and she knows better than to mess with me."

"Yeah, sure." He crossed his arms and waited as I pulled Mystic aside.

Waving my arms angrily for Jugger's benefit, I whispered to her, "I need you to agree to come back and do this ritual thing tomorrow night. Tell him you understand how important it is, and you're sorry. Tell him tomorrow is more auspicious or something, but tell him you'll do it up right."

"But ..."

"Don't argue with me, Mystic. I'm not saving your butt twice. Just lie like a dog, then get out of here and get out of the Quarter for a few days, any way you can." At the hesitation in her face, I added sharply, "This isn't up for debate."

I turned back to Jugger. "Okay. She gets it now. She'll do your voodoo thing or whatever. But it will have to wait for tomorrow."

Thankfully Mystic jumped in. "Yes. The *loa* are displeased tonight, and will not grant what you seek. I will calm them, and tomorrow the spirits will be ready to answer your call."

She added some more voodoo lingo, apologized and groveled a little. Fortunately Jugger seemed to buy her performance.

"Well, now that that's solved," I said, then thumped him on the back, good-old-boy style, "you owe me a game and I owe you a drink! I know this place ..."

Jugger laughed and reverted to the big, obnoxious puppy I knew so well. We left the Moonwalk and headed into the Quarter. I led the way, my sights set on a pool bar where neither of us were likely to be recognized. But when we reached St. Philip, the Juggernaut suddenly ducked out from behind me, making a beeline down toward Chartres. I rushed to catch up just as he ducked into a squalid little joint I didn't know. Glancing around, I couldn't see any pool tables. Why pick this bar?

"Dunk!" Jugger roared, closing in on a scruffy, dark-haired kid and a slim girl with long blond hair and very tight jeans. "You fuckin' two-timin' bitch! Who the hell is your skank this time?"

Dunk? Sunshine's boyfriend? And the girl? She looked up, and I realized with horror that the slim blond was Alex, her eyes wide at the sight of the angry behemoth charging towards her.

Chapter 38

Bone

"They didn't give you a hard time? Not going to get in trouble?"

Alex touched my hand gently. "Bone ... who cares?"

She was right. It *did* matter about her job, about her calling in sick, about there not being a backlash. But what we were doing tonight was of a whole different magnitude of importance.

I'd been smoking steadily all day and lit another now. I was smoking tips I wasn't making. I followed Alex's lead and thought, *Who cares?*

We had waited on the night, and now it was here. We hadn't been outdoors much the whole day. We had gone out for coffee early in the afternoon but hadn't gone for a stroll like we normally would when we were both off from work. Didn't want anybody from Pat O.'s seeing her walking about the Quarter in apparent good health, not with the "food poisoning" she had gotten from some bad clams.

She wore a somewhat ratty, dark red T-shirt, her snug black jeans, and very becoming black suede mid-calf boots. She looked ordinarily and believably enticing; it was nothing like a hooker's fake allure. She also wore that long blond wig that gave her bangs, long sides and back, and was such a startling contrast to her short, dark haircut I'd been stunned into a silent study of her when she'd emerged from her bathroom after half an hour of fiddling with it.

"Do I pass?" Alex asked.

"Definitely!" *Way too good for the likes of Dunk,* I thought. "He won't be able to resist you. What about me?"

I wore dark clothes, a threadbare hoodie from the thrift store and dark sneakers, not my customary boots. My hair was pulled back and tucked into an old ball cap. My right front pocket sagged with the weight of something the Bear had given me. Alex had used some of her makeup to smear shadows on my face, to black out some of my teeth. I looked older, like a homeless person. The oversized hoodie added at least fifty pounds.

She looked at me in critical appraisal and nodded. "You need to remember to slouch, so you don't look so tall. And shuffle your feet and look at the ground a lot."

I practiced, exaggerating each movement until Alex laughed.

I was actually glad when Maestro called. Despite the risk of being recognized, I preferred to be the one watching her back. Besides, Dunk was *mine*. I'd found him. I'd hunted him. And I intended to take care of him.

I glanced at her—as I'd been doing all day—to see if Alex was nervous, if there were misgivings or indecision on her face. I had seen and felt nothing but preparedness from her since we'd gotten out of bed, since the night before last when we'd all convened at the Calf, the five of us, to map everything out and to nail down the details. The plan for tonight's job had come from her.

I left first, cup in hand. Once I reached the bar on Chartres, I settled into place in the spot I had scoped out earlier—a doorway, mostly in shadow at this hour, on the opposite side of the street from the bar. I maneuvered until I had a good view into the place. Small as it was, I could see almost all the way to the back. Pulling the hoodie partway over my face, I drew out a cigarette, lit up and puffed on it, concentrating on looking and acting like one more derelict street person looking for handouts. I knew I had succeeded when people passing by either made an effort to avoid me or ignored me completely.

A few minutes later, Alex arrived at the bar, found a spot inside that was well within my view, and ordered a drink. I settled in to wait, watching as she deftly deflected guys trying to hit on her. The minutes ticked by. I shifted several times to allow feeling back into my legs, and waited. I don't wear a watch, but I have one. Someone left it on one of my tables at the restaurant. I took it from my pocket now and then, hit the tiny button that lit the digital display. After almost an hour I spotted Dunk coming up the sidewalk. He had finally traded the cargo pants for denim cutoffs and was weaving slightly, his center of gravity not quite where it should be, not quite fixed. Already stoned, drunk, or both. He walked right past me—homeless bums are even one level lower than waiters— and across the street into the bar.

It took him only a moment to spot Alex, and saunter up to her. She smiled in recognition, a coy, flirty, seductive smile. She held up an unlit cigarette. He rooted around in his jeans, finally came up with a book of matches. She put the cigarette in her painted lips and leaned in to him ...

And my view disappeared as something large blocked the doorway.

"Dunk!"

It was the Juggernaut. I immediately pushed away from the wall, my gut twisting as he bore down on Dunk and Alex. I saw her look up and drop her cigarette as the man-mountain loomed over them. Juggernaut grabbed Dunk by the shirt, lifting him off his feet and shaking him violently. I ran into the street, barely feeling my feet touch the ground, knowing I would blow my cover if I went in. That didn't matter. I wouldn't let Alex face that monster alone. I had no idea what I could do, but that didn't matter to me, either.

I was no more than two steps into the street when I saw Maestro, who had apparently been right behind Juggernaut, scoot into the bar. He quickly changed his hurried steps to a casual saunter as he moved up beside the big man. I stopped, held my breath, and waited—but I would only wait for a fast, adrenalized heartbeat or two. I would not leave Alex in danger.

After only a slight hesitation, Maestro stepped in front of Juggernaut and grabbed Alex by the upper arm, and jerked her to one side. I heard him shouting at her, but could only make out a few words.

" ... catch you with some other guy again ... my woman ... you forget it!! ... teach you a lesson..."

He escorted her roughly out of the bar and around the corner until they were well out of sight of anyone inside, then released her. I started after them, but he raised his hand slightly to stop me, never once looking in my direction. He said something quiet to Alex, who nodded and pulled back into the shadows of the next doorway.

Maestro looked toward me, moved his hand a little to let me know Alex was okay, and walked back into the bar. I waited until Alex made a small, furtive gesture of her own—a tilt of her head, a quirk of her lips that slowed the runaway, urgent pounding of my heart.

Dunk was climbing up off the floor, which was apparently where Jugger had dropped him. The monster looked mad enough to pound nails with his fist. Maestro imitated a similar angry stalk and came up beside Jugger. They talked, gesturing at Dunk, who cowered behind a chair, and then they walked out the door, apparently commiserating about their "bitches." After a few moments Jugger pounded Maestro on the back, nearly knocking him off his feet, and laughed—a coarse, surprisingly high-pitched sound that made the hair prickle on the back of my neck. Maestro gestured out the door and together they left the bar, walking in the opposite direction from where Alex waited.

I let them get around the corner, then flashed an all-clear signal to Alex. She stepped out on the sidewalk and headed back to the bar, her walk casual, an unlit cigarette in her hand.

Dunk stuck his head out of the bar, glanced in the direction Jugger and Maestro had gone, and headed the other way—towards Alex.

I huddled against my wall, eyes tracking, my breathing silent and very deep. I was coiled tight. I felt I could make the street in one leap.

I heard her voice—that familiar musical inflection—but not the words as she stepped into Dunk's path, stopping him. She lifted her hand. Dunk swayed a little in place for a second or two, then came up with a book of matches, struck one, and lit her cigarette. Alex struck an effective pose, showing off without being glaringly obvious. She took a drag, blew out smoke, and her head tilted slightly and coyly. Her body language shifted a bit more, and I heard more of her voice, then a soft sweet giggle, which *wasn't* her normal laugh.

I heard Dunk's slurring, stunted enunciation. He laughed, a rattling chuckle.

Alex's hand lifted again, touching his arm, then trailed a fingernail across his chest. She slid a step closer to him.

Half a minute later, he had his arm around her shoulders. He made an evident effort to walk steadily as they moved away from the bar, down Chartres. Not back to his nearer apartment, but toward Alex's. Alex had said she had any number of good ideas how to bring him there instead of going to his place. She would use the one that seemed appropriate when the time came. I hadn't argued. Hadn't asked.

Her hip pressed against him as they walked. Her arm settled around his waist. I gave them a half-block lead before I followed, and still I could hear her giggle-girl laughter float over the empty night street.

By the time they reached Burgundy, Alex's blond-wigged head was nestled against Dunk's shoulder. It lifted as she got out her keys, opened the gate. When it closed, I was outside it, listening to their steps going up. Then her apartment door opened on the building's third story, clicked shut, and the overhead light in the front room went on. I slotted my key soundlessly into the gate's lock.

I came up the stairs on the edges of the risers, knowing which ones made noise, putting on the Bear's brass knuckles as I went. Brass knuckles—like, say, a blackjack—are one of those street-fighting weapons that everyone has heard of but no one has ever laid eyes on. I hadn't asked the Bear where he'd gotten his set, but I'd worn them around my apartment today a few times, getting familiar with the weight. I was comfortable with them, and confident.

Alex hadn't locked her apartment door behind her. I turned the knob with my left hand and swept forward into the front room. I jabbed Dunk hard on the crest of his left cheekbone just as his head came around at the door's opening. His fingers still clutched Alex's red T-shirt, which he'd pulled free of her jeans.

I saw a surprised, if dope-muddled, expression on his face just before the ridge of heavy metal caught him. He made a surprised *"ga-lawp"* of noise, then went down hard.

Alex ducked down the hall to her bedroom. I reached behind me, closed the door, and flipped the lock without taking my eyes off Dunk. I had swung on him with maybe a third of the muscle I could muster for my best slamming punch. I wondered why the hell brass knuckles had gone out of style.

Unlike my apartment, Alex's apartment is usually neat and uncluttered. For this evening we had cleared the front room of even the decorative rugs, leaving the wood floors bare. Dunk lay on the floor, on his side, rocking back and forth and moaning, nowhere near able to get back on his feet and not even yet trying—still absorbing the hurt and the shock. I watched and waited outside the range of his legs.

Alex came back into the room carrying her shotgun and a towel. As she entered she tossed me the towel so I could wipe off my disguise. She gave the gun a good, loud pump. She'd had it a long time in a box in her bedroom closet, disassembled, a gift from her father on her eighteenth birthday. Keeping a good distance back, she aimed at him from the hip.

Dunk held his head in both hands as he rocked. His long, dirty hair brushed the floor. He was wearing a stained purple T-shirt that advertised some heavy metal band I didn't know. He heard the shotgun's pump-action, and got his eyes open and saw. Understanding seemed to slice straight through the pain and his dopey fuzziness.

"Whoa ... no. Nuh-nuh-no way ..."

His head whipped my way.

"Oh, uh, see. She, um, it was her, dude. *She* picked *me* up."

I had removed the hood and took off the hat, wiped the makeup off my face, and waited, gazing back, letting him see me. Then, I saw, he had it.

"You ... yer that *Bone* dude ..."

"Why did you sic the Juggernaut on me?"

His head shook side to side with the heartfelt denial of a three-year-old trying to escape blame. "Nuh-nuh-nuh-nuh—"

"Did you ask him to kill me?"

"No."

"He was looking for me. You were looking for me. Why? For what?" My tone was level, almost neutral, not aggressive.

"The ... drawing." His cheek was red, getting redder and swelling. "Y'know, those dragons. Yuh-yuh-you took it. I mean, yuh *did*. Right? Offa the door of the apartment. I—I—I wanted it back ... and Jugger made me tell him about yuh, why I was lookin' for yuh, everything. He was mad ... wanted to know why yuh was snoopin' ..."

For a moment, I felt like I couldn't breathe. "Why? Why was that drawing important to you?"

Dunk's eyes twitched toward the barrel of the shotgun, then hurried back to me.

"It ..." He licked his lips repeatedly. His eyes were growing shiny. "That drawing ... it had *her* in it."

"Sunshine," I said, and then I realized how hateful it was to be saying her name in the same room with him.

"Yeah." A tear rolled from his eye. "See ... I didn't have any, like, pictures of her. No photos. Nothin'. I jus' wanted ..."

"Why did you give me that envelope with the photograph?"

He stared back at me, clueless.

"The envelope," I said. "Had an M drawn on it. You handed it to me at your place. Why?"

I saw it catch up to him. "Oh ... right. Sunshine said to give it to—somebody. It was, like, some family thing. I dunno. She told me, if she ever, y'know, disappeared ... or whatever ... that I should give it to ... " Confusion clouded his face. "I couldn't remember. So I just gave it to you. 'Cause you were, well, *there*."

He was useless. Breathtakingly useless.

I watched another tear drop, then pressed him. "How did you get Sunshine to go out there by the river? What did you tell her, what kind of setup? What was she doing on the Moonwalk after midnight?"

He started shaking his head again, frantically this time. The tears were now accompanied by a sickly, squirming whine.

"No. No. *No no no no*—"

"You're going to answer," I cut through his whining. "You understand that, so don't give me this 'no-no' shit. Answer. How did you get her out by the river?"

His eyes went over, studied the shotgun again in Alex's very sure hands—she knew how to work the gun, not me. Then, with the tears still coming but no longer indicating grief for Sunshine, and with his upper lip—dusted with a trail of downy fuzz—quivering, Dunk answered.

"Juh-Juh-Juh-Jugger ... Jugger was back. He found out about ... me an' Sunshine. An' ... fuck, it made him, like, crazy. He wuh-wuh-wouldn't let no *girl* touch me. Never. I tol' Sunshine about him, about my, y'know, my past with him. Jugger said he had to meet her. If she wanted me an' I wanted her, then we could have each other ... but he had to meet her first. He tol' me to tell her that. Tol' me to tell her when an' where."

The brass knuckles hung heavy at my side. I flexed my fingers slightly within the hoops.

His wet eyes looked up desperately at mine.

"That's all."

"What day?" I asked.

"Huh?"

"What day of the week—when did Jugger tell you to pass on the meeting time to her?"

He had to think a moment; think hard through the fear.

"Uh, Thursday, he tol' me. For a meetin' Sunday night."

Maestro had gotten that phone message from Sunshine two days before her murder. She had doubtlessly smelled a rat. A middle-of-the-night meeting on the Moonwalk with the assault-happy ex-lover of her boyfriend? Sure she was suspicious. She had perhaps thought about enlisting help or advice and had picked Maestro because he seemed a level head, somebody who could handle himself? Or because of that photo—maybe she thought he might be her father? When she couldn't get in touch, she had ... reconsidered? Dropped it? Figured the Juggernaut was all bluff and she had no reason to be afraid of him? Maybe. However it had gone, Sunshine had not tried to contact me, had not turned to me for help.

"That's all," Dunk said. "That's *all* I did. I swear, dude."

"Get on your feet," Alex said, and there was nothing about that harsh voice that could have produced that sweet girlish giggling earlier. "Stand up."

His teary eyes widened, and he was shaking his head again.

"Do it," I said.

Dunk slowly pulled his feet under himself, then, even more slowly, stood on legs that shook like a newborn deer's.

"That's all I did ..." His voice was a reedy little whisper now.

"I know it is," I said, nodding. "Put your hands behind your back, lock the fingers together."

He shook as he did so and looked very, very frightened. I stepped forward and threw a hard, fast roundhouse that smashed him on the temple, and he caromed off the wall and went down a second time. The many rings in his earlobes jingled, then were still.

This time he was unconscious. I pulled him out into the middle of the floor. I set the brass knuckles out of reach, got the square of duct tape I'd already cut and laid it over his mouth—the mouth that had blown such amazing, soulful music from his saxophone. I thought, *How could someone as repellant and cowardly as Dunk be given such a gift?*

I didn't want to think about it. I shook my head, clearing it, then neatened the edges of the tape, straddled his chest, and looked up at Alex, who had held the shotgun at the ready throughout this.

"Hand me the pillow," I said. The words hurt my throat. My head, my eyes, felt too tight, too hot.

She laid the gun on the couch, picked up the big feather pillow, and knelt next to me, looking down at Dunk. He hadn't moved during any of this—out cold. I held out my hands for the pillow, but she continued to hug it, pulling it in tight next to her body.

"Do you think he really did love her?" she asked. "At all?" Her words were soft, quiet.

I *loved her!* screamed through my head. I *did, not him!* "She died because of him!" My voice was choked, raw, and I wasn't even trying to hold it steady. "He put her there, Alex. Dunk put her there. Too scared of the Juggernaut to stand up to him. He might've ... loved ... Sunshine. If the selfish son of a bitch could actually feel something like that. But he did the coward's thing. For Christ's sake, he gave her up to make *Jugger* happy!"

"But is that a big enough crime? Being weak? If that's so, Bone, then an awful lot of people deserve to die."

I looked at her. I hadn't expected her to stop me, to take up for *him*. "What are you saying? I thought we agreed."

"We agreed to this when we thought he'd killed her." She took a deep breath. "I'm saying that, however misguided and foolish she was, Sunshine loved this man enough to face the Juggernaut for him. If she was willing to take that risk, do you think she would want this? Do you think she would want this for *you?*"

I looked into her eyes and found nothing judgmental, just love, and I realized, in tiny increments of understanding at first, then all at once, that she was right. I hated Dunk with all my heart and soul, but did I have the right to kill him? Just for my own personal satisfaction? I looked down at his pathetic, skinny body for a long moment.

"Okay," I said, forcing out the sound past a mental scream of rage. "We'll throw him back. He'll probably be too scared to say anything anyway."

I removed the tape, wiped off the fluids that drooled out of Dunk's mouth, stuck my baseball cap on his head and pulled the brim low. Then Alex helped me get him to his feet and take him down the stairs, moving him in that "drunk-assist" way that is to Quarterites what CPR is to paramedics. I had his arm across my shoulder and held him stiff against my hip. Alex steadied him from the other side, keeping him upright while I did all the walking. It's a move you use to get your blotto friends into cabs.

It got Dunk out the gate, across the sidewalk and down the street to the nearest underlit alcove. He started to stir a little as we settled him onto the ground. We left him there, like so much trash.

* * *

Excerpt from Bone's Movie Diary:

The towering screen perfs. are & shall remain: Gloria Swanson's indelible Norma Desmond in *Sunset Blvd.*; Paul Newman, somber & subdued in *The Verdict*; Morgan Freeman (would somebody get this man an Oscar!) in *Shawshank Redemption*; Peter O'Toole as god-like Eli Cross in *The Stunt Man*; David Bowie's brief & magnificent portrayal of Pontius Pilate in *Last Temptation of Christ*; Glenn Close, irresistible & evil in *Dangerous Liaisons*; Paul Sorvino's sidesplitting corrupt evangelist in *Oh, God!*; Jose Ferrer's articulate lawyer in *Caine Mutiny*; Marlene Dietrich's Nazi general's widow in *Judgment at Nuremberg*; Kenneth Nelson, whose tongue drips with poignant acid in *Boys in the Band*; Jane Alexander in *Testament* (the best movie you've never heard of); Joel Grey as master of ceremonies/fiend in *Cabaret*; Melinda Dillon with her UFO-abducted child in *Encounters/3rd Kind*; and Charleton Heston (yes, Heston) in *Soylent Green* (yes, *Soylent Green*). That's that. We may reopen the books on this category one day. Watch. Wait.

Chapter 39

Maestro

The one thing guaranteed to win sympathy with a victim is another victim of the
same thing. Once I realized Jugger thought
Dunk was cheating on him with Alex, the only way out was to make him believe Alex was cheating on me. I hoped our relationship as "pals" would make
Juggernaut leave Alex to me, especially if he thought I was going to do a really
good job of punishing her. There had been no way to warn Alex of the plan. I
had to hope she would catch on and play along when I started tearing into her.
And she did, in a performance worthy of an Oscar.

The ploy worked so well that, once Jugger and I left Dunk, we commiser-
ated about unfaithful lovers for the entire five blocks to the Stage Door. Take
that to mean Juggernaut complained loud and long about his "bitch's" lack of
fidelity, while I threw in an occasional word or comment just so he wouldn't
forget I was there. I comforted myself with the knowledge that there was now
no doubt of Jugger's link with Dunk. I just had to keep Jugger clear of Alex and
Bone long enough for them to get Dunk, and then, at last, I could deal with the
Juggernaut.

I would have preferred to head somewhere besides the Stage Door, where
most of the bartenders knew me, but decided it was more important to get the
Jugger into a situation where he could be contained for a while. As it turned out,
I got lucky. The regular bartender had called in sick and the replacement was a
new guy I had never seen before. I ordered a round and found a table near the
back. Jugger slugged back his drink in one motion. I quickly ordered him another. He wouldn't be the first man driven to drink by a faithless lover, but the
tipsier I could get him, the better. Once I had an opening, I planned to duck into
the sandbox, call the Bear, and set the final phase in motion.

Halfway through his second drink, Jugger saved me the hassle, going for his
own sandbox run. I used his bathroom break as an opportunity to make the call
to the Bear. I would call again once the target was in range.

I sipped my drink sparingly, careful to stay clear-headed. It was almost over.
Now that I was sure we had the right guy, it was just a matter of taking care of
business.

Ten minutes passed, then fifteen, and Jugger had still not emerged from
the men's room. Suspicious, I did a quick check and confirmed my fears. Jugger

had done the same thing I had once done to him—used the sandbox run as an excuse to duck out, undetected. Alarmed, I tried to imagine where he would go. Normally I couldn't peel him off with a crowbar. What would be more important than the companionship he wanted from me? The answer: his "bitch." He was going after Dunk—and Dunk was with Bone and Alex. I left my drink mostly untouched and quickly headed towards Bone's place, using my ground-eating "late to meeting" stride, though I didn't really care who saw me rushing this time.

I turned the corner on Burgundy in time to see Bone disappear quietly into his gate. There was no sign of Juggernaut. I moved closer and found a secluded place to keep watch, scanning the street for any sign of the big man. Some thirty minutes later Bone, and Alex—now without the blond wig—emerged from the gate, half dragging a very groggy but surprisingly alive Dunk between them. They deposited Dunk in the nearest recessed doorway, went back inside. I watched long enough to see Dunk crawl out of the niche and struggle to his feet—with lots of help from the wall nearby. He leaned on the wall for a while, obviously not in the best shape, before he started stumbling slowly down Burgundy toward Barracks. Once I was sure no one was watching, I gave Bone a quick call on his landline. He met me at his gate and led me up to his apartment where Alex waited amid a comfortable clutter of clothes, pillows, books, and movies. A small, green-eyed black cat lurked at the far end of the hallway.

They told me about Dunk. They had spared him, and I had to admit their reasoning made sense. It was their decision, anyway.

Juggernaut's fate was mine to decide.

"Yeah," I said, "I saw Dunk head off to his place. I'm just glad you're both safe."

"Why wouldn't we be?" Alex asked from where she sat on the overstuffed couch, snuggled close to Bone. "Certainly not because of Dunk."

I had to tell them.

"Because ..." I took a deep breath. "I lost the Juggernaut."

"You *what?*" Alex looked stunned. "But you're a super hunter-tracker wise-guy or whatever. You're the pro, right? How could you lose him?"

Bone blinked at me, probably thinking the same thing.

I proceeded to tell them what happened. "So I want you both to stay here by the phone—especially since you no longer have a cell phone. I don't think he knows where you live, but we can't count on that. I'm going to find him."

Bone frowned. "You're going to hunt him down alone? Is that wise?"

"Not really, but the Jugger still thinks we're friends, I'm sure of that. And I've got an idea where to look. Trust me, if I need you, I'll call. I have no delusions of being a hero."

I left Bone and Alex holding each other on the couch. If nothing else, this hunt had certainly opened Bone's eyes. Now the bond between them was practically visible, no doubt strengthened by what they'd undertaken together.

* * *

I followed the track Dunk had taken, down Burgundy toward Barracks street. If I was right, Jugger would head for Dunk's place and wait. Since Dunk was only a few minutes ahead of me, I figured I had a good chance to catch him there.

At the edge of the park I slowed, surreptitiously looking through the fence to Dunk's building. No sign of movement there. A couple of kids walked by on Barracks, heading toward the river. A derelict sat slumped on the steps a few doors down. Still no sign of Jugger. I decided to do a casual pass-by to see if I could pick up anything closer to the building. Without changing stride I crossed Barracks and turned toward the river on a path that took me in front of Dunk's building. I stopped, bending to pretend to tie my shoe, and listened. The place was dark and silent. I continued past, glanced at the derelict on the steps, and froze in my tracks. I recognized the partially shaved, greasy dark hair, cutoffs, and stained purple T-shirt. It was Dunk.

Glancing around to make sure there were no eyes on the street, I knelt down for a closer look. He wasn't breathing. Careful not to touch anything, I pulled out my lighter and flicked it. In the glow from the flame I saw two bloody punctures in Dunk's chest. He wore a cord with a dried chicken's foot around his neck, just like the one I had seen on Jugger—I was fairly sure he hadn't been wearing it earlier. He also had one of those tourist trinket voodoo dolls clutched in his fist.

The examination took only seconds. No pulse, two wounds straight through to the heart. It had been so quick that his ruptured heart hadn't had time to pump out much blood. Dunk was dead, that was certain. I was equally certain I wanted to get as far away as possible before someone else noticed. Jugger had definitely been here. He couldn't be that far ahead. Making sure that I'd left no sign of my presence on the murder scene, I stood up and continued casually down Barracks. To anyone watching, I would have simply been a passerby who'd stopped to give a light to a bum.

I decided to head back to the Stage Door, hoping to get lucky. I turned up Bourbon, mixing in with the party crowds to throw off anyone who might have seen me on Barracks, and glanced in the Bourbon street bars as I passed. Fortunately Jugger's unusually large size made him easy to spot. He wasn't in any of them. I turned on Toulouse and continued on to the Stage Door. This time the gods smiled on me, I spotted Jugger in the back, looking particularly sullen.

"Hey, Jugger," I greeted him warmly, "Where did you go? I waited for you, but you didn't come back."

"Sorry 'bout dat. Had to take care o' some business." He chugged the remainder of his drink. "Fuckin' two-timin' bitch ... got what was comin' to 'im."

I signaled the bartender for another and sat down. "So you showed him, huh?"

"Damn right I did. Damn right. That skank's gonna get hers, too. Bitch's gonna pay for messin' with mine. Gonna do right by you, too, Maestro." He leaned over and whispered conspiratorially, "You don't 'ave ta tell me. I saw where she lives."

The smile froze on my face. He meant Alex. He had seen her with Dunk, followed her, and somehow I had missed him. She was next on his little list, and now he knew where she lived. Now I had no choice. If I were going to do something about the Juggernaut, I had to do it tonight.

"Let me get you another drink. It's on me." I excused myself and went to the bar to collect our drinks. Setting them down in front of Jugger, I waved towards the rest rooms and continued on to the back. I stopped short of actually going in, stood just out of Jugger's line of sight while keeping him in mine. I *would not* lose him again. I made two quick calls, one to Bone and one to give the Bear his "warning order," then rejoined Jugger at the table.

"How about a game?"

Ten minutes later Bone walked into the Stage Door, wearing an unusually brightly colored yellow and blue Hawaiian shirt. Jugger had his back to him, but I caught his eye and nodded. He said something to the bartender, turned and left, heading up Chartres.

Jugger took his shot, and missed. As I moved into place and lined up my own shot, I spoke. "Hey, Jugger, are you still looking for that skinny guy? That Bone dude?" I sank the four-ball and moved on to my next shot.

He looked at me sharply. "Yeah, why?"

"I think I just saw him. He was just in here, wearing a really bright yellow print shirt."

His head whipped around toward one door, then the other. "Did ya see which way he went?"

"Afraid not. He talked to the bartender and left, but I didn't see which direction."

"Thanks, Maestro." He set his pool cue down, started to leave.

"You're not going to run out on me again, are you? I thought you really wanted this game. Or is it just because I'm kicking your butt all over the table?"

The big guy actually looked crestfallen. "Aw, Maestro, you know it ain't that. There's just something I gotta take care of, and it can't wait. How about I meet you back here in, say, half-an-hour, forty-five minutes? Would that be cool?"

I pretended to ponder for a moment, making a show of looking at the run I had carefully lined up on the table. I finally decided I had stalled long enough to give Bone the head start he needed. "Sure, Jugger. Fine." I smiled. "Give me a chance to warm up some more on the table and really kick your butt. But you're buying the round!"

He smiled back and thumped me on the shoulder, nearly knocking me down. He'd done that before, and I didn't like it any better this time. "Thanks, Maestro. You're a real pal."

Yeah, I thought, *a real pal.*

He headed for the Toulouse door, stopping to talk to the bartender who helpfully pointed down Chartres. I watched him duck out, hoped Bone had made good time, and headed out myself—the other direction, down Toulouse. Both Bone and I were heading for the same place, the Bear's bar. But Bone intended to lead Jugger on a merry chase while I took a more direct route.

I had to make one brief stop along the way. My movie would have let out by now, so I needed another solid alibi. It was just after midnight, so I headed for the Dungeon, an infamous bar rumored to be the site of an actual slave dungeon during the early 1800s. Located just a half block off Bourbon on Toulouse, it was on my way, and it opened at midnight, so I knew the crowds would be heavy.

I ducked down the long narrow stone passage that led from the street to the Dungeon door, making certain the security cameras in the passage caught a good view of my face. Once inside, I greeted the bouncer, Butch, and the bartender, Jenny, both good friends, and made certain they saw me head upstairs to the sound bar, again making sure the cameras caught me. There were no cameras pointed at the seating in the corners, so I headed for a back table, out of camera range. As usual at this hour, the place was packed. I waited for a large crowd to head out the exit, and joined them. I had spent many an hour sitting at the end of the bar with Butch, watching him track the security camera, so I knew just where I had to be to avoid being seen on the way out. It worked to my advantage that the cameras were designed to catch people coming in, which gave the bouncer warning of approaching trouble, rather than on the way out.

Alibi established, I ducked out onto Toulouse and turned down Bourbon, heading for the Marigny and the Bear's bar. Bone should be up around Canal Street by now—the opposite direction—and starting to head back. Juggernaut would certainly take Bone in a stand-up fight, but I was pretty sure he didn't have a chance against him in a foot race.

*   *   *

I sidled up on the crowd coming out of the bar, mingling myself reasonably well with the riffraff. The Bear stood in the doorway waving everybody out urgently. "Com'on! Com'on! It's a gas leak! There's nothin' I can do about it! Sorry, all right? Go do your drinkin' somewhere else for a while. *Put that fuckin' cigarette out!* What's the matter with you, Bernie?"

"I left my address book in there," I said. I kept my face down, my posture a bit stooped, going through the crowd up to the Bear. A casual glance wouldn't catch me.

He hooked a thumb over his shoulder without looking at me. "Go get it. Com'on, y'all! Yeah, of course I'm gonna call somebody to come fix it. Soon as I get all you people out!"

I ducked through the door, still hunched. I was breathing a little hard from the fast jog.

Inside the bar as the last of the dozen or so patrons emptied out, I moved quickly. I did a fast check on both rest rooms, and found both unoccupied. Then I took position by the door, dropping money into the jukebox but making no selections. It was hugely unlikely anybody would realize I was still in here, or even remember me being on the scene.

The Bear had concocted the scheme for emptying the place out, and I had to admit it was a beaut. See, this bar is *notorious* for gas leaks. It's got an ancient heating system that the owner, who lives across the river in Gretna, refuses to tear out and replace. So it gets patched here and there and springs new holes at least a few times a year, even in summer when, naturally, the heat's not on. What's more, tonight's gas leak was completely authentic. I could smell it on the air. The Bear had rigged up a deal where he need only press down on a sturdy wrench he had wedged next to a pipe by the floor behind the bar, out of everybody's view. When I had phoned, he had stepped down on the wrench with his boot, and presto! Instant gas leak.

I could hear him dispersing everybody from out front. It was a Monday night, not too many people out. They quickly scattered to Decatur's other available haunts. The Bear stood guard in front of the bar's entrance, shooing away customers.

I preset all but the last button in a series of selections on the juke, found a good vantage point beside the door, and waited.

Chapter 40

Bone

I looked back down the length of Dauphine, waiting for the tell-tale bulk that would be Juggernaut to make the corner. I was three blocks down, and dare not go further less he miss me—though how anyone could miss my garish shirt, even in pitch black, was unfathomable. I had not expected to be involved in a chase with a killer, but now that I was, my adrenaline pumped. Funny how the fear of dying can make you feel really alive.

After Maestro had left, Alex and I had just sat on the couch, comfortable with each other's silence. I held Alex, enjoying her soft warmth and thinking about what Maestro had said. He'd lost the Juggernaut. After watching Jugger's earlier performance, I wasn't thrilled with the thought of that monster running around loose out there, especially knowing that he wanted a piece of me. I wasn't particularly worried about our safety inside the apartment, but it did bother me that Maestro had managed to loose track of him. Was Maestro losing it? Had he been retired from the Outfit too long after all? Lost his edge? I didn't want to believe that. I had pinned a lot on his knowledge and experience, wanted to believe he would manage to find Jugger again. I just hoped he wasn't foolish or stubborn enough to take him on by himself.

I got up and walked into the movie room, where Sunshine's drawing hung on the wall. Alex stood behind me, holding me, head resting between my shoulder blades, just like we'd stood there that last time ... the night of my sleepwalking dream about Sunshine.

"It's almost done," she said, and all the edges were showing in her voice, too. That was okay, even a good thing. "We did the right thing. Maestro will get him."

The red thumbtack hung loosely in the lower left corner. I pushed it back in, but it dropped to the floor in a tiny sprinkle of white wall plaster, bouncing behind a messy stack of videotapes.

I folded Alex into my arms. I was almost ready to blow off Maestro's instructions, to send Alex up to her own apartment with the shotgun and go out looking on my own, when the phone rang. Maestro had found Jugger, but he needed my help to bring him to ground. He outlined his plan.

"It will be dangerous. You'll have to stay well ahead of him while making sure you don't completely lose him."

"No problem. I know just the thing."

Five minutes later, after I'd persuaded Alex to go upstairs—she'd promised to do so, and I didn't doubt her—I stepped out of my gate onto Burgundy. I'd dressed in comfortable jeans and an obnoxiously loud shirt Sunshine had bought me as a joke Christmas gift back in San Francisco. It was one of those awful shirts tourists wear on tropic vacations to show they can compete with the local flora. I had kept it only because I'd intended to donate it to the local homeless shelter, but I'd never quite gotten around to delivering it. The mission required me to be the prey in a cat and mouse game, but I had no intention of getting too close to this particular cat. This shirt, with its day-glow bright flowers, made me visible from space, much less from a few blocks away in the Quarter.

I made the extra block to St. Louis, so I could come up on the bar without being spotted, turned on Chartres and ducked into Keuffer's, kitty-cornered from the Stage Door. From there I could see Jugger and Maestro at the pool table. The Juggernaut's attention seemed riveted on the game. Once I was certain Jugger had his back to me, I hurried across the street and stepped up to the bar. Maestro made eye contact and nodded, never breaking the motion of his shot. I signaled the bartender, some guy I didn't know.

"Can you tell me the way to Canal Street?"

"Sure, just head up that way on Chartres five blocks or so. You'll come to Canal."

"Thanks." I glanced at Juggernaut to make sure he hadn't spotted me—Maestro still had his full attention—then headed down Chartres toward Canal at a rapid pace. It being Monday, there weren't a lot of people out, so I figured I could get a fairly good head start and still be seen by someone looking for me.

I made Canal and turned away from the river, then slid back over to the corner and peeked around the building. Jugger wasn't too hard to spot amid all the normal-sized pedestrians. He was several blocks back, close enough to have seen which way I turned, but far enough back so I was safe. I headed over to Dauphine, but Jugger had still not made the corner at Canal, so I pretended to look in the window of the GNC on the corner.

I wanted a cigarette, but didn't think I had that much time. A moment later, I spotted him coming around the building at Chartres. After a second more to be sure, I turned on Dauphine and headed back into the Quarter. Hated to admit it, but I was having fun—so long as I didn't slip up and let him actually catch me. Whatever difficulty I might have with this chase, bad smoker's lungs and all, I was fairly certain it would be worse for someone the Juggernaut's size.

I kept the chase going for about twenty minutes—ten shy of the amount of time Maestro said he needed—then ducked over to Decatur and turned toward the Marigny. I stayed under the streetlights as much as possible, to make certain Jugger could see me from a long way back, and picked up the pace. In short order, I found myself hurrying past my restaurant. I caught a glimpse of my reflection in the big windows and beyond them saw the dance going on between the waiters and the feeders. The reflected face didn't look familiar, and the scene behind the windows looked improbably alien to me, like a ritual viewed through a museum exhibit's glass. For that instant I felt, keenly, like I didn't belong in there, had *never* belonged to that world.

I'd built up a considerable lead by the time I reached the Bear's bar. Glancing back, I spotted a shape that could only be the Juggernaut about three minutes behind. I made sure he saw me, then nodded to the Bear and ducked inside.

The place was so dim that at first that I couldn't see anything beyond the lights over the bar. The sound system played something soft and low. The jukebox was lit up as if it had been slotted with quarters and primed with selections, but it played nothing.

"How far back?" Maestro's voice came from behind me, by the door. I had completely missed him.

"Two to three minutes, I'd guess." I finally spotted him at a booth, sitting in the shadows just to the side of the door. He sat with his hands folded in front of him on the table. There was something odd about them, though, something different. *Oh,* I thought. *Surgical gloves.*

"There's a back exit through the storeroom behind the bar," he said. "Duck out there. I'll take it from here." His voice was calm and sure, but it, too was oddly different. Flat. Emotionless.

I'd thought long and hard about this moment, ever since Maestro had called to ask me to play a part in the final chase. The original plan had called for each of us to focus on our "own" suspect. But things had definitely not gone according to the plan. Now that I was involved, I realized I needed something more.

Something for Sunshine.

Instead of heading toward the storeroom, I turned to face him. "No, Maestro," I said. "I'll be staying."

"You'll be *what?*" His voice dropped even lower. The tone I heard in it gave me a chill. But I knew what I wanted, and after what we'd already been through, I wasn't going to back down now.

"I'm staying," I said. "I want to talk to him, first."

"You're out of your fucking mind!" I could hear the anger coming through now. "He's already killed Dunk! He left him lying in the street, two holes in his heart. Do you understand this is not a game?"

A cold calm filled me—a fine, icy grip. Soothing, in its way, and far removed from sadness and grief and anger.

I didn't want to fight Maestro over this, but I was not going to back down.

"How can you ask me that?" I said. "Sunshine was my *wife*. Jugger killed her. I have to face him. That's what this has been about, all along—not just revenge, but *justice*." Without waiting for what he might say to that, I walked over to the bar and climbed up to sit on it, settling myself under the brightest light to be sure I would be the first thing Jugger saw. And the last thing. "You'll want him distracted. Let me talk to him. Then do what you want. If we're partners, you owe me this."

Something shifted behind Maestro's eyes. My final words had hit the right target, had clinched something between us. They'd been meant to.

"Hey, brother-man," the Bear's voice came from just outside. It was the signal.

"Hey," the Juggernaut returned the Bear's greeting, then pushed open the door, and entered.

He stepped into the dim light and stopped, spotting me immediately. He was obviously surprised to find me alone and waiting for him. "What the *hell*?"

"You must be the Juggernaut," I said. My voice was surprisingly calm and strong. "Well, I'm Bone. I hear you've been looking for me. Why?"

He hadn't expected a conversation, but he recovered from his surprise quick enough. "You got something I want," he said. "You stol' that picture from Dunk. Want it back, an' maybe want to teach you a lesson about messin' in my business, boyo." He took a threatening step forward, then stopped. I saw Maestro twitch, then grow still. He was giving me my time.

"Yeah," I said. "You killed the woman who drew that picture. You remember Sunshine? Or maybe you never even knew her name. Well, she was once my wife."

"She was a *whore*!" Jugger spat on the floor and took another stomping step towards me. "A whore who tried to steal my bitch. Nobody fuckin' steals my bitch! She got what was comin' to her. I hexed her good, too, made sure she got a bad death and a bad time in the afterworld."

"And Dunk?" I held my place, kept my voice perfectly calm but hard as stone, as Maestro began to move again. I watched as he came up out of the booth with no more weight or presence or sound than a shadow. I didn't so much see him as I felt him glide up behind Jugger. "What about Dunk? You killed him. Now you've got no ... bitch." I found the ugliness of the word, the way that Jugger used it, staggering and foul. I leaned forward, just a degree or two, and looked right into Jugger's mad eyes. "Are you really surprised that Dunk preferred Sunshine to you?"

"You ... mother-fuckin' ..." Jugger choked out, then he roared. It was a primal sound, like the yowl of a big predator. He drew a large, wickedly pointed weapon, not an ice pick unless it was on steroids, from a pocket hidden somewhere in the expanse of his overalls.

Tripwire ...

I froze as he lunged for me, *fast*. *Christ*, was he fast, like a moving wall, and he held his steel pointed directly at my heart. I'd wanted to confont him, to make him face what he had done. I'd known he might attack, but I had not been completely prepared for the reality of it. It was like what facing a bull in the *corrida* must be like for a matador. Death came for me on huge, stomping boots, and I couldn't move, couldn't think. I could only watch.

And the thought that came to me then, in that shattered fragment of time in which death rushed toward me, was that it had been worth it to face him. It had been essential. I hadn't said the words for him. I hadn't said them for myself. I had said them for Sunshine.

And then, before that terrible, lightning-fast lunge could puncture my heart, Maestro was on him, sailing in from his right like a viper striking its prey, slicing his neck with a shining razor of a knife.

Maestro's steel bit into Jugger's thick neck, slid through in a flash, and left a sudden red line behind it. The line widened instantly. Blood gushed with dismaying force from the wound, spraying everywhere in a shocking scarlet plume. Blood like that, a river, a waterfall of blood, belonged in a Sam Peckinpah film, not in this quiet bar in the Quarter.

But this was no movie.

Maestro pivoted out of the move like a ballet dancer in the midst of some *danse macabre*, releasing the dripping razor to clatter on the floor. The lighting was dim, but not so dim that I couldn't see faces. The Juggernaut's eyes got wide. He clapped his hands over the sudden, gaping wound in his neck, and spun to look at Maestro. As he recognized his attacker, his eyes bulged even wider, like they were going to pop out of his skull. His mouth worked, but nothing came out other than obscene gurgling and whistling sounds.

On his face I saw an expression of absolute, astonished betrayal.

And Maestro ... his face had twisted from its normal, bland expression into a strange, cold grin that belonged on a pagan icon. Or a death's head. Here was a different, deadly, singular, focused person, someone or something that I had never seen before. It is one thing to know someone can kill. It is quite another to come face to face with that killer. His years, his practiced, easy calm had fallen away to reveal ... something else. A predator. A raptor caught up in the joy of its killing dive, flexing its talons as it grasped its prey. Exhibiting, for that moment, a predator's joy.

Then, Maestro stepped back from his work and slapped a final button on the jukebox, starting the speakers blaring to life. *Metallica*, I thought as I smothered a hysterical giggle. *"No Remorse."* Old stuff. How had that gotten into the Bear's jukebox?

With a wound like that, it had to be over. No way could someone, even someone as big as Jugger, survive having his throat cut, through and through, from one side to the other. I was wrong. As Maestro triggered the jukebox—something he'd obviously preset before I'd forced him to change his plan—Jugger pounced.

Maestro must have been expecting something. He spun, and with a speed I had not believed he—or anything human—possessed, he glided back out of range of Jugger's lunge. A second long, wicked blade appeared in his hand as if he'd conjured it out of thin air. The Juggernaut, covered with blood, still held his own long knife.

Perched on the bar top, I was within easy reach of Juggernaut's blade. I hoped Maestro knew what he was doing. If not, nobody was going to walk away from this.

* * *

Excerpt from Bone's Movie Diary:

> Movies are escapism. That's wisdom as commonly accepted as you can get. But what are we escaping from? ... I've just spent 3 full minutes staring incredulously at that *we* I flung in there so casually. Who the hell am I to anoint myself spokesperson on so profound a point, to put words into anybody else's mouth, no matter how sincerely I think I know best? But, anyway ... what am *I* escaping from? I think I can finally say, after viewing what may be thousands of films over the course of my years, it is the fundamental dissatisfaction of reality. Oh, not to go all black-beret existentialist: I don't

mean life is cruel or bleak or hopeless, or any of those adolescent fallback terms. Of course, there's cruelty & bleakness & hopelessness. What did you think? But reality doesn't tidy itself up the way films will—even bad movies usually have appropriate endings. Reality isn't even satisfyingly dissatisfying. It's streaming with loose ends, with unexplained motivations, with improbable turns of events. And it ends more like the smash-crash outta nowhere finale to *Dirty Mary Crazy Larry* (1974, classic Peter Fonda) than the beatific twisted wreckage wipeout that finishes off *Vanishing Point* ('70s again). The latter quenches a need for culmination. The former just makes me want to look both ways before crossing the train tracks.

Chapter 41

Maestro

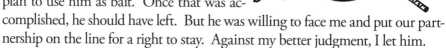

I was furious with Bone. It was bad enough that we'd had to change the game plan to use him as bait. Once that was accomplished, he should have left. But he was willing to face me and put our partnership on the line for a right to stay. Against my better judgment, I let him.

Once the Juggernaut stepped through the door, he focused all of his attention on Bone, who sat calmly on the bar, taunting him. I realized that could work to my advantage. Jugger never saw me come up behind him. When he attacked Bone, I was in a perfect position to strike. My steel bit into his thick neck and pulled through the flesh like a hot knife through butter. The spray, which splattered me with blood as I went past, told me I'd hit the carotid. I'd also gone right through the larynx.

He stumbled, but he didn't go down. Turning, he faced me, eyes wide with disbelief. I was his only friend—at least, the only one he hadn't killed—and I had betrayed him. I took the moment to lean over and hit the last button on the juke. If Bone had not intervened I would have started the loud music the minute Jugger came through the door. As it was, I took a risk turning my back on him, even for a second, even when I'd given him a mortal wound.

He lunged, his steel perfectly directed at me. Kill shots are great, but you don't always get the immediate kill. Early on in my days with the Outfit, I'd once seen a man take a .38 slug in the heart. He still found the time and strength to empty his 9-millimeter at my "trainer" and then change magazines for several more shots before he finally keeled over. The trainer had been showing me, the newbie, the ropes. He took a round in the cheek, one in the elbow. I quickly decided to transfer over into the hunter/tracker branch of my organization.

I had learned my lesson from that. I never truly dropped my guard. I sensed the big man move, and I glided back from his leap. I'd already cleared my Quicksilver. It might not be as sharp as the razor, but it gave me an extra inch or so of reach, and it had a needle point. Loud, harsh metal music pounded the air as Jugger brandished his weapon in his bloody hand. That was going to screw up his grip ... that, and the pints of blood he was rapidly losing. His overalls were already soaked with it.

I had betrayed him. He probably realized I'd tagged him fatally, but the one hair-trigger thought now burning out of control through his suffocating brain was revenge. He was dying, but he meant to take me with him.

One thing in my favor, however, was what I had discovered long ago while working with swords: your average street fighter has no concept of how fast or how far a fencer can lunge. Right now the Jugger, who was plainly getting ready for another pounce, probably thought he was currently at a safe distance. In actuality, he was nearly ten inches inside my range. He'd told me when I first met him that he hadn't picked up a sword since he was eighteen. His lack of practice worked to my advantage. I noted with some surprise that he held his weapon left-handed. He had always shot pool right-handed. He was versatile, I guessed.

I couldn't run the risk of his deciding to turn tail and run out into the street. The Bear was under my orders to stay guard out there, to keep anybody from coming in during the show. But even he wouldn't be able to stop the Juggernaut if he hit the door with the full weight of his massive body. And that would be ... messy.

Before he could complete his strike, I moved. Bone, thank all the gods, stayed put.

Long lunge. My point penetrated Jugger's right eye. Don't step back—fall and roll sideways to avoid the thrust from his weapon side.

I came up on one knee, knife ready for another lunge.

It was over.

He did a three-step stagger, a little weave, then dropped. His body hit the boards, actually shaking the place. He landed on a hip and rolled onto his broad back, thrashed forcefully for a few seconds, then weakly for a few more. He'd dropped his weapon, had a hand on his throat and one clapped over where his eye had been. His remaining eye wasn't looking at me.

Thankfully.

I waited with a kind of totally detached and serene horror for a full minute after all movement had stopped. Even then, my first move was to step on his knife hand and pin it down while I withdrew my handkerchief, picked up his weapon—an oversized ice pick or a sharpened whetting steel, maybe—from the floor. Then I removed the envelope from my hip pocket, shook the card out onto his chest, and spiked it there with his own weapon.

Bone came up beside me and put a hand on my shoulder. He looked down at my work. The tarot card was the Sun.

"Maybe the cops will get the hint when they find the body." Bone's voice remained surprisingly steady.

I had several spare pairs of surgical gloves in my pocket. I handed a set to Bone.

The Bear had told me where he'd stashed the plastic tarpaulin behind the bar. We spread it on the floor and rolled Jugger onto it, onto his side. I picked up my razor and pocketed it. Then I grabbed the expensive, absorbent paper towels, handed some to Bone, and mopped. Jugger could bleed all he wanted to now. At least he wasn't spouting anymore. I only had to worry about the red stuff he'd dropped on the floorboards, and some bleach and Pine Sol would take care of what I missed. Even before seeing to the floor, though, I meticulously wiped off the few drops I could feel already congealing on my face.

We worked in silence. It seemed like forever, but at that moment the juke-box clicked off. I realized the song I'd played to cover the noise of the fight had only just finished. The winking display told me to make the rest of my selections.

We tied up the wide tarp with coarse hemp ropes. The tarp covered the Juggernaut entirely. We threw the used towels into a bag for the incinerator. I stripped off my gloves and tossed them in, too, and directed Bone to do the same.

"Bone," I said, "you don't need to know the rest. Go out the back. And burn that shirt."

He nodded, gave me his version of the warrior's handshake, and headed out.

I rapped sharply on the inside face of the front door. Two short, pause, two short. Then I waited. The Bear regularly carried a cell phone. It was nothing odd for him to make a call from out in front of the bar.

By my wristwatch it was ninety-five seconds before the van rolled up to the door—and I mean *to the door*. It used the driveway and swung up onto the sidewalk, braking with about a foot and a half of clearance from the entrance. The big side door opened just as the Bear pushed open the bar's door. He reached into the van and pulled out a plywood ramp.

We grabbed the Juggernaut, dragged him up the ramp, and heaved his tarp-covered body into the van. I hopped in after, pulled up the ramp after me, and slid the door shut. No windows opened onto the bare bed of the van. The front seats were screened from the rear by a black curtain.

Padre took the wheel and sent us lurching off the sidewalk and down Decatur. He had made up the phony signs for the sides of the van—big magnetic sheets that peeled right off. They said PRIMEAUX GAS EXPERTS. Even had a phone number. If anyone asked, the Bear would say he had called the bar's owner in Gretna after first calling for the repair crew, and that the owner, tight-wad that he was, had ordered the Bear to cancel the professional repairs. The Bear would then go in and patch the leak up himself. No big deal. He'd done it before.

Meanwhile, I heard no sirens as Padre drove at a modest, normal speed. Beside me in the darkness of the van's rear, the Juggernaut remained a large dead mound ... and I didn't feel too old to be doing this.

No, not too old at all.

* * *

I'd ordered a full week to cool-off, so seeing everybody again at once was a pleasant shock.

We'd coordinated our schedule at that last all-present summit conference, after the operation, so that our crew would not cross paths for a week. Of course, I did put in one appearance at the Calf, since my total no-show would seem strange, but I did it on a night when Alex was off work and Bone wasn't there to collect her. I stayed long enough for one drink and had a brief conversation with Padre about our eight-ball team, within earshot of several regulars.

I had missed seeing Bone the most.

I hit the Calf at about two-thirty. The Bear was punching numbers on the jukebox, throwing comments over his shoulder at Padre behind the bar about the "wimp-ass selection." Padre chuckled and set a fresh cocktail in front of Alex, who was in her black-and-whites. I glided up and tossed a bill on the bar top.

"Let me get it," I said as I nodded to Padre, which got me a hardy hug and a sound kiss on the cheek from Alex. Though I probably would have gotten those anyway. Padre said a casual hello.

The Bear and I shook hands, and we got into an almost immediate argument about college football draft picks. It was actually an argument from several years ago, and people were used to us trotting it out every so often. I picked up my Irish, and, nodding more hellos to the tipsy regulars, wandered down to where Bone sat at the trivia machine.

"How's it going, Bone?" I said, glancing at the screen over his shoulder. Movie trivia, of course.

"I hate my fucking job," he said around the cigarette burning between his lips. He glanced at me, and a definite flicker of warmth showed in his eyes.

I nodded. The gripe was practically his mantra. I suppose I might feel the same way if I had a square job, or if I needed to be working any job at all to make ends meet. Fact was I had left Detroit with a good nest egg, as well as a few ... treasures, so to speak. Even after buying my new identity from Padre I'd had a solid amount left over. My first year in New Orleans, I had made a fluke killing on the stock market, one of those ridiculous, overnight fortune deals.

Five months before that, I'd been a dabbling investor. Now I had ... well, I had *enough*.

"Although, I figured out how to make up for lost tips," Bone said. He hesitated and grinned. "Alex and I decided we could save money if we shared an apartment."

I congratulated them both and ordered drinks all around to celebrate the happy news.

Padre closed it down at about a quarter after three, which was about the earliest he could get away with it, what with the grill working again and the Calf serving its topnotch burgers. When the shutters were pulled, we assembled with our various drinks in the back booth. The Bear sat next to me, Bone and Alex snuggled opposite, and Padre pulled up a chair.

"To a job, I think, well done," I said, lifting my glass. Everybody drank to it, smiling and grinning.

Then we reviewed thoroughly. Padre had returned the van to its place of origin, which was at a friend of his in Mid-City. Gone were the PRIMEAUX GAS EXPERTS signs. Also, Padre had put the original authentic license plates back on the vehicle.

I'd tossed the straight razor and my Al Mar Quicksilver into two different segments of the Mississippi. The cell phone had gone in too, per Padre's instructions. I hated to lose the Quicksilver, but I could and would get another.

No one at Alex's job had questioned her absence. Food poisoning happens. Bone, obviously, was back to work.

The corpses of both the Juggernaut and Dunk had been dutifully discovered—Dunk's where he had fallen, Jugger's where we had placed it on the Moonwalk—and the events splashed briefly across the evening news programs. The police had made their standard request for anyone with information to come forward. So far as what had turned up in the paper or any news show, nobody had. It was never even mentioned that there was a link between the two murder victims.

Around the Quarter it became part of the gossip, but not so long and not with as much feeling as Sunshine's murder. Now we were a week away from it all. Things had cooled.

We sat in our booth, and we talked and laughed, like we were all decompressing from our work ... and I guess, in a way, we were. I knew the Bear could handle what he'd done without blinking. I knew Padre, too, had been a pro, had started and finished his original career outside the civilian life. I quietly watched Bone and Alex. They looked like they were hanging on to each other a bit for comfort, though that was to be expected. Good for them. It must be nice to have somebody around like that, somebody that's *always* around.

For no good reason—or maybe a perfectly good reason, after all—I thought of Hope, Sunshine's mother. And Sunshine hadn't been my daughter. Couldn't have been. The fates just didn't work like that. Did they?

"So," I said as I raised my glass, "everything looks clear and kosher. Don't you think?"

Everyone nodded.

"I can't see where we missed a stitch," the Bear said.

"Like clockwork," Padre put in.

I agreed. It had almost blown up in our faces, but we turned it back into a successful operation.

Eventually, the camaraderie turned to yawns and owl-eyes. We'd put away a few rounds. It was late. Alex had worked tonight. So had Padre, and so had Bone. We started making our goodbyes, reluctant to do so, drawing it out. Everyone got a warrior's handshake from the Bear, including Alex, though she gave him a friendly peck on the cheek as well. Naturally, the two of them had hit it off.

We started shuffling toward the door. The Bear was going to run Bone and Alex to their apartment in his Impala. I was going to walk. It had rained hard a little before midnight, and even though the streets would be steamy, they would still smell better than they normally did. For a little while, anyway.

Bone and I lingered together a moment.

"Did you notice that 'For Rent' sign on that apartment house on Dumaine Street?" Bone asked. "So long to meth-man Lester and his junkie crew."

"Yeah," I said. "Nice little bonus."

Shifting gears, he said, "I really do hate my job, you know."

"Believe me, I've never doubted you did."

"What we did, Maestro—for Sunshine, what we did to avenge her—it was good. In a lot of ways. I felt, for the first time in my whole life, that what I was doing meant something worthwhile. I love Alex, but that's a *state*, not an *action*. Doing what we did, the hunt, it was the best."

I eyed him levelly, but he wasn't talking about the thrill of the kill. Not at all.

I nodded. "You can make money committing crimes, Bone. Or you can make money preventing them or catching the culprits, provided of course you've got a badge or a PI license. But ... I'm afraid nobody pays a vigilante a salary."

I said it gently, but he wasn't stupid and it wasn't news to him. He just chuckled and lit a smoke. We did a warrior shake ourselves, eyes locking briefly for a second of pure understanding. Then my friend picked up Alex's knapsack, put an arm around her shoulders, and walked out with the Bear as Padre unlocked the door and shutters. "Later days, Maestro!" Bone threw back at me, and then they were gone.

"You definitely haven't lost your chops, Maestro," Padre said as I stepped out onto St. Peter, automatically scanning the street and deeming it all clear.

"Thanks, Padre. See you at pool tomorrow night."

"We're playing the Fink Ployds at home. Vulture's on that team, so sharpen up your stick."

"I'll start whittling when I get home," I said, and I headed off.

Bone was, of course, completely right. It had felt good. It had *been* good. The hunt had been a worthwhile undertaking, worth the risks. I had something now that I'd been without for ... I didn't really know how long. But feeling alive and lively and like I had a purpose on this planet, that was a fine feeling. I savored it, even as the hunt started its slow fade into the past.

At home, I reached for the saber I kept mounted on the wall, then stopped my hand and left the sword hanging there. I'd had a drink or two tonight. Probably should leave the live steel alone. I shrugged and started getting ready for bed.

Then I noticed the answering machine and hit the button.

"Just thought you'd like to know, Maestro. The case on that Moonwalk knifing is still *officially* open. There're some happy detectives on the force lately, though."

The message clicked to an end.

That "officially" meant the evidence against the Juggernaut just wasn't firm enough to hold legal water. The rest of the message meant the Sun tarot card had done the trick.

I sat down slowly in my chair in the front room, staring at my phone, wondering just how in the *hell* Sneaky Pete had gotten my number.